LADY ELEANORA

MICHAEL O. GREGORY

Inks and Bindings
888-290-5218
www.inksandbindings.com
orders@inksandbindings.com

CONTENTS

ABOUT THE AUTHOR

Raised on ranch in north Texas, Michael entered military service in 1956. He served two tours in Vietnam. The first with the Airborne Brigade of the 1st Cavalry Division. The second as an infantry heavy weapons advisor on a mobile advisor team (MAT-105). Retired from military service in 1977 as a Sergeant First Class. Michael won the 2009 Beach Book Festival award in the history category for "SHINY BAYONET". A first-hand historical account of the first combat operation of the Vietnam War of the men of the 1st Battalion (Airborne), 12th Cavalry Regiment, 1st Cavalry division (Air Mobile), 10 to 14 October 1965. Michael now lives with his wife Jeanne in Evans, Georgia.

DEDICATION

I would like to dedicate this book to my wife Jeanne. My partner in life for these last fifty-four years.

JUTE
EMPIRE
GRAND
CITADELS
Arlistun
Quendara Pass
Stone Bridge
Marvelia
AIBER RIVER
Dunkern
Durnat Ford
MAGN RIVER
KINGDOM
TUBIN KINGDOM
VERNLAND
Taverna
Salizburg
Star Lake
Venedan on the lake
TUBIN
CHANNEL
PALISADES
Arssabash
Hadlendel
GREAT
OCEAN
SEA
Notterby
RED
Alder Vine
Kimtar
STRAIT OF
BALTHASAR
Quasar
JADE SEA
Malcran
Kazajiro
XANATAR

PROLOGUE

Interment rain swept the dark surface of the sea. A mass of grey-black clouds covered the vault of the sky, to a point that blotted out the horizon. The only colour in this grey world a bright-green bireme with bronze clad ram. A geometric band of yellow, black and red ran around the upper edge of the hull and the archer's catwalk. Eyes painted in black and white were on each side of the bow. At the peak of the mast flew a purple flag with a golden dragon passant, the standard of the Emperor of the Jutes. The only sound besides the wind and water was the beat of a drum marking cadence as the oars dipped in unison to propel the bireme through the water.

On the forward part of the archers catwalk, in the ships bow, stood three men. They were Emperor Eimion of the Jute Empire, Lord Marshal Rhodri his top commander and, Master Arfon his sorcerer. Emperor Eimion and Lord Marshal Rhodri both wore chain mail, surcoat, sword and helm under their dark-grey heavywool cloaks with cowl. Under his dark-grey heavywool cloak with cowl, Master Arfon wore a dark-blue robe decorated with embroidered arcane symbols in golden-yellow thread. Emperor Eimion and, Lord Marshal Rhodri were both in their mid-forties and of average height. They both had the powerful physique of warriors, having trained since childhood in martial arts. Emperor Eimion had a clean-shaven face with light-brown hair greying at the temples and brown eyes. He had a dour temperament and hardly ever smiled. Being suspicious of everyone close to him, he dealt mercilessly with anyone that he felt a threat to himself. Lord

Marshal Rhodri had black hair and close-trimmed beard shot through with grey and grey eyes. Lord Marshal Rhodri was one of the few men that Emperor Eimion felt that he could trust near the throne. Master Arfon, an older man of almost sixty years, was also of average height, but less robust, more scholarly in appearance, with long-grey hair and beard and dark-brown eyes. Knowing the limits to his authority and power, Master Afron was always quick to his loyalty and give advice.

As the bireme neared the beach they looked forward anxiously at a cave in the face of the cliff. The cave, being the home of the oracle of Narvis. Emperor Eimion, planning a military campaign of conquest, wanted a seeing by the oracle. Being overly superstitious, he was a man who always liked to hedge his bets.

Just before grounding the order to back oars was given, allowing the ram of the bireme to nudge gently into the sand. As soon as they grounded a ramp lowered from the bow to the beach. Emperor Eimion walked down the ramp to step ashore, followed by Lord Marshal Rhodri and, Master Arfon.

The stone face of the mountain behind the beach soared at a seventy-degree angle to a height of over two thousand feet. The oracle's cave opened onto a ledge more than three hundred feet up from the beach. A narrow trail with many switch-backs connected the ledge before the cave to the beach.

Without delay, they mounted the trail and begin to climb. Upon reaching the ledge in front of the cave, they looked about for any signs of life. A minion of the oracle came forth from the cave to greet them saying, "Good-day, Sirs. How may I assist you?"

Emperor Eimion looked at the oracle's minion before he answered. The minion was diminutive in stature. A large robe with cowl that the minion wore hid everything, even the face, giving no clue as to the gender of the minion. Even the thin and reedy voice could be that of an ancient male or female. Emperor Eimion then said, "We have come to see the oracle."

"Then follow me, Sirs." the minion said, turning to walk back into the cave.

Within the cave stood an altar to Eloisa, goddess of wisdom. Seeing the bowl on the altar, Emperor Eimion dropped several gold coins into it; feeling that a generous offering may bring about a favorable seeing.

The minion then led Emperor Eimion and his party through a small opening at the rear of the main chamber, into a smaller chamber. In the centre of the chamber, near a natural vent, a young woman with long-brown unkempt hair, and dressed in a dirty-grey shift, sat on a stool. They could hear the lass humming an incoherent strain.

Waving at the lass, the minion said, "Gentlemen, the oracle. I will now withdraw. You may ask her any question. She may answer you, and then she may not. However, keep this in mind. For every question answered, there could arise another question. Many leave here with more questions than they came with. When you are finished just return to the main chamber." Having finished the minion turned and left the chamber.

As soon as the minion passed from sight into the main chamber, Emperor Eimion and his party approached the oracle. Addressing the oracle, Emperor Eimion said, "I'm Emperor Eimion of the Jutes. I am about to embark on a bold military venture. I would like to know my chance of success."

The oracle continued to rock from side to side while humming. After a few seconds the oracle giggled, then spoke, "I see fighting. I see your banners advancing in triumph."

The men looked at each other with relief clear on their faces. However, their feelings of relief turned out to be premature. The oracle giggled again then said, "The prince of Dunboro."

Emperor Eimion looked again at the oracle with concern, then exclaimed, "The prince of Dunboro! What of the prince of Dunboro?"

The oracle giggled as she continued to rock from side to side. She then said, "Danger lies with the prince of Dunboro."

Concern now showed on Emperor Eimion's face and in his voice as he responded, "What is this about danger? What can the prince of Dunboro do to disrupt my plans?"

Rocking from side to side the oracle giggled, then said, "The danger from the prince of Dunboro is not certain, only a possibility."

Breathing easier, Emperor Eimion remarked to his companions, "We should have another look at our plans to ensure that the prince of Dunboro can't interfere with our plans until it's too late for him to prevail."

Master Arfon was about to reply when the oracle giggled, then exclaimed, "The Youth!"

Emperor Eimion's head snapped around to look at the oracle again. "What Youth!" he exclaimed.

The oracle giggled again, rocking from side to side. "The Youth." she repeated.

Emperor Eimion had no idea what the oracle meant by' the youth'; could this youth portend an ill omen? He had to know all that he could about this youth. He asked, "What about this youth? Is he a young man, or a lad?"

Rocking from side to side and giggling, the oracle said, "No." "Then it must be a young woman, or lass." Emperor Eimion said. Rocking from side to side and giggling, the oracle again said, "No."

By now, Emperor Eimion had become confused by the oracle's responses. He exclaimed, "What do you mean by 'no'! There are only two genders! This youth has to be one or the other!"

The oracle giggling rocked from side to side as she replied, "The gender and age of the youth is hidden from me."

Emperor Eimion started to ask another question when the oracle continued, "The youth together with the prince of Dunboro will be your undoing."

"What!" Emperor Eimion exclaimed loudly, "What do you mean by my undoing! You must tell me more!"

For several minutes, Emperor Eimion, Lord Marshal Rhodri and Master Arfon tried to get more information from the oracle to no avail. The oracle had started to hum her meaningless melody. The seeing had come to an end.

Emperor Eimion wanted more information, but knew that he would get no more from the oracle. After a few minutes he gave up and led his party back to the main chamber.

Leaving the cave, Emperor Eimion took the lead followed by, Lord Marshal Rhodri. Master Arfon brought up the rear as they started to descend the trail to the beach.

When they were half way down the trail, Emperor Eimion stopped, then turned to face the other two men, saying, "Gentlemen, we have something to discuss, and I don't want to do it in front of the men. So, I'm open to any ideas that you may have about this unexpected development."

"I take it, Your Majesty, that you mean the youth." Lord Marshal Rhodri said.

"Yes, I mean the youth!" Emperor Eimion exclaimed through clenched teeth, "Who else do you think that I mean? I want ideas!"

Lord Marshal Rhodri could see that Emperor Eimion had been shaken by the unexpected revelation of the oracle. He knew that Emperor Eimion felt most comfortable when there was a plan with everything tucked away in its own place. He didn't react very well to unexpected surprises. Lord Marshal Rhodri spoke, "Your Majesty, I know that you speak of the youth. However, with just the oracle's statement, the youth, we have nothing to go on. Not only do we not know the age or sex, but also the class is not known. Is the youth of noble birth and living in a palace? Is the youth a kitchen drudge, a beggar in the streets, a farmer's child working in the field? We have no clue. How are we ever expected to find this youth if we know nothing about him or her?"

Master Arfon's lips curled into an evil grin as he had a thought. He then said, "Your Majesty, we do not know who the youth is, we may never know. But, we do know the prince of Dunboro. If the prince dies, then it will not matter who the youth is."

Emperor Eimion smiled, then said, "I like it, Master Arfon. A simple solution to a vexing problem. Yes, the death of Prince Hugh of Dunboro would add another distraction for our enemy. The pigeons we have on the bireme. How many are for our agent in Dunboro?"

"We have three pigeons for Dunboro, Your Majesty." Master Arfon said. "Good," Emperor Eimion said, "use all three pigeons. I want a message sent to our agent in Dunboro. He is to arrange the assassination of Prince Hugh D'Croix, the prince of Dunboro." Pulling his cloak close about himself against the chill, Emperor Eimion continued, "Now let us hasten to the ship. I have need of a strong drink to warm my insides."

CHAPTER 1

The portly middle-aged woman moved about the cobblers shop, as she took her time to inspect the samples of the cobbler's wares. Within a couple of minutes, Chester the cobbler realized that she wasn't a serious customer, but merely browsing. He had been ready to close up the shop when the woman had entered. She had so far spent over half an hour looking at everything, but not showing an inclination to purchase anything. Every time that the woman had started for the door, something had caught her eye and she had turned aside to look. Chester had reached the limit of his patience. He thought, *gods, is this stupid, fat old cow ever going to give up and leave?*

Chester hovered close to her elbow hoping that she would hurry up and make a purchase so that he could get her out the door and close the shop. "Is there anything in particular that madam has in mind?" Chester asked, trying without much success to keep his irritation in check.

The woman however picked up on his ill mood. "Well, I don't see anything that I really like." she said in a tone of voice to show her displeasure. "Good-day, sir." She then moved to the door and left the shop.

As Chester closed the door behind the woman and throwing the bolt, he muttered under his breath, "Bitch!"

Turning the sign in the window to read closed he thought that over half an hour had been wasted on that stupid old cow for nothing, not even a boot lace sold. Turning to the stair at the back of the shop he said again, this time out loud, "Bitch!"

Chester took the stairs up to his living quarters over the shop. After lighting a lamp, Chester built a fire in the stove and put water for tea; he went up to the attic to check the pigeon coop. The messages could wait until after he had had his supper.

After making his tea, Chester took from the cupboard a wedge of cheese, a link of sausage and a loaf of dark bread. He then ate his meal alone, washing it down with tea.

Chester now lived alone. He had tried marriage once as a young man. It had been a calamitous affair from the start. All he and his wife ever did was argue. There had never been any love in the marriage. Finally his wife had left him.

After his wife had left him, he had not tried to get her back. He felt a lot better off without a wife. He only needed one thing from a woman; and that was negotiable with any prostitute.

Having finished his dinner, Chester got up from the table. He took from a cabinet a bowl of dried berries and nuts and a bottle of wine, then sat back at the table. After pouring a glass of wine, Chester reached for one of the tiny harnesses, saying to himself, "Now, let's see what we have here." Opening a small tube on the harness; he then extracted a slip of very thin paper covered with many groups of numbers. The second harness held the same message. Two pigeons had been used to insure delivery.

Retrieving the cipher from its hiding place, Chester decoded the message. He then sat back in his chair with a groan. "Damn!" He exclaimed, "Why this now?"

He read the message again, letting the enormity of the message sink in. "Why does Lord North want the prince of Dunboro assassinated?" He said to himself, "That's like shoving a stick into an ant hill." Well, it wasn't his place to question the orders from Lord North. He would have to arrange a meeting with Gerone.

It had been Gerone who had first contacted him with an offer to work for Lord North, and another person whom, Gerone did not know, called Hammer. The gold was good, but he had accepted mainly for

other reasons. He also knew that Gerone had been recruited by Hammer, through a woman at the White Dove brothel. In their organization he was the messenger between Lord North and Hammer. Gerone carried out the orders from Hammer or, Lord North.

Chester's pigeons came in by ships, mostly ships from Zanatar that traded with and smuggled for the Jutes. Gerone would smuggle the pigeons off the ship and deliver them to him. Gerone would then take pigeons raised by him to be smuggled onto ships bound for the Jute Empire. Chester thought that it all worked very well.

Chester got up from the table, and went back downstairs to the shop. From a cabinet in the shop he took a pair of black leather riding boots with red leather trim around the tops. He then placed them in the left rear corner of his display window, as viewed from the street. The boots in the display window being the prearranged signal that he needed to meet with Gerone. He knew that Gerone checked the window every day and would see the boots in the window tomorrow. He would then have dinner at the Red Ox Inn.

The next evening after closing the shop, Chester went up the stairs to his living quarters. There he put on a heavy-wool tunic, a wool beret and heavy-wool cloak with cowl. After having dressed for the cold night air, Chester checked to make sure that he had sufficient coin in his purse to cover the meal at the inn. He then went back down stairs and left for the inn.

Chester locked the door to his shop. Pulling his cloak snug about himself against the cold night air he started off for the inn. Unknown to him eyes followed his movements from the shadow of an alleyway. Eddy the cat knew that the cobbler lived alone; taking his meals and staying at home most evenings. When the cobbler did feel the need to go out, it would be for dinner first. He would then find a whore to bed for the evening. Eddy the cat knew that the cobbler could be expected to be gone at least till midnight. Now would be the best time for him to make entry into the cobbler's shop and home to look for his stash. Eddy the cat smiled, even the weather would cooperate; keeping the casual strollers off the streets. On a night with a cold wind blowing off the sea, few people would venture far from the home fires.

Keeping to the shadows, Eddy the cat moved to the alleyway behind the cobbler's shop. Then climbing the stone wall, made entry through a second storey window. Starting in the shop on the first floor, Eddy the cat made a thorough search of every conceivable location where the stash could be secreted without results. Finding nothing in the shop, Eddy the cat then moved to the second floor to search the cobbler's living quarters.

After a few minutes of searching, Eddy the cat found a loose wall panel behind a large armoire. Pulling the armoire away from the wall, Eddy the cat removed the panel. The panel had concealed the hiding place for a small book. Being fascinated by books, Eddy the cat looked at it, but found it to contain only a series of numbers, with corresponding letters, words and phrases. Taking the book and dropping it down the front of the tunic, Eddy the cat replaced the wall panel and armoire, then continued to look for the cobbler's stash.

Chester arrived at the inn. Over the door hung a sign with a red bull on a green field, the letters on the sign in dark-yellow read The Red Ox Inn.

Pushing the door open he entered the tap room of the inn. The bar took up the left-rear corner of the room, with the door to the kitchen next to the end of the bar. A large fireplace took up the center of the right wall. Across the room from the front door was the stairs to the upper floor; all the open space in the room being taken up by tables and chairs.

At this hour the tap room was a little more than half full with patrons having dinner, or just drinking. Chester spotted Gerone at a table next to the kitchen door having dinner.

Taking a seat at a table close to the fireplace, Chester signaled for the waitress. When the waitress arrived at the table, Chester asked, "What are you serving for dinner this evening, lass?"

The waitress replied, "We have a very good lamb stew, with fresh baked bread and baked apples."

Nodding with pleasure, Chester responded, "That sounds good. Bring me a tankard of dark ale now, and the rest as soon as it's ready."

"Yes sir." the waitress said. She then went to the bar to get him a tankard of dark ale. She then went to the kitchen, returning soon with his meal.

As she bent to place the tray on the table, Chester got a look down the front of her bodice at the swell of her breast and wondered how she would be in bed. Perhaps he could find out some other time.

As they ate dinner, Chester and Gerone were aware of, but did not acknowledge one another. Their actual meeting would occur after they left the inn.

After finishing his dinner, Gerone got up from the table, put on his cloak and hat, and then left the inn. Chester took about fifteen minutes longer to finish his meal. He then got up from the table, put on his cloak and hat, then left the inn.

Gerone having left the inn first; took a route to the cobbler's shop, making sure that no one had followed him. Arriving at the cobbler's shop, Gerone checked to make sure that no one had the shop under surveillance. He then secreted himself in the shadows near the door to await the arrival of, Chester.

Chester arrived back at his shop a few minutes after Gerone's arrival. He had been careful on his way home from the inn to be sure that he had not been followed from the inn. He unlocked the door and entered the shop. Gerone quickly slipped from the shadows, entering right behind Chester before he closed the door. Chester took a flint and steel and struck a spark to light a lamp. He then led Gerone to the stairs.

Eddy the cat having found the cobbler's stash under a loose floor board under the bed, had dropped it down the front of the tunic. The cobbler was no more creative than most other people were. A loose floor-board under the bed was something that Eddy always looked for.

Eddy the cat had then moved to the attic to see if there was anything of value there.

Eddy the cat found the attic to contain little more than a pigeon coop and a few trunks of old clothing. The attic had two windows set in dormers. One in the front and one in the back, the window in the back being partially open to allow the carrier pigeons ingress to the coop. One of the pigeons in the coop, most likely being a recent arrival, wore a tiny harness with a small message tube on it. Being curious, Eddy the cat removed the harness, and was about to leave when the down stair door of the shop opened. Moving silently to the rear window, Eddy the cat opened it enough to allow an easy exit. If need be escape could be made over the roofs of the buildings.

Soon, Eddy the cat could hear the voices of two men coming up the stairs. To climb out the window now could make noise that would be heard by the men. Eddy the cat just stood in the shadow near the window and froze.

Reaching the top step to his living quarters, Chester waved at the table saying, "Take a seat, Gerone. I can get a fire going in the stove for tea, or if you prefer, I have a fine port. It's an excellent vintage."

Settling into a chair, Gerone responded, "I would prefer the port." "Good choice." Chester said with a smile.

Using the flame from the lamp, Chester first lit a taper, then lit a candle that sat in a holder in the center of the table. He then took a bottle of port and two glasses from the cupboard. Pacing them on the table, he sat down across from, Gerone. After pouring for both, Gerone and himself, Chester raised his glass. Chester then said, "To the future."

"To the future." Gerone responded lifting his own glass.

They touched their glasses together then drank. Gerone then asked, "The future, what does it mean to you, Chester?"

Chester had a ready answer for that question. It had started when, despite his best efforts, the royal patent as the cobbler for the prince of Dunboro and his court had been awarded to the cobbler, Morris. Chester had been outraged. Clearly in his mind he was the better

cobbler, and the royal patent should have been his. Chester now loathed royalty, especially the prince of Dunboro. Chester said, "For me the future means that I will have my revenge on those who have wronged me, cheated me out of what was rightfully mine. I live to see the prince of Dunboro, and all of his kin ruined."

Gerone nodded, having heard all this before. Clearing his throat, Gerone said, "As for me, I'm only in it for the money. I'd say that I'm more likely to get what I want than you are. Now, why did you call this meeting?"

Chester took another sip of wine then spoke, "There has been a message from, Lord North. He has ordered an assassination."

When Chester didn't continue immediately, Gerone asked, "Who, might I ask, is the target for the assassination?"

Looking directly at Gerone with a smile on his face, Chester replied, "The target of the assassination is, Prince Hugh D'Croix, the prince of Dunboro."

Gerone's cheeks puffed as he blew out a breath with an audible sigh, then exclaimed, "The prince you say!" Calming down he continued, "That will be an order that will be difficult to carry out."

Nodding, Chester said, "Yes I know. Will you be able to do it?"

"No!" Gerone exclaimed shaking his head, "My lads are good for knocking in heads, or a dagger between the ribs, but not for this. There's another reason that I can't use them. They don't know of our involvement with, Lord North or, Hammer, and I want to keep it that way. We need a professional assassin, someone who can actually get close enough to the prince to do the job. We need to make a contract with the Brotherhood of the Black Rose for an assassin."

"That will be very expensive, won't it?" Chester said.

Gerone replied with a nod, "Yes it will. I will have to contact Hammer to arrange for the funds to pay for the contract."

Having overheard the topic being discussed by the two men down stairs, Eddy the cat realized just how dangerous the situation had become. These men would do anything, even resort to murder to keep their secrets. Eddy the cat, fearing being caught in the attic, started to steal silently toward the window when a floor board creaked. Without delay, Eddy the cat was through the window, and moving quickly over the rooftops.

"What's that?" Both men exclaimed, pushing back their chairs and standing. Grabbing the lamp, Gerone rushed for the stairs with, Chester close behind. Coming into the attic and seeing the open window, Gerone knew that it was the only way out of the attic. Gerone looked out the window in time to see what appeared to be a young lad scamper over the roofs to vanish into the night. Gerone started to climb out the window to give pursuit, but then thought better of it. Seeing how the lad easily ran over the rooftops; he knew that he didn't have the agility to give chase across the rooftops.

"Damn it!" Gerone exclaimed with bitterness; slamming his fist on the window sill, "Of all the gods cursed luck! How long was the lad up here? What did he hear?"

Chester could only shrug his shoulders with regret saying, "Who knows. We must assume that the lad had been up here all along. If so, he must have heard most of what we said. What should we do now?"

Being very concerned for the breach in their security, Gerone remarked, "The lad's most likely a thief."

With alarm Chester exclaimed, "My cache!" as he started to rush back down the stairs to his living quarters.

Reaching his living quarters, Chester grabbed the foot board of his bead, pulling it aside. He then dropped to his knees, prying up the loose floor board. He searched inside the cavity in the floor to no avail, it was empty. "My cache!" Chester exclaimed loudly, "That little bastard stole my cache!" Then something else came to mind, "The cipher!"

Chester jumped up, grabbed the corner of the armoire and pulled it away from the wall. Quickly removing the loose wall panel, he looked into the wall cavity. When he spoke it was almost with a sob, "The cipher, he has taken the cipher."

Now, Gerone was distressed, but better able to control his emotions than Chester was. He knew that they had a crisis on their hands. He also knew that they had to act quickly to minimize any damage done by the thief of the cipher. Looking at Chester he said, "Calm down, Chester. There can't be that many lad cat burglars in Dunboro. I'll put the word out. By morning every information peddler, rumor monger and beggar will know who we are looking for. We'll get him, you can be sure of that."

"Should we notify the Hammer?" Chester asked."

"No, not yet." Gerone responded, fearing reprisal from Hammer if he were to learn of this breach of their security. Gerone, feeling that he could take care of it himself decided that Hammer need not know.

CHAPTER 2

Once back at the shanty called home, Eddy the cat examined the haul from the cobbler's home. The leather purse was large and heavy with many coins of gold and silver. Eddy figured that even subtracting the fee that would have to be paid to the guild of thieves, there would still be plenty to live on for quite a while.

Next the book and pigeon harness. Eddy the cat knew that most thieves in the guild would have considered it a mistake to have taken it, but, Eddy had a passion for books and had not been able to resist taking it. The conversation that Eddy had been privy to had been the act of two men committing treason. Eddy now felt that if proof were ever needed of what had been overheard, the book and pigeon harness would provide it.

Eddy the cat thought while getting ready for bed that it might be a good idea to lay low for a few days, even delaying the fee to the guild of thieves for a couple of days. The cobbler, Chester and his co-conspirator would be desperate. And being that they plotted the assassination of the prince, they wouldn't give a second thought to murdering anyone that got in the way to keep their activities secret.

The next morning Eddy the cat took the time to make sure that the shanty wasn't being watched before leaving. Eddy, not wanting to take any chances on being found, planned to change location, at least for a few days. Too many people knew of this location for it to remain safe. Eddy left the shanty wearing extra clothing, boots, slouch hat, heavy-wool cloak with cowl and haversack with personal items and provisions. Eddy knew of the basement of a burned out house in the labyrinth of alleyways called Fisherman's camp that would make a good temporary home, as long as it didn't rain too much. Best of all it would be a place least likely to be searched.

Eddy the cat went first to the burned out house in Fisherman's Camp. With the fishermen already on the water at first light, and being too early for any shops to be open, there were few people on the street. After checking that no one seemed to be watching, Eddy entered the basement of the burned out house. The place was a mess, and there wasn't much there, but it would have to do. After all it would be only for a few days. That is if it would ever be safe to return to that home again. Eddy had endured worse than this before.

After dropping off the extra clothing and other items, Eddy the cat went back out into the city to see what was going on, keeping to the shadows as much as possible to be inconspicuous. For sure those two men would be desperate to get their property back, especially the book. They would certainly be looking for the thief that had taken their property.

Eddy kept thinking of the two men. Eddy knew the cobbler, Chester well, having kept him under surveillance for several weeks before the break in. The other man, the one called Gerone, was the mystery. The voice seemed to have a familiar ring, although at the same time being disquieting. Just that voice for some reason conjured up black thoughts and nightmares.

Eddy the cat first purchased one muffin from a street vendor for breakfast, at the cost of six and one half coppers. Then still keeping in the shadows and alleyways as much as possible so as not to be recognized, Eddy moved through the city. Finally, Eddy found an acquaintance, a street urchin by the name of, Jimmy the deft; a toe-headed lanky lad of sixteen years with grey eyes. Jimmy was a successful cut purse who worked other scams on occasion. "Jimmy the deft." Eddy called out just loud enough for, Jimmy to hear.

Turning his head and seeing, Eddy the cat in the shadow of an alleyway, Jimmy the deft came over to greet his friend saying, "Hi, Eddy the cat. What do you need?"

Eddy the cat shrugged nonchalantly saying, "Oh, nothing really important, Jimmy. I'm just curious as to what's new on the street this morning."

Jimmy the deft looked around to make sure that no one was close enough to overhear. He then looked at, Eddy the cat saying, "Eddy, you didn't by any chance do a job last night?"

"Why do you ask that question, Jimmy?" Eddy the cat asked, trying to appear casual about the whole thing, but now realizing that the word had already been put out on the street. Chester and Gerone were really desperate and had wasted no time in starting the search. They really wanted the book back, and to silence anyone that has knowledge of it.

Looking around again to make sure that their conversation wouldn't be overheard, Jimmy the deft responded, "Word went out early this morning. There is an interested party looking for a certain lad cat burglar."

"So," Eddy the cat said, "I'm not the only cat burglar in Dunboro. There are others you know."

Nodding, Jimmy the deft said with a smirk, "That's true, but it's a short list, and your name is close to the top, if not number one. Also the description of this lad could fit you"

"Did they say what this was all about?" Eddy asked, trying to show ignorance of the whole thing. "Perhaps this lad stole some lady's virginity?"

Chuckling at Eddy's humour, Jimmy replied, "They're not saying, but they want to get their hands on this lad quick. They are spreading money around like icing on a cake for information. They also have some guild enforcers, and other men out looking for this lad. If I were you I'd disappear for a while. You may even think of leaving Dunboro, if you can. If you're the lad that they are looking for and they catch you; you will end up floating in the harbor with your throat cut."

Nodding, Eddy the cat said, "Thanks, Jimmy." Taking some coins from a purse, Eddy gave Jimmy three silver royals. Then thinking of one last detail, Eddy handed Jimmy two gold half sovereigns saying, "It would be good if you would forget that you have seen me, at least for a couple of days."

Looking at the coins, Jimmy smiled and nodded. "You can count on me, Eddy." He said, "I'll not give you away. The gods know that you have watched my back on occasion, and even helped me out of some close scrapes. I'll not give you away."

Giving Jimmy a pat on the shoulder, Eddy the cat said, "Thanks Jimmy. Now, go ahead and get along. I'll see you again later."

Turning away, Jimmy said, "So long, Eddy."

With a wave of the hand, Eddy said, "Take care of yourself, Jimmy." Jimmy the deft started to walk up the street. After a few paces he looked back. Eddy the cat had already vanished into the shadows of the alleyway.

The rest of the morning into the afternoon, Eddy the cat prowled about Dunboro looking for a way out of the city, but finding only surveillance at every turn. The surveillance was so heavy along the docks and at all the city gates that no one could get near without being seen. At other key locations about the city, at a street corner, or at a shop front men took their ease. However, as relaxed as they appeared, their eyes never stopped moving.

Eddy the cat had been trapped in the city, and the trap was slowly being drawn tighter. What to do? That was the question. Eddy knew that with all exits from the city barred, it would only be a matter of time before they found their quarry. Eddy the cat being optimistic and resourceful knew that there had to be a way out, and given enough time it could be found.

The sky had by now turned from orange to red. In a few minutes it would go from red to purple and indigo, then fade to black. Eddy the cat now stood in front of a hovel in the working quarter of Dunboro; a small wattle and daub structure, with thatch roof and stone chimney. It had a door and one window on the front. The owner had the reputation of being a seer. Eddy had decisions to make, and felt the need of the seer's prophecy. Eddy knocked on the door. A small lass of about eight to nine years and dressed in a patched-brown shift opened the door.

Eddy the cat said, "I'm here for a seeing."

The lass stood aside saying, "Please come in, young sir."

Eddy the cat entered and looked about. The hovel had a single room, with a dirt floor, the front door and window being the only window and door in the structure. The fireplace took up the centre of the left wall. The fire in the fireplace provided most of the light in the room. The furniture consisted of an old cabinet, a simple three leg table, several three leg stools, two chests and two sleeping pallets on the floor.

An ancient crone in a black shift sat on a stool next to the fireplace, stirring what smelled to be a pot of stew. The crone motioned the child over to the fireplace. She then stood, letting the child take her place by the fire.

"Have a seat at the table, young sir." The crone said. Then taking a cane, she walked over to the cabinet. From the cabinet she took a clear-crystal bowl and a small silver cup. She then paced them in the centre of the table, and sat on a stool across from Eddy.

Eddy took a good look at the crone. She had a short-scrawny build. Her face was so wrinkled that even her wrinkles had wrinkles. Her long-straight hair was completely white. The visible teeth in her mouth could be counted with little more than the fingers of one hand. The skin on her hands was nearly translucent, with blue veins. But the eyes, they were like clear-blue crystals that shone with intelligence and curiosity. The old crone didn't give a price for the seeing, but, Eddy the cat wanting a good seeing, handed over three silver royals and one gold half sovereign. The crone smiled as the coins vanished into a fold of her shift.

"Now, lad I'll need something from you." The crone said. She reached up under, Eddy's hat, gave a jerk, and came away with a few strands of hair. "This will do." The crone said. She placed the strands of hair into the small silver cup in the centre of the table, and inverted

the crystal bowl over the cup. She then reached across the table and took, Eddy's hands into hers.

The crone started to incant a spell. Nothing seemed to happen for a few seconds, then the room seemed to darken. Threads of white smoke started to waft out of the cup. Soon copious amounts of smoke poured from the cup. The surface of the bowl became opaque. Then sparks of colour started to dance about the surface of the bowl. The sparks of colour coalesced into a kaleidoscope of all the colours of the rainbow; that arranged and rearranged themselves over the surface of the bowl. The colours bathed everyone and everything in the room in shifting colours of light. The crone gazed at the shifting colours, seeing what only she could see in them. Finally the colours faded, the bowl cleared of smoke and the level of light returned to normal.

Releasing Eddy's hands, the crone looked up from the bowl saying, "Young sir, you now stand at a juncture in your life. From this juncture there are many paths. You may take any of the paths, but one. The one path that you can't take is the path back. Your life must change. I see danger, strife, adventure, opportunity and happiness. However, you must choose well. The choice is yours alone to make."

Eddy the cat tried to get the seer to give guidance, or to just give some clarification to the seeing. The seer however had nothing further to add. That was all that, Eddy would be getting from the seer.

Eddy the cat left the seer's house just as confused as before; the only certainty being that the old life had come to an end. Another path would have to be walked now. Eddy tried to think of what to do next. There would be no going back to the old shanty. The only option now would be to return to the basement of the burned out house in the Fisherman's Camp. Tomorrow, Eddy the cat would have to give serious thought as to what to do next. If only a way could be found out of Dunboro. A new start could be made in Sallasburg, Stone Bridge, or some other city. Eddy would have to give it more thought.

The trip back to the basement of the burned out house in the fisherman's Camp took a twisted route through dark side streets and

alleyways, constantly checking that no one followed. All the caution and stealth took time and effort to be safe.

Near midnight, Eddy the cat approached the basement of the burned out house with extreme caution and stealth, trying to push back the darkness as much as possible with sight and hearing. Being fully on guard against ambush, Eddy had a dagger in hand for added security.

Suddenly, Eddy the cat heard the faint sound of the crunch of a boot as someone shifted his weight. Instantly, Eddy squatted. Something heavy swung past overhead, delivering a glancing blow to the top of the head. Pain exploded in Eddy's head. Fighting to remain conscious and alert, and sensing the position of the assailant; Eddy thrust out with the dagger and felt the blade drive deep into something firm, like a human body. There followed a grunt, then a cry of pain from a male voice. With a sudden burst of speed, Eddy ran away into the night. As Eddy fled the scene answering calls could be heard from two other men coming from the other side of the burned out house. There would be no going back to the basement, but where to go now that would be safe?

After a few minutes of flight, Eddy the cat slowed down and started to look for a place to holed up for the night. Eddy finally found a place of refuge behind some crates, in an alleyway that smelled like the final resting place for a few days of dead cat. As deplorable as it was, it would have to do.

CHAPTER 3

Despite Eddy the cat being exhausted sleep would not come; due to the scant comfort provided by the cloak on the hard, cold and damp pavement of the alleyway, a pounding headache and fear of discovery. Then there was the problem of what to do. With the docks and all the city gates being covered, Eddy now knew that getting out of Dunboro had become impossible. However, remaining in the city would eventualy lead to capture and death. There could be only one place of sanctuary now. No matter how personally distasteful it would have to be taken. Eddy had run out of options.

Two hours before first light, Eddy set out by clandestine route toward the main gate of the palace of Dunboro. Moving with stealth, every sound being heard, and every perceived movement having to be scrutinized, Eddy the cat finally made it to a place of concealment in the shadows near the main gate of the palace.

Finally at first light; taking advantage of an early morning delivery to the palace commissary, Eddy had tried to get past the gate by walking next to the wagon, only to be stopped by a guard. Blocking Eddy's way, the guard said, "Now lad, where do you think you're going?"

With respect, Eddy said, "Sir, I must see someone in the palace. I have some very important information to tell someone about."

The guard looked at the scruffy, smelly lad in front of him with scepticism. How could a worthless street waif have anything important to convey. He was most likely a thief that wanted nothing more than to pilfer some of the silver. "Now what important information can a lad like yourself possibly have?" The guard said with a patronizing tone.

Eddy could see that this guard would be difficult to get past. Still showing respect for the guard, even more than would be expected, Eddy said, "But, sir, I have information concerning the prince."

"Oh, and how does it concern the prince?" The guard asked sarcastically. Eddy, fearing being turned away by the guard became desperate. Eddy kicked the guard hard in the shin and bolted through the gate into the bailey, only to be stopped be soldiers standing close to the gate.

A corporal in the group of soldiers said to Eddy, as he was being held by two other soldiers. "Well lad, you wanted in so bad. Striking a soldier in the performance of his duty is a punishable offense."

Struggling to get loose from the grip of the two soldiers, Eddy cried out loudly, "But, they plan to assassinate the prince!"

Sir Walter, a knight of the court of Prince Hugh and his squire, Hal stood next to a pell close by that, Squire Hal had been hacking at with a practice sword, and couldn't help but to hear the lad's excited exclamation. If there were a plot to assassinate the prince, Sir Walter wanted to know about it. Stepping over to the soldiers restraining the lad, he asked, "You, lad, what's this about an assassination plot against the prince?"

At the approach of Sir Walter, all the soldiers, except for the two holding Eddy came to attention.

Eddy, seeing someone of authority willing to listen said, "Sir, I overheard two men plotting to assassinate the prince."

Knowing that some people made statements that later proved to be erroneous, Sir Walter said with authority, "You say that you overheard such a plot against the prince. What proof do you have to back up your statement?"

Eddy, trying to get the soldiers to loosen their grip, said, "Well, Noble Sir, I do have proof. It's inside the front of my tunic."

Sir Walter, nodding at the soldiers holding Eddy to relax their grip a bit said, "This proof, I will see it now."

Eddy withdrew the cipher and pigeon harness, then handed them over to, Sir Walter.

It took, Sir Walter less than two minutes to realize what he had. He addressed the corporal, the senior soldier present, "I will take charge of the lad, corporal. Duke Bran and Knight Marshal Simon must see this and question the lad."

Looking at Eddy, Sir Walter saw a young lad dressed in baggy pants, cut off above the ankles, too large tunic with whip-cord belt, much worn and scuffed boots, a slouch hat, with ragged cut auburn hair sticking out from underneath the hat at odd angles, and a heavy-wool cloak. The clothing, hands and face were smeared with soot, like he had been sleeping in a chimney. And the smell of the lad was strong, from Eddy having had to spend the night laying in the alleyway. Before the soldiers could move away, Sir Walter said, "Corporal, the lad must have been sleeping in the bait well of a fisherman's smack. Take him to the bath house, give him a bath, and find him something decent to wear."

Hearing this, Eddy jerked back, trying to break the grasp of the two soldiers, while yelling, "I don't need no bath, Noble Sir. Just give me a rag and some water and let me wash some of the grime off myself."

Ignoring Eddy's protestations, the soldiers dragged Eddy struggling and howling to the bath house.

As they were dragging Eddy to the bath house, Sir Walter turned to his squire and said, "Squire Hal, run to Duke Bran's office. Tell him of the lad, and tell him that I will have him there, as soon as he is cleaned up."

Bowing to Sir Walter, Squire Hal said, "Yes, Sir Walter." He then turned and started to move quickly in the direction of the main palace.

Squire Hal had hardly left for the duke's office, when the corporal burst from the bath house door in a panic, running up to Sir Walter. "Sir," The corporal exclaimed, "the lad isn't a lad, she's a lass!"

"What!" Sir Walter exclaimed, "How can that be?"

"It's true, Sir." The corporal said, "She's a lass. It quickly became apparent when we tried to undress her."

By now, Sir Walter and the corporal were over the shock of the event. Sir Walter, said, "Corporal, put a guard on the door. Keep everyone out, and her in. Send a man to fetch some of the maids to bathe her, and tell them to bring proper clothing for her. We can't have her masquerading as a lad."

The corporal raced off to carry out his orders. A little while later a group of women came from the main buildings of the palace, some carrying bundles of clothing, and entered the bath house.

About twenty minutes later the women exited the bath house. Two of the women were escorting a young woman between them; the other women returning to the main palace. The young woman was dressed in a dark-brown skirt, buff color blouse, green snug-fitted front laced bodice, brown leather slippers and russet color wool cloak with cowl. The metamorphosis from a dirty, smelly, unkempt lad dressed in rags, to a clean and well-dressed young woman was startling. Her body, although slender, wasn't delicate. Under the soft-feminine curves were muscle and strength. She had the light step and sense of balance like that of a dancer or an acrobat. The face of light complexion with a sprinkling of freckles, although not goddess like, had a balance of features and symmetry that gave her a very pleasing appearance. Sir Walter thought that in two to three years, when she was fully mature, she would be a very beautiful woman.

As the two women approached with the lass, Sir Walter could see that even though the lass was subdued, she was still angry. When they reached him the two women curtsied. The lass just stood erect, looking at Sir Walter with sapphire-blue eyes as hard as flint. Pointing to an object of cloth that one of the women were carrying, the lass spoke with barely contained rage. "You have forced me to dress like this, but I absolutely will not wear that wimple."

"But, Sir," The woman holding the wimple said in a beseeching tone, "the lass's hair is cut so short, it's unseemly. She must be made presentable."

"And my property," The lass said with anger in her voice, "my clothing, my purse with my money and my dagger. I want them back."

Finding a bit of humour in the lass's distress, Sir Walter had to keep a straight face. He could see that the lass had a strong will. Even after having her true identity revealed and having to submit to the will of others, she had the audacity to demand the return of her property. He said, "The clothing will be burned. As for the purse and dagger, we will see to that later." To the two women he said. "Burn the clothing, then deliver her property to me."

"Yes, Sir Walter," The two women replied.

Sir Walter, continued, "As for the wimple, we can do without that. You may go now. I can take it from here."

The two women curtsied, glad to be rid of their charge, then departed.

Sir Walter then addressed the lass. "Well, now that you have had a bath and have on good, clean clothing, how do you feel?"

Still upset by the coarse treatment at the hands of the maids, the lass literally spit out the words. "I feel like a complete idiot! I come to the palace in good faith, and what do I encounter, all manner of rough handling and indignities!"

Sir Walter, tried hard not to burst out with laughter. He knew that the lass felt ill treated by this unexpected change in situation, but he couldn't help but see some humour in it. He said, "Now, you say that they call you Eddy the cat, on the street. I take it that Eddy isn't short for Edward or Edwin?"

The lass replied in a matter of fact tone of voice, "My name is, Eleanora." "Eleanora," he said. "That's a lovely name. We can talk more later on, Eleanora. Right now we have a meeting with Duke Bran, and Knight Marshal Simon."

The duke's secretary, a young knight, escorted, Sir Walter and, Eleanora into the duke's office. Duke Bran, a tall man of advanced years, with gay hair, sat behind a trestle table that he used as a desk. Knight Marshal Simon sat in a chair next to the table. Sir Walter bowed. Eleanora gave a passing imitation of a curtsy.

Duke Bran looked at, Sir Walter and, Eleanora and said, "Oh, Sir Walter, where's the lad that you were to bring to me?"

Indicating Eleanora with a wave of his hand, Sir Walter said, "Your Grace, this is the lad."

Knight Marshal Simon, a stocky built man of middle years, with light-brown hair grying at the temples, sat regarding Eleanora, "What's this all about?" the Knight Marshal asked, with raised eyebrows, "Your squire said that you had a lad. Now you show up with a lass, even my eye sight isn't that bad. Could you explain that to me?"

Sir Walter said, "Well, My Lord, she hid her true identity, masquerading as a lad on the street. When we first got her she was dressed as a lad, and no one suspected anything different. We didn't discover the truth to her identity until I ordered the soldiers to give her a bath."

The Duke and Knight Marshal both laughed. After the mirth subsided, Knight Marshal Simon said, "I can well imagine that the soldiers were taken aback by this revelation."

With a short display of mirth, Sir Walter responded, "You can believe that, My Lord. You should have seen the corporal. The way that he came bursting through the bath house door, like the seat of his pants was afire."

Everyone roared with laughter, even Eleanora. After the laughter subsided, Duke Bran said, "I say, that must have been quite a performance to have fooled everyone." Looking at, Eleanora, he asked, "How did you manage to fool everyone."

With a faint smile and shrug of the shoulders, Eleanora responded, "It's not so difficult, Your Grace. Most people tend to see what they are looking for. If they think that they are looking at a lad, they will see a lad."

Knight Marshal Simon now spoke up. "Now, lass, it is one thing to look the part, but you're still a lass."

"My Lord," Eleanora said, "from my fourth year I have lived my life only as a lad. My mother felt that it was safer on the street to be a lad, than a lass. I now think and act as a lad." "This is the only female clothing that I can ever remember wearing," taking the skirt in her hands for emphasis.

Nodding, Duke Bran said, "I understand that you say that you can think and act as a lad, but how do you handle the personal conversations between men or lads about the opposite sex?"

With a little chuckle, Eleanora replied, "You mean that when men or lads talk about women and sex, Your Grace. I am well aware of the fantasies and fallacies of men and lads when it comes to the feminine gender. Some are a little scary, and some I have to bite my tongue to keep from laughing."

"Well, that's very interesting." Duke Bran said.

Looking at, Sir Walter, Duke Bran said. "Now, Sir Walter, what do you have for us?"

Eleanora gave this to me, Sir Walter said, handing over the cipher and pigeon harness to Duke Bran.

Duke Bran, looked at the cipher first. "Very interesting," he said. Putting the cipher down, he picked up the pigeon harness. Removing the cap on the message tube and looking inside said, "Now, what do we have here."

Taking tweezers, he withdrew a long-rolled strip of very-thin paper. Unrolling it he found a code of numbers written on the paper. Using the cipher, Duke Bran soon had the message decoded. Handing the cipher and message over to Knight Marshal Simon, Duke Bran said. "Simon, you have to take a look at this. It's very serious, it's an order to assassinate, Prince Hugh."

Duke Bran then looked at Eleanora saying, "Now, Eleanora, I want to know everything that you know about this. Leave nothing out, even if you don't think it very important."

Eleanora, having made the decision to be honest and candid with them, started to tell them about entering the cobbler's shop and living quarters. She left nothing out as she told her story of how she had found the cipher and pigeon harness. She then told them about overhearing the conversation between the cobbler, Chester and the unknown person called, Gerone. She finished by telling them of her escape over the rooftops, and the efforts of her adversaries to find her before she came to the palace.

When she had finished, Knight Marshal Simon said, "We know who the cobbler, Chester is. However, this other man that was called by the name of Gerone, do you have any idea who he could be?"

Eleanora thought for a few seconds before answering. "No, My Lord, I don't know him, although his voice gives me a feeling, like there's something locked away in my memory, something very terrible. As for the others that were mentioned, Lord North, and Hammer, I have no idea who they are. I do however know that Lord North sent the message, and that, Hammer is someone here in Dunboro. There is one other thing to consider. By the next morning the word was already out all over the city. In order to react so quickly, Gerone had to have an organisation, or crew to do his bidding."

"What do you mean by this?" Lord Marshal Simon inquired.

"Well, My lord," Eleanora responded, "it means that treason isn't his only activity. He could also be into smuggling, or other things."

Pushing back his chair and rising, Duke Bran said, "Eleanora, you have convinced me that there is a grave threat to the prince. Now let's be off. Prince Hugh, is waiting for us in his library." Everyone followed Duke Bran as he set out for Prince Hugh's library.

Entering the library, Duke Bran and, Knight Marshal Simon and Sir Walter bowed, Eleanora curtsied. Prince Hugh stood in front of the trestle table that he used for a desk. He was a man of thirty-two years, very handsome and in the prime of his life. He stood two inches over six foot with broad shoulders. He had light-brown hair, hazel eyes and was clean shaven. He had dressed in an unadorned tunic and trousers of indigo-blue with black boots.

After the introductions, Eleanora again told her story, this time to Prince Hugh, as he examined the cipher, pigeon harness and message. By now the stress, aching head, lack of sleep and nothing to eat for twenty-four hours had started to catch up with her. It had become hard for her to concentrate on what she was saying. Suddenly, she started to lose colour in her face, and sway on her feet.

Sensing Eleanora's distress, Prince Hugh grabbed her by the shoulders. "Are you ill, lass?" He asked.

Eleanora answered, "My head hurts badly, Your Highness." "Where at?" Prince Hugh, said. "On the top." Eleanora, said.

Prince Hugh reached up and felt the large bump from the blow that she had received the night before. "Wow," Prince Hugh said, "that's a real goose egg. How did you get it?"

Eleanora, replied, "Well Your Highness, some men were lying in wait for me last night. I detected one man close by me just in time to barely avoid a blow to my head by something heavy."

"Well, not quite avoided I would say." Prince Hugh remarked.

Eleanora managed a short laugh, then said, "Your Highness, as I squatted to avoid the blow, I thrust out with my dagger. I felt the blade strike deep, then a man's voice cry out in pain. I'm sure that he's hurting more today than I am."

"When was the last time that you ate, or slept?" Prince Hugh asked.

"About a day, Your Highness." Eleanora responded.

Pointing to a door, Prince Hugh said, "Sir Walter, take the lass to the sitting room, and make her comfortable. Then send a page to the kitchen for a tray for her."

Sir Walter, bowing to the prince, said, "Yes, Your Highness."

He then took Eleanora by the arm, and escorted her into the sitting room.

As soon as Sir Walter and Eleanora left the library, Prince Hugh, said. "Well, gentlemen, thanks to the lass we have been forewarned of an assassination plot. Now Bran."

"Yes, Your Highness." Duke Bran, responded.

"Bran," Prince Hugh said, "I want you to increase palace security, and do it without any fanfare. We don't need anyone asking questions."

"I'll have it done right away, Your Highness." Duke Bran, replied.

"And also," Prince Hugh, continued, "get with Sheriff Ancel in Dunboro. I want to know of anything unusual that is occurring in the city. Again, you don't need to give a reason why."

Duke Bran, nodded saying, "Done, Your Highness."

Prince Hugh now turned to Knight Marshal Simon, saying, "Simon, no one would go to all this trouble for no reason. We must consider that there could be an invasion of the kingdom in the near future. We must make our army ready."

"I'll take care of the army, Your Highness." Knight Marshal Simon said. Prince Hugh now said, as much to himself, as to the other two men,

"Now, what should I do with the lass?"

Neither Duke Bran, or Knight Marshal Simon answered the question knowing it to be rhetorical.

Prince Hugh, thought for a short time, then said, "Gentlemen, you may go now and attend to your duties. Also, send a page to ask my wife and Mistress Caitlin to attend me here."

Bowing, they both said, "Yes, Your Highness."

Twenty minutes later, Prince Hugh's wife, Princess Juliana, and Mistress Caitlin, his adviser for magic, were with him in his library. Looking at both of them he said, "Thank you for coming. We had an incident this morning. A lass, her name is Eleanora, came to the palace. She brought with her information of an assassination plot on myself." Prince Hugh saw his wife blanch, but continued, "There is little to worry about at this time. Now this lass is being hunted by the plotters, so I can't just let her go back into the city, she would most likely be dead in a days' time. Therefore, my dear, Juliana, I have decided to

place her with you as a personal companion. This is the only way that I can keep her safe, and to avoid questions being asked about her. Can you do that for me?"

His wife, Juliana, responded, "Yes, I can do that. Now, tell me a little about the lass."

Prince Hugh, continued, "As I said before her name is, Eleanora. I would say that she is between fourteen and sixteen years. She is in the next room, so you will be meeting her in a few minutes. Now, she is a bit unorthodox. To start with, the clothing that she is now wearing is the first female clothing that she has ever worn in her memory. Since the age of four she has lived on the streets as a lad, known as, Eddy the cat. And that's not all, she's also a cat burglar, she climbs walls, and runs over rooftops to steal people's property. Now, knowing this, do you still want her?"

With a smile, Princess Juliana said. "Oh, Hugh, you know that I can't turn down a challenge, I'll take her. Is the clothing that she is wearing is all that she has; we will have to provide a wardrobe for her. I shall have the maids get on it right away. I want to have everything ready before I take her in hand."

"Thank you, dear," Prince Hugh said.

Looking at Mistress Caitlin, he continued, "Mistress Caitlin, I also have need of your services. When Eleanora came to the palace this morning, she had contact with several soldiers and palace staff. Now I could swear them to silence, but that's not enough. Sir Walter can tell you who they are. Can you make them forget how, Eleanora came to the palace this morning?"

Nodding, Mistress Caitlin said, "Yes, Your Highness, I can do it. I can take them one at a time. There are ways to expunge those memories. Afterwards that time will just be a part of the day, being so routine as to not even leave a memory. Will that do?"

Smiling, Prince Hugh said, "That will do just fine. You can take care of it as soon as you are finished here." Prince Hugh, continued, addressing both Mistress Caitlin and his wife. "Now, Eleanora is waiting

in my sitting room. Since both of you will be working with her, I would like for both of you to go in to take charge of her when you're ready."

CHAPTER 4

Sir Walter escorted Eleanora to Prince Hugh's sitting room and invited her to make herself comfortable on a divan. Grateful to be away from the scrutiny of the prince and other nobles, Eleanora settled onto the divan with an audible sigh. He then went to find a page to send to the kitchen for a tray, leaving her alone.

As exhausted as she was, Eleanora found it hard to relax. With her true identity being exposed she felt alone and vulnerable. She also found it overwhelming being in the palace, with all the soldiers and nobility scrutinizing her. She had no idea of what was to become of her. She had willingly come to the palace, putting her fate into the hands of others. There would now be no going back to her old life on the street. She would now walk a new path. Would it be the right path? She now hoped that she had made the right decision.

Having seen the library of the prince, Eleanora had marvelled at so many books and scrolls in one place. Ever since she had been taught her letters and numbers, and had been shown how to make words with letters, she had been fascinated by books. That was what had prompted her to take the cipher when she found it. She would love to have the time, and the opportunity to spend time, in that library.

In less than twenty minutes a servant delivered a tray from the kitchen. The tray contained scrambled eggs, sausage, toast, butter, fruit preserves and hot tea. Being famished, Eleanora quickly consumed the meal. Now being warm, comfortable and fed, she could no longer fight her weariness and soon dozed on the divan.

The opening of a door brought, Eleanora awake and to her feet. Two women had entered the room. Eleanora, believing that at least one to be of noble rank, curtsied. Eleanora noticed that the two women were very different in appearance, the youngest being in her late twenties, not yet thirty; Very fair complexion, long-blonde hair and pretty face. She was slender of build, with a noble carriage, and elegantly dressed. The second woman was older, perhaps forty, dark complexion, with jet-black hair. Her face was handsome, with a look of mystery to it. This second woman, also of slender build, wore a vermilion-colour robe, with arcane symbols embroidered on collar and cuffs with purple thread, with a purple sash about the waist.

The two women stepped up to Eleanora and stopped. The younger woman then spoke, "I am, Princess Juliana," indicating the other woman, "and this is, Mistress Caitlin. She is a sorceress and an adviser to my husband, Prince Hugh. And you are Eleanora I presume?"

With a nod, Eleanora responded, "Yes, Your Highness, I am, Eleanora." Princess Juliana continued, "From what my husband has told me about

you, you have, let us say, a very unique background. Well, you can consider all that behind you now. My husband had decided to place you under my care." After looking into Eleanora's eyes for a few seconds, Princess Juliana continued, "You are, from this time onward, my personal companion. You are now a lady of the court and will learn to conduct yourself as such. Mistress Caitlin and I will give you all the help that you will need to perform your duties. Now, Eleanora, do you have any questions?"

Eleanora could hardly believe what she was hearing. A lady of the court and the personal companion to the princess. Her world had just completely changed, like she was now living in a dream. "Oh, Your Highness, do you think that I can do it?" Eleanora asked with a look of astonishment on her face.

Princess Juliana could since, Eleanora's confusion and gave her a warm smile to booster her confidence. "Don't worry," Princess Juliana,

said. "I'll take good care of you. Now, I need to know something about you. Do you have any family here in Dunboro?"

Eleanora responded, "No, Your Highness, I have no family in Dunboro, I'm an orphan."

Princess Juliana thought for a few moments, then said, "That will make it a bit easier. Okay, Eleanora, from now on you are the daughter of an influential merchant from Marvella. That should be far enough away that no one will think of knowing you. But just in case, make up a family history that you can remember. Now, remain aloof to the servants and they will not bother you. The ladies of the court may be curious, but have enough manners not to pry. Do you understand?"

Eleanora nodded saying, "Yes, I understand, Your Highness."

"Good." Princess Juliana said, "Now, you seem to be in need of rest. I understand that the last twenty-four hours have been very stressful for you."

Eleanora replied, "Yes, Your Highness, it has been very stressful." Princess Juliana then said, "Then I will show you to your apartment. You may have all day to rest. I will have a servant awaken you in time to get ready for diner. You will dine with us this evening. It will be informal, so just watch me if you need to, and do as I do. Now, follow me." Princess Juliana, along with, Mistress Caitlin led, Eleanora to a two room apartment close to Princess Juliana's own apartment. It consisted of a sitting room and bed chamber. It was lavishly decorated with frescoes, expensive furniture and furnishings. It even had a feather bed.

Eleanora viewed the apartment with eyes wide with wonder, then said, "Is this all for me?"

Smiling at how Eleanora had reacted when shown her apartment, Princess Juliana responded, "Yes, it is all for you. This will be yours for as long as you are with us."

Princess Juliana then opened the doors of the large armoire in the bed chamber. It was filled with very splendid clothing, gowns, skirts, blouses, and all manner of feminine apparel. "I also had this delivered for you." Princess Juliana said.

"All for me?" Eleanora said, with a hint of disbelief in her voice.

Patting Eleanora on the arm and smiling, Princess Juliana said, "Yes, this is all for you, and you will need it all at court. Mistress Caitlin and I will leave you now, so that you can rest before diner. I will send the maid in to help you undress. I'm sure that you would like to sleep before dinner."

Eleanora replied, "Thank you, Your Highness, I would like that." Princess Juliana and Mistress Caitlin left the apartment. Two minutes later a maid entered and curtsied to Eleanora. "My Lady," the maid, said. "May I help you in any way?"

Quickly recovering from the surprise of being shown deference toward her by the maid, Eleanora replied. "Yes, I wish to sleep for a while. You can help me out of these clothes."

In a few minutes the maid had Eleanora out of her clothing, into a nightgown and the bed covers turned back. The maid then curtsied to her again and left the apartment. Eleanora had never had such a bed before, having for all her life slept on a sleeping pallet on the floor. The bed proved to be so soft and comfortable that she was asleep almost immediately.

Chester had just finished taking the foot measurements of a woman, when the bell over the door to the shop jingled as someone entered. Chester looked up to see Gerone standing in the shop and said, "I'll be with you, sir, as soon as I have taken care of this lady."

Waving a hand, Gerone said. "Take your time, cobbler. I'm in no hurry." As Chester went back to serving his customer he wondered why Gerone had come to his shop in the middle of the day. He had never done that before. Chester became nervous thinking that Gerone's visit did not bode well for him.

As Chester finished serving the woman, Gerone casually inspected some of the cobbler's production that was on display.

Chester finished with the woman. As she started to leave, Chester turned to Gerone. "How can I help you, sir?"

"I need a new pair of boots." Gerone responded.

Indicating a chair, Chester said, "Then have a seat sir, and I'll measure you for a new pair of boots."

As soon as the woman left the shop, they dropped the verbal charade. Chester did however keep going through the motions of removing Gerone's boots and measuring his feet for a new pair of boots. Why, Chester wondered, had Gerone come to his shop in the open, in the afternoon. Before he could ask, Gerone said, "We know now who took your stash and the cipher. He's a thirteen or fourteen-year-old cat burglar. On the street he's called, Eddy the cat."

Chester, smiling for the first time since the loss of the cipher, said "Then you will soon have him?"

"No, I think not." Gerone said shaking his head. Chester, starting to imagine the worst asked. "Why not?"

"He's a slippery one." Gerone replied, "We found out who he was, that was easy enough. We even found out that he had moved to a new place to hide out. We laid a trap for him, but he stuck a blade in the gut of one of my men, dealing him a wound that will prove fatal, and slipped away. We tried to follow him in the dark, but he was too quick and got away.

"Now he has vanished. No one has been able to find him. Some way, he must have been able to slip past my men, and found a way out of the city. I must admit that because of his age I underestimated the crafty little imp."

Now worried, Chester exclaimed, "We must do something to find him!

We must recover the cipher!"

Gerone sighed, then spoke, "Forget the cipher, we have bigger problems." "What problems?" Chester asked with fear now clearly showing in his voice.

Gerone said, "You have been watched since mid-morning. There is a street vendor across the street, near the corner. He is selling meat pies, but mostly he is watching your shop."

"What are we to do?" Chester asked nervously, with an image of the prince's gibbet on his mind.

Gerone said, "You will have to leave Dunboro. There's a ship in the road stead that will be leaving on the morning tide. The captain is in debt to me, and will be willing to give you transit to a place out of the reach of the Prince of Dunboro."

"But what about my business, I can't just leave it behind. It's all that I have." Chester said.

"Don't worry," Gerone said in an encouraging tone. I'll see that you have funds enough for a fresh start. After you leave, my men will take everything of value to sale before the Prince's agents seize everything. You know that you must go, you have no options."

Chester realizing that Gerone was right nodded saying, "You are right. I have no choice, I must flee."

With relief, Gerone said, "Now we haven't much time. When you close your shop this evening, you will go to an inn for dinner. It doesn't matter what inn that you go to, or even that you are followed. Just have a good time at dinner and remain at the inn until at least two hours after sundown.

"After dinner, you will go to the house of the White Dove, for a night with a woman. I will be waiting for you there. I will lead you out a bolt hole into the sewers, that's not known to the city watch. We will proceed through the sewers to the dock. Then from the docks, by boat to the ship."

As Gerone got up to go, he said. "I wish you good fortune, Chester." Chester replied with sincerity. "Thank you Gerone for all that you are doing for me, I'll not forget it."

Eleanora was awakened by a maid. "My Lady," the maid said, "it's time to get ready for dinner."

Eleanora threw the covers off, and swung her feet to the floor. She felt very refreshed after a few hours of sleep, and hungry.

The maid spoke, "My Lady, I have set out clothing for you. Do you wish me to help you dress?"

Being unfamiliar about woman's clothing and welcoming the assistance, Eleanora said, "Yes, you may help me to dress."

As the maid helped her to get dressed, Eleanora thought of her suddenly-changing circumstance. As much as she had tried to avoid it, she had known that she could not have kept up the ruse of an orphan lad living on the street much longer. As Eddy the cat, she could have no friends, or close associates. To have anyone close was to risk exposure. The loneliness, as hard as it had been, became even harder with the onset of puberty. Now she had had to fight to keep her emotions and desires hidden. From time to time she would meet a lad of your own age, or a young man a little older than herself, and would become attracted to them. The only thing that she could do had been to ignore her passions and keep her distance from them.

It had at first been upsetting for her to be found out, but at the same time a relief. She now realized that she had been freed to be herself.

Soon, with the help of the maid, Eleanora stood dressed in an unadorned, but well-made gown of light-green silk brocade.

Within a couple of minutes of Eleanora being ready, there came a knock at the door. The maid opened the door. A page stood in the door. He bowed to Eleanora saying, "My Lady, I am to escort you to the dining hall."

As Eleanora exited her apartment to follow the page, the maid curtsied to her. The page led her down to the next floor below, and into another wing of the palace to the dining hall. Entering, Eleanora noticed that most of the diners were already seated. The page showed Eleanora to a table below, but close to the head table. The page then bowed to her, and withdrew.

At Eleanora's table were other ladies and gentlemen of the court, engaged in polite conversation. Being that she had not been introduced, they politely ignored her. Having nothing better to do, she started to look at the other diners. Duke Bran and Knight Marshal Simon sat at the high table. Eleanora noticed that Duke Bran wore an indigo-blue tunic, with silver embroidery at the collar and cuffs, black belt with silver buckle, black trousers and black boots. Knight Marshal Simon wore the uniform of the prince's legion, dark-green tunic with the coat of arms of the Prince of Dunboro, less the heir apparent coronet, on the left breast, brown leather belt with brass buckle, brown trousers and brown boots. Mistress Caitlin also sat at the high table, dressed the same as she had been this morning.

The head steward announced: Gentlemen and ladies, their highness Prince Hugh and Princess Juliana. Everyone in the dining hall stood while the prince and princess entered and took their seats.

Before anyone had started to eat, the Master of Ceremony Baronet Bartholomew, stepped forward and struck the floor with the butt of his staff three times; the dining hall fell silent. He then spoke, "Gentlemen and ladies, his Highness Prince Hugh, wishes to introduce to the court the most recent addition to the court, Lady Eleanora of Marvella. She is joining the court as the personal companion to Princess Juliana. Lady Eleanora, please stand."

Eleanora stood and was greeted by a round of polite applause from the court. She then took her seat and the meal began, with servants bring the meal to the table.

The Master of Ceremony, Baronet Bartholomew took a good look at her as he wondered why he had not been given advanced notice of her arrival. He would have to check on this. He didn't like it when protocol wasn't followed.

During the meal, Eleanora's table mates slowly started to warm to her and to include her in their conversion. Being that the topic of conversation dealt mostly with the most recent court gossip, Eleanora didn't speak much, except to answer questions directed towards her.

After dinner a page escorted Eleanora back to her apartment. Once in her apartment she sat in a chair in her sitting room, next to the window. The sun having set, she looked out over the battlements of the palace, to the lights of the city of Dunboro and the lights of the ships anchored in the road stead. In less than twenty-four hours her

life had changed beyond recognition. The seer had been right, the one path that she could no longer walk was the one back to her past life.

Eleanora still sat at the window looking out at the lights of the city when the maid entered to help her get ready for bed.

She thought as she undressed and got into her nightgown that her first day at court went rather well. Eleanora, being all too aware that she had been given an opportunity that few people of her social position and circumstance dare even dream of, knew that much would be expected of her. She had determined to do her best to justify Prince Hugh and Princess Juliana's faith in her and become a lady of the court worthy of her position.

Chester closed his shop at the regular time, as if there was nothing at all different about this day. He then went upstairs to get ready to go out.

Knowing that he would be leaving for the last time he changed into his best clothes. He then put on his hat and cloak. He then took a few small items important to him that he could easily carry on his person. When he left he didn't look back. His life in Dunboro was at an end.

From his shop he casually walked to the Wagoner's Rest Inn. If he had cared to look back, he might have noticed the two men following him, keeping to the shadows as much as possible.

At the inn he ordered an ale and dinner, not knowing or caring about the two men who had entered shortly after he had. They had occupied a table close to him. Not caring if he was being watched, Chester took his time to enjoy his diner. After dinner he ordered two more tankards of ale before leaving.

From the inn, Chester walked leisurely to the house of the White Dove. By now he had spotted the two men following him. Acting as though he hadn't noticed them, he smiled at the thought of them waiting outside the house of the White Dove on this cold night. They would be trying to keep warm as they watched the door waiting for him to come out as he slipped away to begin his new life.

Chester entered the entry lounge of the house of the White Dove. The house madam stood to greet him as he entered the lounge saying,

"Good evening, Chester. We have not seen you for a couple of weeks. How have you been doing?"

"Well enough," Chester said, keeping up the ruse on the chance that an agent of the sheriff posing as a customer was listening, "I felt the need for feminine pleasure this evening. Is Lucia available?"

Smiling and giving him a playful poke in the chest with her finger, the madam said, "Lucia is here, but I have someone special for you tonight. She is young, fresh and exotic. She has skin the color of amber, long-raven hair, large-dark eyes and the body of a goddess."

Smiling, Chester said, "My manhood already swells at the thought of this rare gem. Please lead the way."

The madam led Chester through a door into the interior of the building. She led him down a long hall, with doors on both sides. Behind some of the doors could be heard the sounds of couples copulating. At the end of the hall the madam opened the door on the left. Behind the door stood a woman in her late twenties to about thirty years, dressed in a dark-brown gown and black heavy-wool cloak with cowl. Without preamble the woman said to, Chester, "Follow me, sir."

The woman stepped through the door with Chester falling in behind her. The woman led Chester to a flight of stairs that led to the basement. In the basement the woman pointed to a heavy-oak tap door in the floor saying, "Would you please open this trap door, sir."

Chester reached for an iron ring set in the door and pulled. The trap door swung open on well-oiled hinges to just past vertical, where it stood held in place by a chain.

Starting to climb down through the trap door, the woman said, "Please follow me, sir."

Chester followed the woman down through the tap door, into the cities sewers, closing the trap door behind him. As Chester's eyes adjusted to the darkness of the sewers, he noticed three men standing close by. One of the men held a shuttered lantern with the shutter opened enough to be able to make out the people standing in the darkness. One of the

other men was Gerone. "Good-evening, Chester," Gerone said, "good to see that you made it. Did you have any problems?"

Shaking his head, the motion barely perceivable in the darkness, Chester replied, "No, there were no problems. However, there are two men who have been following me."

"Did they follow you into the house of the White Dove?" Gerone asked. Chester answered, "No, they stayed outside."

Gerone laughed, then said, "That's good, they say that cold-night air is good for the constitution."

Chester, feeling really good by now, said, "Let's hope that they freeze their private parts off. By the way, who are they?"

Gerone responded, "Most likely agent of the sheriff, from the city watch. It's for certain that that little bastard, Eddy the cat, got to someone. For sure it's time that you leave Dunboro."

Gerone took a small- leather bag with a shoulder strap and handed it over to, Chester saying, "Here's the gold that you will need to get started over again as soon as you are settled."

Chester took the bag and opened the flap to check the contents. The man with the lantern held it high so that Chester could check the contents of the bag. Seeing the glint of gold, Chester smiled with pleasure saying, "I knew that I could count on you, Gerone. I'll never forget this."

Gerone replied still smiling, "Okay, but we must be off now. I want you safely aboard the ship as quickly as possible."

Without further words they set off through the sewers, headed for the docks. The woman came with them so that she would not be seen leaving the house of the White Dove. When they emerged from the sewers, she would leave them to go to her home.

Chester said, "I didn't know that the sewers were so large."

Gerone responded, "Yes they are. Most of the time there's just a little water running down the center channel, with the sides mostly dry enough to walk on. Only during heavy rains is the water too deep for anyone to come into the sewers."

"Do many people use the sewers?" Chester asked.

Gerone answered, "Smugglers use them to bring in goods from the ships, to avoid paying customs duties. You also have thieves, muggers, assassins and others who don't want to be seen moving about the city."

Nothing more was said until they came to a ladder that led up to the basement of an inn near the docks. The stairs from the basement came up behind the kitchen. From there they exited through the rear door of the inn, the woman going her own way. Gerone, with his team, kept moving toward the docks.

Half an hour later, Gerone and his party approached a deserted pier. Neither of the two moons being in the night sky as yet, the only light being that distant light from the city and the stars in the sky. As they started down the pier, Gerone spoke, "We're almost there. The boat is tied up to a floating dock, just below the ladder at the end of the pier. Once in the boat my men will row you to the ship."

"You're a true friend, Gerone." Chester said, "I'll never forget what you have done for me."

In his excitement, Chester pulled a little ahead of Gerone. Looking at the lights from the ships at anchor, Chester asked, "Which ship is it?"

With his left arm, Gerone pointed just past Chester's left shoulder saying, "It's that one over there."

"Which one?" Chester asked.

Suddenly, Gerone grabbed Chester by the jaw and yanked his head back at the same time driving the long blade of a dagger through Chester's back, between his ribs and through the heart, with the point of the dagger protruding from his chest. Chester didn't even have time to struggle, or to cry out. He lost consciousness almost immediately and was dead in minutes.

"Sorry Chester, nothing personal, you just became a liability. You know the old saying, you don't throw good money after bad." Gerone said.

Gerone, wiped the blood from the blade of his dagger on Chester's cloak and put it away. He then said to his men, "Get the gold and

anything else of value off the body and throw it in the water. If we're lucky the tide will carry it out. If not, they may think it a mugging that went bad."

CHAPTER 5

When the maid arrived at Eleanora's apartment the next morning, she found Eleanora already awake. Eleanora sat in a chair, in her nightgown and robe, next to the window in her sitting room, watching the dawn break over the city of Dunboro. Curtsying, the maid asked, "Is, My Lady, ready to get dressed now?"

Eleanora, taking her eyes from the scene outside the window to focus on the maid replied, "Yes, I wish to dress now. You may lay out clothing for me."

Eleanora followed the maid into the bed chamber, where the maid selected clothing from the armoire, with Eleanora's approval; then helped her to get dressed.

When, Eleanora had finished dressing, the maid asked, "Does My Lady, wish to send for a breakfast tray now?"

With a nod, Eleanora said, "Yes, I would like to have breakfast now." The maid curtsied, then turned and left the apartment to send a page to the kitchen, to have a breakfast tray sent up to, Eleanora.

After breakfast a page arrived to escort Eleanora to Princess Juliana's apartment. It was but a short walk, being that Eleanora's apartment was close to the princess Juliana's apartment. Arriving at a door, the page knocked. A woman's voice from within said, "Enter."

The page opened the door and motioned for Eleanora to enter. Eleanora entered the room, the page closing the door behind her. Eleanora found herself in an opulently furnished sitting room. Princess Juliana and, Mistress Caitlin sat on a divan near a window.

Eleanora Curtsied saying, "Your Highness."

Waving her hand at a chair next to the divan, Princess Juliana said, "Please have a seat, Eleanora."

As she took her seat in the chair, Eleanora noticed that Princess Juliana was dressed in a splendid gown of cobalt (kings) blue silk brocade. Mistress Caitlin wore a dark-green robe with red-orange embroidery and sash.

Looking at Mistress Caitlin, Eleanora wondered if she ever wore anything other than those robes.

When Eleanora had made herself comfortable in the chair, Princes Juliana said, "Well, Eleanora are you comfortable in your apartment?"

Eleanora responded enthusiastically, "Oh yes, Your Highness, most comfortable. It's the best that I have ever had. I was especially amazed by all the clothing. How could you have gotten all that for me so quickly?"

Smiling, Princess Juliana answered, "Getting the clothes was easy. Nothing is ever thrown away as long as it can be used again. We have clothing stored in trunks, in basements and attics all over the palace. Fine clothing in good repair, just waiting for someone to need it again. All I had to do was to send the maids to find an appropriate wardrobe for you in your size."

The next question that Eleanora asked was the question that had been on her mind since she had come to the palace yesterday. "Your Highness," Eleanora said, "why has all this been done for me? I'm not high born, or have any family of influence. I'm just a thief living on the streets."

Princess Juliana could understand Eleanora's confusion over her sudden rise in social status. It was, however, a very unusual occurrence. It may even be unprecedented. Certainly Princess Juliana had never seen or heard of it before. She said. "Well, Eleanora, that was my husband's decision. As for why he decided to put you into my care, you will have to ask him. He could have just as easily assigned you as a maid, or a kitchen drudge, or even confined you. I'm sure that he had a very good reason for what he did."

Eleanora thought for a minute, then responded, "Yes, I understand, Your Highness. However, I will have to ask your husband about it when I can."

Princess Juliana said, "Mistress Caitlin, I believe that you have something to say to, Eleanora."

With a nod to Princess Juliana, then smiling to Eleanora, Mistress Caitlin said, "Good-morning to you, Eleanora."

"Good-morning to you, Mistress Caitlin." Eleanora replied.

Mistress Caitlin continued, "I had to see to it that no one, except those that have a need to know, retained any memory of the circumstance of your arrival here at the palace yesterday. The only ones who know of your true identity is Prince Hugh, Duke Bran, Knight Marshal Simon, Sir Walter and the two of us. Everyone else believes that you arrived from Marvella."

Eleanora, being curious about magic and magicians, wanted to know how Mistress Caitlin had done it. She asked, "How did you make all those people forget, Mistress Caitlin?"

"Let me show you something." Mistress Caitlin said, pulling a small object from a hidden pocket in a fold in her robe. "This is a device, or talisman if you want to call it that. It is what I used as an aid to expunge the memory of your arrival from the memory of all those that had no need to know."

Holding the device out towards Eleanora, Mistress Caitlin asked, "Would you like to have a look at it, Eleanora?"

Reaching for the object, Eleanora said, "Yes, thank you, I would love to see it."

Taking the object in her hand, Eleanora could see that it was a highly-polished stone about the size of a hen's egg. The stone felt warm to the touch, but comfortable in the hand. The stone was opaque-white with tiny flakes of color, like an opal. Eleanora became fascinated by the stone.

When, Eleanora looked up all she could see was, Mistress Caitlin's face, as if she were viewing it at the end of a long-dark tunnel. The

face moved forward until it seemed to be almost touching hers. Now all that Eleanora could see was Mistress Caitlin's dark-mesmerizing eyes. An alien presence seemed to enter her mind. It didn't seem to be malicious, just curious. No secret could be denied it. How long it stayed could not be determined. When at last the entity withdrew it seemed like less than a moment had passed, not even enough time to warrant a memory.

Eleanora turned the talisman in her hand admiring it; having no memory of the mind probe. She said, "Oh, it's beautiful, Mistress Caitlin." handing it back, Eleanora continued, "Thank you for letting me look at the device."

Taking the device, Mistress Caitlin said, "I'm glad that you like it, Eleanora. A good many people don't trust those of us who practice the arts.

They would find the handling of a talisman discomposing."

Princess Juliana now spoke. "Well, Eleanora, now that you have seen Mistress Caitlin's toy, we can discuss other things. The first thing we need to cover is your duties at court. As my personal companion you will be available to me when I need you. That is why your apartment is close to mine. Now do not misunderstand, you are a lady of the court, not a servant. Now as a lady of the court, but without title, you have the rank equal to a squire. Your main task for now will be to master the social skills that you will need at court."

Looking Princess Juliana in the eyes, Eleanora said, "Yes, Your Highness, I understand. I will do my best to justify your faith in me."

Princess Juliana responded, "Yes, I'm sure that you will, Eleanora. Now, I would like to know about you and your family."

Eleanora said, "I have no family, Your Highness, I'm an orphan." Princess Juliana continued, "You may be an orphan now, but you did have a father and mother at one time. Can you tell me about them?"

Eleanora took a few moments to order her thoughts, then began. "Well, Your Highness, most of my family like grandparents, uncles, aunts, cousins I have no memory of. I don't even know from what shire I was born in, or came from. I only remember my parents. My father and mother were farmers. The only recollection I have of my father is of a very large person with large hands, rough with callouses, who made me happy. He would lift me in his arms and tickle me until I would laugh. Then in my forth year he was gone."

"What do you mean, gone?" Princess Juliana asked.

Eleanora answered, "Mother told me that father was crushed by a falling tree while clearing new land for pasture."

By now starting to feel sorrow for Eleanora, Princess Juliana asked, "What about your mother, Eleanora?"

With a sigh, Eleanora said, "Well Your Highness, when father died the lord of the shire gave the land for another man to work. Destitute, mother and I moved to Dunboro. She felt that here she could find work and provide for the both of us.

"In Dunboro the only work that mother could get was serving in the inn. However, that wasn't enough to live on so mother was forced to whore for men. Mother feeling it being safer for a lad on the street than a lass, had me dress and act as a lad. Eventually I even started to think as a lad.

"Then one night, it was about this time of year, three months before the summer solstice festival when I would be counted nine years old, a man came to the house. Being that I was in the back room, I only heard his voice. Mother, never wanting me around when she was whoring for men, sent me away before I could see him. Taking my hat and cloak, I went out to walk the streets. When I returned a crowd of people and the city watch were at the house. My mother had been murdered."

By now Princess Juliana was shocked, with tears starting to trickle down her cheeks. Even Mistress Caitlin showed some signs of distress. Princess Juliana said, "You poor child. You must have cried a lot for your mother."

Looking at Princess Juliana, Eleanora said, "Yes, Your Highness, I cried all that night. That's the last time that I have cried. Life is hard on the street, you have to be tough to survive. You cannot show weakness."

Princess Juliana felt the need to change the subject now. She could learn more about Eleanora's life on the street later. She said, "Tell me about your education, Eleanora. How much have you had?"

Eleanora, also wanting to change the subject, took a deep breath then replied, "Well, Your highness, I never had a regular teacher and my mother couldn't read or write. However, the inn keeper that my mother worked for taught me the letters and numbers and showed me how to use letters to make words."

Princess Juliana said, "So you can read and write?"

"Yes, Your Highness," Eleanora said, "I love to read. Whenever I find a book I want to know what is in it. That is why I took the Cipher that I gave to your husband."

Nodding, Princess Juliana said, "Yes, I've heard of the cipher that you speak of. It's good that you can read. Now, how are you with numbers?"

Eleanora answered, "I can do basic mathematics like add, subtract, multiply and divide."

"Fine," Princes Juliana said with a smile, "We will have the tutors that teach my children also work with you. You will also be taught etiquette. Since my husband has made me responsible for you, it will be my task to make you a proper lady of the court."

Eleanora could not help but to smile. Suddenly she could see opportunities that she could never have imagined opening up for her. She said, "I am very grateful to you and your husband, Your Highness. I shall do my best to justify your faith in me."

"I'm sure that you will." Princess Juliana said, "Now, just one last question. What age will you be counted at the coming summer solstice festival?"

"I will be counted sixteen, Your Highness." Eleanora said.

Princess Juliana said, "You may withdraw now, Eleanora. We will speak again later."

Eleanora got up from the chair and curtsied saying, "Your Highness." She then turned and left the room.

When Eleanora had left the room, Princess Juliana turned to Mistress Caitlin saying, "You used the query device on Eleanora. What is your assessment of her?"

Mistress Caitlin took a few seconds to order her thoughts. She then spoke, "I must say, Your Highness, the lass may not be counted sixteen yet, but in life's experiences she is old far beyond her years. She has a strong personality and will. She has survived the streets on her own for seven years, she's a fighter. Although she turned to being a thief to survive, given the chance she would rather have been a productive citizen. If you treat her fairly her loyalty to you will be beyond question."

Princess Juliana nodded, then said, "That is very interesting. It seems that my husband made the correct judgment in giving her over to me for training."

"That's not all of it, Your Highness." Mistress Caitlin said.

"Oh," Princess Juliana responded, "what more is there?"

Mistress Caitlin continued, "Eleanora walks a perilous path fraught with strife and peril. If she prevails we will all be better for it."

"What does that mean?" Princess Juliana asked with a puzzled look on her face.

Mistress Caitlin replied, "That, Your Highness, I do not yet know. But there is one thing that is quite clear. The destinies of Eleanora and your husband are, for some unknown reason, intertwined."

With a worried look on her face, Princess Juliana asked, "What do you mean by intertwined?"

Looking directly into Princes Juliana's eyes, Mistress Caitlin said, "Your Highness, it could mean that the survival of your husband, your family and even the survival of the kingdom may rest on the shoulders of Eleanora. I tell you now and I shall also inform your husband, train her as a member of the court, but if she shows an interest in anything else, don't try to discourage her, give her all the cooperation she needs. Who knows, it may be a skill that she will need."

Realizing the gravity of the warning, Princess Juliana made a decision. To Mistress Caitlin she said, "Thank you, Mistress Caitlin, I will do as you advise."

Thirty minutes later, Mistress Caitlin knocked at the door to Prince Hugh's library. A male voice from within called out. "Enter."

Mistress Caitlin opened the door and entered, closing the door behind her. Prince Hugh stood near a window speaking with Duke Bran. Mistress Caitlin curtsied to Prince Hugh saying, "Your Highness, I've just come from a meeting with your wife and Eleanora. I must say that the lass has had a most interesting life. I also used the query device to probe her mind. In the query I found something quite unexpected that concerns you."

Giving Mistress Caitlin his attention, Prince Hugh asked, "What may this concern be, Mistress Caitlin?"

"Your Highness," Mistress Caitlin replied, "For some unknown reason, that only the gods know, the destinies of Eleanora and yourself are joined. And that's not all of it, there is grave danger ahead. Your survival, the survival of your family and perhaps even the survival of the kingdom may rest on, Eleanora's shoulders." By now she had the attention of both men.

Duke Bran asked, "Are you sure of this, Mistress Caitlin?"

Looking at Duke Bran, but addressing both men, Mistress Caitlin said, "Your Grace, in all my years I have never had a probe more clearly as this one. I am certain of it."

"Then what do you suggest, Mistress Caitlin." Prince Hugh asked. Mistress Caitlin answered, "The same as I advised your wife, Your

Highness. If Eleanora should show an interest in anything, do not try to discourage her, but encourage her. It may be something vital that she will need."

After a minute of consideration, Prince Hugh nodded to Mistress Caitlin saying, "Thank you Mistress Caitlin, Your advice is always well received. I will see to it that no one stands in her way."

Turning to Duke Bran, Prince Hugh said, "Bran, you heard what Mistress Caitlin said. See to it that everyone knows to assist Eleanora if she should make a request."

"Yes, Your Highness." Duke Bran said.

CHAPTER 6

T he morning of the tenth day after her arrival at the palace, Eleanora had just finished breakfast when Princess Juliana entered her apartment. Eleanora quickly rose to her feet and curtsied saying, "Good-morning, Your Highness."

Princess Juliana sat in the chair next to the chair that Eleanora had been sitting in when she entered the apartment. She then said to Eleanora, "You may take your seat, Eleanora."

"Thank you, Your Highness." Eleanora said as she sat back down in her chair.

"Well Eleanora," Princess Juliana asked, "have you ever been on a horse?"

With a shake of her head, Eleanora responded, "No, Your Highness, never in all my life. Horses are most often the privilege of the more high born." Eleanora wondered what this was all about.

Looking at Eleanora, Princess Juliana asked, "What do you know about horses?"

Eleanora thought for a moment, then answered, "Well, Your Highness, they are large, fractious animals with bad habits that manifest themselves at the worst possible time for the rider."

When Princess Juliana stopped laughing, she said, "I'll have to remember that one so that I can tell it to my husband, but now for what I'm here for. Eleanora, the one thing that every lady must know is how to ride. I have spoken with, Horse Master Osburn, he is expecting you at the stables. If you have any apprehension about being on a horse just put your fears aside. Horse Master Osburn will take good care of you and teach you the proper way to ride. Now, what do you think?"

Eleanora asked, "Your Highness, I'm sure that it should be a thrilling experience to learn how to ride a horse. The one question that I have is, how should I dress?"

Noticing that Eleanora was dressed in a plain, but well-made gown of jade-green linen, Princess Juliana said. "It will be alright to wear what you already have on. Of course you shall need boots. They have pairs of riding boots in the tack room for use by those who do not have their own boots. You can get boots and spurs there. Now, I must be going. Now you dress warmly and get along to the stables."

Eleanora rose from her chair and curtsied saying, "Your Highness." Princess Juliana rose from her chair and headed for the door.

By the time Eleanora reached the stable, she had become really excited about riding a horse. Horse Master Osburn, a slight built man, no taller than herself, of fifty years, with salt and pepper hair and beard and grey eyes greeted her. He had already had a roan palfrey tacked up with a side-saddle waiting for her. "Lady Eleanora," Horse Master Osburn said, "you're right on time. Have you ever been on a horse before?"

Shaking her head, Eleanora said, "No, Master Osburn, I have never been on a horse before. I have never had the opportunity to learn."

Horse Master Osburn, with a smile that radiated confidence, said, "You will be just fine, Lady Eleanora." Waving a hand at the palfrey, he continued, "Porky here is a gentle soul. He's as benign as your favorite lap dog. You need not fear being upon his back."

Fighting to control her excitement and nervousness, Eleanora allowed Horse Master Osburn to show her how to mount and sit side-saddle. When she felt comfortable he showed her how to use the reins to control and guide the animal. Horse Master Osburn then let her ride around the stable paddock at a walk.

After a few minutes, Eleanora became comfortable as she gained confidence. She found it exhilarating to be up on the back of the horse,

above everyone around her. Riding a horse had to be one of the most thrilling experiences so far in her life.

The riding lesson lasted for well over an hour. Horse Master Osburn watched her carefully as she mastered the art of controlling the horse by neck reining and slight shift of, or leaning in the saddle. The horse, being well trained, responded instantly to every command. Horse Master Osburn could tell that Eleanora had an extraordinary sense of balance, and a natural ability as a horse woman.

Horse Master Osburn believed that to be a good rider, you also had to know how to care for your horse. He showed Eleanora how to untack the horse, changing the bridle for the halter. He also showed her how to brush down the horse. By the time she left the stable, Eleanora considered herself a budding horse woman.

The next morning, Eleanora returned to the stables to continue her riding instruction. Arriving at the stables, she found that Porky had already been tacked up for her. Horse Master Osburn and two soldiers also had mounts tacked up and ready. Both Master Osburn and the soldiers were armed with sword and dagger.

"Good-morning Horse Master Osburn." Eleanora said, noticing the two soldiers and their mounts, "What do we have for today?"

Horse Master Osburn responded, "Good-morning, Lady Eleanora. Today we will be riding with you. We will leave the palace through the postern gate. Then through the city and out through the river gate. We will then ride up the river road for about five miles, then return to the palace."

The idea of riding outside the city thrilled, Eleanora. Since coming to Dunboro with her mother at age four she had not been outside the walls of the city. She said, "That's great, Master Osburn. I may have a chance to gallop, Porky."

Feeling some of Eleanora's enthusiasm, Horse Master Osburn smiled saying, "I will let you trot him and even take him up to a canter, but I do not believe you are ready to go galloping over the country side yet."

Eleanora realizing that Horse Master Osburn was a better judge of her ability as a rider than she was, nodded saying, "Yes, you're right, Master Osburn. I will be sure to do as you say."

Horse Master Osburn assisted Eleanora to mount her horse. He and the two soldiers then mounted.

After passing through the postern gate, they moved through the streets of Dunboro, Eleanora marveled at how quickly the citizenry moved to make a passage for them. From time to time, Eleanora would see a familiar face in the crowd of someone that she had at least a passing acquaintance. The weather still being cool, she rode with the cowl of her cloak over her head. As unlikely as it was, she didn't want anyone to recognize her as, Eddy the cat.

They passed through the river gate into the foul burg, an expansion of the city beyond the wall. Eleanora had never visited the foul burg before. Looking about she saw nothing of interest, it being just a squalid sprawl.

Once through the foul burg and into open country, Horse Master Osburn picked up the pace to a trot. The countryside rolled by, the river to the right and open fields to the left. Eleanora watched the farmers in the fields as they worked to get the land ready for planting. Eleanora had no memory of such a pastoral scene, but she had a feeling that she should, being that her parents had farmed the land. She wondered how her life would have been if her father had not died. Would she be like one of these in the field? Would she now be looking to marry the son of another farmer and begetting a brood of children to work the land? She knew that she could never go back to that life.

The last half mile before the turnaround point, Horse Master Osburn picked up the pace to a canter. To, Eleanora the road seemed to pass by in a blur. She felt the wind in her face and pulling at her cloak and skirt. For her it was like flying, she loved it.

At the turnaround point they dismounted to give the horses a rest. Horse Master Osburn took the time to comment on her progress,

saying that she had a good seat. After a few minutes they remounted for the return to the palace.

After caring for her horse, but before returning to her apartment, Eleanora stopped at the tack room to see Hansel, one of the palace harness makers. She had asked him to devise a way for her to carry her dagger strapped to her leg, concealed under her skirts. She didn't think that she would ever need it in the palace, but when she left the palace to venture into the city, as she would eventually do, she wanted the secure feeling of having it on her person. Hansel had been able to devise straps that allowed her to wear the dagger comfortably. Being very pleased with his efforts, Eleanora gave him three silver royals and thanked him for his efforts. For Hansel her thanks was worth more than the silver.

Prince Hugh sat at the head of the large table in his conference room. With him were Duke Bran, Knight Marshal Simon, Sheriff Ancel and Mistress Caitlin. Looking at Sheriff Ancel, Prince Hugh asked, "Sheriff Ancel, what do you have to report today?"

Feeling uncomfortable under the gaze of the prince, Sheriff Ancel responded, "Well Your Highness, to recap on the last meeting; when my men lost contact with the cobbler, Chester at the White Dove, we continued surveillance of his shop and home, expecting him to return. After two days without him returning we made entry. As you know, it seemed that he had just walked away. At the time we had thought that he had left Dunboro for places unknown, most likely by ship. Then three days ago fishermen recovered a body floating in the road stead. The body has since then been identified as the cobbler, Chester. The body had been badly damaged by the elements and marine life, but it appears that he had been stabbed to death.

"According to your orders, all of his property is now forfeit to the crown. We made a complete search of his shop and domicile, but found no evidence of who any of his contacts were. He kept no records or journal of his treasonous affair. All that we know from your informant is the name of the other man, Gerone. There are many men in Dunboro with the name of, Gerone. We need more than that to track him down. Now of these other two, Lord North and Hammer, we have nothing on them. I have my agents out, but I don't think that we will get much more than we already have.

"The forfeited property will be auctioned off tomorrow. We will see who makes bids, especially for the pigeons. It will be interesting to see who would want them."

"I'd bet, Your Highness," Duke Bran, with a bit of levity in his voice, remarked, "that if you were to purchase a meat pie from a street vendor in the next few days, one of the pigeons is likely to be in it."

Everyone laughed at Duke Bran's humour. "No bet," Prince Hugh said, "I doubt that any accomplice would risk exposure just to gain control of a few pigeons. However, there are stupid people in this world." Addressing Sheriff Ansel, Prince Hugh continued, "Thank you, Sheriff Ancel for your report. Keep me informed of any new developments. You may withdraw now."

Sheriff Ancel rose from his chair and bowed to the prince saying, "By your leave, Your Highness."

Prince Hugh nodded, Sheriff Ancel turned and left the room.

Prince Hugh addressed those remaining at the table. "With the death of the cobbler we have lost our best lead. However, it does confirm what Eleanora has told us. Now that this conspiracy has been confirmed, what steps do we take to ferret it out?"

After about a minute or so, Knight Marshal Simon said, "Your Highness, the two persons referred to only by code names. Now the one referred to as, Lord North. The only thing that comes to mind when you say Lord North, is the, Jutes. Could this, Lord North be some Jute noble? Could this mean that they plan invasion? If it does, your assassination at an opportune time could throw the kingdom into disarray."

"That's true," Prince Hugh said looking at Knight Marshal Simon, "if this, Lord North is a Jute, even if we knew who he was, there would be no way to get to him."

Knight Marshal Simon responded, "Your Highness, even if this person is out of our reach, we must assume that they plan invasion."

Prince Hugh sat for a minute in thought. He then looked back at Knight Marshal Simon saying, "You're right, Simon, even if the evidence isn't overwhelming we must act with prudence. We will not alarm the public by putting the army on a war footing, but make everything ready to go with little notice."

Nodding, Knight Marshal Simon said, "It will be done, Your Highness. I will also need additional funds for the fletchers. In war you can't have too many arrows."

"Just let me know what you need, Knight Marshal Simon I'll see to it that you get it." Prince Hugh said. Then looking at the others, he continued, "Now. Who has any idea who this, Hammer could be?"

"Who knows, Your Highness," Duke Bran said, "the name could mean that he's a carpenter, shipwright, cabinet maker, or none of the above. The name could just be an attempt to mislead."

"Your Highness," Mistress Caitlin said, "we still have the man called Gerone, if that's his real name. Now as I recall, Eleanora said that she didn't recognize the name, but that the voice filled her with anguish. Like she should know the voice. I sense that she has something locked away in her mind, it being too painful to recall; some trauma that for a long time she hasn't been willing to face. Perhaps she is ready to face it now, and that I may be able to help her to recall it now. It could give us a lead on who the voice belongs to."

Prince Hugh weighed the consequence to Eleanora of being forced to face a memory so painful that she has kept it locked away in her mind. His wife had become very fond of Eleanora, as he also had. He did not want to do anything that would cause her distress or harm. Finally he said, "Mistress Caitlin, could this cause great trauma for Eleanora? Could there be any danger for her?"

"Your Highness," Mistress Caitlin replied, "it will be distressful for her, but I believe that she is mature enough to face it now. I will however be very careful. I also care for the child's wellbeing."

Prince Hugh gave it a little more thought, then nodded to Mistress Caitlin saying, "Go ahead and do it, Mistress Caitlin."

CHAPTER 7

The next morning, Eleanora had just finished her breakfast when there came a knock at her door. "Enter." Eleanora called out. The door opened and Mistress Caitlin entered the apartment. Eleanora, getting to her feet, said. "Good-morning, Mistress Caitlin." Eleanora noticed that today, Mistress Caitlin wore a dark-blue robe, with golden-yellow embroidery and sash. Eleanora had yet to see her wear anything other than those robes.

Mistress Caitlin, motioning Eleanora back to her chair, responded, "Good-morning Eleanora. How has the riding been going so far?"

"Oh Mistress Caitlin," Eleanora responded with a feeling of elation, "It's wonderful. Charging down the road with the wind in your face and your cloak flapping behind you, it's almost like flying."

Remembering how it had been when she had first learned to ride a horse, Mistress Caitlin said, "Yes, I know the feeling."

Mistress Caitlin being one of her tutors, Eleanora assumed that she was here to give a lesson. "What am I to study today, Mistress Caitlin?" Eleanora asked.

Mistress Caitlin regarded Eleanora for a moment to discern her disposition, then spoke, "There will be no instruction for now. I would first like to just talk. But first," Mistress Caitlin said, indicating the divan in the room with a wave of the hand, "Let us move over to the divan where we may be more comfortable."

Consenting to Mistress Caitlin's request, Eleanora moved over to the divan with Mistress Caitlin following to sit next to her. When they were both comfortable, Mistress Caitlin said, "Eleanora, you remember when you first came to us and you were describing the meeting between the cobbler, Chester and the other man known only as, Gerone."

Sensing the direction of the conversation and not wanting to go there, Eleanora started to feel uneasy. Mistress Caitlin continued, "This man that is called Gerone, we need to have more information on him. I would like to question you more about him."

"No!" Eleanora exclaimed as she started to rise from the divan.

Taking Eleanora by the hand and gently, but firmly keeping her in her seat, Mistress Caitlin said, "I understand, Eleanora that there is something in your past, something about this man that frightens you. I am sure that you know of this man, but have for some reason blocked any memory of him. I want to try to help you to remember him."

With a shake of the head, Eleanora said, "No, I can't do it. I just can't." Taking both of Eleanora's hands into her own, Mistress Caitlin looked directly into Eleanora's eyes and said, "Eleanora, I know that it frightens you. It would be frightening to me if I had experienced the same, but it is something that you must face. Do not be afraid. I will be here to shield you. You will come to no harm."

Since coming to the palace, Eleanora had come to know and trust those around her, to include, Mistress Caitlin. Eleanora didn't want to do it. Even the thought of it caused anguish in her. However she had been treated well since coming to the palace. She felt that she owed it to her new friends, and perhaps even to her mother and to herself to try. Finally, Eleanora nodded acknowledging her willingness to try. "Yes, Mistress Caitlin I'll do it." Eleanora said with a sigh, "I owe it to my mother. Perhaps it will bring justice for her."

"Thank you, Eleanora," Mistress Caitlin said, "I will make sure that no harm comes to you."

Taking the talisman from a pocket in a fold in her robe, Mistress Caitlin put it in Eleanora's hand. Eleanora felt the warmth of the talisman in her hand. Then everything in the room seemed to go out of focus, except for the face of Mistress Caitlin. As Eleanora's attention focused

on Mistress Caitlin's face, it seemed to come closer until all she could see were the eyes. Those dark, mysterious eyes.

Eleanora sat on her sleeping pallet in the back room of her mother's home. Soon it would be the summer solstice festival and she would be counted nine years old. The hour being late, Eleanora was about to get ready for bed when a knock came at the front door. She heard her mother open the door, then the voice of a man. She knew the voice, having heard it before. It was a deep-strong baritone voice that projected arrogance and authority. Eleanora had never seen the man who owned the voice, but she didn't like him. At least once before after this man had visited her mother, Eleanora had observed bruises on her mother's body. Her mother had tried to reassure her; telling her that there was nothing to worry about. However, Eleanora also knew that her mother feared him. Her mother had also told her that the man worked on ships.

Her mother came into the back room and said, "Eddy," Her mother always called her by her street name when anyone was present. "You have to leave for a while. Mother has business with the gentleman."

Eleanora being tired and wanting to go to bed objected saying, "But, mother, it's cold outside."

"Then dress warmly, my dear." Her mother said, "I'm sorry that you have to go out on a cold night, but you know that you can't stay when I have men here."

As much as Eleanora didn't want to go out into the cold night, she knew that she had to. "Yes, mother." Eleanora said. She then got up, dressed in extra layers of clothing, and left home to roam the streets as her mother serviced her male client.

At that hour all the retail shops were closed. However, there were still many people on the streets. The inns were busy, with the sound of voices speaking, or singing being heard on the street. She envied those who could live their lives openly, not having to fear discovery. If only she could be herself.

After about an hour of wondering the streets, Eleanora decided that enough time had passed and started back home. As she neared the hovel where she and her mother lived she could see many people milling about, some with lanterns. She could also see two men in front of their home wearing the tabards of the city watch. Eleanora thought, *why are all these people here? I can't go home with all these people here. Where is my, mommy?*

Eleanora was wailing, Mummy...Mummy. Tears were running down her cheeks, and her body trembled. Mistress Caitlin held Eleanora in her arms to comfort her. Tears were also running down Mistress Caitlin's cheeks. As the tears and trembling subsided, Eleanora noticed that she no longer held the device in her hand. Mistress Caitlin asked, "Are you all right, Eleanora?"

After a few seconds, Eleanora nodded saying, "Yes, I believe so. My mother, I remember now. I never got back into our home. There were just too many people about. I just stayed back in the shadows until they brought out my mother's body, wrapped in one of our old blankets. They put her body in a two wheeled cart pulled by a mule and took her away. I never saw her again. I don't even know where she is buried.

"The first night on the street was the worst. All I had was the clothes on my back. I was cold, hungry, frightened and totally alone. I cried the whole night, as much for myself as for my mother.

"The next day, with the help of some of the lads that I knew on the street, I started to work as the hand off for a cut purse. That is how I first earned money to live on."

Mistress Caitlin's heart went out to Eleanora. To survive such a tragedy as this speaks well for Eleanora's strength of character and will to survive. Mistress Caitlin said, "Well, Eleanora, how do you feel now?"

Eleanora broke the embrace and they both sat back in the divan. Eleanora then said, "I'm angry at you for what you made me go through. I'm angry at my mother for getting killed and leaving me alone. But most of all I'm angry with, no, I'm enraged with the man who murdered my mother."

"So, then you remember him now?" Mistress Caitlin asked.

"Yes, I remember him." Eleanora said, "I know his name and I will never forget his voice. If I ever find him, I'll kill him with my own hands."

Mistress Caitlin knew that Eleanora would be all right, that the spell had had no lasting effect on her. Eleanora would however need some time to recover her composure after the remembering spell. She said to Eleanora, "There will be no lessons today, Eleanora. Why don't you take the day to do whatever you want to do? We will continue with you studies tomorrow."

Having the day to herself, Eleanora went first to the stables. In the short time that she had been riding, she had started to think of the roan palfrey, Porky, as her own. She would not ride him today, but she did brush him down and put some grain in his feed trough. Performing these simple chores and speaking to Porky, even if he didn't understand her, had a calming effect on her.

Horse Master Osburn watched her as she cared for the horse. Most of the ladies didn't want to be bothered with caring for a horse. They just wanted the animal tacked up and waiting for them. As soon as they were finished they just wanted to turn the horse over to a groom to take care of it for them. He liked this young, Lady Eleanora. She was willing to take responsibility for her own animal. A rare quality in such a young person. Since she had obviously formed a bond with Porky he would make sure that Porky would be the mount reserved for her whenever she went riding.

From the stables, Eleanora begin to stroll about the bailey. Still discomposed from the episode with Mistress Caitlin, she was just wandering about aimlessly. In the bailey soldiers of the household guard were training with weapons. Recognizing her as the companion of Princess Juliana and a lady of the court, the soldiers would pause in what they were doing and bow to her. Even though she didn't have to, Eleanora would return the courtesy with a nod of the head, or a pleasant word. After all it didn't cost anything to be polite.

Eleanora found Sir Walter in the bailey drilling, Squire Hal in the use of the broad sword. They were using wooden practice swords, weighted to give the feel of a real sword.

Squire Hal, seeing Eleanora approaching became more spirited in his sword work. Sir Walter was thrown on the defense, but not for long. He was soon back on the offense. Squire Hal finally ended the contest by yielding to Sir Walter.

Sir Walter then told his squire to take a break to catch his breath. He then came over to speak with, Eleanora. "Goodday, Lady Eleanora." Sir Walter said.

"Goodday, Sir Walter," Eleanora replied, "I just came over to watch you and Squire Hal. Squire Hal really works hard with the sword."

Sir Walter laughed, then said, "His tempo with the sword was really brisk. That started as soon as he saw you coming. Your champion in the making is smitten by your beauty."

Eleanora blushed saying, "I'm not beautiful I'm just plain looking. My hair is too short, as some have said, scandalously short. It's cut to just above the shoulder with bangs like a lad. I'm not what you would call a classic beauty. Also, I haven't learned yet how to comport myself in a way to attract men."

"Oh, lass," Sir Walter said, giving Eleanora's figure a quick appraisal, "do you have a lot to learn. You are like a breath of fresh air. You are genuine, without guile. There are many men here in the palace that have noticed you, and would like to get to know you."

Sir Walter's praise had helped to improve Eleanora's disposition, she said, "I thank you, Sir for your praise. You do have a way of making a lass feel better about herself. Now, I have a largess to ask of you."

Having his interest heightened by Eleanora's request, Sir Walter asked. "And what would that be, Eleanora?"

"I would like for you to teach me to use the sword." Eleanora said.

Sir Walter was taken aback by her request. Normally he would have said no, it being an improper interest for a woman. However, it had been directed by Duke Bran that she was to be allowed to pursue

any interest. He said. "Why do you want to learn to use the sword, Eleanora?"

"I want to kill a man." Eleanora responded in a voice that conveyed determination and purpose.

Eleanora's answer wasn't what Sir Walter had expected, but then he knew that Eleanora wasn't the average young woman. He said, "Before I answer, who might this man be?"

Without hesitation, Eleanora replied, "He is the man that murdered my mother."

Sir Walter knew better than to even try to debate her on this. If he were in her place he would be thinking the same thing. Looking into her eyes and seeing the resolution there, Sir Walter replied, "Well, Eleanora, that's a good enough reason for wanting to learn to use the sword, I'd not argue with you on that. Now, I haven't the time to do it myself. I already have my squire to train. However, I will go with you to speak with Master Ralph, the Master of the Sword. He is the person that instructs members of the court in the use of weapons. Just give me a minute to give Hal some instructions, then we can be on our way."

Eleanora said with a broad smile, "Thank you, Sir Walter, you are very kind."

While Eleanora waited, Sir Walter went over to where Squire Hal stood and said, "You can let some of the air out of your lungs now, Hal."

"Sir, what do you mean?" Hal responded.

With a grin, Sir Walter said, "You're like a rooster parading before a hen. You do this every time that Eleanora comes around."

With downcast eyes, Hal said. "But, Sir Walter, I don't mean her any disrespect. I didn't think it improper to just look."

"Well, I guess that you can dream," Sir Walter said, "but that's all you'll do. Unlike other lasses of her age, whose minds are filled with romance and happily ever after, she has but one man on her mind, and he had better start to watch his back.

"I need to go with Eleanora now to see Master Ralph. It will soon be time for the mid-day meal. We will resume training after the mid-day meal."

Master Ralph, Master of the Sword, a large man above average height with blonde hair and beard and green eyes, sat in his office going over training reports for Duke Bran when a knock came at the door. "Enter." He called out.

The door opened and, Sir Walter entered accompanied by Eleanora. Sir Walter said, "Good-morning, Master Ralph," Indicating Eleanora with a wave of the hand, Sir Walter continued, "I'd like to introduce, Lady Eleanora, personal companion to, Princess Juliana."

Master Ralph stood and bowed to Eleanora saying. "Good-morning, Lady Eleanora. I've heard a lot about you since you came to the palace. It's good to finally meet you".

Eleanora curtsied saying. "Good-morning Master Ralph."

Sir Walter said. "Master Ralph, Lady Eleanora came to me to ask that I teach her how to use the sword. Since you are responsible for the training of the members of the court I have brought her to you."

Master Ralph took another look at Eleanora. He wondered if she could even hold a sword horizontal for more than a minute before letting the point drop. Looking at Eleanora, Master Ralph said. "Well, Eleanora, what do you know about weapons, other than the knitting needle?"

Eleanora bent at the knee, reaching up under her skirt, then coming erect with amazing speed the point of her dagger levelled at, Master Ralph's throat.

Seeing the started look on Master Ralph's face, Sir Walter laughed, then said, "If you anger the lass; then turn your back on her, you will have a blade between your ribs. She has used that dagger to defend herself before. Believe me when I say that she's really good with that blade."

Master Ralph viewed Eleanora with new found respect saying, "I say, you're right handy with that thing."

Eleanora raised the hem of her skirt to put her dagger away, the two men could see the sheath for the dagger strapped neatly to the calf of her leg.

When Eleanora had put her dagger away, Master Ralph spoke. "All right, Lady Eleanora, I'll teach you as much about the sword as you can learn."

Smiling, Eleanora exclaimed, "Oh, thank you, Master Ralph!"

"Now, if you want," Master Ralph said, "We can start after the mid-day meal today. I'll be waiting for you in the indoor training hall."

CHAPTER 8

aster Ralph had been training Eleanora for a month now in the use of the broad sword. After the second day, Eleanora had replaced her skirts for a man's tunic and trousers with her riding boots while training with the sword. She trained with the broad sword whenever her schedule of other duties didn't conflict. She had learned all the moves with the broad sword, but as much as she tried, she didn't have sufficient upper body strength to wield the sword with force. There were other swords, like the shorter sword with a blade of about twenty-six inches long; used by the infantry and ships crews. There were also other swords made mostly for the private trade that had lighter blades, but they were inferior to the broad sword. Master Ralph thought that there had to be another answer to the problem.

Eleanora entered the training hall prepared for her training with the broad sword. Seeing Master Ralph standing next to a bench close to the wall, Eleanora went over to him. "Good-afternoon Master Ralph."

"Good-afternoon Eleanora, I have a gift for you."

With ill-concealed interest Eleanora said, "A gift, you didn't have to get a gift for me." Reaching for a long object on the bench wrapped in a cloth, Master Ralph said, "Eleanora you will never have the strength for the broad sword. Finally, after some thought I went to see Master Angus, the master armorer and blacksmith. Together we came up with this." He handed the gift to her.

Removing the cloth, Eleanora had a quick intake of breath in amazement. It was a beautifully made sword and scabbard. It had a slender blade, longer than that of a broad sword. The handle was long with a long-slender cross guard and basket guard. The handle had been weighted to give the sword a point of balance at the base of the blade, next to the guard. "It's beautiful, Master Ralph," Eleanora said, "much too an extravagant gift for me."

Master Ralph beamed with pleasure at Eleanora's reaction to the gift and said, "It is a pleasure for Master Angus and I to present this gift to you."

With tears of emotion glistening in her eyes, Eleanora reached up and kissed Master Ralph on the cheek. "Thank you, Master Ralph," she said, "it's the grandest gift that anyone has ever given me. I will cherish it always."

Clearing his throat nervously, Master Ralph said, "Okay, now as to how to use this new sword. Although the blade is double edged, it is not a slashing weapon. Like the dagger that you are so fond of, this sword is a thrusting weapon. Instead of brute strength you will need speed and finesse. You cannot use this as you would use a broad sword."

Nodding, Eleanora said, "Yes, I understand, Master Ralph. Unlike the broad sword that you draw back to deliver a crushing blow; with this sword you kill with the point."

"Good," Master Ralph said, "now I have some ideas on how to use this new weapon. Let's get to work."

The next three weeks were spent by Eleanora learning how to use her new sword. Slowly with the guidance of Master Ralph she developed the technique to win against the broad sword. Word of the new weapon had spread through the court drawing spectators, mostly men, but some ladies too observing the training sessions. Some of the men of the court expressed a desire to acquire this new weapon that some were starting to call a rapier for themselves.

Ten days before the summer solstice festival, Eleanora sat with Princess Juliana having tea and shortbread in the princess's apartment. They both enjoyed the mid-morning teas. A strong bond had developed between the princess and Eleanora. Even Princess Juliana's children,

Isabelle age seven and Mark age five enjoyed, Eleanora's company. For Eleanora it was the only family, except for her mother, that she had ever known. She loved having been made a part of the family, even if being only a minor part and would do anything for them.

As they sipped their tea and nibbled at short bread, Eleanora said, "Your Highness, I need new riding boots. The boots that were given to me when I started riding are old boots taken out of storage for my use. However, time has caused the leather to dry out and crack."

Princess Juliana continued to sip her tea as she gazed out through the open window over the rooftops of Dunboro. After about a minute she turned to face, Eleanora and spoke, "Then if you need new boots you should have them. I will make arrangements with the palace guard to have an escort for you waiting at the main gate after the mid-day meal. They will escort you to the shop of Master Morris the court cobbler."

Eleanora had become accustomed to the policy that any lady of the court going outside the palace be escorted by at least two soldiers of the palace guard. Eleanora said, "Thank you, Your Highness, It shouldn't take too long."

With a wave of the hand Princess Juliana said, "Don't worry about it, Eleanora. Take the whole afternoon off to enjoy your excursion in the city.

You push yourself too hard. You need to take some time off."

"Thank you, Your Highness," Eleanora said, "I'll do that."

After the mid-day meal, Eleanora arrived at the main gate of the palace. Two soldiers wearing the tabard of the palace guard and armed with sword and dagger were waiting for her. With the two guards escorting her, Eleanora passed through the gate into the city of Dunboro. The cobbler's shop wasn't far from the palace, less than a thirty minute walk.

For her afternoon in the city, Eleanora had chosen to wear a plain, but well-made gown of fine light-blue linen, white linen-lace Shaw and white-silk wimple. With the make-up and lip rouge no one would ever

recognize her as Eddy the cat. Even though Gerone was still looking for Eddy the cat, she felt safe hiding in plain sight.

The bell over the door jingled. Master Morris looked up to see a young lady come through the door followed by two soldiers of the palace guard. Bowing, Master Morris said, "How may I be of help, My Lady?"

"Master Morris," Eleanora said, "I am Lady Eleanora. I am in need of a new pair of riding boots."

Indicating a chair with a wave of his hand, Master Morris said, "Then please, Lady Eleanora, have a seat. Then I will take measurements of your feet for the boots."

Eleanora took a seat in the chair and removed the black-leather shoes that she had been wearing. Master Morris sat on the bench in front of her and started to measure her feet, writing the numbers in the book along with her name. Looking up at Eleanora he said, "What colour of boots would My Lady like?"

Eleanora answered, "I would like them black, Master Morris."

"And the leather trim around the tops of the boots," Master Morris said, "what colour do you want them?"

Eleanora replied, "Yes, Master Morris, I would like that to be a russet." Writing this in a book, Master Morris said, "I can have your boots ready in two to three weeks and what a splendid pair of boots they will be. I shall notify the palace when they are ready."

With a smile, Eleanora replied, "Thank you, Master Morris, I'm sure that I shall be really pleased with them."

Once they were done with the fitting, Eleanora left the cobbler's shop with her escort. Back out on the street she didn't want to return to the palace right away. She turned instead to stroll further into the city. It felt good to see familiar sights again. She recognized several people on the street, but made sure that she gave no sign of recognition. A few looked right at her, but didn't make the connection between this young lady from the palace, and the ragamuffin known as, Eddy the cat.

Then as she passed an inn she could hear through the open window the sound of male voices and laughter. Then for a few seconds she heard the sound of a loud voice over the murmuring of the other voices. Her blood seemed to freeze in her veins. It was the voice of the man that had murdered her mother. She paused to look in the window to see if she could see the owner of the voice.

One of the soldiers took her by the arm. "My Lady," The soldier said, "it is not wise to tarry here."

Realizing that to be too inquisitive now could lead to exposure, Eleanora said. "Yes, you're right. Let us return to the palace quickly. I must see Duke Bran as soon as possible."

As they started back to the palace, Eleanora looked back to make sure of the name of the inn. The sign over the door showed a man standing on a quay with his foot resting on a cleat. The name on the sign read, Quay Side Inn.

After listening to Eleanora's report, Duke Bran took her to see Prince Hugh. Duke Bran knocked on the door to, Prince Hugh's library. A voice from within called out. "Enter."

Duke Bran and Eleanora entered Prince Hugh's library. The prince sat at the trestle table that he used as a desk going over written reports. Duke Bran bowed while Eleanora curtsied. 'Your Highness," Duke Bran said, "Lady Eleanora came to me this afternoon. She said that she heard the voice of the man that we have been searching for." Indicating Eleanora, Duke Bran said.

"Your Highness, I'll let Lady Eleanora tell you about it."

The paperwork forgotten, Prince Hugh gave, Eleanora his full attention. Taking a deep breath, Eleanora began. "Well, Your Highness," she said,

"I went into the city this afternoon to order a new pair of riding boots. After conducting my business with the cobbler, I decided to take a stroll through the city before returning to the palace. As we passed an open window of an inn I heard the voice of the man called Gerone, whom I overheard speaking with the cobbler, Chester. The same man who murdered my mother. I wanted to pause to try to get a look at him through the window, but my escort wanted to keep moving."

With his interest heightened, Prince Hugh asked, Eleanora, "How sure are you of this voice, Lady Eleanora?"

"I am certain of it, Your Highness." Eleanora said, "That is one voice that I shall never forget." Prince Hugh then asked, "Where is this inn?"

"It's down close to the docks, Your Highness." Eleanora responded, "The name of the inn is the Quay Side Inn. I know of it, it is favored by a lot of longshoremen."

Prince Hugh turning his attention back to Duke Bran said, "At last, Bran we have another lead. We need to get Sheriff Ancel in on this. He can have his agents keep the place under surveillance." "May I speak, Your Highness?" Eleanora said.

Prince Hugh looked back at Eleanora and nodded saying, "Yes, Lady Eleanora you may speak."

Hoping that she had not overstepped her prerogative, Eleanora spoke, "Your Highness, I believe that to let agents of the city watch near the Quay Side Inn would be a mistake. This man is very street smart. He would smell an agent of the city watch two blocks away."

Regarding Eleanora with an intense look, Prince Hugh asked, "Then, Lady Eleanora what do you suggest that we do?"

On impulse, Eleanora said, "You could send me, Your Highness." "What!" Prince Hugh exclaimed in amazement, "That's out of the question!"

Having broached the idea, Eleanora had no option but to carry on. "Your Highness," she said, "I would go incognito. I would wear a wig, make-up and dress as a commoner. No one would recognize me. After all, they are looking for a lad known as Eddy the cat, not a lass."

"Okay, so they're looking for a lad, not a lass." Prince Hugh said, However, Lady Eleanora I will not let you go in alone. You must have an escort."

"I agree, Your Highness," Eleanora said, "one man will do. He should look mean enough to snap a sword in half with his teeth."

Both Prince Hugh and Duke Bran broke out in laughter. When the laughter subsided, Prince Hugh said, "You're a clever one, Lady Eleanora. I like your idea. When would you like to do this?"

"The summer solstice festival starts in ten days." Eleanora said, "That will give us three days to watch the Quay Side Inn. My escort and I can pose as brother and sister, father and daughter, or whatever, having come to the city for the festival."

Prince Hugh turned to Duke Bran and said, "You know, Bran I think that it might just work."

"Yes, Your Highness," Duke Bran said, "and I have just the right man in mind for the job. He's a soldier in the palace guard. He is a very reliable man who can think on his feet."

Eleanora spoke up, "That will not do, Duke Bran. I do not think that we can use any man from the palace guard. There would be too much of a risk that he would be recognised. I suggest that we let Knight Marshal Simon provide a man from the legion that spends little or no time in Dunboro."

Prince Hugh thought it over for a few seconds. He then turned to Duke Bran saying, "Lady Eleanora is right, Bran. I will have Simon provide a man from the legion as Lady Eleanora's escort. Is that all you have for now?"

The meeting being at an end, Duke Bran bowed while Eleanora curtsied, both saying, "By your leave, Your Highness."

"Granted." Prince Hugh replied.

Six days later a soldier wearing the tabard of the Prince's Legion entered the indoor training hall of the palace. The man stood six-foot four inches and was massively built. He had black hair with a thick-black beard, streaked with grey and grey eye. There were scars on his hands from sword cuts. He also had a scar on his left cheek, covered mostly by his beard. He had a rough appearance that no one would ever call handsome.

Looking about he noticed two lads engaged in a training match with swords. Several spectators stood around watching the match. He could

also see that several were making bets on the outcome. As he watched the match a tall, slender-built man of about forty years, wearing dark-blue tunic with black trousers and boots approached him and said, "I am Master Ralph, Master of the Sword. May I help you, corporal?"

The corporal responded, "Yes, Master Ralph, you may. I am Corporal Giffard and I have orders from Knight Marshal Simon to report to, Lady Eleanora. I have been told that she is here."

With a nod, Master Ralph said, "Yes, Lady Eleanora is here. If you wait here I'll inform her that you have arrived, as soon as she is free." Master Ralph then turned and walked away.

A few minutes later the contest ended, the lad in the dark-red tunic, buff colored trousers and black boots the clear winner. Corporal Giffard watched as Master Ralph spoke to the two lads, then the one in the red tunic started to approach him. When the lad drew close, Corporal Giffard noticed with a start that the lad was actually a young woman.

Coming up to stand in front of Corporal Giffard, Eleanora said, "I am, Lady Eleanora, you must be Corporal Giffard."

Bowing, Corporal Giffard said. "Yes, My Lady, Corporal Giffard at your service. I have orders from, Knight Marshal Simon to report to you."

Eleanora studied Corporal Giffard for a few seconds, then smiling said, "You will do just fine. I asked, Knight Marshal Simon to get me someone that looked mean enough to be able to snap a sword in half with his teeth."

Corporal Giffard couldn't help but to laugh at Eleanora's remarks. When he could speak, he said, "My Lady, I have been chosen for duty for a lot of reasons, but not for that one."

"Well Corporal Giffard," Eleanora said, "when I explain your duties it will be clear as to why I asked for someone like you."

Seeing a page close at hand, Eleanora waved him over, then said, "Page, go to the kitchen and have them send a pot of tea with two cups and shortbread to my apartment."

The page bowed, saying, "Yes, My Lady." He then turned and hurried off to the kitchen.

Eleanora then turned back to Corporal Giffard and said, "I know that you are a little confused now. If you will accompany me to my apartment, we can have tea while I explain your duties to you."

As they walked through the palace, Corporal Giffard noticed the sword that hung at Eleanora's left side from a baldric. He found it strange to see a woman wearing a sword. That she was proficient with the weapon had been made clear by her performance in the training match in the training hall. That she could make request of Knight Marshal Simon for resources and personnel, and wear man's clothing meant that she must have a special status in the court. What he found most amazing was her age. She seemed so young to be given such trust. He wondered what made this lass so special.

Arriving at her apartment, Eleanora had Corporal Giffard take a seat in a chair in her sitting room as she put her sword away. By then there was a knock at the door, Eleanora called out. "Enter."

The door opened and a servant from the kitchen entered carrying a tray. The servant sat the tray on the table, then bowed saying, "Your tea, My Lady." then withdrew.

Eleanora performed the duty as hostess serving tea and shortbread to Corporal Giffard. She then said. "Well, Corporal Giffard you must be wondering why you are here."

Corporal Giffard, clearly uncomfortable sitting in a ladies sitting room, having tea and shortbread said. "Yes, My Lady, I am a bit confused."

Sitting her tea cup down on the saucer, Eleanora said, "I will be going into the city during the summer solstice festival, and you shall be my escort. There is a man that I expect to find somewhere in the city. Now I don't want anyone to suspect that we are from the palace. That is why I asked for someone from the legion to be my escort. We shall dress as common people from the provinces. You will go armed with sword and dagger, but nothing else that would mark you as a soldier. We will just be two people that have come to the city for the

summer solstice festival. Now you are too old to be my brother. You can be my father or uncle."

"Make it your uncle." Corporal Giffard said with a chuckle, "I don't know the first thing about being a father."

"Okay, Uncle Gifford," Eleanora said smiling, "starting now you will address me as, Eleanora. I shall address you as Uncle Giffard. We must get in the habit of treating each other as family."

"Alright, Eleanora," Corporal Giffard said, "now I have a question. Who is this man that we're looking for?"

Eleanora said, "Three months ago I overheard two men plotting against the Prince of Dunboro. A few days later the body of one of the men was found floating in the road stead. Now, the other man. No one knows what he looks like, but we have a name and I know his voice. The other day I was in the city and heard that voice again. We now believe we know his occupation and at least one inn that he frequents. I will try to find him again."

Looking at Eleanora with wonder and respect, Corporal Giffard said, "You are taking a risk by going after this man, why?"

Looking right into Corporal Giffard's eyes, Eleanora said, "I want to see this man dead. If not by the hangman's rope, then skewered on the blade of my sword."

All that Corporal Giffard could say was, "Why?" "Because," Eleanora said, "he murdered my mother."

CHAPTER 9

Eleanora left through the main gate of the palace before dawn. She had dressed in the same dark-brown skirt, buff colour blouse and green front laced bodice that she had been given to wear when she had first come to the palace. She also wore a long-black wig that cascaded down her back and over her shoulders. She had blackened her eyebrows with a black pencil, eyelashes with a tiny brush with charcoal dust and put on make-up to darken her skin and hide her freckles. Corporal Giffard accompanied her dressed in plain grey tunic, black trousers and black boots. He was armed with sword and dagger.

Once away from the main gate of the palace, Eleanora headed for the workers quarter of the city. They paced themselves so as to arrive in the workers quarters just after sunrise. As they moved into the city, Eleanora and Corporal Giffard engaged in casual conversation. Corporal Giffard asked, "Eleanora, what age are you counted today?"

"I am counted sixteen years today." Eleanora said, "How many years are you counted today?"

"I am counted thirty-four years today." Corporal Giffard said, then looking at Eleanora he continued, "Eleanora, I know that this is important for you to find this man during the festival. However, most people want to spend the festival with family and friends, but I have yet to hear you even mention your family."

Eleanora thought for a moment if she should say anything about herself. She wondered if it were prudent to become so familiar with

Corporal Giffard. She made the decision that if they were to rely on each other, then she should tell him something about herself. Looking at him as they walked along the street, Eleanora said, "I don't have any family. I was alone before I came to court."

Corporal Giffard exclaimed. "You have no family! How can that be, you're a lady of the court?"

Eleanora said. "It's true, I have no family. My father died when I was four. My mother was murdered about three months before I was counted nine by the man that we are looking for."

Corporal Giffard responded, "At that age, Eleanora there must have been someone to take care of you."

Shaking her head, Eleanora replied, "There was no one, I lived on the street and took care of myself."

All that Corporal Giffard could say was, "How?"

Glancing at him, Eleanora answered, "I was a thief. I started out as a hand off for a cut purse, then became a burglar."

Looking at Eleanora a little amazed, Corporal Giffard said, "But how could so young a lass, as you were at the time, live on the street?"

"I didn't live on the street as a lass." Eleanora said giving, Corporal Giffard a sideways glance, "I lived as a lad. I was known on the street as Eddy the cat, the best cat burglar in Dunboro. These clothes," Eleanora emphasized by grabbing at her skirt, "were the first woman's clothing that I have ever worn. That was three months ago. From the time that I was four, I dressed, thought and acted as a lad."

Corporal Giffard just shook his head in wonder saying, "All this is so bizarre. Then how did you end up a lady of the court?"

Eleanora responded, "That was the decision of Prince Hugh. He needed to make Eddy the cat disappear. Being a thief he could have just locked me up, or he could have made me a servant in the palace. Instead he made up a background on me, then made me a lady of the court, the personal companion to Princess Juliana. Perhaps he thought that he could keep a close eye on me that way."

Corporal Giffard, after hearing her story had to respect Eleanora for her strength at being a survivor. That she was not the pampered daughter of the high-born, but a commoner like himself. This divulgence left him in awe of Eleanora. She definitely was more than she appeared to be.

"What about your family, Uncle Giffard?" Eleanora asked.

Corporal Giffard responded. "My family are commoners much like your own, my father is a farmer. He kicked me out of the home when I reached my majority at fifteen. He said that I was too lazy to be a good farmer. I needed a home so I became a soldier. I've been a soldier ever since. I am soon to be promoted to sergeant."

Eleanora looked around and noticed that they were entering the workers quarter of the city. The sky had lightened to a predawn glow. People were starting to move about on the street. The inns would be open to serve breakfast. Eleanora said. "We are not far from the Quay Side Inn. Let us breakfast there at our leisure. Then stroll about along the docks and through the workers quarter."

"Okay, Eleanora," Corporal Giffard said, "you lead the way."

At the Quay Side Inn they were served hot tea, fresh-baked bread, sweet butter, fruit preserves, soft cheese and hard sausage. They took their ease at breakfast, displaying a nonchalant demeanor as Eleanora listened to the voices of the inns patrons. After breakfast they relaxed with a second cup of tea drawing out the occasion as long as they deemed prudent, as Eleanora continued to listen to the voices in the inn.

Upon leaving the inn, Eleanora and Corporal Giffard wandered down to the docks. There they rambled about goggling at the ships as if they were fresh off the farm for the first time. They seemed to be very interested in the ships and the activity on and around them. The whole time that they went about taking in the panorama of the docks, Eleanora kept listening for the voice locked in her mind.

They took the mid-day meal at the Mermaid Inn. The sign over the door showed a mermaid sitting on a rock with waves washing up on it. It was not far from the Quay Side Inn. The Mermaid Inn was also known to be frequented by longshoremen. They had a simple meal

of bread, cold meats, cheese and a fresh-green salad. As with breakfast they lingered over their meal. After the meal, Corporal Giffard had a second tankard of ale. Instead of a second glass of wine, Eleanora had a cup of tea. Many men came and went while they were at the Mermaid Inn, but not the one that they were looking for.

By the time they left the inn the festival celebration had started. On the streets were jugglers, acrobats, musicians and other entertainers. There were now more than the usual number of people on the streets. Eleanora noticed and alerted Corporal Giffard to several young lads that she knew to be cut purses so that they could avoid them. As they moved about the workers quarter in hope that they could chance upon the person that they were seeking, Eleanora noticed many people that she knew. Some of them looked at her and Corporal Giffard briefly, but none ever recognised her.

For the evening meal they returned to the Quay Side Inn. Eleanora having heard the voice of Gerone there before, she felt this the best place to look for him. They had timed their arrival to catch the early crowd in the middle of their meal, before the later diners arrived. Before they ordered dinner, Corporal Giffard had a tankard of ale while Eleanora had a glass of wine. They then ordered dinner of roast pork, bread rolls, fresh vegetables, green salad and more ale and wine. They lingered over diner as much as they could without attracting undue attention. After dinner they relaxed with a cup of tea. During the time that they spent in the Quay Side In, Eleanora paid close attention, but did not detect the voice that she sought.

After dinner they drifted around the streets. The street dancing had started and everyone was merry making. Corporal Giffard and Eleanora got caught up in the festivities and danced a little. Eleanora kept listening to the voices in the crowd, but did not detect the voice that continued to elude her. They finally ended their quest for the day and returned to the palace, making sure that they were not followed.

The next morning before dawn, Eleanora and Corporal Giffard left through the main gate of the palace and ventured through the city toward the workers quarter. They arrived at the Quay Side Inn for breakfast. Their breakfast was the same as the day before. Eleanora listened carefully to the voices in the inn, but could not detect the one that she was listening for.

The second day of the festival, Eleanora and Corporal Giffard spent much as the first, roaming the workers quarters and the docks. The midday meal they took at the Golden Dolphin Innm another inn known to be frequented by longshoremen. The sign over the door showed a golden-yellow dolphin on a blue field. By dinner time, Eleanora had begun to wonder if their mission had been such a good idea. What were the odds that you could by chance find one man in a city as large as Dunboro. Eleanora knew that having made the commitment they would have to return the third day.

By early evening they were back at the Quay Side Inn for the evening meal. This evening the inn had a troubadour that would perform for the patrons for the remainder of the festival. The same as the day before, Eleanora and Corporal Giffard started out with wine and ale. They then ordered dinner consisting of lamb stew, fresh-baked bread, green salad and wine for Eleanora and ale for Corporal Giffard. They had taken a table in the centre of the inns taproom so that Eleanora could better hear anyone speaking anywhere in the room. Sitting at the table, Eleanora faced the fireplace where the troubadour performed while, Corporal Giffard faced the bar at the other end of the room.

During the meal, Eleanora had to leave the table to visit the privy. She returned to the table just as the troubadour finished singing a ballad. After the applause patrons started to call out requests. Then one loud voice from behind, Eleanora called out the name of a popular folk song. At the same time a silver half royal was flipped from the bar across the room to land at the feet of the troubadour. Inwardly, Eleanora flinched fighting hard to keep from turning to see the source of the voice. "That's him." She said barely above a whisper.

"Where?" Corporal Giffard said softly while looking down at his plate so that no one would read his lips.

Eleanora said, also looking down at her plate, "Behind me. The man who requested that the minstrel sing that song and pitched that coin."

Corporal Giffard knew whom she spoke of, having noticed him pitching the coin from the bar. Lifting his tankard to take a drink of ale, Corporal Giffard looked over the rim of the tankard to get a better look at the man at the bar. Lowering the tankard and paying attention to his meal again, Corporal Giffard said in a soft voice. "Average height, stocky, chestnut-brown hair and beard, dark-blue tunic, grey trousers and black boots."

Eleanora responded in a low voice, while picking at her food with a spoon. "Yes, I noticed him when I went out to the privy."

"Okay, what do we do now?" Giffard asked.

"We finish our dinner," Eleanora said, "then get up and leave. We then find an inconspicuous place to watch the inn. Perhaps we can follow him home."

They finished their dinners as though they were just visitors to the city for the festival. They then left the inn as if going to take part in the street celebrations.

About one and one half hours later, Gerone left the inn and started to walk home. With the celebrants in the street he didn't notice the couple that started to follow him.

Eleanora and Corporal Giffard followed Gerone for three blocks, staying within the crowd of street revellers as much as possible. They didn't want Gerone to spot them if he chanced to look back. Gerone then turned right onto a street with roll houses on each side of the street. Eleanora reached the corner then stopped, Corporal Giffard stopping next to her. "What's the problem, Eleanora?" Corporal Giffard asked.

Watching Gerone walking down the street, Eleanora said, "We can't follow him down the street. The street is deserted. Everyone is on the main streets where the party is. We would be the only people on the street behind him." Spotting an alleyway about thirty feet away, Eleanora continued. "We need Eddy the cat. Now, follow me."

Eleanora rushed down the street and ducked into the alleyway with, Corporal Giffard right behind her. Without pause, Eleanora reached up under her skirt, loosened her two petticoats and let them slip to the ground. Picking them up, Eleanora handed them to, Corporal Giffard saying, "Hold on to these for me."

Corporal Giffard took Eleanora's petticoats timidly as if they would burn his fingers. Eleanora had to use all her will power to keep from laughing at him.

Then reaching down between her ankles, Eleanora grabbed the back of the hem of her skirt. She then pulled it up between her legs and tucked it under her belt buckle. Eleanora then grabbed the drain pipe running down from the roof of the corner building and started to climb the four stores to the roof.

Once on the roof of the corner building, the corner building and the roll houses being of the same height, Eleanora got a running start and cleared the alleyway to the roll house.

Eleanora felt at home scampering over the roof tops as she followed, Gerone down the street. She had to clear two more alleyways as she continued the pursuit. Gerone finally entered the sixth door down the third block of roll houses, across the street from where, Eleanora observed him. A few minutes later the shutters of the fourth floor apartment were opened and a lamp was lit. Eleanora now knew where Gerone lived.

Giffard heard a slight noise as Eleanora cleared the alleyway, landing on the roof of the corner building. A minute later, Eleanora climbed down the drain pipe to the alleyway. Releasing her skirt from her belt, Eleanora said, "You may give me my petticoats now."

Eleanora quickly put her petticoats back on under her skirt, then said. "We may return to the palace now, Corporal Giffard. I now know the apartment where he lives."

CHAPTER 10

The next morning after breakfast, Eleanora went to Duke Bran's office. Upon arrival, Eleanora found Knight Marshal Simon and Corporal Giffard already there with Duke Bran. Curtsying to Duke Bran, Eleanora said. "Good-morning, Your Grace."

Duke Bran responded. "Good-morning Lady Eleanora. Now that you are here we all can go, Prince Hugh is waiting for us in his library."

Duke Bran led the way to Prince Hugh's library. Arriving there, Duke Bran knocked on the door. The princes voice from within bid them to enter. Upon entering the men bowed while, Eleanora curtsied.

Prince Hugh sat behind the table that he used as a desk with a cup of tea. Waving at Duke Bran and his party, then at a tea service with several cups, Prince Hugh said, "Please, Gentlemen and Lady, have a cup of tea, then take a chair."

Everyone helped themselves to a cup of tea, then took a seat in one of the many chairs in the library. Everyone seemed to be at ease except for, Corporal Giffard. He felt uncomfortable around so many people of high office. When everyone was settled, Prince Hugh asked, "Well, Bran, what do you have for me?"

Duke Bran responded, "Your Highness, upon her return to the palace, Lady Eleanora left a message with the officer of the guard for me. The message just said that she had been successful, and that she needed to see me this morning. Since I have not as yet debriefed Lady Eleanora or Corporal Giffard, I feel that you should hear the story first hand from them."

Prince Hugh nodded at Duke Bran then looked at, Eleanora saying, "Lady Eleanora, you may start when you are ready."

"Well, Your Highness," Eleanora said, "we left the first morning before dawn on foot. To the best of my knowledge we were not noticed or followed. We had breakfast at the Quay Side Inn, as well as the evening meal. For the mid-day meal we went to another inn close by. The rest of the day we spent moving through the workers quarter and along the docks. The first day ended without finding our quarry.

"The next morning we again set out before dawn. The second day was much as the first. By the evening meal I had started to wonder if we were being too optimistic in our ability to find this, Gerone. Then after visiting the privy at the Quay Side Inn during dinner, and returning to the table I heard the voice coming from behind me. Corporal Giffard confirmed that the voice belonged to a man standing at the bar.

"After dinner we waited outside and followed the man that we now know as Gerone, when he left the inn. We were able enough to follow him without being seen until he turned onto a side street of roll houses. I then climbed onto the roof of the corner building and jumped the alleyway to the roll houses. I then followed him from the roof tops, jumping two more alleyways before I observed him enter a roll house. A few minutes later he opened the shutters of the fourth floor apartment and lit a lamp. We now know where he lives."

With a look of approval on his face, Prince Hugh said, "Excellent work the both of you for finding this man. And especially you, Lady Eleanora for being able to follow him to his home." Prince Hugh paused for a few seconds, then continued. "I do have one question. While you were coursing about on the roof tops, what was, Corporal Giffard doing?"

There was an awkward silence for several seconds, then Corporal Giffard nervously cleared his throat, and said, "Well, Your Highness, I was in the alleyway holding my ladies petticoats."

There was no sound for a moment, then the room erupted with laughter.

Corporal Giffard just sat mute with a red face.

When the laughter subsided, Eleanora said, "Your Highness, I had to remove my petticoats to be able to climb. I gave them to Corporal Giffard to hold for me, knowing that he wouldn't be able to make the climb with me."

With a short laugh, Prince Hugh said, "I doubt, Lady Eleanora, that anyone in the palace could have made that climb with you. Both of you have done excellent work. To be truthful better than I expected."

Prince Hugh then looked at Duke Bran saying, "Okay, Bran you have it now. Get Sheriff Ancel to put this man, Gerone, under surveillance. I plan to hang him, but first I want to know who his conspirators are, then I'll hang him. If Sheriff Ancel needs, Lady Eleanora can point out the roll house."

Prince Hugh looked at everyone, then said, "Is there anything else?" Eleanora spoke up, "Yes, Your Highness, this man is always looking over his shoulder. If you have men following him he will spot them. Sheriff Ancel will have to use agents at strategic points to track his movements, and to see who he associates with."

Prince Hugh pondered this for a minute, with his hand to his chin. Then putting his hand down on the table he said, "Good point, Lady Eleanora. Bran, make sure that Sheriff Ancel conducts the surveillance as Lady Eleanora suggests. All right, Gentlemen and Lady, we know what has to be done. Everyone is dismissed, except for Lady Eleanora."

The men got to their feet, bowed and left the room. When the last man left the room, closing the door behind him, Prince Hugh addressed, Eleanora, "Lady Eleanora, you have done well. To be truthful with you, I didn't give your idea much of a chance for success. Fortunately you prevailed."

Eleanora nodded with a little blush of self-consciousness, then said, "Thank you, Your Highness, we got lucky. The God Teige (god of fortune) must have been with us. I had begun to think that perhaps we were on a fool's mission when we found our man."

Prince Hugh was about to speak when Eleanora continued, "your Highness, I've given some thought to this man, Gerone. The next morning after I overheard the conversation between him and the cobbler, Chester, they were looking for me all over the city. Now it takes more than just one man to organize a search that quickly. Also I would say that the men who were lying in wait for me that night were bashers. I believe that this man, Gerone, isn't just a smuggler, but is high up in the bashers."

"Then, Lady Eleanora, you think that the bashers are in on this treason?" Prince Hugh asked with a wrinkle in his brow.

Eleanora responded, "No, Your Highness, I don't believe so. They just follow orders, not always knowing the reason why."

Prince Hugh regarded Eleanora as he spoke, "I sense that you have something in mind, Lady Eleanora."

"Yes, Your Highness," Eleanora said, "I want to go into Gerone's apartment to have a look around. Perhaps I can get something about this assassination plot, Lord North, Hammer, or the reason for all of this."

"Do you really think that it's worth the risk to get a look inside his apartment, Lady Eleanora? Isn't that dangerous? What if they catch you in the apartment?" Prince Hugh inquired.

"Yes it is, Your Highness." Eleanora responded, "That's why I will need to know his routine before I attempt it. Once the city watch puts him under surveillance they can work out his routine. I know that the apartments where he lives are small two room bachelor or spinster apartments. It is unlikely that he ever shares it with anyone."

Prince Hugh finished his tea that had grown cold, then said, "Alright, Lady Eleanora I'll tell Duke Bran what you need. Now, anything else?"

Eleanora took a minute to study Prince Hugh's face before she spoke, "Yes, Your Highness, there is. Corporal Giffard is someone that I can trust to watch my back. Could you have him transferred from the legion to the palace guard?"

Prince Hugh nodded saying, "Yes, Lady Eleanora, I can do that." Eleanora continued, "Your Highness, I understand that Corporal

Giffard is soon to be promoted to sergeant. Will the transfer effect the promotion?" Smiling, Prince Hugh said, "Well then, Lady Eleanora, why don't we let him have his promotion now."

"Thank you, Your Highness," Eleanora replied with pleasure, "I'm sure that he will be pleased."

Prince Hugh now stood to get another cup of tea. Eleanora started to rise from her chair, but he motioned for her to keep her seat. Once seated again behind his table, Prince Hugh said, "Now to change the subject. You have been with us for over three months now. When you came to us I had to decide what to do with you. I had many options to choose from. Upon my instinctive feeling, then later on advice from Mistress Caitlin, I decided to make you a member of the court. At that time I had no idea of what to expect from you. I must admit that you have really surprised me in your ability to adapt to your life at court. You have shown an eagerness to adjust to and learn what is expected of you as a lady of the court."

Feeling pleased with Prince Hugh's praise, Eleanora responded, "I thank you, Your Highness, for the complement. I know that I have been given preferential treatment. I just wanted to justify your faith in me."

Regarding Eleanora with a friendly manner, Prince Hugh said, "Lady Eleanora, Juliana and I have become fond of you. After this business with this person, Gerone, and this assassination plot is ended, we want to keep you at court. It is our desire that when the time comes to make sure that you find a good man and make a good marriage."

What Prince Hugh had just told her seemed too good to be true, Eleanora said, "But, Your Highness, I have no family and no dowry. How can I find a good husband?"

"You just let me worry about that, Lady Eleanora." Prince Hugh said, "You are our ward now, you don't have to worry about that."

This revelation took, Eleanora by surprise. It took a few seconds before she could respond. "Your Highness," Eleanora said, "I don't know what to say. I am but an orphan of the streets. I have done very little to deserve such favorable consideration."

Prince Hugh got up from his chair and came around the table to stand in front of Eleanora, who had stood with him. Putting his hand on her shoulder, Prince Hugh said, "Oh, Lady Eleanora, you are much more than you suspect. The kingdom is facing a perilous threat, and you have as yet some unknown role to play in the salvation of the kingdom. That is the reason why you have been allowed to pursue any interest that you have."

"I do not understand, Your Highness?" Eleanora said.

Prince Hugh responded. "I know, Lady Eleanora. No one as yet knows, but we believe that when the time comes you will do the right thing. Now I believe that you have enough to think about. You may withdraw, Lady Eleanora."

"Yes, Your Highness." Eleanora said. She curtsied then turned and left the library. Prince Hugh watched Eleanora go and wondered if he had done the right thing by trying to inform her of her destiny.

As Eleanora headed for Princess Juliana's apartment she thought of what Prince Hugh had told her. What was this role that she had to play? Would she have the knowledge and wisdom to see what had to be done, and do the right thing? She would have to make devotions to Geraint (the god of knowledge), and Eloisa (the Goddess of wisdom) for guidance.

As for the other subject, the prospect of a good marriage in the future. It had been more than she had dared not even think about until now. Even as she had lived her life on the street as a lad, she could not ignore her true nature. Her desires and emotions had been even harder to control as she got older. She had wanted what every other lass wanted. Now at last she could hope.

CHAPTER 11

The next five weeks seemed to go by quickly for Eleanora. Riding, weapons training with her sword and her other studies took up a lot of her time. She also spent a lot of time with Princess Juliana and her children, Isabelle and Mark. Eleanora found the children adorable and played with them whenever she had the time. The children in turn had started to think of her as they would an older sister, or aunt. Even if not her own family, Eleanora had started to think of them as her surrogate family.

Eleanora had also gotten to know the rest of the court. Duke Bran and Knight Marshal Simon always had time for her when she wanted to talk with them. They also had libraries with many interesting books that they were willing to lend her. The ladies of the court still had some resentment toward her, feeling that she were being shown too much favour, but having the good grace to be polite to her. The court barons and Knights, who mostly served with the palace guard or legion, treated her well. Some had even started to show an interest in her as a young woman. Although all were older than she was, some by several years, she still found a couple of them attractive. However she knew that now wasn't the time to get tangled up in an affair, there still being too many unsettled issues in her life. Perhaps later she could find a man whom she could love, and would love her.

The one person in the court that she had a disliking for was, Baronet Bartholomew the Master of Ceremonies. He was friendly, even more so than to her liking. He was very accommodating. Even to the point at times of being patronising toward her.

He wanted to keep everything orderly, to be a moderator. However, there was something about him that made her wary, like the way that he would ask a direct question from time to time about her family. She always had to be on her guard with him. She couldn't put words to it, but something didn't ring true about him.

The first work day of the sixth week after locating Gerone, Eleanora was called to Duke Bran's office. Arriving there she found Sheriff Ancel in conversation with Duke Bran. After she curtsied, Duke Bran waved her to a chair. Eleanora took a chair and made herself comfortable.

Duke Bran then said, "Lady Eleanora, Sheriff Ancel has brought to me a report on the longshoreman, Gerone." Picking up a folder and handing it to Eleanora, Duke Bran continued, "This is a summary of his movements over the last five weeks."

Eleanora took the folder, opened it and started to read. She soon found what she was looking for. Indicating the report, she said, "I see here that he visits the White Dove brothel every sixth day. He arrives after he has had dinner and drinks at an inn. He spends most of the night there, arriving back home shortly before sunrise. This is the best time for me to make entry into his apartment and have a look around. I don't know what I may find, if anything, but I must do it."

Sheriff Ancel, amazed that a young lady such as Lady Eleanora would even consider entering the apartment of such a dangerous man as Gerone, now spoke up, "Your Grace, is it proper, or even safe to let, Lady Eleanora try to gain entry to the apartment of such a dangerous person as this, Gerone?"

With a crafty smile, Duke Bran said, "Tell me, Sheriff Ancel, do you think that such a person as Eddy the cat could do it?"

Sheriff Ancel exclaimed, "That little felon, I've been trying to catch him for years!"

"Well, Sheriff Ancel," Duke Bran replied, "Do you think that he could do it?"

With a nod, Sheriff Ancel replied, "Yes, Your Grace, as much as I dislike giving him credit for it, he could easily do it. However, he is no longer in Dunboro. There is even a rumor that he is dead."

Looking at, Eleanora, Duke Bran said, "Lady Eleanora, should I tell him, or do you want to?"

Giving Duke Bran a nod and a smile, Eleanora said, "You may do so, Your Grace."

With a smile and a wave of his hand toward, Eleanora, Duke Bran said, "Sheriff Ancel, I would like to introduce you to, Eddy the cat."

With a look of astonishment, Sheriff Ancel responded, "Surely you jest, Your Grace, how can that be?"

Trying to control a fit of giggles, Eleanora said, "It is true, Sheriff Ancel, I was known on the street as, Eddy the cat."

Duke Bran then said, "Well, Sheriff Ancel, now that you know the secret, you can do all you can to keep the rumour that, Eddy the cat is dead. That is what the prince wants."

With a glance at Eleanora and a nod to Duke Bran, Sheriff Ancel said, "It will be done, Your Grace."

Facing Eleanora, Duke Bran said, "Lady Eleanora, is there anything that we can do to help you?"

Eleanora replied, "Well, Your Grace, all that I need is the services of Sergeant Giffard as an escort." Turning her head to face Sheriff Ancel, she continued. "There is one thing that I need to bring up with you, Sheriff Ancel."

"What is that, Lady Eleanora?" Sheriff Ancel said.

Indicating the report, Eleanora replied, "Sheriff Ancel, according to this report, Gerone has hardly any callers at his apartment. He takes his meals daily at one of the inns close to his apartment. However, I'm sure that he considers the tap rooms of the inns too public for clandestine meetings. I would be willing to bet that he doesn't always go to the White Dove just to avail himself of the tender services of some doxy. I believe that he also conducts meetings there. That was also the last place that the cobbler, Chester was seen alive. I'm sure that you know of everyone that works there."

Sheriff Ancel nodded saying, "That we do, Lady Eleanora."

Eleanora continued, "We need to know who Lord North and Hammer are, and how they are communicating without the cobbler Chester, and his pigeons. One suggestion is that you start by identifying anyone who visits the White Dove at the same time as Gerone does on a regular basis."

With a nod, Sheriff Ancel said, "Yes, Lady Eleanora, I've already thought of that." Then shaking his head he continued, "I still can't believe it, you're really Eddy the cat. How did you get away with it for so long?"

"It wasn't that difficult, Sheriff Ancel." Eleanora said, "I just dressed and acted as a lad. Everyone saw me as a lad that being what they expected to see. Well that's all behind me now, thanks to Prince Hugh."

With a sigh, Sheriff Ancel replied, "Yes, Lady Eleanora, it's true that it's all behind you. Now I shall never have the pleasure of catching you."

Duke Bran guffawed, then said, "Sheriff Ancel, just look at it this way. Every fisherman has to have the tale about the big one that got away."

With a chuckle, Sheriff Ancel responded, "I guess you're right, Your Grace. From now on, Eddy the cat will be my big catch that got away" Eleanora then said to Duke Bran, "Your Grace, I would like to make entry to Greone's apartment this coming sixth day. I will do it as soon as I'm sure that he's settled in the White Dove for the evening. You can tell Sergeant Giffard to meet me at the main gate two hours after the mid-day meal this coming sixth day, dressed much as he was the time before. That will give us plenty of time to get in position."

"Okay, Lady Eleanora, I'll take care of it." Duke Bran said, "Now if there is nothing more that you have for me, you can withdraw."

Eleanora got to her feet, curtsied, then turned and left Duke Bran's office.

On the sixth day, at two hours after the mid-day meal, Sergeant Giffard waited at the main gate to the palace. He had dressed plainly in dark-brown tunic and trousers, and was armed with sword and dagger.

Eleanora approached the gate wearing the same black wig and the same make-up as the time before. Her clothing was very dark, a black skirt, dark-grey blouse and indigo-blue front laced bodice. She also carried a small bag with shoulder strap.

As, Eleanora approached, Sergeant Giffard said, "Good-afternoon, My Lady, I'm ready to go."

Eleanora responded, "That's good, Sergeant Giffard. Now once through the gate it's just, Eleanora and Giffard as before. One other thing, do you know much about the White Dove?"

"Yes, Eleanora, I do know of the White Dove." Sergeant Giffard said sheepishly.

Eleanora gave Sergeant Giffard an inquiring look then said, "Giffard, if I have embarrassed you by asking you of your knowledge of the White Dove I apologise. I may be young, but I have not lived a sheltered childhood. I know the nature of men. I also know that men have certain needs that only a woman can satisfy. So with me you have no reason to be embarrassed for being a man. Now, we need a place near the White Dove where we can observe who enters and leaves without anyone seeing us."

Sergeant Giffard smiled at Eleanora, relieved at her candour, then said, "Yes, Eleanora, I do know of a place where we may watch the White Dove without being noticed."

Eleanora responded. "That's good, Giffard, we can go into the city now. We will take the evening meal at one of the cities inns, but not one near the Quay Side Inn, or the docks. We don't want to chance being seen by Gerone, or any of his men. Every sixth day, Gerone spends most of the night at the White Dove. After we know that he is at the White Dove for the evening, I plan to make entry into his apartment to see what I can find. Now, what inn do you recommend that we dine at this evening?"

Giffard said, "Yes, Eleanora, I recommend the Dented Barbut Inn." Nodding, Eleanora said, "Yes, I know of it, they do have an excellent reputation. Now let us be on our way."

Eleanora and Sergeant Giffard waited deep in the shadows of an alleyway about two hundred feet from the front entrance to the White Dove brothel. They had been in place for the surveillance of the main entrance to the White Dove for close to two hours now. The last gleaning of twilight had long since faded, and the larger moon, Marta and the smaller moon, Dora had yet to rise. The night was very dark.

Sergeant Giffard spoke, "If the agents of the city watch are correct, Gerone should be getting here soon."

Eleanora knew that Sergeant Giffard was impatient. This had been the fifth time that he had made the same statement, she said, "In my former trade I had to conduct a lot of surveillance before a job. You learn that an impatient burglar is soon a dead burglar. He will come when he comes."

It amazed Sergeant Giffard how calm, Eleanora always seemed to be. He had never before seen anyone, lad or lass, so mature at such a young age. No wonder the prince favoured her so much. He felt sure that he still had a lot to learn about this astonishing young lady.

Nudging Giffard's arm with her elbow, Eleanora said, "Here he comes." Sergeant Giffard looked to see their subject enter the White Dove. Eleanora continued to speak, "Okay, Giffard, let's give him a little time to get settled in with his honey; then we'll go to pay him a visit at home."

Eleanora and Sergeant Giffard entered the alleyway between the corner building on the main street and the first roll house, on the same side of the street as Gerone's apartment. Eleanora quickly removed her petticoats, handing them to, Sergeant Giffard who still felt a bit reluctant to hold them. She then pulled the hem of her shirt through her legs and tucked it under her belt. She then pulled a length of rope in a coil from the bag and put it over her shoulder. Sergeant Giffard then handed her a small-shuttered lantern they had lit and shuttered

before they had entered the alleyway. She hooked the lantern to her belt, then without delay started to climb to the roof of the corner building, using the aid of a drain pipe.

Once on the roof, Eleanora jumped the alleyway to the roll houses. She moved along the roof of the roll houses, jumping two more alleyways, until she stood on the roof directly over Gerone's apartment. So far, Eleanora hadn't seen anyone in the street below. Tying the rope off to a chimney, she lowered herself down to the window ledge of the rear window of Gerone's apartment. After tripping the shutter latch with a short length of twine and a small hook, she entered the apartment, closing the shutters behind herself.

After making sure that the shutters were secured, Eleanora opened the shutter on the lantern just enough to be able to move around without disturbing anything. She found the apartment rather spartan. She could tell that Gerone never did much cooking. About all that he had was a teapot, cups, glasses and a few plates. All that he had in the cupboard were tea, sugar, cheese, sausage, bread and some wine. He was also not much of a house keeper. The apartment seemed to be used for little more than a place to sleep, and to deposit personal items and clothing.

For over an hour Eleanora searched Gerone's apartment. She found his stashes easily enough, he had three. She had been tempted to take them, but that wasn't what she was there for. She had to leave no trace that she had been there. After a thorough search of the apartment, Eleanora had found no cipher, other codes, or journals. It was clear to her that if he had any of these things, which she doubted that he did, he was smart enough not to keep them in his home.

Eleanora exited Gerone's apartment through the same window that she had made entry, closing and latching the shutters behind herself. She had been very careful in Gerone's apartment not to disturb anything and felt that no one would ever know that she had ever been there. Using the rope she climbed back upon the roof. After recoiling the rope, Eleanora proceeded back to where Sergeant Giffard waited for her.

Sergeant Giffard noticed when Eleanora cleared the space between the buildings overhead. She then quickly scurried down the drain pipe to the ground. As Eleanora put her petticoats back on, Sergeant Giffard blew out the flame in the lantern and repacked it and the rope back in the bag.

As they exited the alleyway five men stepped forth from the darkness into the light of a street lamp. They were all armed and had swords drawn.

Eleanora and Sergeant Giffard automatically took a couple of steps away from each other. As the men approached, Sergeant Giffard drew his sword, Eleanora crouched with her right side slightly turned away from the man close to her. The man didn't see her hand slip up under the hem of her skirt.

Thinking that the lass had cringed in fear, the man nearest to Eleanora lowered the point of his sword as he reached out towards her, to take her by the arm. Faster than a viper, Eleanora struck, so fast that the man didn't even see the blade that buried to the hilt just below his sternum at an upward angle into his heart. The man started to collapse dying as his sword slipped from loose fingers to clatter on the cobble stones.

Eleanora's sudden attack stunned the other men to inaction for a moment, and that was all that was needed. Sergeant Giffard swung with his sword, decapitating the man nearest to him. Stepping over the body, Sergeant Giffard engaged the closest man to him. There surviving adversaries had by now recovered and were starting to fight back, a second man engaging Sergeant Giffard.

After dispatching the first man, Eleanora quickly switched the dagger to her left hand and retrieved the fallen sword. She then engaged the last man. Eleanora found the sword heavier than her own sword, but not as heavy as a broad sword. She would be able to fight with it.

Finding himself facing a lass, Eleanora's opponent feeling contempt for her tried to defeat her with brute force, rather than with skill. He soon found to his dismay that he faced a skilled adversary, and that he was in a fight for his life. He had tried to take a swing at the lasses neck, only to be awarded by a slash across the ribs. The way that she fought with the sword as a thrusting weapon, he could only defend and look for an opening.

Eleanora had to end her fight quickly, Sergeant Giffard was defending against two swords. Taking a step back with her right foot she seemed to stumble. Sensing an opening her opponent drew back his sword to deliver a killing blow. In doing so he had left himself undefended. Eleanora's stumble had only been a ruse, she lunged forward thrusting with her sword. The point of her sword stabbed deep into his solar plexus, a killing blow. The man cried out in pain and collapsed to the pavement.

Hearing their comrade cry out, the two men fighting, Sergeant Giffard looked to see, Eleanora advancing on them. The distraction caused one man to drop his guard with fatal results. Seeing the opening, Sergeant Giffard struck cleaving the man from the shoulder to the sternum. The last man seeing his position hopeless turned to flee. Dropping her sword, Eleanora took the blade of her dagger in her right hand and cast it at the fleeing man. The dagger flew true, plunging deep between the shoulder blades. The man stumbled and fell dead in the street.

After cleaning their blades on the tunics of the dead men and putting them away, Eleanora said, "We need to go now, Giffard. We can report this to Duke Bran later. I don't want to be here in public view explaining all this to the city watch."

"You won't get an argument from me on that, Eleanora." Sergeant Giffard said as they started to walk quickly away from all the carnage.

When they were a couple of blocks away, they turned in the direction of the palace. By now they could look back on the fight with relief. Sergeant Giffard spoke, "Eleanora, I never thought that I would be saying this. If I'm ever in another fight like that I would like you at my side."

Placing her hand on his arm, Eleanora responded, "thank you, Sergeant Giffard. I know what a compliment that is and I'm really flattered."

Smiling, Sergeant Giffard said, "That bunch thought you only a defenseless young female. You are a kitten with real claws."

Eleanora said, "I shall make devotions to Farquhar."

Sergeant Giffard inquired, "Why make devotions to the God of chaos and trickery, Eleanora?"

With a smile, Eleanora replied, "So that my enemies always think me a defenseless female."

Sergeant Giffard erupted with a barking laughter. When the laughter subsided he asked, "Who were those men anyway, Eleanora?"

"They were bashers, Giffard, and their intention was murder." Eleanora replied.

"How could you have been so certain of that, Eleanora?" Sergeant Giffard asked.

Eleanora replied, "Well, Giffard, they were armed with swords. If the intent had been to rob us they would have had truncheons. Someone wants us dead. We must have attracted more attention than we thought. Or perhaps they were keeping a close eye on Gerone's apartment. We need to bring this up with Duke Bran."

CHAPTER 12

After breakfast the next morning, Eleanora went to Duke Bran's office. Sergeant Giffard had already arrived. After Eleanora curtsied to Duke Bran with a greeting, Duke Bran said, "Thank you, Lady Eleanora for being punctual. Sergeant Giffard has been filling me in on the initial report that you gave to the guard commander last night."

Eleanora said. "That report mostly covered the fight with the bashers. There's more than that, Your Grace."

Duke Bran responded, rising to his feet, "I'm sure there is, but wait until we see the prince. He's waiting for us now in his library." Duke Bran then led the way out of his office door.

Prince Hugh sat at his table in his library when there came a knock at the door. Clearing his throat, he called out. "Enter."

The door opened and Duke Bran entered followed by Eleanora, and Sergeant Giffard. The men bowed while Eleanora curtsied, all giving salutations to the prince.

Looking at them, Prince Hugh said, "Gentlemen and Lady, please be seated."

When everyone had taken a chair, Prince Hugh looking at Eleanora said, "Lady Eleanora, Bran has relayed a copy of your report to me. Perhaps you could expand on it for me."

"Yes, Your Highness," Eleanora said, "the report last night covers mostly the fight with the bashers, that being the most urgent. As for the rest, I did gain entry into, Gerone's apartment. I spent over an hour searching everything. I found no notes, journals, ciphers, or any other evidence of a conspiracy. The one thing that he had plenty of was gold and silver coins. I found three stashes amounting to a small fortune. I would say far more than a longshoreman could make in honest labour."

Nodding, Prince Hugh said, "That's very good, Lady Eleanora. Did you by chance find anything about the assassins?"

Shaking her head, Eleanora said, "No, Your Highness, I didn't, but then I didn't expect to find anything. After all, the Brotherhood of the Black Rose doesn't make written contacts with their clients. I believe that the only way to get information from Gerone is to arrest him."

Smiling, Prince Hugh remarked, "Since when did you start reading minds, Lady Eleanora."

"What do you mean, Your Highness?" Eleanora asked with a puzzled expression.

Prince Hugh chuckled, then said, "Just kidding about the mind reading, Lady Eleanora. I plan to arrest this person, Gerone, today." Turning to Duke Bran, Prince Hugh said, "Are the soldiers ready, Bran?"

"Yes, Your Highness," Duke Bran said, "I have sixty men ready to go. That should be more than enough to effect the arrest."

"That should be sufficient," Prince Hugh remarked, "even if, Sheriff Ancel requests a few of them to set up his cordon."

"You must let me go, Your Highness," Eleanora said, aroused by the thought of seeing Gerone finally being brought to justice, "I must be there to witness it. I owe it to my mother. I have wanted to kill him myself, but I'll be satisfied to see him hang." Eleanora then blushed realizing that she had spoken out of turn. She then said, "Excuse me for my impetuous outbreak, Your highness."

Prince Hugh drummed his fingers on the table as he thought. Eleanora's attendance would not be required to make the arrest, but he understood her desire to be there. After a minute he said, "All right, Lady Eleanora, you have earned the right. You can come with us."

Eleanora squealed with delight, then jumped up out of her chair, threw her arms about Prince Hugh's neck and kissed him on the cheek.

"Oh thank you, Your Highness." Eleanora said, then recovering her poise, she said, "Excuse me, Your Highness, I got carried away."

Prince Hugh looked at Eleanora, then smiled saying, "I should do that more often. It feels good to be kissed by a pretty young woman."

The other men laughed as Eleanora blushed. She then went back to her chair, sat back down and made herself comfortable. About a minute after Eleanora had taken her seat, there was a knock at the door. "Enter." Prince Hugh called out.

The door opened and Sheriff Ancel entered, and bowed to, Prince Hugh saying, "Your Highness."

Pointing to a chair, Prince Hugh said. "Take a seat, Sheriff Ancel."

When Sheriff Ancel had settled into his chair, Prince Hugh continued, "Well, Sheriff Ancel, I hear that you had an incident in Dunboro last night."

"I would hardly call it an incident, Your Highness." Sheriff Ancel said, "It was bloody murder. We had five men murdered and left lying in the street in the workers quarter last night. By the looks of it they were set upon by a superior force. I am investigating it now and hope to have some suspects soon."

Prince Hugh and, Duke Bran roared with laughter. Eleanora and Sergeant Giffard merely smiled.

Sheriff Ancel obviously confused said, "I see nothing amusing about murder, Your Highness."

Getting himself under control, Prince Hugh said, "Excuse me, Sheriff Ancel, I wasn't laughing about murder." Indicating Eleanora and Sergeant Giffard with a wave of his hand, he said, "This is your superior force, Sheriff Ancel; Lady Eleanora and Sergeant Giffard. They were there on business for me when they were set upon by those five men, with the intention of murder. Lady Eleanora and Sergeant Giffard only defended themselves."

Sheriff Ancel saw in Eleanora and Sergeant Giffard, a slender young woman and a menacing giant of a man. Sheriff Ancel said, "That was amazing work dispatching those five men, Sergeant Giffard."

Sergeant Giffard chuckled, then said, "Don't give me all the credit, Sheriff Ancel. I only killed two of them, Lady Eleanora killed the other three."

Sheriff Ancel had to take a second look at Eleanora. It became evident to him that her pretty face, feminine charm and young years could be very deceptive. Lady Eleanora could be a most dangerous adversary.

Prince Hugh said, "Now, let's get down to business. Sheriff Ancel, the man, Gerone that you have been keeping under surveillance, I plan to arrest him as soon as possible, before he runs. This is the seventh day, he should be back home now, sleeping off his episode with the prostitutes at the White Dove."

Sheriff Ancel said, "Your Highness, do you want that I make the arrest?" Prince Hugh responded, "No, Sheriff Ancel, my own palace guards will make the arrest. What I need from you is a cordon around the area of Gerone's apartment."

Sheriff Ancel nodded saying, "I can do that, Your Highness. However, it's a large area, I could use some additional men."

"Will twenty men do?" Prince Hugh asked.

"Twenty men will do, Your Highness." Sheriff Ancel said, pleased with the generosity of the prince.

Prince Hugh now asked, "How long will it take you to get the cordon set up, Sheriff Ancel?"

Sheriff Ancel answered, "Your Highness, give me three quarters of an hour head start and I will have your cordon in place when you arrive."

"Good," Prince Hugh said, "then I shall not detain you any longer, Sheriff Ancel. There will be twenty soldiers at the main gate for you shortly."

Sheriff Ancel got up from his chair, then bowed saying, "By your leave, Your Highness." He then turned and left the room.

Prince Hugh then said, "Bran, see that there are twenty guards at the main gate for, Sheriff Ancel."

Duke Bran replied, "I have already taken care of it, Your Highness. Anticipating Sheriff Ancel's needs, I already have twenty men from the sixty-man force waiting for him."

Prince Hugh now continued, "That will do, Bran, we have more than enough to effect the arrest with forty men. Now, let us be ready. We will be mounted while the soldiers will be on foot. Lady Eleanora, I assume that you will be more appropriately attired."

"Yes, Your Highness," Eleanora said, "I will change before we go."

"Then, Lady Eleanora," Prince Hugh said, "I shall have the stable tack up your horse with a man's saddle."

"Thank you, your Highness." Eleanora said.

Prince Hugh then said, "Be at the main gate in three quarters of an hour. You are all dismissed."

Three quarters of an hour later everyone had assembled at the main gate. Eleanora had changed into a dark-green tunic, grey trousers and black riding boots with bronze spurs. Her sword hung from a black leather baldric with bronze buckle. Her dagger hung from a black leather belt with bronze buckle. Her red hair that was now long enough to rest on her shoulders, had been pinned up and covered by a wide brimmed black-felt hat. To the casual observer she could be seen as the son of a noble in the company of the older men.

Prince Hugh gave the order and they moved out through the main gate. Prince Hugh, Duke Bran, Eleanora and Sergeant Giffard on horseback at the walk, with forty soldiers of the palace guard marching in formation behind.

Being a member of a force of armed men, on a mission for the first time, felt both strange and thrilling for Eleanora. She felt grateful to Prince Hugh for allowing her to be a member of the arresting force, even if she didn't have a clear role to play.

As they advanced into the city, the citizens seeing men on horseback leading a formation of men at arms, suddenly found that they had to be someplace else right then. The crowded streets cleared ahead of them, as if by magic; the progress to their destination being unimpeded.

Arriving at the head of the residential street that led to Gerone's apartment they dismounted, turning their mounts over to two of the soldiers.

As they were getting ready to move up the street, Eleanora spoke to Prince Hugh, "Your Highness, I know this area very well. There are alleyways between the roll houses on this street and the next street over. I can take a few men to cover the alleyways, to block off that route of escape if he sees us coming and tries to duck out the back way."

Prince Hugh thought for a moment, then turned to Duke Bran saying, "Bran, give, Lady Eleanora six men to cover the back way."

"Yes, Your Highness," Duke Bran said. Then picking out six men he told them, "You men, go with Lady Eleanora and follow her lead."

Without further delay, Eleanora drew her sword and set out for the alleyway to the rear of Gerone's apartment at the run, with her six men close behind her.

Gerone having come home that morning from the White Dove, found out that five of his men had been cut down in the street. As tired as he was, after a night of carousing at the White Dove, he couldn't go to bed. This being a major blow to his crew of bashers he needed to find out what had happened. Whoever was responsible for this dastardly act had to be found and dealt with. He brought six of his men to his apartment, while sending other men out to try to find out who had been responsible for this tragedy.

He now had four men in his apartment and two men down stairs at the front door, watching the street. Finally he had become so exhausted that he had started to doze in a chair.

One of the men stationed downstairs at the front door came bounding up the stairs, bursting into the apartment. "Soldiers are coming up the street!" He exclaimed breathlessly.

Gerone snapped awake, springing to his feet exclaiming, "Quick, out the back way!"

They all rushed out of the apartment and took the stairs down, two and three steps at a time. Rushing out into the garden, they ran for the gate in the back wall that led to the alleyway.

Eleanora had just neared the gate behind Gerone's apartment at the head of her soldiers, when the gate started to open. The first man came through the gate and seeing Eleanora started to draw his sword. Eleanora immediately lunged forward, taking the man in the throat with the point of her sword, dealing him a killing blow. The man fell to the ground clutching his throat, trying to staunch the flow of blood.

The second man came through the gate with his sword already drawn. Eleanora attacked, quickly working past his guard to drive the point of her sword through his heart. By then her men were in position to support her, as more soldiers were entering the alleyway from another direction.

Gerone coming out the gate and seeing that they were hopelessly out numbered with no route of escape, threw down his sword. "I surrender," he said holding up his hands, "don't hurt me."

Eleanora had dreamed for a long time of having this man at her mercy. To look into his eyes as she impaled him on her sword. Now all she saw before her was a coward. It would be better for the prince to hang him. Turning to one of her men, she said, "Disarm and bind them."

As Gerone and his surviving men were being bound by the soldiers, Prince Hugh and Duke Bran came into the alleyway. Prince Hugh asked, "Did we get him, Lady Eleanora?"

Eleanora, pointing at Gerone, answered, "Yes, Your Highness, that's him there."

Prince Hugh turned to Duke Bran saying, "Well, Bran, he's yours now. Get all the prisoners back to the palace quickly. I want this man, Gerone, isolated from everyone. No one is to come near him, unless authorized by you or myself. He is to be kept under maximum security. I will keep Lady Eleanora and Sergeant Giffard and fifteen men here. You take the rest of the men, plus what guards that you can gather from the sheriff's cordon in the next few minutes."

Duke Bran gave a shallow bow saying, "Yes, Your Highness." He then started to issue orders to move the prisoners back to the palace.

Prince Hugh then spoke to, Eleanora, "Lady Eleanora, I would like to see the apartment now." Eleanora followed Prince Hugh up to the apartment.

There she conducted a tour of the apartment for Prince Hugh, showing him everything that she had found, to include the three stashes of gold and silver coins.

After Prince Hugh had seen everything of interest, he had guards posted so that no one would disturb anything until a detail could be sent to collect everything. He then returned to the palace with Eleanora, Sergeant Giffard and the remainder of the escort.

After dinner, Eleanora went to the cell at the lowest level of the old keep where they were holding Gerone under guard. She had been given clearance from Prince Hugh to visit the prisoner. Upon arrival the senior guard bowed saying, "Good evening, Lady Eleanora, we received word that you would be coming."

"Is the prisoner well restrained?" Eleanora asked.

The guard nodded saying, "Yes, My Lady, he is shackled by a chain to his ankle. He can lay on his sleeping pallet and use his soils bucket, but he can't reach the door of his cell."

"Then open the door," she said.

Gerone had been sitting on his sleeping pallet in the low light of the cell. As exhausted as he was fear kept him from sleeping. He knew that he was in a critical situation and feared for his life. The door to the cell opened and he looked up to see a young woman standing in the door. From her poise and elegant gown she had to be a lady of the court. He wondered why a lady of the court would trouble herself to come here. "Who are you?" Gerone said, trying to show defiance in his voice, but not showing much success.

"Don't concern yourself with who I am," Eleanora responded, "I am the person that has brought you down. I have dreamed of killing you for a long time. After killing two of your men in the alleyway today; I wanted to run you through, but I knew that Prince Hugh wanted you alive."

"That can't be!" Gerone exclaimed in disbelief, "That was no lass in the alleyway today! I know what I saw!"

Smiling, Eleanora said, "The night that you plotted treason with the cobbler, Chester, I was there and heard every word that you and Chester said. For that the prince will hang you."

"You are lying," Gerone said in disbelief, "you were not there."

"Oh, but I was." Eleanora said, "On the street I didn't look as I do now. On the street I was known as, Eddy the cat."

Gerone still didn't want to believe it. However, this young woman seemed to know a lot about him. She must be telling the truth that she was, Eddy the cat. It would explain why, Eddy the cat had simply vanished, he said, "How did you do it, I mean get away with pretending to be a lad?"

When Eleanora answered him, she regarded him with eyes hard and cold. "I have my mother to thank for that. You do remember my mother, don't you?"

Confused by the question, Gerone responded, "Your mother, how would I know your mother?"

With a smile that radiated no warmth or cheer, Eleanora said, "Oh, but you do know her. Think back about seven and a half years ago. My mother had auburn hair like mine. You came to our home to see her one night. Did she argue with you? Did she belittle your manhood? Did you blame her for your inability to perform? Why did you murder my mother?"

All the colour drained from Gerone's face. He did remember her mother, and he knew that he was doomed. He didn't answer. How could he?

Eleanora continued to turn the blade, enjoying his agony, "The prince's inquisitors will be here soon to interrogate you, and they will not be gentile with you. They will get what they want from you. I hope that you hold out for a long time and suffer much, but knowing the coward that you are, I doubt that you will last long. I will leave you to your fears and misery now." Eleanora then turned and left, the guard slamming the cell door shut.

CHAPTER 13

Four days later, after the mid-day meal, Eleanora was summoned to Prince Hugh's library. She knocked on the door and heard the prince's voice call out. "Enter."

Eleanora opened the door seeing Prince Hugh seated behind his table. She entered and curtsied saying, "Your Highness."

Prince Hugh looked up from a document that he had just signed and sealed and with a smile said, "Lady Eleanora, please have a seat," as he indicated a chair close to the table.

After Eleanora had settled herself into the chair and made herself comfortable, Prince Hugh held up the parchment saying, "I thought that you would like to see this. It is the death warrant for, Gerone. He is a traitor, but publicly we are hanging him for the murders of the cobbler, Chester and your mother."

With the realization that her mother would finally get justice, Eleanora was overcome with emotion, almost to the point of tears. Understanding how Eleanora felt about her mother, and the man that murdered her, Prince Hugh gave her the time that she needed to regain her poise. After taking time to get herself under control, Eleanora said, "Thank you, Your Highness, it means a lot to me that my mother will have justice. I had wanted to kill him myself. For a long time I have dreamed and fantasised about what I would do when I found him. However, when I had him in the alleyway, to run him through would have been too easy on him. He would not have had the time to ponder his own death. I want him to lie in his cell at night unable to sleep, thinking of the rope that will strangle the life from him. Hanging is better for him."

Prince Hugh chuckled, then said, "Oh, Lady Eleanora, you do have some hard edges. I'm lucky that you work for me."

Eleanora asked, "Your Highness, did you get the information that you wanted from Gerone?"

Prince Hugh with a look of displeasure said, "Well, Lady Eleanora, we tried our best, but got little more than we already knew. From what he told us about the messages received from Lord North by the cobbler, Chester, we believe that, Lord North is someone close to, Emperor Eimion of the Jutes. As for the person referred to as Hammer, Gerone has no idea who he is. Gerone said that Hammer recruited him through a woman at the White Dove."

"Does the woman work at the White Dove, Your Highness?" Eleanora asked.

Prince Hugh answered, "No, Lady Eleanora, she doesn't work there. Whenever she had something to pass on to Gerone, or to receive something from him, she would make contact with him inside the White Dove. There were also drops where messages could be left, or received. Hammer took precautions not to have his identity known by Gerone, or Chester."

"Do you plan any punitive action against the White Dove, Your highness?" Eleanora asked.

"No, Lady Eleanora, not now. Some of the people in the White Dove have to be assisting Hammer, but it would be hard to ferret them out. Later, if I can separate the sheep from the goats, I will take action." Prince Hugh said.

"What about the assassin, Your Highness." Eleanora asked, "Did we find out anything about them?"

Prince Hugh responded, "Yes we did, Lady Eleanora, Gerone told us that he left a note naming the target at a secret drop at the temple of Odila (goddess of the dead). He then went back the next day to pick up a note naming the price and how to deliver it." Prince Hugh slapped

his hand on his table in ire, then continued, "Damn that, Gerone and his kind. So we now know that there is an assassin, but we don't know who he is, or when or where he will strike."

Eleanora thought for a minute of their problem of a lack of information, then spoke, "Your Highness, I have an idea. We need information about unusual persons, or occurrences in the city. I know that the city watch has its agents and informers. I also know that they are known by many who live on the streets. I would like to recruit certain former associates of mine to keep their eyes and ears open, and to report anything unusual to me."

Prince Hugh sat back in his chair rubbing his chin with thumb and forefinger as he thought for a few minutes on Lady Eleanora's request. Eleanora sat quiet in her chair next to his table as he thought. Finally, Prince Hugh said, "Lady Eleanora, can these people be relied upon?"

Eleanora took a few seconds to compose her answer before she spoke.

She then said, "Well, Your Highness, I would say some more than others. I would have to evaluate the information against the person as I know them."

Prince Hugh considered what Eleanora had said, then asked, "Who are these people anyway?"

"Mostly street kids, Your Highness." Eleanora said, "They are just part of the background, unless they cut your purse, or get sticky fingers with some street vendor's merchandise."

Prince Hugh laughed at Eleanora's humour, then responded, "Sounds like a ragged bunch of spies to me, Lady Eleanora."

Eleanora said, "Yes, Your Highness, they do, but for that reason no one would suspect them. No one would pay much attention to them as they move about the city."

Prince Hugh got to his feet and turned to look out the window in thought as, Eleanora waited patiently. Finally after a couple of minutes he turned back to her and said, "Okay, Lady Eleanora, I will go along with this plan of yours. What will you need?"

Eleanora responded, "Not much to start, Your Highness, mostly some silver and a little gold coin to entice those that I choose to work for me. Then I will have to go into the city to recruit them."

"Will you take Sergeant Giffard with you, Lady Eleanora?" Prince Hugh asked.

Eleanora responded with a shake of her head, "No, Your Highness, I must go alone. If I have an escort with me no one will want to approach me. I will go right after the evening meal." With a smile, Eleanora continued, "Your Highness, Eleanora will not be going. It will be, Eddy the cat. After all, that is who they will expect to see. Besides, with Gerone to be hung tomorrow, no one will be looking for me. And I will also be armed."

Prince Hugh with a nod said, "Well, Lady Eleanora, after all that you have done this week, I'm sure that you can take care of yourself. You are a terror with a blade, both long and short. I know that as good as I am I wouldn't want to face you. You can go by yourself as, Eddy the cat, but be careful. I will have a purse ready for you filled with half royals, royals, a few double royals and two half sovereigns."

"That should be more than enough, Your Highness," Eleanora said.

"Oh, by the way," Prince Hugh said, "the gold and silver coins in Gerone's apartment totalled to more than two hundred and seventy-one double sovereigns. I am giving you thirty double sovereigns as a reward for finding them. The rest will go to the royal treasury."

Eleanora grinned with appreciation saying, "Thank you, Your Highness, I am very grateful."

Prince Hugh then said, "You may withdraw now, Lady Eleanora, to get ready for your excursion."

Eleanora stood and curtsied saying, "Your Highness." She then turned and left the room.

Prince Hugh watched her go thinking of the discussion that he had with his wife about, Eleanora. Since coming to them, Eleanora had done everything she could to show her gratitude for having been given such an opportunity to better herself. He had to agree with his wife that

Eleanora had shown true devotion to them, and should be rewarded for it. He would have to do something about it at the first opportunity.

Back in her apartment, Eleanora dressed in an indigo-blue tunic, black trousers and black boots. Her sword hung from her baldric and her dagger from her belt. She pinned up her hair and covered it with a black beret. The nights starting to be cool, Eleanora wore a black cloak with cowl.

Just as she had finished dressing a knock came at the door, she called out. "Enter."

The door opened and a page entered and bowed. He then held out a purse saying, "My Lady, Prince Hugh instructed me to deliver this to you."

Eleanora accepted the purse saying, "Thank you, you may withdraw now."

The page bowed saying, "My Lady." He then turned and left her apartment.

The sun stood low to the western horizon when, Eleanora left through the main gate of the palace. By the time that she reached the workers quarter the setting sun had turned the sky to shades of orange, purple and indigo. The oil wicks in the street lamps glowed with a yellow flame. Lights were seen in the inns and many of the shops. The streets were full of people going about their business, or just out for an evening stroll.

It had been many months since Eleanora had been alone on the streets at night. However, she soon became reacquainted to the bustle and noise of the street after dark. She realised that she had missed it, and at the same time felt grateful to be away from it. Her place was now the palace, not the streets of Dunboro.

Soon after entering the workers quarter, Eleanora found one of the persons that she was looking for. Moving up close in the shadow of an alleyway, Eleanora called out softly, "Hi, Jimmy the deft."

Jimmy, hearing his name being called, looked about to see who it was that had addressed him. Seeing a well-dressed young lad standing in the shadow, he took a hard look then exclaimed, "Eddy! Eddy he cat!"

Smiling, Eleanora said, "Yes, Jimmy the deft, it's me, Eddy the cat." "What happened, Eddy?" Jimmy said, "One day you were here, then you were gone. People started to believe that you were dead."

Jimmy now took a good look at, Eleanora. He noticed the fine clothing, sword and dagger. With a little wonder he said, "Wow, Eddy, you look really great. Are you some kind of a gentleman now? How did you do that?"

Smiling, Eleanora said, "Well, Jimmy, let's just say that I got lucky. Now, what I'm here for is that I need your help."

"You need my help," Jimmy said with raised eyebrows, "what for?" Eleanora answered, "I need information, and I'm willing to pay for it. I need to know if anything unusual happens in the city. Like if a man, or men come to Dunboro and say that they are on certain business, or of a certain trade, but do not do what would be expected of them to do. Also any suspicious comings or goings in the sewers. Or anything else that seems odd, or out of place. I'm sure that you will know what to look for."

"What's all this about, Eddy?" Jimmy asked.

Eleanora, taking out three royals and one double royal and handing them to, Jimmy, said, "Look, Jimmy, all that you need to know for now is that I need the information. And I also need for our arrangement to remain confidential, so don't be looking to make more on the side by selling the information to someone else. If you do and I find out that will be the end of our arrangement, understand?"

Nodding, Jimmy said, "Yes, I understand."

Eleanora patted Jimmy on the shoulder saying, "Good, now I'll check with you from time to time. I also plan to get others to work for me. You will be the head of my network, everyone will report to you. You may also recruit others as needed, just let me know who they are so that I can provide for your expenses. If you have something for me

we can arrange signals and drops. Now, if you happen to come upon something that's an emergency and you have to get in touch with me immediately, go to the main gate of the palace and ask for, Eddy the cat, understand."

Jimmy regarded Eleanora with a look of wonder and respect saying, "Wow, Eddy, are you a squire, or something like that now?"

Eleanora with a sort of half-smile and another pat on the shoulder responded, "Well, Jimmy, you might say it's something like that. Now just remember what I said."

After leaving Jimmy, Eleanora contacted four more people. Two were lads living on the street, their names, Alan and Thomas, both were cut purses. One was a lass of thirteen years her name, Brenda. Eleanora felt sorry for her. At thirteen years she had just started to show the signs of womanhood. A family that owned a tailor shop and dry goods store now gave her room and board for her labour. Soon there would be unscrupulous people trying to force her into prostitution. Eleanora wished that there were something more that she could do for her.

The last person that she was able to recruit was Owain, the inn keeper that had employed her mother to serve his customers in the taproom of his inn. He had also taught Eleanora her letters and numbers. And had shown her how to use them to read and write. She now had the start of an intelligence network. Jimmy would coordinate the network on the street. Owain with his ties to other inn keepers could keep her informed as to anything unusual occurring in the inns.

The next morning, one hour after sunrise a formation of soldiers from the palace guard marched out of the main gate to the beat of a drum. They took up position around the gallows outside the palace wall, close to the main gate. Within a few minutes a crowd started to assemble. There were always plenty of people eager to watch some poor soul go to meet Odila (goddess of the dead).

Soon the slow roll and beat of another drum could be heard coming from inside the palace gate. A minute later the condemned, walking slowly beside a priest of Raginfrid (god of the underworld), surrounded by a detail of palace guards and following the drummer, passed through the palace gate. At the sight of the gallows, Gerone's pace slowed, having to be prodded by the butt of a spear by the guard behind him to keep moving.

At sight of the condemned most of the crowd cheered. Some of the spectators knowing Gerone for a cruel man jeered and cursed him. For most of the crowd the hanging was entertainment and they wanted to see a good show.

Reaching the gallows the drummer ceased his tattoo. The guards then prodded Gerone up the steps, where the hangman and his assistant, their heads covered by black hoods, grabbed him by the arms and bound them behind his back with rope. They then maneuvered him to the spot under the noose. An officer of the guard then read the death warrant for the murder of two citizens of Dunboro. The hangman then put a black cloth bag over, Gerone's head and adjusted the noose around his neck. The drum rolled, then on a signal the drum stopped and the trap was sprung. Gerone dropped a short distance where he kicked and twisted for a short time, then hung still.

Eleanora had watched the hanging from atop the gate tower close to the gallows. Eleanora didn't care to watch hangings, but had felt that she had to watch Gerone hang out of respect for the memory of her mother. Now that it was over she felt relief that her mother had gotten justice. Even so, she still didn't feel any better for having gotten revenge, and her mother was still gone.

CHAPTER 14

The fall season came upon the land, then the first snowfall. Eleanora worked at building her intelligence network in Dunboro. She now received reports of strangers arriving in Dunboro, but none turned out to be the assassins that she was looking for. Each of the people that she had first recruited now had their own agents that reported to them. If anyone in the network needed to get information to her, they went through Jimmy the deft. Eleanora would meet with him often on the street in the evening, always dressed as, Eddy the cat.

Eleanora also wondered if the elusive Hammer had tried to replace his lost agents in Dunboro. She knew that Hammer used a woman to insulate himself from his agents. The key to finding Hammer would be to find the woman, but where to look. The White Dove figured in this, but how do you find one woman in a house full of women.

With the coming of winter most activities moved indoors. Eleanora kept with her studies and weapons training. She even found time to take a short ride on, Porky from time to time. She even found more time to play with Isabelle and Mark, the children of Prince Hugh and Princess Juliana. Eleanor had grown to love the children who returned the love, even starting to call her, aunt Eleanora. One month before the mid-winter feast, Princess Juliana announced that she was with child. The court was very pleased with the announcement. Eleanora celebrated the mid-winter feast with Prince Hugh and his family. At last she felt that she had a family.

Eleanora stood in the corner of Mistress Caitlin's study watching her as she prepared to cast a weather spell. Eleanora had watched Mistress Caitlin cast spells before, but this would be the first time that she would watch her using the far seeing basin. The basin being an elaborately carved and polished pedestal and basin of alabaster, much like a large bird bath. Duke Bran and Knight Marshal Simon had also joined them for the weather seeing; each needing the weather forecast for the palace guard, or for the prince's legion.

When Mistress Caitlin was ready they all gathered around the basin, Mistress Caitlin and Eleanora facing each other across the basin with Duke Bran and Knight Marshal Simon at their sides. Mistress Caitlin took a small bottle from a pocket in a fold of her robe. She pulled the stopper from the bottle and let two drops of an oily liquid drip into the water in the basin. She then replaced the stopper in the bottle and put it back into the pocket in her robe, then said. "Now, everyone hold hands."

When everyone was holding hands with the person on each side of them, Mistress Caitlin started to incant a spell in an ancient language known to few outside the priesthood, or the community of magicians. A shimmer developed on the surface of the water in the basin. Then a glow began to issue from the basin, as the light of the chamber dimmed. Then the shimmering in the basin coalesced into an image from above showing them standing around the basin. As Mistress Caitlin continued to incant, the view point started to rise until it was outside looking down at the roof of the tower that housed the basin. As the view point continued to rise, the whole palace, then the city of Dunboro came into view.

Mistress Caitlin continued to incant as the angle of view angled to the west and started to move across the land while accelerating. They soon left the land, heading out to sea at an increasing speed. Soon clouds came into view. As they moved west the clouds became thicker and darker. Mistress Caitlin incanted again and the speed slowed. The clouds became even darker and heavy with snow, as strong winds whipped the waves. The image faded and the light came back to the room. Addressing Duke Bran, Mistress Caitlin said, "A storm comes from the west, out over the ocean sea, Your Grace."

Knight Marshal Simon asked, "Mistress Caitlin, when will it hit?" Mistress Caitlin replied, "In three days, My Lord, there will be high wind and heavy snow."

"Thank you for the seeing, Mistress Caitlin," Duke Bran said, "It is very helpful for us. Simon and I have a lot to do to be ready for the storm. We will be going now."

Mistress Caitlin and Eleanora curtsied as, Duke Bran and Knight Marshal Simon left the room.

When the men had left the study, Eleanora turned to Mistress Caitlin and said, "Thank you for letting me be a part to the seeing, Mistress Caitlin. It's amazing what you are able to do with magic."

Mistress Caitlin responded, "It was a pleasure to have you here with me, Eleanora. I like the way that you show interest in everything." "I do have one question, Mistress Caitlin." Eleanora said. "What is that, Eleanora?" Mistress Caitlin asked.

Eleanora replied, "Mistress Caitlin, do you use the basin only for the weather?"

Giving Eleanora a friendly pat on the arm, Mistress Caitlin said, "Even though I use it mostly to see the weather, I can also use it to look for a person, or object. All that I need to know is where to look. Now, are there any more questions that you have about magic?"

With an inquisitive look, Eleanora responded, 'Yes, Mistress Caitlin, there are many questions that I have about magic. First of all, there are certain people that for a fee will give you a love potion, place a curse on your enemies, or other such things."

Mistress Caitlin laughed, then responded, "Oh, Eleanora, don't pay those people any mind, they are all charlatans. All they want is your money, so stay away from them. There is a lot that magic can do, but it has its limitations. You can't call down fire from the sky, or make the earth move, or make a river run uphill. Also you can't use magic to sweep enemy armies from the field. There are however many things that you can accomplish if you can incant the proper spell, or have an amulet that has been properly prepared."

"What about seers, Mistress Caitlin?" Eleanora asked.

"Well, Eleanora," Mistress Caitlin said, "The seers have their own magic. This magic will not let them have a clear picture of the future in detail. What it does allow them to do is to see many possible futures in a vague sort of way. They also at times give warnings, but this warning will also be ill-defined, like you are being allowed to see only a part of the puzzle. With it they can make a person aware of their options. The priesthood of the temples also have their own magic. There are many kinds of magic, but they all are limited in one way or the other."

"Thank you for that explanation of magic, Mistress Caitlin." Eleanora said, "Perhaps you can tell me more about magic later on."

Eleanora spent a few more minutes with Mistress Caitlin, then left for her own apartment.

Two days later, at mid-morning, Jimmy approached the guard at the main gate to the palace. The guard stopped him asking, "Now what could your business be, lad?"

Feeling foolish for being here, Jimmy said, "I need to see Eddy the cat, it's an emergency."

The guard's demeanor immediately changed. He said, "Wait right here, lad."

The guard then conferred with a second guard, who then set out for the palace.

Fifteen minutes later the guard returned with a maid of the household staff. The guard then instructed Jimmy to go with the maid. Jimmy followed the maid into the main palace, along corridors, and upstairs, finally coming to a door. The maid knocked at the door, a woman's voice called out. "Enter."

The maid opened the door and entered the room, followed by, Jimmy. A young woman sat in a chair reading a book. The maid curtsied saying, "My Lady, the lad, Jimmy."

Jimmy, taking his cue from the maid, bowed saying, "My Lady."

The young woman dismissed the maid and laid her book aside. She then looked at, Jimmy with a smile and said, "Well, Jimmy, what do you have for me?"

Jimmy looked at her with confusion. Then a look of astonishment came over his face and he exclaimed, "No! No, it can't be! You're a woman!"

As hard as she tried not to, Eleanora had to laugh at Jimmy's discomposure. She then said, "I'm sorry if I gave you a shock, Jimmy the deft. I am however, Eddy the cat. You may now call me by my true name, Eleanora."

Shaking his head, Jimmy said, "I still don't understand. All those years on the street, we thought you a lad. Clearly that was a masquerade on your part. But now you have people bowing and curtsying to you as if you were high born."

Eleanora responded, "That's honorary due to my position as personal companion to her highness, Princes Juliana. Now, Jimmy, what is so urgent as to bring you here."

"It's, Thomas," Jimmy said, "he's dead."

"What!" Eleanora exclaimed startled, "How did it happen?"

Jimmy answered, "It all started when Thomas noticed a man new to the streets of Dunboro. This man told people that he was a cooper by trade, and had come to Dunboro to seek employment. However, as much as we could tell, he wasn't really trying to find a job. Thomas decided to keep an eye on him, then Thomas disappeared. We found him yesterday evening. He had been severely beaten and his throat cut. It wasn't robbery, his purse was still on him. Perhaps he was about to, or had found out something that someone didn't want him to know."

Eleanora was now fully alarmed by the report on Thomas' death, she asked, "Where was the body found?"

"In the sewers." Jimmy said.

"Tell me, Jimmy," Eleanora asked, "was, Thomas found near the White Dove?"

Nodding, Jimmy answered, "Yes, about three blocks from there." Eleanora now asked, "This man, the one that calls himself a cooper, what does he look like?"

Jimmy replied, "I'd say about thirty years, short, not much taller than you, brown hair and eyes, slight build and he is also clean shaven."

Continuing to appraise the information related by Jimmy, Eleanora asked, "Has this man been seen by anyone since, Thomas was murdered?"

Jimmy responded, "No one has seen him since, Thomas died. He has just disappeared."

Getting to her feet, Eleanora said, "Come with me, Jimmy, we must relay this to Duke Bran."

"The duke!" Jimmy exclaimed, "Do we have to?"

Eleanora chuckled at Jimmy's uneasiness, then said, "Don't worry, Jimmy, you will get along with the duke just fine. All you have to do is tell your story just as you have told it to me."

Before Jimmy could complain further, Eleanora led him from her apartment.

Jimmy related his story again to Duke Bran while Eleanora added a comment from time to time. After the presentation by Jimmy there were some follow up questions until Duke Bran was satisfied. For the information, Duke Bran rewarded Jimmy with two gold double sovereigns. Jimmy left the duke's office very pleased with two gold double sovereigns, thinking of all that he could buy with them.

After, Jimmy had departed, Eleanora spoke, "Your Grace, I believe that the assassin is now in Dunboro, and that he has a plan to get into the palace." Nodding, Duke Bran said, "I'll not dispute you on that, Lady Eleanora. Thanks to your intelligence network we are forewarned. We now have a description of the potential assassin. I will alert Sheriff Ancel to get the city watch looking for him. I also need to put on extra guards here at the palace.

Now, let's go up and tell the prince about this."

The storm hit two hours before sunrise the next morning, with howling winds and blowing snow, the temperature and visibility dropped

to freezing and almost a whiteout. The conditions were miserable for anyone who had to be out in the weather. It was almost impossible to look into the icy wind and blowing snow. Even with the added guards it was hard to completely secure the palace perimeter. Extra guards were also posted within the palace.

Eleanora, with a feeling that danger lurked in every shadow, roamed the palace corridors and common spaces. She had been at it all day, taking time only for meals and a short rest from time to time. Her intuition told her that the assassin would strike this day. She didn't know from where the threat would come from, but she had to be ready.

She was now close to the princes apartments. Turning a corner she expected to encounter a guard. No one was there. Eleanora thought, *now where could the guard be?* It would be unthinkable for a palace guard to leave his post. She looked down the corridor that was illuminated by oil lamps set in brackets at regular intervals. She noticed that one of the lamps had gone out. Most likely a gust of wind had snuffed it out.

Just then the door right in front of her, that led to the princes library opened and, Prince Hugh started to emerge from his library into the corridor. Eleanora was just a couple of steps from the prince when she saw movement in the shadow of a window recess, created by the extinguished lamp. Without thought she lunged forward catching Prince Hugh by her shoulder, knocking him sideways to the floor. As they were both falling, Eleanora felt a sting across her shoulder blade. Hitting the floor hard, Eleanora rolled a few feet between the assassin and Prince Hugh, in a flurry of skirt and petticoats, then lay still.

The assassin having missed his target with the dart, dropped the blowgun, pulling his dagger. Prince Hugh, having hit the floor hard and been momentary stunned, slowly rose to his feet while reaching for his dagger. With murder in his eyes, the assassin advanced on Prince Hugh who still struggled to be ready to defend himself. Seeing the inert body of a young woman between him and his target, the assassin went to step over the body of Eleanora to get to the prince. There was a sudden movement and the assassin screamed out in pain, dropping his dagger and grabbing his groin where the hilt of a dagger protruded, the blade buried deep into his innards. The assassin crumpled to the floor mortally wounded.

Prince Hugh shouted out as loud as he could, "Guards, to me! Guards, to me!"

In moments the pounding of boots could be heard as guards within earshot answered the call of their prince. As the first guard arrived, Prince Hugh, checking that the assassin was no longer a threat said, "See to Lady Eleanora."

The guard bent down to check on Eleanora. Seeing the guard, Eleanora asked with a weak voice, "Is my prince safe?"

Nodding the guard said, "Yes my Lady, the prince is safe." Eleanora showed a faint smile of relief, then lost consciousness.

The guard turned to Prince Hugh saying. "She is alive, Your Highness, but she needs medical attention."

By now several guards were on the scene. Prince Hugh turned to a guard next to him and said, "You, go and get my healer. Tell him to come to the apartment of Lady Eleanora, and make it quick."

He then detailed a group of guards to gently carry Eleanora to her quarters.

After assigning other guards to pick up everything from the scene for examination, Price Hugh went to Eleanora's apartment to see how she was doing.

When, Prince Hugh arrived at Eleanora's apartment, Mistress Caitlin was already there. Father Damon of the order of Urian (the god of physicians) and healer to, Prince Hugh, arrived right behind him. Without delay, Mistress Caitlin and Father Damon set to treating Eleanora.

After dressing the wound, Father Damon turned to Prince Hugh saying, "Your Highness, I have dressed the wound. The wound its self isn't serious, but something is causing her condition to deteriorate. Do you know the weapon that caused the wound?"

"Yes, Father," Prince Hugh said, "it was a dart from a blowgun."

Father Damon said, "May, Mistress Caitlin and I see the dart that caused the wound?"

Price Hugh responded, "Of course, Father Damon, I will get it for you." Prince Hugh turned to a guard and sent him off to retrieve the dart. Just

then, Duke Bran entered the room. Seeing him, Prince Hugh asked, "What do you have so far, Bran?"

"We found the missing guard, Your Highness," Duke Bran said, "We found him dead in an unoccupied chamber. He had been stabbed in the heart. Also in the chamber were woman's clothing, like those worn by the serving staff and a wig."

Rubbing his chin with thumb and forefinger, Prince Hugh said, yes, that's the reason for a small, slight-built, clean shaven assassin. All he had to do was wait for really dreadful weather, then just walk in like a maid coming to work.

"I'm glad that we caught him." Duke Bran said.

Prince Hugh replied, "We didn't catch him Bran, Eleanora fouled his attempt, then brought him down. Her devotion to me is exemplary. I must reward her for that."

Father Damon and Mistress Caitlin examined the dart delivered to them. They could feel the arcane spell imbued in the dart. Finally, Father Damon said, "With your help, Mistress Caitlin, we can counter the magic. I will send my accolade for what we need, then we can affect the cure."

Mistress Caitlin replied, "I will gladly assist, for the lady is very dear to me."

They first got everyone out of the apartment. By that time the accolade had returned. At each corner of Eleanora's bed they set a candle on the floor. They then drew a symbol around each candle with chalk and lit the candle. Father Damon then opened a small satchel and removed a multitude of small bags, ranging in size from that of a lemon, to that of a walnut. Taking each bag, Father Damon would say a short incantation, then place the bag at a specific point on Eleanora's body, that lay in repose on her bed.

When all the bags had been placed, the accolade held a large blue-leather bound book, so that Father Damon and Mistress Caitlin could read from it. As they started a long incantation, a golden nimbus started to glow faintly about Eleanora's body. The brightness of the nimbus continued to increase as they incanted. When they had finished their incantation the whole room was bathed in light from the nimbus.

The nimbus glowed brightly for a few minutes, then slowly faded until it was completely gone. Father Damon and Mistress Caitlin then took the bags, one at a time and burned them in the fireplace. Father Damon then said, "Well, it's done, Mistress Caitlin, the lady was very lucky. She was only partiality affected by the spell. It wasn't specific to her, but someone else."

"Like the prince." Mistress Caitlin said.

"Yes, the prince." Father Damon responded.

"Them," Mistress Caitlin said, "the magician that fashioned this spell had to have an article that Prince Hugh had touched; which means that we have a traitor in the palace."

Mistress Caitlin adjusted the bed covers round Eleanora. She then turned back to Father Damon saying, "She sleeps well now, and will sleep through the night to awaken sometime tomorrow. I will stay with her until she awakens."

Bidding Mistress Caitlin good night. Father Damon and his accolade left her alone in the apartment with Eleanora.

CHAPTER 15

Eleanora came awake. She could tell that she lay in her own bed. The last that she could remember was the assassin. She could see light coming in through the window. From the angle of the light, she deduced that it had to be late afternoon. The crackling of a fire burning in the fireplace came to her ears. She started to move, and cried out. "Oh, I hurt!"

Hearing Eleanora, Mistress Caitlin rose from the chair that she had been resting in. "Oh, good," Mistress Caitlin said, "you're awake. How do you feel?"

Reaching over her shoulder, Eleanora felt the poultice over her shoulder blade and said. "My back hurts, what happened?"

Mistress Caitlin responded, "You were struck by the assassin's dart from a blowgun. The dart was meant for Prince Hugh and would surely have killed him. When you pushed the prince aside at the last moment, the dart struck you a glancing blow on the shoulder blade. You are fortunate that the wound is clean and will heal well." Thinking of Princess Juliana's children that had been waiting in the corridor for most of the day, Mistress Caitlin asked. "Eleanora, do you feel up to having visitors?"

"And who could that be?" Eleanora asked.

Mistress Caitlin replied, "The children, they have been very worried about you."

"Then send them in." Eleanora said with a smile, as she moved to sit more upright in the bed.

Mistress Caitlin went to open the door for the children. Within seconds they were through the door and standing beside Eleanora's bed. Mark started to cry. Isabelle was holding the tears back, but barely. Eleanora patted the bed on each side of her, and the children climbed onto the bed and snuggled up next to her on each side. She put her arms around them and held them close.

Eleanora now found herself a celebrity around the palace. By now everyone had heard that she had saved Prince Hugh from an assassin. She found herself a little embarrassed by her notoriety. Even the cooks in the kitchen wanted to prepare for her anything that she wanted.

On the morning of the fifth day after the assassination attempt, maids came to Eleanora's apartment with the most beautiful gown of azure-blue silk brocade. With the dress came a gift from Princess Juliana. A gold necklace set with lapis lazuli, and matching earrings. She was to wear the gown and jewelry at court that day. Eleanora was amazed by such a precious and generous gift. She appreciated the gift, but wondered if she were worthy of such consideration.

More people than usual, of both the peerage and commoners had found a reason to be present at court, having heard that something special was to occur that day. Mistress Caitlin escorted Eleanora to the main hall, keeping the more curious at a respectful distance. Eleanora immediately noticed that Mistress Caitlin wore not her usual robes, but a lovely gown of burgundy-red silk. She had also had her hair done up in an elaborate coiffure. She wondered as to what special occasion would prompt her to dress this way.

Prince Hugh took care of some urgent court matters first, then nodded to the Master of Ceremonies Bartholomew. The Master of Ceremonies struck the floor three times with the butt of his staff. The chamber fell silent, with all eyes turned to the throne. The Master of Ceremonies called out. "Gentlemen and Ladies of the court draw near and witness a proclamation under the seal and signature of, Prince Hugh D'Croix of Dunboro, commander of the king's army in the western realm and heir apparent to the king."

With a gentle prodding from Mistress Caitlin, Eleanora moved forward, everyone stepping aside to clear a path for her. Prince Hugh and Princess Juliana stood as she approached. Eleanora curtsied saying, "Your Highness." Prince Hugh nodded to a herald who held a document. The herald cleared his throat then started to read. "To all within the realm. Whereas the, Lady Eleanora of the court of Dunboro has given full love and devotion to the royal family. Taking many risks in her service, without thought of reward. And most recently saving the life of a member of the royal family from assassination, at great risk to her own life. For this we wish to show our gratitude and love for her. For this let it be known that the, Lady Eleanora, be given a place in the court with the rank of baronet, with all rights and privileges pertaining thereunto.

Furthermore, we grant to the baronet, Lady Eleanora the title to Hawkers Dale, to be held by her and her descendants for as long as they shall live, with servants and properties thereupon."

Eleanora stood before Prince Hugh stunned. It was all that she could do to maintain her composure as the ceremony continued. She could hardly believe it. She was now nobility, a member of the peerage, a baronet with an estate.

A page now stepped forward to stand next to Prince Hugh. He held a small blue-satin covered cushion, upon which rested an oval pendant badge on a red satin ribbon. At the centre of the pendant badge was a golden lioness rampant holding a dagger. The lioness was centered not on a man's knight shield, but on a sanguine (reddish purple) woman's diamond shaped lozenge. Over the blazon was the cornet of a baronet. Prince Hugh took the ribbon and tied it around Eleanora's neck, so that the pendant badge hung at her throat.

Another page then came forward with a small blue-satin cushion. Upon the cushion rested a pair of silver spurs. Taking the spurs, Prince Hugh said, "These are now yours, Lady Eleanora. You now have the right to wear silver spurs." He then handed them to Eleanora.

Taking the spurs from Prince Hugh, all that, Eleanora could manage to say was, "Thank You, Your Highness."

Prince Hugh now grinned saying, "Now, Eleanora, go and enjoy the adulation of your peers. Come to my library in one hour. There are things that we need to discuss."

Eleanora then curtsied saying, "Yes, Your Highness."

As, Eleanora turned to fade back into the crowd, Prince Hugh nodded to the Master of Ceremonies. The Master of Ceremonies struck the floor three times with the butt of his staff then said, "Gentlemen and Ladies, court is now concluded for the day. Anyone with business for the court should return tomorrow morning."

Eleanora moved among the court members that were still milling about the main hall. Many came up to congratulate her on her elevation to baronet. Of those that she now out ranked, the men bowed and the women curtsied to her.

Two people that she was delighted to see there were, Sir Walter and Squire Hal. Sir Walter was the first to befriend her when she had come to the palace. Sir Walter and Squire Hal bowed to her, Sir Walter saying, "Congratulations on your elevation to baronet, Lady Eleanora."

Smiling, Eleanora said, "Please, don't be so formal. I like it to be like old friends between us. I'm still the same Eleanora that you rescued from the clutches of the guards that first day. I value your friendship and advice. I very much want that we remain friends."

Squire Hal spoke up, "I'm glad for you, Lady Eleanora. I am to be knighted soon. I also want to keep you as a friend."

Sir Walter laughed, then said, "Its true, My Lady, Hal is to be knighted this coming summer solstice. Then I will be able to get a new squire that will be worthy of the title."

A hurt look crossed Squire Hal's face and Sir Walter laughed again.

The one man that went out of his way not to congratulate Eleanora on her elevation was, Baronet Bartholomew the Master of Ceremonies. Eleanora thought that perhaps he felt bitter over the fact that she had been elevated to a rank equal to his while being about half his age. It was common knowledge that he considered himself better than his present station in life.

By now, Eleanora had formed a very low opinion of Master of Ceremonies Bartholomew. He ran the palace staff with a heavy hand. The pages of whom he had direct control feared him. As for the knights and other nobles in the palace, they had little respect for him. He had a longing for fine food and wine. It showed on him by a well-developed paunch. As for weapons training, he did barely enough to maintain a marginal proficiency with the sword.

One hour later, Eleanora stood in Prince Hugh's library. Sitting behind his table, Prince Hugh, indicating a chair, said, "Have a seat, Lady Eleanora."

Eleanora sat in the chair, arranging her skirt, then looked at him.

Holding up a parchment, Prince Hugh said, "Lady Eleanora this is the deed to your estate. It is a small barony, but a rich one. It is known throughout the kingdom for its fine wines. It will provide you with a comfortable income. I had planned at first to make you a dame, but after consulting with my wife, I decided to make you a baronet. It is felt that since you have some unknown destiny the higher rank may be needed some day." He then handed the deed to her estate over to, Eleanora.

Eleanora said, "thank you, Your Highness, I will do my best to live up to your expectations."

"I know that you will, Lady Eleanora." Prince Hugh said, "It's your nature to do so."

Eleanora then remarked with levity, "The only thing that I worry about is that I will wake up in the morning to find this all a dream."

With a laugh, Prince Hugh said, "It's no dream, Lady Eleanora, you are a baronet. Oh, the lioness with a dagger on your blazon, that was my idea, I thought it very expressive of you. How do you like it?"

Touching the pendant badge at her throat, Eleanora said. "I just love it, Your Highness, I can't think of anything better."

Changing the subject, Prince Hugh said, "Lady Eleanora, you remember that we talked about a dowry, and you finding a good husband."

Nodding, Eleanora responded, "Yes, I remember, Your Highness."

With a smile, Prince Hugh said, "Well, Lady Eleanora, now that you have a title and estate, you could end up attracting a viscount, earl, marquis, or even a duke. What would you think about being a duchess?"

"You jest, Your Highness." Eleanora said with a blush, "I am already far more than I ever dreamed that I would ever be."

"Oh, one last thing, Lady Eleanora," Prince Hugh said, "as a member of the peerage, above the rank of knight or dame, you must in the first year of your elevation journey to the king's court at Vanaden on the Lake, there you will swear fealty to the king."

Eleanora with a look of surprise and placing a hand to her breast exclaimed, "Me, see the king!"

Prince Hugh just had to laugh at Eleanora's surprised reaction. Then thinking that until just recently she had been a young lass living on the streets of Dunboro, her reaction seemed quite normal. With a reassuring smile he said, "Don't worry, Lady Eleanora, I have told father a lot about you in my letters to him. He is anxious to meet you, as is also my mother. You can make the journey to Vanaden on the lake after the summer solstice festival. Now, I believe that's enough for today. We will talk more at a later time. You may withdraw now, Lady Eleanora."

Eleanora got to her feet, then curtsied to Prince Hugh, saying, "Your Highness." She then turned and left the library.

CHAPTER 16

Emperor Eimion of the Jutes paced the polished marble floor of the audience hall, his footfalls echoing across the room. The two black uniformed guards of the emperor's immortals could see that the emperor was furious about something and were being correct and proper in their duties. Knowing the emperor's wrath they didn't want to give him a reason to turn on them.

The Emperor turned at the sound of footsteps as, Lord Marshal Rhodri and Master Arfon passed through the large double doors and between the two guards. When they got close, Emperor Eimion exclaimed, "It's about time!" Waving a parchment that he had been holding in his hand, he continued, "This just arrived by ship from Dunboro! It is from our agent, Hammer! He reports that our plan to assassinate the prince of Dunboro has failed!"

"But Your Majesty, how can that be? How could it have failed?" Master Arfon exclaimed, "We had been assured of success!"

Waving the report again, Emperor Eimion said, "The assassin got into the palace without difficulty as expected. He reached the apartments of the prince without detection. The assassin even surprised the prince and launched his attack. At the last moment a lass intervened, first to save the prince, then to kill the assassin." Emperor Eimion then threw the parchment on the floor, exclaiming with anger. "A lass, mind you! A lass of only sixteen years, not even fully a woman yet! An assassin of the Brotherhood of the Black Rose! How in the names of all the gods did she do it?"

Lord Marshal Rhodri and Master Arfon didn't try to answer the question, knowing it to be rhetorical.

"The youth!" Lord Marshal Rhodri said, as much a question as an exclamation. He recalled the oradle's prediction about the youth. This lass mentioned in the dispatch from Hammer could be that youth. He would like to say something about it, but feared to enrage, Emperor Eimion further.

"That's not all," Emperor Eimion said, starting to curb his temper a little, "this lass is also responsible for the death of Hammer's agent in Dunboro. She is also responsible for the death of several of the agent's men, some by her own hand. Hammer also said that this lass is deadly with the blade, both long and short. When she trains daily with the blade she wears man's clothing. She even led the soldiers that captured Hammer's agent.

"For saving the life of Prince Hugh from the assassin, and killing the assassin, the lass has been elevated to the court rank of baronet."

Lord Marshal Rhodri now felt that he had to speak his mind. "She must be the youth that the oracle warned us about, Your Majesty." Lord Marshal Rhodri said, slamming a fist into the palm of his other hand. "Where does this lass come from anyway?"

Shrugging his shoulders, Emperor Eimion said, "According to Hammer she just appeared in the palace one day as the companion to, Princess Juliana. It is said that she is the daughter of a wealthy merchant from Marvella, but no one knows for sure. Hammer has tried to find out about the lass's family, who is supposedly in Marvella, but has found nothing."

Master Arfon now asked, "Your Majesty, should we try to assassinate Prince Hugh again, or the lass?"

Emperor Eimion thought for a while, then shook his head saying, "As much as I would like to I must say no. First, it would be much harder a second time. They would be expecting it. Second, Hammer has lost his agent in Dunboro. Without this agent, Hammer has no way to contact the assassins. Third, another attempt would only convince them that something major is afoot. No, we have to have them complacent until we make a move."

Lord Marshal Rhodri now spoke, "Your Majesty, we were counting on the death of Prince Hugh to provide the distraction needed for our plan to work. If the assassination had succeeded, every noble in the kingdom would have been in Vanaden on the Lake for the prince's funeral and interment in the family crypt when we struck at Questers Pass. We will now need another distraction."

Master Arfon looking at Emperor Eimion said, "Your Majesty, the part of the plan that I would have been responsible for will still work. What we need is another diversionary plan. I have an idea, but I will need a little time to work on it. Then I would have to coordinate my plan with that of Lord Marshal Rhodri's plans."

Emperor Eimion looked at his two advisors, then said, "Okay, I will have the army stand down. As the army has not yet staged for the invasion, only a few high-ranking noblemen had certain knowledge of the invasion plan. It was a mistake to rely too heavily on Hammer. He may still be useful, but I want a better plan this time. Now go and return when you have something to show me."

As, Lord Marshal Rhodri and Master Arfon bowed and left the hall, Emperor Eimion brooded. He knew that his reign as emperor of the Jutes stood in peril. He had made too many promises to just call everything off. As much as he feared the prediction of the oracle, he feared his people more. If he couldn't deliver on the victory that he had promised, the men that now insured his continued existence on the throne could become his executioners. His only option then would be to fall on his own sword. At least that would insure his families continued well-being. Then the empire would be plunged into civil war that would rage until one man vanquished all of his rivals to become the next emperor. In the end this new emperor would rule over a people so shattered by civil war that it would take a generation or more to recover. He had no other options, he had to prevail.

CHAPTER 17

The time passed after the spring equinox. Eleanora made a decision on something that she had been considering for a while. The next time that Jimmy came to the palace to make his report to her she asked that Brenda be sent to the palace for a meeting with, Eddy the cat.

The next morning a young lass in a patched gown approached the main gate of the palace with trepidation. Brenda had never had to go to the palace to report to Eddy before, and wondered why she had been sent for now. Brenda had tried to get the reason from Jimmy the deft to no avail. All that she got from Jimmy the deft was that Eddy the cat wanted to see her. Stopping before one of the guards she said, "I'm here to see Eddy the cat."

The guards had been told to expect her. The guard turned the girl over to the commander of the relief. The commander of the relief then turned Brenda over to a maid that had been waiting to escort her to Eleanora's apartment. The maid said, "Come with me." The maid continued to speak as they started toward the main palace. "Now listen, lass, you are to see a noble woman. She is the Baronet Eleanora, so you need to watch your manners. Do you know how to curtsy?"

"I think so," Brenda responded, "I've seen other women do it before." The maid said, "Well, then just watch me and do as I do."

"Why do I have to see this noble woman?" Brenda asked nervously. With a shrug of her shoulders the maid replied. "I don't know why you have to see her. I was just told to pick you up at the main gate and deliver you to her."

They went up flights of stairs and along corridors. The imposing size and splendour of the main palace almost overwhelming Brenda's senses. Everywhere that she looked she could see soldiers, or well-dressed men and women going about their business. Finally they came to a door where the maid stopped and knocked. A feminine voice called out. "Enter"

The maid opened the door and entered the sitting room of an apartment followed by Brenda. A young woman with red hair, wearing an elegant jade-green gown, stood at the window. The maid curtsied saying, "My lady, this is the lass, Brenda."

Brenda imitated the maid, but not with such poise while saying, "My Lady."

After dismissing the maid with instructions for the kitchen to send up tea and shortbread, Eleanora sat in a chair. Indicating the chair next to hers she said, "Brenda, come have a seat here and relax."

Brenda looking at the lady noticed the pendant badge at her throat suspended from a golden-yellow ribbon. She had heard of these pendant badges that the nobility wore, but this was the first that she had ever seen. Taking a close look at the woman, Brenda started to get a feeling that everything wasn't all that it seemed to be. There was something about this woman that seemed vaguely familiar.

Eleanora spoke, "Thank you for answering my summons, Brenda. I want to talk with you."

Brenda responded, "But, My Lady, it is, Eddy the cat that I have come to see." Brenda stopped speaking, noticing a broad grin on the ladies face.

Still grinning, Eleanora said, "Brenda, look at me. Take a good look. Who do you see?"

Brenda looked at Eleanora with a puzzled look that suddenly turned to one of amazement. Her mouth moved, but for a few seconds, Brenda could make no words. Finally, Brenda said, "How can it be? I must be dreaming. You look like, Eddy the cat, but you're a woman, and Eddy's a lad."

Trying not to laugh at Brenda's discomposure, Eleanora said, "Yes, Brenda, I am, Eddy the cat, or I once was. On the street I grew up as a lad, acting and thinking as one until it became second nature to me. However, I have always been a lass.

"Now, Brenda, as to why I called for you. If you stay on the street they will soon be forcing you into being a whore. To service every man that comes to your door. To have nothing in your future, except maybe a miserable and short life. I want to save you from that. I want to make you my personal companion. You will live with me here in the palace. I will see that you are trained well and educated. And when the time comes, I'll arrange for you a good marriage. Now, Brenda, do you accept my offer?"

Brenda looked at, Eleanora, almost in shock at what she had been hearing. Then tears came to her eye and she started to cry. Eleanora took

Brenda's hands in hers, to comfort and reassure her. Finally, Brenda got herself under control enough to speak. "My Lady, why would you do this for me?" Brenda asked, "We are not family. You don't owe me anything."

Eleanora responded, "I do this for you, Brenda because someone gave me the chance to be the person that I am. So now that I can I want to save you from the street. Will you accept my offer?"

With a broad smile, Brenda nodded saying, "Oh, yes, My Lady, I will be your companion. I will be the best companion that I can be."

Just then a knock came at the door. Eleanora called out. "Enter."

The door opened and a servant entered with a tray holding a teapot under a cozy, cream, sugar, two cups with saucers and a plate of shortbread. "Your tea and shortbread, My Lady." the servant said.

After setting the tray down on the table, the servant stepped back and bowed saying, "By your leave, My Lady." Nodding, Eleanora said, "Granted."

The servant then turned and left the room.

When the door closed Eleanora said, "Well, Brenda, let's have our tea and shortbread. Then I shall take you to your apartment."

"You mean that I'll have my own apartment!" Brenda exclaimed. Still finding it hard to adjust to her sudden change in fortune, "Oh, My Lady, all that I have ever had is an old sleeping pallet and blanket in a small room with a dirt floor, and a wicker basket to hold my meagre possessions. I never dreamed that I would ever be living in the palace, with my own apartment."

With a smile, Eleanora replied, "Yes, Brenda, you shall have your own apartment. Also your status at court is now equal to that of a squire. Here in the palace to address a person by their title, or honorific is as automatic as breathing, so get used to being addressed as, My Lady, or, Lady Brenda. Now let us enjoy our tea, then I'll show you to your apartment."

After they had their tea, Eleanora took Brenda to the apartment that would be hers. Upon entering, Brenda looked around in astonishment and said, "This is all for me?"

Struggling to keep from laughing at Brenda's excitement, Eleanora said, "Yes, Brenda, this is all for you."

They stood in the sitting room, that wasn't much different than Eleanora's. Eleanora opened another door and beckoned Brenda to enter saying, "This is your bed chamber, Brenda."

As Brenda felt the softness of the feather bed, Eleanora stepped over to a large armoire and opened it. It was filled with gowns and other woman's apparel, all of quality fabric and well made. Overcome, Brenda started to cry again. Eleanora handed her a handkerchief of linen to dry her tears. Eleanora then said, "Brenda, I have taken the liberty of providing you with a wardrobe. I have tried to get everything right for you. If anything doesn't fit, or you don't like it, we will have it exchanged."

"Oh, My Lady," Brenda said, "I'm sure that I shall like everything here. It is far more than I ever dreamed of having."

With a nod, Eleanora said, "I'm glad that you like it. I will now have the maids draw you a bath. Then you can dress in something more appropriate for court. Then we can get rid of those rags that you are wearing."

As the spring season progressed towards summer, Eleanora found Brenda to be very eager to master her new duties. Brenda worked tirelessly to show Eleanora that she appreciated the opportunity given her. She threw herself into her new duties with a zeal that was commendable.

Eleanora got Horse Master Osburn to teach Brenda how to ride a horse. After at first being apprehensive of the size of the horses, Brenda took to the equestrian training with a natural ability that surprised even Horse Master Osburn. Eleanora was pleased that Brenda would now be able to accompany her on the trip to the king's court at Vanaden on the Lake.

Eleanora had also noticed that Brenda had taken a notice of Squire Hal. It also appeared to Eleanora, seeing how Squire Hal acted whenever Brenda came around, that the attraction was mutual. However, Brenda being young, shy and still unsure of herself around the other members of the court, and Squire Hal not making the first move, fearing rejection. Eleanora could see that she would have to make something happen.

Eleanora, with the help of Brenda kept close supervision over her intelligence network in Dunboro. Since she had recruited her first agents the network had really blossomed. Jimmy the deft now had direct control of the day to day operations in Dunboro, taking direction from Eleanora. Jimmy the deft now had most of the children on the street coming to him when they had something of value. He would pay them for good information. Jimmy had now set up his own business as a street vendor, selling sausage, cheeses, breads, cakes, pies and candy. That way it wasn't unusual to see children hanging around his vendor's cart. Jimmy, having left his larcenous past behind him, no longer wanted to be called, the deft.

So far there was no evidence that the phantom individual called Hammer had tried to resurrect his organization. Perhaps this wasn't the only organization that Hammer had. There was also the unknown woman who would show up at the White Dove. So far they hadn't been able to find out when she came to the White Dove, or how she would arrive or depart. Who she was, where she lived and worked, if she did have a job outside the home. Those were the questions that Eleanora wanted answers for."

The summer solstice festival arrived. On the first day everyone was counted one year older. Eleanora was now seventeen and Brenda fourteen. Squire Hal was now nineteen and would be one of four squires to be knighted. He was the only one from the palace guard. The other three were from the prince's legion. The ceremonies would take place in the main hall during morning court.

Brenda, having a fondness for Squire Hal was determine to witness the ceremony. For court, Brenda wore her best gown of cardinal-red satin brocade. The gown really complimented her dark complexion, green eyes and very-long raven hair, that had been done up in an elaborate coiffure, interwoven with a long strand of red-coral beads. Around her neck she wore a gold chain from which hung a heart shaped blood stone pendant.

Eleanora wore an emerald-green silk gown, with her pendant badge held in pace at her throat with a golden-yellow ribbon. As for her hair, although it was now below the shoulder, it still wasn't long enough for the elaborate coiffure that Brenda wore. Instead she wore it lose about her shoulders, with just a simple gold circlet set all around with small-oval jade stones on her brow.

Throughout the ceremony in the main hall, Brenda never took her eyes off of Hal. At the end of the ceremony the newly sworn knights joined their families, or friends that had come to witness their ascension to knighthood. Sir Hal came over and bowed to Eleanora saying, "Lady Eleanora."

Smiling, Eleanora said, "Sir Hal, I am pleased to have witnessed your elevation to knighthood." Seeing Brenda's interest in Sir Hal,

Eleanora continued, "Brenda, is there anything that you would like to say to Sir Hal?"

Although nervous at the presence of Sir Hal, Brenda appeared to be calm as she said, 'Oh, Sir Hal, how handsome you look in your guards' uniform with your pendant badge and silver spurs."

Giving a courtly bow, Sir Hal said. "I thank you for your compliment, Lady Brenda. And I must say that you are a truly exquisite young lady." Eleanora saw Brenda blush at the compliment. She knew that from the first day that they met, Brenda could think of no one but Hal. She had decided to help Brenda out. "Sir Hal," Eleanora said, "if you have nothing else planned, Brenda and I would be pleased if you would join us for the mid-day meal in two hours. I will have the kitchen serve us in my apartment so that we may dine in private."

Suppressing a grin and trying to show proper demeanor, Sir Hal nodded politely at Eleanora saying, "I would be pleased, My Lady, to join you and Lady Brenda for the mid-day meal. Now if you will excuse me, I must see Sir Walter."

He then bowed his head at Brenda saying, "Good-day to you, Lady Brenda."

Brenda curtsied to Sir Hal saying, "Good-day to you, Sir Hal."

As Sir Hal moved away, Eleanora heard Brenda sigh. She knew that Brenda was still a young lass, but it wasn't too early to start thinking of a match for her. In one year, Brenda would be fifteen years and reach her majority and be able to marry. Eleanora felt sure that Brenda would be pleased with a betrothal to Sir Hal.

Eleanora had known Sir Hal for over a year now and considered him to be an honorable man. Now that Sir Hal had become a member of the peerage, his liege lord, Duke Bran would have to approve the marriage. It would be a year or two before Sir Hal would be allowed to marry, but there could be a betrothal before then.

At the mid-day meal, Brenda became very quiet, giving an answer only when Eleanora, or Sir Hal addressed her. She mostly just picked at the food on her plate as she watched Sir Hal; either looking to the side, or down at her plate when he looked at her.

"Sir Hal," Eleanora said, "I am leaving three weeks after the summer solstice festival for the king's court at Vanaden on the Lake to see the king. Accompanying me will be Brenda, Sergeant Giffard and ten soldiers of the palace guard. We will go by barge up river to Stone Bridge. Then cross country to Duman Ford, then by barge down the Mon River to Star Lake and Vanaden on the Lake. Prince Hugh has also agreed that I may take a knight with me. Would you like to accompany Brenda and me to Vanaden on the lake?"

This was one question that Sir Hal didn't have to think about. With an eye on Brenda he responded, "Yes, Lady Eleanora, I would be honored to accompany you and Lady Brenda to Vanaden on the Lake." Glancing at Brenda, Sir Hal saw her smile.

Feeling a little mischievous, Eleanora said, "Well, Brenda, it looks like you will have Sir Hal all to yourself for a long time."

Brenda blushed furiously, unable to say a word. Sir Hal reached out to take Brenda's hand in his own, giving a slight, reassuring squeeze. Brenda at last looked into Sir Hal's eyes and smiled. Looking back into Brenda's eyes, Sir Hal smiled back at her.

Seeing the silent exchange, Eleanora knew that there was a mutual attraction between them; even though neither one nor the other had made the first move fearing rejection. "Sir Hal," Eleanora said, "I believe that we are finished with the meal. Why don't you take Lady Brenda for a stroll? I'm sure that she would enjoy your company for the afternoon."

Brenda looked at her with a broad smile that reassured Eleanora that she had done the right thing.

Smiling as he rose to his feet, Sir Hal said, "Yes, My Lady, I will." Brenda stood, taking the arm that Sir Hal presented to her. He then escorted her from the room.

Eleanora watched them go, knowing that they did have strong feelings for each other.

On the tenth day after the summer solstice festival, Princess Juliana went into labor. After nine hours she gave birth to a healthy son. All through labor, Eleanora remained at Princess Juliana's side. After witnessing the labor and birth, Eleanora knew that someday she wanted to experience the birth of a child of her own.

At the naming ceremony, three days later, Prince Hugh named the child, Fergus.

CHAPTER 18

The sun had just appeared above the eastern horizon when Eleanora's honor guard departed through the main gate of the palace. In the lead rode Sir Hal and Sergeant Giffard. Sergeant Giffard carried Eleanora's personal standard, a golden-yellow lioness rampant holding a dagger, with a baronet coronet over the lioness, on a reddish-purple flag. Behind them, mounted side saddle, rode Eleanora and Brenda on their palfreys. Behind them were ten mounted soldiers of the palace guard. Bringing up the rear were three baggage wagons, each pulled by two mules. All the men were dressed in the uniform of the palace guard of dark-blue tunic, black trousers and black boots. They also wore burnished cuirass and helm and carried lance and shield. Eleanora had dressed in a yellow gown trimmed in black, with matching hat. Brenda wore a pink gown trimmed in purple, with matching hat.

As they moved through the streets of Dunboro, the citizenry seeing palace guards escorting two ladies and seeing the personal standard of a baronet scattered to give them the right of way. As they rode by some of the men would bow and the women would curtsy. Watching the people, Eleanora recognized some of the faces in the crowd; and thought that if only they knew that she was the person that they had known as Eddy the cat. Thinking of it now it seemed as though it were another lifetime. The persona of Eddy the cat was now dead.

Reaching the docks they started to load everything onto a river barge for the trip up the Aber River to the City of Stone Bridge. The river barges were large flat-bottom boats that could be propelled by oars or sail. They had side boards that could be lowered to act as a keel when under sail. Eleanora and Brenda would share a cabin in the stern of the barge. The horses and mules were kept in the cargo hole. The men would sleep on deck, under, or alongside the wagons. The master of the barge told them that with the favorable winds that they were getting, the trip up river to Stone Bridge should take about three days.

From Stone Bridge they would go cross country to the city of Duman Ford. The trip by horse, Sergeant Giffard said, should take five days; more if the weather turned bad on them. Then by barge again, down the Mon river to Vanaden on the lake.

Within the hour all the horses, mules, baggage, wagons and the soldiers were on board the barge and ready to depart. The master of the barge gave the command to take in all morning lines. They then used long polls to push the barge away from the dock. Once clear of the dock the crew set to the oars to move the barge out into mid channel. Once in mid channel the barge master ordered the side boards to be lowered and the sails set. Soon the barge was moving up river under sail.

The trip up river to Stone Bridge was uneventful. They made good progress during the daylight hours. At night they tied up to the bank of the river. Eleanora had only ventured a few miles upriver during her rides on Porky. She spent a lot of daylight hours at the rail watching the scenery roll by. There were lush tracks of forest interspersed between picturesque farms and pasture, with the occasional hamlet or village. She wondered if one of these farms seen along the bank of the river had been the farm that her father had worked before he had died. Could there be uncles, aunts, cousins, or grandparents in one of those hamlets, or villages? If they were she doubted that she would ever know.

Eleanora thought back to the time, sixteen months ago, when she had first come to the palace. She had been a youth from the streets, concerned only with her own survival. Now her horizons had expanded. It wasn't just about herself anymore. This was her country now, and she felt an obligation to nurture it, to watch it grow and to defend it if necessary.

Brenda had started to spend a lot of time with Sir Hal. They spent most of their time at the rail with Sir Hal pointing out one thing or the other to her. Brenda had gotten over her shyness and now took Sir Hal's arm whenever she was close to him. Eleanora could also see that Sir Hal had strong feelings for Brenda. She knew that Duke Bran wouldn't let Sir Hal marry for at least one to two years. However, she knew that the Duke would not object to a betrothal.

After three days on the river they arrived at Stone Bridge. There they were met by a reception committee for Earl Gerard and his wife, Countess Natalia of Stone Bridge. Earl Gerard wanted to offer Baronet Eleanora and her party accommodations at the Stone Bridge palace. There would also be a banquet in her honor the next day. Eleanora accepted the offer, thanking the earl for his hospitality.

Eleanora, Brenda and Sir Hal were given luxurious quarters in the palace. Sergeant Giffard and the other men were quartered with the palace guard. Earl Gerard and Countess Natalia proved to be gracious hosts, seeing to their every need.

At the banquet the next evening, Eleanora sat at the head table with Earl Gerard and Countess Natalia. Also at the table was Baron Clerebola - The Commander of the fortress at Questers Pass. Questers Pass being a narrow pass cut through the Grand Citadels mountains by the Aber River. The river drops hundreds of feet through the pass, and is not navigable due to the rapids. The only way through the pass is a trail between the west bank of the river and a near vertical cliff that rises over two thousand feet in some places. Most of the passage is no more than twenty to thirty yards wide. As the pass broadens out at the southern end, the river is forced to flow hard against a near vertical six hundred foot cliff on the west side by a hillock on the east side of the pass. At this point the trail crosses over a wooden bridge to continue south. The fortress of Questers Pass commands the hillock with the bridge being in range of their war engines.

To the south of the fortress is the town of Questers Pass. It had grown up to provide logistical support for the fortress. It is also home for families of a lot of the soldiers serving at the fortress. There are also many soldiers that after retiring from service at the fortress now own land or have businesses in or around the village of Questers Pass.

Eleanora found Baron Clerebola and Questers Pass very interesting, speaking with him at length to learn as much as she could about Questers Pass. Baron Cerebella told her that the pass was used by caravans moving north to the Jute Empire, or south into the kingdom. Trade was allowed between the Jute Empire and the kingdom. However, if a large army tried to invade the kingdom through the pass, the narrowness of the pass, and the Questers Pass fortress would hold them until the prince of Dunboro could be in the field with his legion, and the garrisons of other towns and cities.

Not being able to get past the Grand Citadels mountains with their army; the Jute Empire turned to piracy, using their biremes and triremes to capture ships, and raid coastal towns. So far the kingdom had been able to keep the damage from the incursions of these pirates at a minimum.

Earl Gerard and Baron Cerebola had heard of the new sword that, Eleanora had. The story of how she had saved the life of Prince Hugh, and her prowess with that new sword of hers had spread from Dunboro and they were eager to see it. Eleanora had to send a servant to her quarters to fetch her sword. Eleanora had brought her sword with her to have when they rode cross country. She carried it attached to her saddle, under the stirrup leathers.

When the servant returned with the sword, Eleanora showed it to Earl Gerard and Baron Clerebola. After, Earl Gerald and Baron Clerebola expressed amazement with her sword, Eleanora agreed to give a demonstration of the swords use.

The next day, Eleanora demonstrated the fighting technique with the sword. Not wanting to go into her baggage for men's clothing, Eleanora wore a gown while demonstrating the fighting technique with her sword. Even in a gown her speed was little diminished. She easily defeated all her sparring opponents. Sergeant Giffard added considerably to the weight of his purse by placing bets against her opponents. He called it easy money.

After a three day stay at Stone Bridge, Eleanor and her party set out across country for Duman Ford. They rode over a broad plain in the gap between the Grand Citadels Mountains to the north, the Red Palisades to the south, the Aber River to the west and the Mon River to the east. This was the most productive land in the kingdom; being referred to as the bread basket of the kingdom. Eleanora would occasionally pass through a stand of forest, but mostly they rode past fields of grain. The grain stood as high as the belly of a horse. The grain had started to ripen. The fields, now green, would soon turn a light golden-brown; then the harvest would begin.

The road that they travelled, being the major east-west route between the Aber and Mon rivers, was heavily travelled. They encountered trade caravans of many wagons, coaches, carriages, single travellers on horseback and local traffic on foot. With all the traffic there were inns at regular intervals to accommodate the travellers. Sergeant Giffard, having travelled the road many times, knew the better inns, and would send a rider ahead to secure the best lodgings for the night. With, Eleanora and Sir Hal's rank, the inn keepers made sure that they got the best of service and accommodations. Eleanora found that the news of her heroic acts had spread through the kingdom. Everyone was eager to cater to her every need.

Late in the fifth day, Eleanora and her escort arrived at Duman Ford on the Mon River. Having been alerted by one of their patrols of the approach of Eleanora and her party; Count Edred of Duman Ford had a welcoming committee to meet them as they reached the gates of the city. They were invited to take accommodations at Duman Ford palace as the guest of Count Edred and Countess Rowena. Eleanora accepted their invitation and was provided with luxurious accommodations for Sir Hal, Brenda and herself. The rest of the escort was quartered with the palace guard.

The next evening, Count Edred and Countess Rowena had a banquet in Eleanora's honor. All through the meal the count and countess questioned her about the latest gossip from the court of Dunboro. Eleanora kept them entertained with the latest rumours of the court of Dunboro. She also told them about Prince Hugh and Princess Juliana's latest child, Prince Fergus. In turn, Eleanora learned a lot about the eastern part of the kingdom, and about the king's court at Vanaden on the Lake.

After spending two days at Duman Ford as the guest of, Count Edred and Countess Rowena; Eleanora, with her escort departed by river barge for Vanaden on the Lake. Going down river the barge used little sail, as this time of year the prevailing winds were most often against them. Most of the time the crew used oars, or poles to give the barge enough additional headway to maintain steerage.

For the three days that they were on the river, the barge master proved to be an excellent host. Less than two years ago, Eleanora hadn't known, or cared about anything that happened outside the city of Dunboro. How things had changed since then. Now she had a hunger for information and knowledge about the kingdom. She found the barge master, with his travels up and down the river, had a wealth of knowledge about the kingdom. Eleanora spent many hours listening to what the barge master had to say about the workings and politics of the kingdom.

As for Sir Hal and, Brenda, they were rarely separated. Eleanora wondered if perhaps, Sir Hal would be willing to make a commitment by the time they returned to Dunboro, and ask for a betrothal. Eleanora knew of Brenda's feelings for Sir Hal and would agree to the betrothal. Everything would then depend on Duke Bran.

On the third day the barge entered Star Lake. The barge continued south, staying close to the east bank of the lake. As they continued south along the east shore of the lake, the west shore receded until it was out of sight over the horizon. Eleanora could see many boats out on the lake fishing. All the activity on the lake fascinated Eleanora. She could really see that the lake was indeed a rich resource for the kingdom.

Toward late afternoon a town came into view. As they approached closer, Eleanora could see river barges tied up to piers, loading or unloading cargo. Mixed in with the river barges were ocean- going ships that had sailed up river to discharge their cargoes. These ships were cogs of sixty to eighty foot in length, with beams of from twenty-four to thirty-two foot. Larger ocean going ships did not come up river, but discharged their cargoes at Natenfor.

The barge master told Eleanora that the name of the town was Norgate. It was the town at the entrance to the north causeway. Eleanora knew that the king's palace stood at the center of an island, connected to the shore by three causeways from the north, east and south.

After arriving and tying up at the pier, Eleanora and her party disembarked from the barge. They then took rooms at one of the inns for the night. In the morning they would ride across the causeway, to present themselves at the king's court.

CHAPTER 19

A s Eleanora and her escort proceeded across the four-mile causeway, they had a clear view of Vanaden on the Lake. It was a circular island of just over a mile in diameter. A twenty-foot-high stone wall encircled the island, with towers at regular intervals. The king's palace, a marvellous edifice of high white-washed walls, turrets and steep-pitched red-tile roofs, dominated the central high ground of the island. The rest of the island had been taken over by housing for palace staff and guards, stables, workshops, storage facilities and other structures.

Eleanora's escort was in full dress uniform with burnished cuirass and helm. All the guards, to include Sergeant Giffard carried a shield bearing the blazon of the Dunboro palace guard, a purple shield with two golden-yellow lions rampant counter charged. Sir Hal carried a shield with his own blazon, a yellow shield, with black chevron, a red star at each top corner and a green clover at the bottom. Sir Hal and Sergeant Giffard led the way with, Sergeant Giffard carrying Eleanora's personal standard. Eleanora and Brenda followed them, with the rest of the soldiers following behind. Eleanora wore an exquisite gown of sapphire-blue satin brocade. She had her pendant badge suspended at her throat with a reddish-purple ribbon. Her long auburn hair, now well below her shoulders, was held in place with a gold circlet set with garnet stones. Brenda wore an elegant gown of lavender silk. With the gown she wore gold and amber necklace and earrings, with a long strand of small-amber beads interwoven into her coiffure.

As they drew near to the north gate, a guard called out, "Halt! Who goes there?"

Sir Hal responded, "Sir Hal, officer of the Dunboro palace guard and knight of the court of Dunboro. I escort, Lady Eleanora, a baronet of the court of Dunboro to the court of the king."

The guard spoke again, "You may proceed through the gate, Sir Hal. Then wait for the corporal of the guard to provide you with escorts."

Within minutes the escorts were there. Sergeant Giffard, the soldiers and teamsters would be quartered with the palace guard. Eleanora, Sir Hal and Brenda would have quarters in the palace. Their baggage would be delivered to their quarters in the palace.

As Sergeant Giffard and their soldiers were led off to the soldiers' quarters; a page led Eleanora, Sir Hal and Brenda into the palace. Eleanora had thought the palace of Dunboro really grand, but the king's palace was truly amazing. The palace was full of paintings, sculpture, frescoes and tapestries of value beyond belief. Gold or silver leaf covered every carved surface. Eleanora saw alabaster, marble and other fine stone in the architecture. The only word that came to Eleanora's mind to describe it all was, exquisite.

After climbing many stairs and walking down several corridors, Eleanora and her party came to a set of double doors, with guards posted on either side. Passing through the double doors they entered the king's grand hall. Eleanora was impressed by the size of the grand hall, it being easily the size of a large barn, but that was where the comparison ended. The grand hall being just as opulent as the rest of the palace, with many banners and other war trophies displayed. Eleanora noticed that there had to be at least two hundred people, all richly dressed, in the king's grand hall, and it didn't even seem to be half full. At the far end of the room, King Harold D'Croix II and Queen Serafina D'Croix sat their thrones on a dais three steps above the floor.

Upon entering, a page in the service of the Master of Ceremonies noticed Eleanora and her party and led them to where they should stand until called. The king was now in the process of elevating a baron of the court to the rank of count. There followed two petitioners with request of the crown.

The Master of Ceremonies then struck the floor three times with the iron shod butt of his staff then called out, "Lady Eleanora, baronet of the court of Dunboro, come before your king!"

Eleanora advanced to the foot of the dais, then curtsied to the king saying, "Your Majesty."

After swearing fealty to the king and kissing his signet ring, King Harold said, "I'm pleased to meet you at last, Lady Eleanora. Is it true that you killed five men in a fight in an alleyway?"

"That's not true, Your Majesty," Eleanora said, "I only killed three of them. Sergeant Giffard killed the other two."

King Harold, with a short laugh, slapped his thigh saying, "That's even better than the rumours, Lady Eleanora, knowing it to be the truth."

"Your Majesty," Eleanora said, "I did however kill two more men the next day when we arrested the traitor, Gerone."

"I am also in your debt, Lady Eleanora," the king said, "for saving the life of my son. How did you do that?"

Eleanora responded, "Well, Your Majesty, at the last moment I pushed your son aside, taking the assassins dart. When the assassin went to step over my body to get to your son, I buried the blade of my dagger to the hilt in his groin."

King Harold was about to ask another question when, Queen Serafina said, "My dear, Eleanora, why don't you join us for the midday meal tomorrow. We can then talk at our leisure."

Addressing Queen Serafina, Eleanora said, "Thank you, Your Majesty, I will look forward to it."

King Harold, taking the hint from his wife said, "You may withdraw now, Lady Eleanora."

Eleanora curtsying said, "Yes, Your Majesty." She then backed away from the throne until she was back in the crowd.

As the business of the court continued, Eleanora tried to remain inconspicuous to no avail. The report of her saving Prince Hugh from

assassination, killing the assassin of the Brotherhood of the Black Rose, and of her prowess with the blade, both long and short, had garnered the courts curiosity. As she stood watching the court a page came up to her, bowed and said, "Lady Eleanora, will you please come with me."

Eleanora followed the page to the rear of the grand hall with Sir Hal and Brenda close behind. The page halted before a man wearing a crimson-red tunic, russet- brown trousers and brown riding boots. Bowing to the man, the page said, "Your Highness, the Lady Eleanora."

Taking the cue from the page's honorific that the man was a prince, Eleanora curtsied saying, "Your Highness." Brenda also curtsied while Sir Hal bowed.

Taking a close look, Eleanora saw a quite handsome young man in his early twenties, over six feet tall, with flaxen hair almost to his shoulders, a neatly trimmed beard and the most beautiful azure-blue eyes that she had ever seen. Her heart beat faster just looking at him. He had to be the most beautiful man that she had ever seen.

With a smile the prince said, "Good-day, Lady Eleanora. I am, Crown Prince Ambrose Jorevene. My father is the king of Torin. I have heard many stories about you since I arrived for a visit with your king. When I found out that you would be at court today, I had to come to see you."

Eleanora wanted to get to know more about this man, but having no skills when it came to relationships with men, she had no idea as how to begin. Finally seeing that he expected a response, she said, "Your Highness, I hope that you were not disappointed."

Prince Ambrose giving Eleanora a warm smile said "Indeed not, Lady Eleanora. From the stories of your daring and skill at arms, I had expected an amazon of a woman, standing head and shoulder over everyone in the room, to come striding through the door. Was I surprised to see a goddess, a very lovely young lady with great dignity and poise enter the room."

Blushing, Eleanora replied, "You flatter me, Your Highness. I am but a plain lass, not a goddess."

Still smiling, Prince Ambrose said, "It is no empty flattery, Lady Eleanora, your beauty is as a bright shining light in a dark room. If only half of what I have heard about you is true, you are indeed a very remarkable woman; a woman that I would like to get to know better. That being said, I would like to invite you and your companions to have the mid-day meal with me."

The thought of spending more time with Prince Ambrose made Eleanora's breathing come faster and for her heart to beat harder in her breast. With a friendly smile, Eleanora said, "Thank you, Your Highness, we would like to break bread with you at the mid-day meal."

Pleased that Eleanora had accepted his invitation, Prince Ambrose said, "That's good, court will be concluding in a few minutes. I will have the page with you to escort you to my apartment. I shall see you again in a few minutes."

As Prince Ambrose turned to go, Eleanora and Brenda curtsied while Sir Hal bowed.

The page knocked on the door and a voice called out, "Enter."

The page opened the door then stepped aside to allow Eleanora and her party to enter, closing the door behind them. Eleanora and Brenda curtsied to Prince Ambrose who stood in the center of the room, as Sir Hal bowed.

Prince Ambrose said, "Please, in the privacy of my apartment, I prefer to be informal. So let us dispense with the bowing and curtsying, and just call me Ambrose."

Everyone nodded agreement. They then took their places at the table that had been laid out for their dining. As they started to eat, Ambrose asked "Eleanora, I have heard that you are from Marvella, and that your father is a prominent trader there. Being that Marvella is just across the straight from our island of Turin, perhaps I have heard of him."

For some reason, Eleanora knew that she had to be truthful with Ambrose. Looking into his eyes, she said, "Ambrose, it is not true that I'm from Marvella. That is just the story made up to hide my true

identity. My father died when I was four. My mother died when I was nine. Prince Hugh wanted to hide my true identity because I overheard two men plotting his assassination."

Intrigued, Ambrose asked, "How was it that you were able to overhear the two men plotting the assassination of Prince Hugh?"

Eleanora responded, "Well, Ambrose, I was in the attic of the cobbler's house as they were plotting down stairs. The second man I had never seen before, but I knew his voice."

Ambrose had never heard any of this before, and could understand why it wouldn't be made public. However, his curiosity had been aroused. He had to know more and asked, "Tell me, Eleanora, how was it you came to be in the attic?"

Having decided to tell him everything, Eleanora continued, "Well Ambrose, before coming to the palace at Dunboro, a year and a half ago, I was an orphan living on the streets of Dunboro. I was a thief, a cat burglar. I was known on the street as, Eddy the cat. From the time that my father died, my mother raised me as a lad. I dressed like a lad, acted like a lad, talked like a lad, and eventually I even came to think like a lad. The only woman's clothing that I can ever remember wearing was when I first came to the palace. So the reason I was in the attic that night; I had broken in to steal the cobbler's horde."

Ambrose just sat there for a minute or two. He now realized that the rumours and stories about Eleanora weren't even half of it. Eleanora was more than just amazing, she was a most enigmatic personality. Finally he spoke, "I must say, Eleanora, compared to you I have led a rather dull life. You say that your mother raised you as a lad, why?"

Eleanora, putting her knife and fork on her plate, answered, "I now believe that in some way she knew that she would not be here to look after me. My mother told me that it would be a lot safer on the street as a lad, than as a lass."

"That night in the attic." Ambrose said, "You said that you had heard the voice of the man before, but didn't know his face, how's that?"

Even though it stressed her to think about it, Eleanora answered, "The first time I heard that voice was the night that my mother was murdered. It was the voice of the man that murdered my mother. He is the man that I arrested for treason, and was hanged by Prince Hugh."

Prince Ambrose listened with rapt attention. Eleanora's story was the most fantastic that he had ever heard. He wanted to know everything that he could about this marvellous young woman. She had some mysterious attraction for him. He wanted very much to win her affections.

The talk continued through the meal. Ambrose let Eleanora do most of the talking. He was content to learn as much as he could about her and her exploits. Towards the end of the meal, Ambrose said, "Eleanora, I've heard so much about that sword of yours. If it's not too much of an inconvenience could you show it to me?"

"Why of course, Ambrose," Eleanora said with a smile, "I would be pleased to show it to you. I'll even demonstrate to you the fighting technique with the sword."

Pleased, Prince Ambrose responded, "That's wonderful, Eleanora, they have a very fine indoor training arena here at the palace. What do you say that we meet there in two hours?"

"Agreed," Eleanora said, "in two hours."

Two hours later, Eleanora entered the training arena. She wore a cobalt-blue tunic, black trousers and black boots. Her sword hung from a black-leather baldric, with silver buckle. Her dagger hung from a black-leather belt, with silver buckle. On the left breast of her tunic was an embroidered lozenge with her blazon and baronet coronet. Her now long-auburn hair had been tied back with a blue-satin ribbon.

Prince Ambrose seeing her enter the arena, came over to her.

Eleanora, being dressed in man's clothing, bowed to, Prince Ambrose saying, "Good-afternoon, Your Highness."

With a pleasant smile, Prince Ambrose replied, "Lady Eleanora, I must say that you look really fetching in those clothes."

The compliment drew a smile from Eleanora.

Prince Ambrose continued, "May I see your sword, Lady Eleanora?" Eleanora drew her sword and handed it to Prince Ambrose, hilt first.

Taking the sword from Eleanora, Prince Ambrose first hefted the sword, then executed a few practice moves with Eleanora instructing him of the swords use. He then handed the sword back to Eleanora hilt first. "A very fine weapon, Lady Eleanora." Prince Ambrose said, "The balance is superb, and it's very light, but how would you ever block a slashing blow from a broad sword with such a light blade?"

Eleanora answered, "Your Highness, you do not block, you turn, or deflect your opponents blade. But first you take way his advantage. You make him fight your fight."

"What do you mean by that, Lady Eleanora?" Prince Ambrose asked, showing keen interest in her every word.

Eleanora responded, "It's obvious that I do not have the strength to trade blow for blow with broad sword with a man, and I never will. I take away that advantage. My sword is a thrusting weapon like a dagger, but with a much longer blade. The blade is even a little longer than that of the standard broad sword. The point of my blade is always in my opponents face. If he draws blade back to deliver a slashing blow he leaves himself open, and he's a dead man."

By now a group of onlookers had started to gather around Eleanora and Prince Ambrose. The king's court by now were aware of the baronet, Lady Eleanora from Dunboro, and her sword. Choosing a squire from the onlookers, who was armed with a broad sword, Eleanora asked, "Squire, would you oblige me by participating with me in a sparring match?"

The squire seeing the lozenge with baronet coronet on Eleanora's left breast, knew that she could only be the Lady Eleanora of Dunboro that everyone had been talking about. Bowing to Eleanora, the squire said, "My Lady, I would be pleased to spar with you. I've heard about your sword, and would like to see how it is used."

As they prepared to spar, a circle of spectators started to gather. As they started to spar, the squire not wanting to be too hard on the lady, held back. However, he soon realized that he faced a true master with the sword. He tried every trick that he knew, but could not overcome her skill and technique with the blade. By the time that the exercise ended, he felt no shame at being bested by a woman. He bowed to Eleanora saying, "Lady Eleanora, I salute you as a true master of the sword. I would like to learn to use such a sword as yours."

With a nod, Eleanora said, "Of course I will be willing to show you, squire. I will be willing to show anyone who is interested. As long as I'm here at the king's court, I shall be coming to the arena daily."

After more than an hour of showing Prince Ambrose and others how to use her sword, Eleanora excused herself and left in the company of Prince Ambrose. He had recommended that they visit one of the many gardens on the island. Wanting more than anything else to be in the company of this wonderful man, Eleanora readily accepted his invitation.

As they walked through the garden, Prince Ambrose presented his arm to Eleanora and she took it. He felt a tingling of his flesh where her hand rested lightly on his arm. It was such a marvelous feeling for him to feel her touch. Eleanora wanted so much to lean into him, to feel the warmth of his body next to hers, but she had to maintain the proper decorum.

Walking through the garden, Prince Ambrose revelled at having this extraordinary woman on his arm. Her light touch set his heart to racing. He knew then that his search had ended, that he had found the woman of his dreams. He knew that he had to have her. If he could win her affections, he would set out for home without delay to petition his father to allow him to marry her. That she held the rank of baronet in her own right would be in her favour, when his father decided whether or not to allow the marriage.

Coming to a flagstone rimmed pond, with water lilies on the surface and red carp swimming in the pond, Prince Ambrose, seeing no one else in sight decided to pause for a while. He led Eleanora to a stone bench under a shade tree, where they sat next to each other. He was soon telling Eleanora everything about himself, much more than he had ever told any woman before. Eleanora had been candid with him about her past. He felt that he in turn had to be open to her, holding nothing back.

That evening, Eleanora again dined with Prince Ambrose in his apartment, but this time they dined alone. They ended up talking for almost three hours. They spoke mostly about themselves. They even asked questions of each other, mostly of their likes and dislikes, also of their goals in life and what gave them the most pleasure. By the time that the evening ended, they each felt as if they had known the other for a long time.

As Eleanora got ready to leave, Ambrose asked, "Eleanora, will you join me for the mid-day meal tomorrow?"

Eleanora replied, "I'm sorry, Ambrose, but I can't. I will be dining with the king and queen at the mid-day meal tomorrow. However, I would love to join you for the evening meal tomorrow."

Smiling, Ambrose responded, "Good, then dinner tomorrow it is. Oh, by the way, have you ever been sailing before?"

Eleanora shook her head saying, "No, Ambrose, I have never been sailing. The only boat that I have ever been on is a river barge.

"Then I must take you sailing tomorrow afternoon." Ambrose said, "The palace has sailing skiffs for the use of the members of the court. As soon as you are done with the king and queen, come here. Then we shall go sailing"

"Then, Ambrose, I shall be here tomorrow after the mid-day meal." Eleanora said.

CHAPTER 20

The page led Eleanora through the king's apartment, to a pavilion set up on a patio overlooking the lake. A table under the pavilion had been set for dining. The page stopped a few paces from the table, and bowed saying. "Your Majesty, the Lady Eleanor." He then backed away until he was out of view.

Eleanora advanced two paces then curtsied saying, "Your Majesty." Waving Eleanora over to the table and indicating an empty chair, King Harold said, "Lady Eleanora, please have a seat, then we can break bread." Eleanora sat in the empty chair across from the third person that she had seen sitting at the table when she entered. He was a large heavy-set man of advanced years. His hair, what little that encircled his bald plate, was long and white. He had hooded-bushy brows over dark-brown eyes, a hawk nose, strong jaw and full-white beard. He wore a loose fitted black robe with cowl, whip cord sash and sandals.

King Harold took care of the introductions. "Lady Eleanora, this is my adviser for magic, Master Eamonn." Indicating Eleanora, King Harold continued, "Master Eamonn, this is, Lady Eleanora, the person that my son, Hugh, has written so much about in his letters."

Master Eamonn sat with his elbows on the table, his hands interlocked just below his face. Eleanora noticed a ring on his finger set with a strange stone that reflected the colors of the spectrum as the light hit it. She then noticed his eyes, very dark and vehement. After only a few moments she had to look away. Master Eamonn said. "It's a pleasure to finally meet you, Lady Eleanora. I've heard so much about you."

"It's a pleasure for me to meet you, Master Eamonn." Eleanora responded.

Just then servants started to arrive with bowls, platters and baskets filled with a multitude of savoury dishes. Everyone started to fill their plates and began to eat. Silver buckets of chilled red and white wines were brought to the table. Eleanora found everything very delightful and plentiful.

Once they had settled into dining, King Harold said, "Lady Eleanora, I've been told that you have been busy in the arena instructing members of the court in the use of your sword."

"That is correct, Your Majesty," Eleanora said, "I'm used to it by now. Some of the members of the court at Dunboro have started to arm themselves with this new sword."

"My dear, Eleanora, have you enjoyed your stay with us so far?" Queen Serafina asked.

"Yes, Your Majesty," Eleanora said in response to the queen, "I am very pleased with my accommodations, and the service is excellent."

"And how long do you plan to stay, Lady Eleanora?" Queen Serafina enquired, "We enjoy so much having you here."

Eleanora responded, "I have enjoyed myself so far and would like to stay longer. However, we will be leaving in ten days. We need to get back to Dunboro while the weather is good."

"That's too bad." Queen Serafina said, "We do enjoy your company, but I do understand that you need to travel while the weather is good." Then with a knowing smile she continued, "I also understand that you have been making friends while you have been with us."

"Yes, Your Majesty, I have been making friends." Eleanora responded, reading something unsaid in the queen's remarks. Eleanora was sure that the king and queen would be getting reports about her budding friendship with Prince Ambrose.

The king now spoke, "Lady Eleanora, we are grateful for your aid in exposing the traitors in Dunboro, and your intervention in the assassination attempt on our son."

"I did but my duty, Your Majesty." Eleanora said, "I only did what needed to be done. After all I was also a target for a while."

"Don't be so modest, Lady Eleanora." King Harold said, "You put your own life at risk to save the life of our son. We shall always remember that."

"Your Majesty," Eleanora said, "we got most of the traitors, but not all of them. There is still the one referred to as, Hammer. There is also the mystery woman who is believed to be the intermediary for Hammer. I have had my agents in Dunboro on alert, but so far it doesn't seem that Hammer is trying to replace the agents that he lost."

King Harold now asked for an opinion from Eleanora. "Lady Eleanora, what do you think of all this?"

Eleanora took a few seconds to order her thoughts before she begin.

"Well, Your Majesty," Eleanora said, "as for Hammer, I have no idea who he may be. However, I believe Hammer to be in the palace, or to have access to someone working in the palace. I believe Lord North to be someone close to Emperor Eimion of the Jute Empire, or perhaps even Emperor Eimion himself. I also believe that the attempted assassination of your son to be part of a plot to throw our kingdom into chaos just before an invasion by the Jutes."

"Then, Lady Eleanora," King Harold said, "what you are saying is that stopping the assassin foiled an attempt at an invasion by the Jutes."

Shaking her head, Eleanora said, "No, Your Majesty, what I'm saying is that we only delayed the invasion. The Jutes will try again with a new plan. Emperor Eimion has made promises to his supporters. If he doesn't deliver he risked being deposed. And the only way that you depose an emperor is with the point of a sword."

With a sigh, King Harold said, "Yes, Lady Eleanora, I agree with you. I now understand why my son made you a member of the court and gave you some authority. Even for someone of such a young age, you have a good head on your shoulders. When you leave to return to Dunboro, I will have some dispatches and personal correspondence for you to carry."

Bowing her head, Eleanora responded, "Yes, Your Majesty."

Picking his knife and fork up, King Harold said, "Now, let's get to eating this food before it gets cold."

After the meal had ended and Eleanora had been dismissed, King Harold turned to Master Eamonn saying, "Master Eamonn, when you captured her with your spell she was immobile for at least three minutes. Will she recall any of it?"

With a slight smile, Master Eamonn replied, "No, Your Majesty, all that she will remember is looking at the ring and into my eyes for a few moments."

"And what did you discover about her, Master Eamonn?" King Harold asked.

"Well, Your Majesty," Master Eamonn said, "as for her loyalty to you and your family, it is above reproach. She has made a strong attachment to your son and daughter in law; she now feels as if she were a member of the family. It was this loyalty that compelled her to risk so much to defend your son. I believe that her loyalty and reliability is unquestionable. You can have complete trust in her."

"Thank you, Master Eamonn," King Harold said, "now I know what I can do."

It was a beautiful day on the lake. The wind blew brisk enough to give the skiff good sailing performance. The skiff now sailed on a starboard tack. Prince Ambrose sat on the port side at the tiller. Eleanora sat beside him. At Ambrose suggestion she had dressed casually in plain green skirt and tan blouse.

"How do you like sailing, Eleanora?" Ambrose asked.

Taking in Vanaden on the Lake and other landmarks from their perspective on the water, Eleanora exclaimed. "Oh, Ambrose, I love it!"

Feeling pleased at Eleanora's response, Ambrose said, "Yes, I love it too. Whenever I want to be alone, I get into my boat and go sailing."

"Yes, you do have solitude out here. On the water you need only be concerned for the boat and yourself." Eleanora said.

Ambrose made a sudden decision. "Eleanora, trade places with me." he said, starting to move out of the way so that, Eleanora could take the tiller.

"Oh, no I can't!" Eleanora exclaimed.

"Yes, you can. I'll be right next to you. Do you trust me to keep you safe?" Ambrose said with an air of confidence that began to put Eleanora at ease.

"All right, Ambrose, I trust you." Eleanora said with a nod.

With Ambrose instructing her on how to handle the tiller, and how to keep the sails trimmed using the sheets, Eleanora started to learn how to handle the skiff. By the time they sailed back to the dock, Eleanora felt that she had begun to master the art of sailing.

That evening, Eleanora took the evening meal with Prince Ambrose in his apartment. And for the next four days the mid-day meal and dinner were taken with Prince Ambrose in his apartment. The rest of the time, Eleanora spent in the training arena, or with Ambrose strolling through the gardens, or sailing.

On the fifth day before she was to depart for Dunboro, Eleanora again had dinner with Prince Ambrose in his apartment. From the start there seemed to be something different about this night. For some reason, Eleanora just couldn't settle down. She could feel the beating of her heart in her breast.

There seemed to be a tingling, or fluttering feeling in her body. She had never felt like this before.

All that evening she felt unsettled. She ate the meal without really tasting it. When it came time for her to go, she stood and moved for the door. Prince Ambrose moved to open the door for her. Eleanora just stopped and looked at the door, unwilling to leave. Finally she spoke to, Prince Ambrose, "Ambrose, would you think less of me if I tell you that I don't want to leave you tonight?"

Taken by surprise, Ambrose could only say, "What do you mean, Eleanora?"

Eleanora's eyes now started to glisten with the beginning of a tear as she said. "Ambrose, I must tell you something. For some reason I have a destiny that I cannot avoid. It is a destiny linked with the, Prince of Dunboro. I walk a path fraught with hardship and peril. I do not know what the future may bring, but if I am to know only one man in this lifetime, and for only a brief time, I want that man to be you."

Taken by surprise, Prince Ambrose just stood mute and immobile for a minute or more before finally closing the door. He then said, "You say that you have never known a man before. That you are a virgin."

Looking into his eyes, Eleanora responded, "Oh, Ambrose, I have never even been embraced or kissed by a man before. I need for you to hold and kiss me now. I need for you to love me."

Without further words, Ambrose enfolded her in his arms and kissed her at first softly on the lips, then more ardently. Eleanora wrapped her arms about him, pulling him hard against her body. Their breathing had now become more rapid. Ambrose then gathered her up into his arms and carried her into his bed chamber, where he set her back down on her feet next to the bed. They then kissed again, while disrobing each other with eager hands. Ambrose then picked her up and lay her on the bed, lying beside her.

Eleanora surrendered herself to her passion letting, Ambrose take the lead in the foreplay. His lips were on her lips, eyelids, earlobes, neck, breast and other places. His hands explored her most private places. Taking his manhood in her hand, she felt its firmness and size. She had never known passion like this before. Their skin was now hot and sweaty, their breathing coming in gasps. He was bringing her to the heights of ecstasy, driving her wild. She needed to have him inside of her now.

Ambrose seeing that she was ready, mounted and started to penetrate her.

Eleanora found herself in a state of carnal euphoria as their two bodies were joined as one. Their love making was zealous, leading to a glorious climax.

After a brief interval they made love for the second time. This time their love making was a bit more leisurely, Ambrose taking the time to insure that, Eleanora got the most pleasure from it. After a time they made love for a third time. Afterwards, exhausted, they fell asleep in each other's arms.

Ambrose awoke the next morning as the first light from the new day came in through the window. Eleanora still slept peacefully beside him. He beheld her beautiful face so serene in slumber. With a fan of red hair on the pillow she looked like a goddess.

As Ambrose lay propped up on an elbow watching her, Eleanora's eyes started to flutter, then she opened her eyes. Seeing him, she reached up to put an arm around his neck, then pulled him down to kiss her. This led to foreplay, then another round of love making.

When they had finished they got dressed. Ambrose then had a servant contact the kitchen to send up breakfast for two to his apartment.

As they were eating breakfast, Eleanora said, "I thank you, Ambrose, I am very grateful for last night."

"I should be thanking you." Ambrose replied, "I derived as much pleasure as you did."

"You don't understand, Ambrose," Eleanora said, "A crisis is about to befall the kingdom and I have a vital role to play. The seer has told me that if I prevail then I shall know happiness. However there is no certainty that I shall survive. Our brief interlude may be all that I shall ever know. So it is I that is grateful for this brief chance for happiness." Eleanora paused for a moment, then continued, "One last thing, Ambrose, I love you dearly. You are the only man that I have ever loved, and the only one that I ever shall."

Ambrose had stopped eating and laid his knife and fork on his plate. He just sat there looking at her for two minutes. He then removed a pinkie ring from his little finger. He then took Eleanora's left hand and placed the ring on her ring finger. The ring was of gold, with a flawless square-cut emerald, with smaller round-cut diamonds on each side. He then said, "Eleanora, if you are in agreement, let this ring be a symbol of my love for you, and of our betrothal to each other. Eleanora, I want you in my life. Will you marry me?"

It took Eleanora a few moments to recover her voice. Then bolting to her feet, she exclaimed, "Yes, oh yes!"

She then rushed around the table into the arms of Ambrose, who had also stood. As Ambrose embraced her he could see tears of joy rolling down her cheeks. They kissed passionately, their bodies pressed together as if they would become one. When at last the kiss ended, Eleanora said, "I must speak with Princess Juliana as soon as I return to Dunboro. As a member of the peerage, I must have permission to wed. With her backing I'm sure that her husband, Prince Hugh, will agree."

Ambrose responded, "I'm sure that you will have no problem with Prince Hugh. I must also have permission from my father to wed. He will want to think about it, that's his way, but I'm sure that he will agree. After all, that's the reason for my visit to your king's court. My father wants me to find a wife from your kingdom to strengthen the alliance between our countries."

Nodding, Eleanora said, "Yes, then let us plan for a wedding sometime after the coming summer solstice festival. I will be counted eighteen then. Also, I'm sure that by then everything will be resolved."

Eleanora now used her apartment only to change her clothes, and conduct meetings with Sir Hal and Sergeant Giffard about the return trip to Dunboro. The palace would arrange for the barge to take them up river to Duman Ford.

The evening before her departure, Eleanora was summoned to King Harold's library. A page escorted her to the library and knocked on the door. A voice called out, "Enter." The page opened the door, standing aside for Eleanora to enter, closing the door behind her. King Harold stood in the center of the room looking at her. Curtsying, Eleanora said, "Your Majesty."

Taking a seat in a comfortable leather upholstered chair, King Harold indicated the chair next to his saying, "Come, Lady Eleanor, have a seat. I would like to talk with you."

When Eleanora had taken a seat in the chair next to him, King Harold continued. "Well, Lady Eleanora, I must say that I'll be sorry to see you go tomorrow. You have been quite a novel influence on the court. You have managed to embarrass half of the court who thought that they were really skilled with the blade. The other half are too intimidated to face you."

Eleanora said, "I believe that you are right, Your Majesty. Sergeant Giffard likes to bet on me. He calls it easy money. No one wants to bet with him anymore."

King Harold gave out a short laugh, then said, "Yes, I've heard of your Sergeant Giffard. He has taken members of the court for a lot of money.

Well, enough about your Sergeant, Giffard. I have heard that you have developed another interest like Prince Ambrose."

Blushing, Eleanora responded, "I didn't know that you knew, Your Majesty."

"My dear, Eleanora, if I didn't keep track of what goes on in my palace, soon it would no longer be my palace." King Harold said, "Now, just how serious is this affair?"

Eleanora answered, "Your Majesty, we are betrothed." Showing King Harold the ring, Eleanora continued, "Ambrose gave me this ring as a symbol of our betrothal. I plan to speak to Princess Juliana as soon as I return to Dunboro, then to your son."

With a reassuring smile, King Harold said, "Lady Eleanora, let your mind be at ease. I will approve of your marriage to, Prince Ambrose, but not now." "I thank you, Your Majesty." Eleanora said, "I understand that the time is not right for now. The kingdom faces a terrible trial. The assassination of your son was meant to throw the kingdom into chaos to give a tactical advantage for a Jute invasion. They cannot come now, it's too late in the year to start a campaign. We stopped them this

time. However, Emperor Eimion has made promises, he has to try again. I look for him starting next spring. He won't try assassination again. He will have a new plan."

King Harold thought of what Eleanora had said for about a minute, then said, "You amaze me, Lady Eleanora, how did you come up with all of this?" "Well, Your Majesty," Eleanora said, "Lord Marshal Simon has an impressive library on military tactics and strategy. I have spent countless hours in his library reading."

With mirth, King Harold said, "Perhaps then, Lady Eleanora, I should make you my Knight Marshal."

Blushing, Eleanora said, "You jest, Your Majesty."

Turing serious, King Harold now got to why he had sent for her. Picking up a small leather satchel from beside his chair, he handed it to Eleanora saying, "Lady Eleanora, this pouch contains dispatches and personal correspondence for you to take back to Dunboro."

King Harold then produced a small leather tube, with leather caps on each end. Pulling off one of the caps, he removed a parchment from the tube. He then said, "Now, Lady Eleanora, before I give this to you I want you to read it." He then handed the parchment to her. Eleanora took the parchment and started to read.

To whom it may concern,

Let it be known that the, Lady Eleanora, baronet of the court of Dunboro, as my agent in all matters concerning security of the kingdom, acts in my name and speaks with my voice. Her authority in all matters of security of the kingdom is absolute, she answers only to me. You are commanded to render any and all assistance asked of you by, Lady Eleanora to the best of your ability. Given under my signature and seal.

Harold d' croixIIrex

Eleanora read the document three times to make sure that she wasn't mistaken. She then looked up at, King Harold her eyes saying everything.

King Harold then said, "Lady Eleanora, I know what you're thinking, but be sure that you have that document with you at all times. You have some important role to play in the coming crisis. I want you to have every advantage. And I'm sorry to say that you may need it with some of the more senior members of the peerage."

Nodding, Eleanora said, "Yes, Your Majesty, I will always have this with me, but I hope that I never have to use it."

With a satisfied smile, King Harold said, "That's good, Lady Eleanora, I would be worried if you didn't feel that way. Now I think it time for you to run along to spend your last night with your prince."

Taking everything, Eleanora rose from her chair and curtsied saying, "By your leave, Your Majesty." She then turned and left the room.

When Eleanora arrived at Prince Ambrose's apartment she still had the dispatch case and the document with her. She let Ambrose read the document. By the expression on his face, Eleanora could tell that it had much the same effect on him as it had on her. As he finished reading the document he exclaimed, "This is unbelievable! Eleanora, if you had not shown it to me, I would have not believed that such a document could exist. Believe me when I tell you, kings do not delegate authority like this, it's too dangerous."

Sighing, Eleanora said, "Yes, I know what you mean. I'm not sure if I want the responsibility. I hope that I never have to use it."

Ambrose, still looking at the document, shook his head saying, "Eleanora, every time I think that I know everything about you, you surprise me with something different. Do you know what this means?" Eleanora didn't answer, knowing it to be a rhetorical question. Ambrose continued, "It means that you are now the most powerful person in the kingdom, aside from the king. With this document you could raise and command an army"

Looking Ambrose in the eyes, Eleanora said, "Yes, Ambrose, that's what frightens me. Am I worthy of such trust?"

Ambrose had to look at Eleanora in awe as he spoke, "Eleanora, believe me when I say, kings do not do things like this. I have never heard or seen of such a document before. King Harold must have complete faith and confidence in you to trust you so completely."

He now took her into his arms, continuing to speak, "Eleanora, knowing you as I have come to know you, I can see why King Harold trust you so completely. You are the most extraordinary person that I have ever met. To have won your love, it makes me feel more like a man."

Putting her head on his shoulder, Eleanora said, "I thank you for your inspiring words, Ambrose. A time of peril is coming that will test our resolve. I pray to the Gods that I shall be equal to the task. I shall remember your words and draw strength from them." Embracing Ambrose more firmly in her arms, Eleanora continued, "Enough of this gloom for now; I have good news. I told the king of our betrothal. He is in favor of it, and will grant permission for us to wed."

With a kiss on her forehead, Ambrose said, "Wonderful! Now I must get my father to agree. Although my father will probability want to think about it for a while, but I'm sure that I can convince him to allow us to marry."

"Then, Ambrose my love, I shall make devotions to Idonea (goddess of the hearth) for your success. Now this being our last night, I want as much pleasure from it as we may have."

CHAPTER 21

The next morning, Prince Ambrose saw Eleanora and her party off for their return trip to Dunboro. Their last night together had been filled with passionate love making, or just laying arm and arm. Eleanora, for the most part had kept her emotions under control, however there were a few tears shed. Wanting to make their parting memorable for Ambrose, Eleanora had worn her most attractive riding ensemble, an orchid colour gown with purple trim and matching hat. She had paid careful attention to her hair and make-up to look her best for Ambrose.

Prince Ambrose, wanting to look his best for Eleanora, wore a scarlet-red tunic with golden-yellow embroidery on collar and cuffs, black trousers and boots. He also had on a black cavalier hat with red plume; the final touch being his ceremonial sword and dagger, with hilts and scabbards decorated with precious metal and gem stones.

After seeing Eleanora off, Prince Ambrose departed Vanaden on the Lake by fast river boat down river for the port city of Natenfor. From there he would take ship to Taverna the capital of the island kingdom of Turin.

Within a day by fast river boat, Prince Ambrose arrived at the port city of Natenfor. From the boat he went directly to the office of shipping master at customs. There he found that a Turin ship, the Red Enchantress would be sailing on the morning tide for Taverna. After making arrangements with Captain Evan, the ship's captain, Prince

Ambrose had his baggage transferred from the boat to the ship. Once settled aboard ship, he was eager to be at sea.

By barge the trip up river to Duman Ford took four days. With Vanaden on the Lake and the king's court behind her, Eleanora was anxious to be back in Dunboro. She needed to check on what her agents in Dunboro were turning up. She still needed to find out who Hammer was. Hammer so far had been too cunning to expose himself. If only they could get a lead on the woman who was his emissary.

Watching Sir Hal and Brenda, only made her long for Ambrose even more. The last look at him standing at the north gate to Vanaden on the Lake, he had looked so splendid dressed in his finest clothing. It would be an image that she shall keep in her mind always. It had been almost more than she could bear to part with Ambrose without shedding tears. Even if she hadn't wept openly, her eyes had all the same glistened with moisture. Would she ever see him again, or would fate keep her from living her dreams. Was she walking the right path, or will her efforts end in disaster. Perhaps she should go to the seer for another seeing.

At Duman Ford, Eleanora and her party spent two days before starting out over land for Stone Bridge. At Stone Bridge they were the guest of Earl Gerard and his wife, Countess Natalia. They were anxious to hear all the latest gossip from the king's court. Even though Eleanora hadn't mentioned it, the earl and countess learned of her betrothal to Crown Prince Ambrose of Turin through other members of her party. From then on the earl and countess showed Eleanora every courtesy. The countess being insistent that, Eleanora tell her everything, how she met him, how he courted her and how they became betrothed. Eleanora told her a good deal, but not all; wanting to keep certain elements of her affair with Prince Ambrose personal.

The last leg of their journey by barge down the Aber River took two and one half days, arriving at the docks of Dunboro in the early afternoon. Everyone, to include Eleanora, were glad to be back home. However, to Eleanora it didn't seem quite the same anymore. It was as if deep in her psyche she knew that no place would be home anymore without Ambrose.

Upon arrival at the palace, Eleanora went first to the apartment of Princess Juliana. Princess Juliana noticed the change in Eleanora almost immediately. With a curious look, Princess Juliana inquired, "There seems to be something different about you, Eleanora. Tell me, what happened at the king's court?"

Eleanora smiled and her whole face seemed to light up. Princess Juliana could clearly see that she was really excited about something. Eleanora responded, "Your Highness, I met a man at court."

The curious look on, Princess Juliana's face changed to a grin as she said. "Well, it took you long enough. I wondered when a man would catch your eye. Who is this man anyway, perhaps I know him?"

Watching for Princess Juliana's reaction, Eleanora said, "Your Highness, he is the Crown Prince Ambrose of Turin."

With an expression of amazement, Princess Juliana asked, "Tell me, Eleanora, how did you come to meet, Prince Ambrose?"

Eleanora, still in a state of bliss, replied, "Well, Your Highness, the day that I arrived at court he was there. Having heard about me, he wanted to see me. He then arranged an introduction. From that introduction we just seemed to spend most of our time together."

"I've not as yet met Crown Prince Ambrose." Princess Juliana said, "What kind of a person is he?"

With a smile that projected happiness, Eleanora replied, "Oh, Your Highness, he's a wonderful man, so handsome and considerate, a person that's a joy to be with."

By now, Princess Juliana suspected that there was something between Eleanora and Prince Ambrose. She kept up the inquiry. "Eleanora, is there anything between you and Prince Ambrose that I should know about?"

With an enthusiastic nod, Eleanora replied. "Yes, Your Highness, there is something that you should know about. Prince Ambrose and I spent most of our time together, taking most of our meals together in

his apartment. Five days before our departure, I had dinner with him in his apartment. When it came time for me to go, I told him that I didn't want to leave. I spent the night in his bed." Holding up her left hand, Eleanora continued, "The next morning, Prince Ambrose gave me this ring as a symbol of our betrothal."

Taken by surprise, Princess Juliana just stood mute for a few seconds. She then embraced Eleanora saying, "Oh how wonderful, Eleanora. How did you get, Prince Ambrose to propose to you?"

"Well, Your Highness," Eleanora said grinning, "I didn't really set out to get a proposal from him. I just let myself be carried away by my desire for him. I expressed my love for him, holding nothing back. He then revealed that his desire for me was just as strong."

"But what about your past life." Princess Juliana said, "What will happen when he finds out who you were before you came to us?"

Eleanora responded, "He already knows, Your Highness, I held nothing back, telling him everything. I wanted to be honest with him. The same day that we left Vanaden on the Lake on our return to Dunboro; Prince Ambrose left to return to Taverna, to get permission from his father to marry. King Harold already knows about the betrothal and has given his blessing."

With a short laugh, Princess Juliana said. "Hugh must know about this. Come, Eleanora, let's go and surprise him."

Prince Ambrose stood on the quarter deck of the Red Enchantress speaking with Captain Evan when the lookout in the main top called out. "Land ho dead ahead!"

Everyone looked ahead. A few minutes passed before anyone on the deck could make out the land, looking like a dark smudge on the horizon, a half hour later the city of Taverna could be seen. Captain Evan then turned to Prince Ambrose saying, "Your Highness, with your permission, I shall now hoist your flag."

Prince Ambrose nodded saying, "Yes, captain, do have it done now." One minute later a cobalt blue flag with silver griffin and heir apparent coronet was hoisted to the top of the main mast.

Captain Evan looked up at the flag, then turned back to Prince Ambrose saying, "Your Highness, it won't be long before the pilot boat spots your flag. It won't be long after that your father will know of your return. Even with priority for docking, your father will have a reception committee to welcome you back home at the dock before we make fast the lines. This young woman that you have told me about."

"Yes," Prince Ambrose said, "Lady Eleanora, a baronet of the court of Dunboro."

"Yes, Your Highness," Captain Evan said, "are you ready to confront your father for the hand of this lady?"

During the trip from Natenfor, Prince Ambrose had told Captain Evan a lot about, Eleanora. Now that he was back home, he was nervous about speaking to his father about her. Looking at the captain, he said, "Well, captain, when you want something from father, no one is ever really ready to face him. He doesn't like to make an important decision without giving it plenty of thought. Even when he does reach a decision right away, he may keep it to himself for a while just to watch you fret."

Captain Evan had a good laugh at this.

When at last the ship had been made fast to the pier, and the gang plank run out and secured, Prince Ambrose was the first to depart the ship. On the pier he was greeted by an elderly man, who despite his advanced years and mostly white hair, displayed a noble bearing. He was dressed in clothing well made of fine cloth. With him were six soldiers, with an extra horse for him and a cart for his baggage. As soon as Prince Ambrose stepped on the pier the elderly man stepped forward with his hand outstretched saying. "Welcome home, Your Highness, I hope that you had a pleasant journey?"

Shaking the elder man's hand, Prince Ambrose said, "Marquis Cecil it's so good to see you again. How is my father and mother?"

Marquis Cecil responded, "Your parents are just fine, Your Highness. How was your visit to King Harold's court?" Picking up on the grin that had appeared on, Prince Ambrose's face, Marquis Cecil continued, "You met someone while at, King Harold's court, am I right?"

Now laughing, Prince Ambrose said, "you could always tell what I was thinking, you old fox. Yes, I did meet someone, and she's someone really special."

Smiling, Marquis Cecil asked, "Who is she, Your Highness, if you don't mind me asking. What's her name?"

"Well," Prince Ambrose said, "she's Lady Eleanora, a baronet of the court of Dunboro, a young woman of seventeen."

"So, Your Highness, her father is a baronet and she uses his title. Or he is deceased and she inherited it." Marquis Cecil said.

Shaking his head, Prince Ambrose replied, "No, that's not it. She's a baronet in her own right. She saved Prince Hugh of Dunboro from assassination, killing the assassin, a brother of the Black Rose."

"The Black Rose!" Marquis Cecil exclaimed in amazement, "How did she do that? They are legendary, most people believing them to be almost immortal"

"She killed him with her dagger." Prince Ambrose said, "And she has killed five, or perhaps six more with sword or dagger. They were men who had plotted treason, or the assassination of the Prince of Dunboro. As I said she's someone special. She has the complete trust and confidence of King Harold; even more so than anyone else in his kingdom. Now, let's get on to the palace. I'm anxious to see father. I'll tell you more about Eleanora later."

At the palace, Prince Ambrose was met by his parents, King Quincy IV and Queen Frederica. When Ambrose was at last alone with his parents he said. "Father, while I was at King Harold's court I met the most remarkable young woman. She is Lady Eleanora, a baronet of the court of Dunboro. On the day of her arrival at court there was keen interest in her, due to her prowess with the blade, both long and short. After all the gossip of the court I had expected to see an amazon of a woman who would dominate the room. To my surprise a goddess entered the grand hall. A young woman of seventeen years with slender figure, auburn hair, fair complexion with a sprinkling of freckles and the most beautiful sapphire-blue eyes. She had a noble carriage and radiated confidence. Father, Eleanora is the woman that I wish to wed."

Ambrose stood silent as his father considered his statement. Finally his father said. This Lady Eleanora, you said that she had a reputation with the blade, tell me about it."

Clearing his throat nervously, Ambrose began. "Well, Father, in the service of the prince of Dunboro she has killed six men with sword or dagger. One was an assassin of the Brotherhood of the Black Rose."

With an expression of amazement, Ambrose's father exclaimed. "How did she manage to do that? How could a lass as you describe overcome an assassin of the Brotherhood of the Black Rose."

"As the account of the event was related to me." Ambrose said, "During the assassin attempt, Eleanora knocked Prince Hugh aside, taking the dart intended for the prince. Then when the assassin closed in for the kill, Eleanora thrust her dagger to the hilt in the assassin's groin."

"Ouch!" Ambrose's father exclaimed, resisting the urge to hold his own groin. "That must be the ultimate kick in the balls." That drew a laugh from both his wife, Frederica and his son. Ambrose's father continued, "You said that there were other men that she had killed. What's the story on those men?"

"Well, Father," Ambrose said, "One night when she was gathering evidence of treason for Prince Hugh, she and Sergeant Giffard, her escort from the palace guard were set upon by five armed men. She killed three of their assailants and her sergeant dispatched the other two. The next day while arresting the traitor, she killed two more of his men."

"It sounds like she's very good with the blade." King Quincy said.

"I'll say," Ambrose said, "I sparred with her with the sword in the training arena one day. She made me look like an ignorant clod flailing about with a club. I never witnessed anyone getting the best of her in a sparring match."

Ambrose's mother now asked. "What about her family, Ambrose. Who are they?"

Ambrose answered, knowing that this would be the most critical part of the interview. Well, Mother, Eleanora has no family. She is an orphan. She has been the ward of Prince Hugh of Dunboro for about a year and a half. She is the personal companion to Princess Juliana. She was elevated to baronet of the court after the assassination attempt."

"So," his mother said, "her parents died about one and a half years ago." Shaking his head, Ambrose replied, "No, Mother, her father died when she was four, an accident while clearing land. He was crushed by a falling tree. Just before she was counted nine years her mother was murdered."

Despite it being a tragic story, his mother continued, "Then, who took care of her before she came to court?"

Looking directly at his mother, but his words also meant for his father, Ambrose answered, "Well, Mother, Eleanora took care of herself. She was an orphan on the streets of Dunboro."

Ambrose's father now took part in the inquiry saying, "Ambrose, how was she able to care for herself at such an early age?"

"Well, Father," Ambrose responded, "Her story is quite an unusual one. Her mother, feeling that she would be safer on the street as a lad than a lass, raised her as a lad. On the street she was known as, Eddy the cat, a cat burglar. That was what she was doing when she overheard the two men plotting assassination and treason. She was discovered and they were trying to kill her. Her only hope was to seek refuge at the palace, and tell Prince Hugh everything that she knew about the plot. Since then she has grown to love the prince's family and to identify with it as her own. The royal family also feels affection for her, knowing that her loyalty to them is without question."

With an inquisitive look, Ambrose's father inquired, "Tell me, Ambrose, how do you know that the royal family trust her so?"

Looking at his father, Ambrose answered, "Well, Father, I have seen the document."

"What document?" King Quincy responded, a little intrigued.

"Well, Father, it is a document given to her by King Harold, it reads. To Whom It May Concern, Let it be known that the, Lady Eleanora baronet of the court of Dunboro, as my agent in all matters concerning security of the kingdom, acts in my name and speaks with my voice. Her authority in all matters of security of the kingdom is absolute, she answers only to me. You are commanded to render any and all assistance asked of you by, Lady Eleanora, to the best of your ability. Given under my signature and seal. It was signed by, King Harold. It also had the seal of his signet ring in wax over a ribbon of purple with gold trim."

Shaking his head in disbelief, King Quincy exclaimed, "That can't be! A king would never give such a dangerous document to anyone!"

Ambrose responded, "I would not have believed it myself, Father, if I had not have seen it for myself. I read it many times to remember what it said. For some reason, King Harold believes that she will have need of such a document in the future, and trust her enough to give it to her."

Still looking at his son, King Quincy asked. "And what does Eleanora think about the king giving her this document?"

"She said that it frightened her." Ambrose replied, "As I said Father, she is the most extraordinary person that I have ever met. She is a person that you only meet once in a lifetime."

Ambrose's father thought for a minute before speaking, "This, Eleanora shows wisdom for a person of such a young age. Knowing her background I would not have felt reluctant to say no to a marriage. However, after hearing all that you have said about her, I will have to give this much thought."

Ambrose felt relieved that his father hadn't said no. There was now a chance that he would be allowed to marry Eleanora. Looking at his mother, and seeing her smile, he knew that with her he had an ally.

CHAPTER 22

Summer faded into fall. The trees took on their hues of yellow and red, then slowly the leaves started to fall to the ground. The winds coming mostly from the northwest, off the Great Ocean Sea, often carried cold rain that would soon become snow.

Eleanora had seen to her network of agents as soon as she had returned from the king's court at Vanaden on the Lake. Jimmy, who ran the day to day workings of the network, had been able to recruit more agents in her absence. He had even been able to enlist the cooperation of one of the prostitutes working at the White Dove brothal. Perhaps now some information could be gleaned about these clandestine meetings that would take place from time to time in the White Dove.

One thing that Jimmy had learned was that there was a trap door in the basement of the White Dove that led to the city sewers. It was used by some of the special clients to come and go without being seen. Jimmy had started to keep it under surveillance.

Eleanora had also started to take Brenda with her when she went to meet with Jimmy. If in the future she did marry Ambrose and live with him in Turin, Brenda would be able to take control of the network and run it for Prince Hugh.

Eleanora continued to work with Master of the Sword, Ralph. She wanted to hone her skills with the sword while wearing chain mail armor, helm, weapons and shield. She felt that this was something that she now had to learn. She also convinced Horse Master Osburn to teach her to ride and control a trained war horse in battle while wearing armor, helm, weapons and shield. From the armorer she got a coat of chain mail with coif. It covered her arm to the elbows, down to just above the knees, with openings at front and back so that she could sit her horse. The armorer also made her a helm with nose guard and chain mail neck guard. He also made her leather bracers covered with small bronze plates like fish scales. She also had made three surcoates of cobalt-blue with her blazon embroidered on the left breast. Prince Hugh seeing what she was doing, presented her with a knight's shield with her blazon painted on it. To get used to the weight of her new armor, she ran one mile each day in full armor. She knew not what she would face in the future, but she was now ready for it.

One day in late autumn a ship sailed into the harbour of Dunboro, flying the flag of the kingdom of Turin from the mast head. A harbour pilot came aboard to pilot the ship into the docks. When at last the ship had tied up to the dock; it commenced to discharge and take on cargo. Once everything was proceeding well the captain had his first officer take charge of the unloading. He then started out for the palace.

Arriving at the palace gate, he informed the guard that he was the captain of the Turin ship Red Enchantress, and that he had business with the Lady Eleanora. The guard had the ship captain wait at the gate while he sent for an escort. A few minutes later a maid arrived to escort the captain to Lady Eleanora. The maid led the captain into the palace, up flights of stairs and along corridors until they came to a door. The maid knocked and a soft feminine voice called out. "Enter."

The maid opened the door, entered the sitting room of an apartment, and curtsied to a young woman standing by the window. The captain one step behind bowed. The maid said, "My Lady, the Captain of the Turin ship Red Enchantress to see you."

Eleanora said. "You may withdraw now."

The maid curtsied again and left the room, closing the door behind her. Sitting in a chair, Eleanora indicated a chair close to hers saying, "You may have a seat, Captain."

When the captain had taken his seat, Eleanora continued, "Now, how may I help you, Captain?"

The captain first cleared his throat, then spoke, "My Lady, I am, Captain Evan of the Turin ship Red Enchantress. The Crown Prince Ambrose took passage on my ship on his return to Taverna. During the voyage he told me a lot about you. When he found that I was about to depart with a cargo for Dunboro, he entrusted a letter to me for delivery to you." Captain Evan then withdrew a folded parchment from his tunic, handing it to Eleanora.

With a slight tremble of her hands, Eleanora took the letter from the hand of Captain Evan. With her thumb nail she broke the wax seal, opened the letter and started to read.

As Eleanora read the letter, Captain Evan scrutinised her. Prince Ambrose had spoken of her often on the voyage back home from Natenfor. As there was a good chance that the Lady Eleanora would become Turin's next crown princess, Captain Evan was understandably curious about her. She was very attractive with her lithe body, long-red hair and lovely face with just a sprinkling of freckles. She had a noble bearing and a pleasing allure. It wasn't hard to see why Prince Ambrose had been attracted to her.

When Eleanora finished reading the letter, she beamed with pleasure. Addressing Captain Evan, Eleanora said, "Captain Evan, may I impose on you to wait here while I pen a letter for Prince Ambrose. I shall send for tea and shortbread. Or perhaps you might like something more, like bread, cold meats and cheese so that you may make yourself a sandwich?"

"Thank you, My Lady," Captain Evan said, "I shall wait for your letter. And the tea and shortbread will be just fine."

Eleanora pulled a bell cord to summon a maid. After instructing the maid to send to the kitchen for tea and shortbread, Eleanora went to her desk where she took up parchment and pen and started to write.

When Eleanora finished writing the letter, she folded it and sealed it with hot wax, pressing her personal seal into the soft wax. She then handed the letter to, Captain Evan saying, "I thank you, Captain Evan for waiting. Please take care of this letter and see it delivered to Prince Ambrose."

With a warm smile for Eleanora, Captain Evan said, "I will, My Lady. That is if I don't run into any more Jute biremes, or triremes."

Eleanora's demeanor instantly changed from that of a charming hostess, to an intense and demanding inquisitor asking, "Captain Evan, you said Jute biremes and triremes, where did you see them?"

"Well, My Lady," Captain Evan said, "I encountered two biremes and one triremes about twenty leagues (sixty miles) off your coast between Haffendel and Kientor."

Showing concern, Eleanora asked, "What were they doing there, Captain Evan? Were they engaged in commerce raiding?"

Captain Evans responded, "My Lady, when we first spotted them I ordered a change of course, taking us further out into the Great Ocean Sea. However, it soon became apparent that they were not interested in commerce raiding, as they didn't even try to cut us off, or give pursuit."

Eleanora took a few seconds to mull over Captain Evan's last answer before she asked her next question. "Captain Even, are they not farther south than you would expect to find them this time of year?"

With a nod, Captain Evan responded, "You are right, My Lady, this is not the time of year to be so far from their base. The weather is more severe and unpredictable during the winter months. They are not as good a sea boat as a cog, or larger ship."

Looking right at Captain Even, Eleanora asked, "Captain Evan, do you have any idea as to why they were there?"

"My Lady," Captain Evan said, "being that they were not there as pirates, then the only other thing that I can think of right off hand would be a scouting mission."

Coming to her feet, Eleanora said, "Captain Evan, you must come with me. There are others that need to hear this."

Wanting to see what she was up to, Captain Evan followed her out of her apartment without complaint.

Eleanora with Captain Evan went first to Duke Bran then to Knight Marshal Simon. From there they all went to Prince Hugh's library. There, Captain Evan repeated what he had told Eleanora. There was then a round of discussions. Captain Evan would be asked a question from time to time that he answered as best as he could.

As the meeting progressed, Captain Evan noticed that Lady Eleanora was an active participant in the meeting; Prince Hugh and the other men inviting her remarks and paying heed to her counsel. It appeared to him that the men regarded her not as a pampered young lady of the court, but more as they would a man holding her rank of baronet. He now realized that Prince Ambrose had not been overstating when he said that she had exceptional talents. If Prince Ambrose did take her as wife, making her the crown princess, then some day she would be queen of Turin. And, Captain Evan could tell that she would be a powerful queen.

For three days after Captain Evan had called on her, Eleanora had brooded over what he had told her about the Jute biremes and triremes. According to Knight Marshal Simon the Jute biremes and triremes were usually not very active during the winter months. Also, working as commerce raiders they like to work closer to shore. There they could trap sailing ships against the shoals, blocking their escape to deep water. In deep water, unless the winds were really light, a sailing ship could usually out run them.

Prince Hugh, Duke Bran and Knight Marshal Simon believed that the Jutes planned an invasion on the coast between Haffendel and Kientor. Once established, using Kientor as a port, they could bring in supplies and reinforcements for their army. Then with a short front, with the left flank secure on the Great Ocean Sea and the right flank guarded by the Red Palisades mountains, they could drive north, clearing the west side of the kingdom. Then if they could capture the fortress at Questers Pass, the way would be open for a mass invasion; one that the kingdom would not be able to resist.

It all seemed so logical, but Eleanora wasn't so sure. For some reason she had that itch behind her ear. That itch that usually meant danger. She had put off going to the seer for far too long.

The next day, Eleanora passed through the main gate of the palace with Sergeant Giffard and into the city. Eleanora had dressed plainly in an unadorned pine-green linen gown and dark-brown cloak with cowl. She also wore her pendant badge suspended at her throat by a maroon ribbon. Sergeant Giffard went armed, but plainly dressed in black tunic, trousers and boots, with dark-grey cloak and cowl. The days were now cold, so they maintained a brisk pace to keep warm.

After a thirty minute walk they arrived at a hovel in the workers quarter of the city. Eleanora knocked at the door. A lass in a well-used and patched grey frock answered the door. Eleanora said, "I have come to see the seer. May I come in?"

Without a word the lass stepped aside to allow Eleanora and Sergeant Giffard to enter. As Eleanora entered the hovel she noticed that everything was much the same as the last time that she was there, except that the lass had gotten a little older, and grown a little taller. The old woman, dressed in a black frock, sat on her stool next to the fireplace turning a spitted roast. The old woman motioned for the lass to take her place at the fireplace. She then greeted Eleanora saying, "welcome to my home, My Lady. How may I help you?"

"I have need of a seeing." Eleanora said.

With a wave of her hand, the old woman responded, "Then, My Lady, have a seat at the table. Your man can have a seat at the table, or stand if he prefers."

As Eleanora and Sergeant Giffard sat at the table; the old woman taking her cane, went to a cabinet and removed a small-silver cup and clear-crystal bowl. She then sat the bowl and cup in the centre of the table and sat on a stool across from Eleanora. Eleanora placed a gold double sovereign on the table. The old woman scooped the coin up and deposited it in a pocket in a fold in her frock. Then looking into Eleanora's eyes, she said, "My Lady, I will need something of you."

Eleanora produce a folded paper that she handed over to the old woman. The old woman unfolded the paper and looked at the few strands of hair. She looked into Eleanora's eyes, then said, "My Lady, you have never been here before, yet you seem to be familiar to me."

Smiling, Eleanora replied, "But I have been here before, less than two years ago. However, I was not as you see me now. I was supposedly the lad called, Eddy the cat. Now I'm Lady Eleanora, a baronet of the court of Dunboro."

With a cackling laugh the old woman said, "Good for you, My Lady. You were right in their faces for all those years and they never thought you a lass."

The old woman placed the strands of hair in the silver cup, then placed the crystal bowl over it. She then reached out taking, Eleanora's hands into her own. She started to incant a spell. Nothing happened for a few seconds, then the room seemed to grow darker. Threads of white smoke started to issue from the silver cup. Soon copious amounts of white smoke poured from the cup. The surface of the bowl became opaque. Sparks of colour started to dance about the surface of the bowl. The sparks of colour coalesced into a kaleidoscope of all the colors of the rainbow that arranged and rearranged themselves over the surface of the bowl. The colours bathed everyone and everything in the hovel. The old woman gazed at the shifting colours, seeing in them what only she could see. Finally the colours faded, the bowl cleared of smoke and the level of light returned to normal.

Releasing Eleanora's hands, the old woman looked up from the bowl and said, "My Lady, you will soon face a great peril and testing. Remember that everything is not always as it seems. Your enemy will show one hand, then strike with the other. One last thing, beware of the treacherous wanderer of false piety. The one that comes under the colors of black and gold over green, white and orange."

Knowing that she would get no clarification on the seeing, Eleanora thanked the seer for her services, then left the hovel with, Sergeant Giffard. On the way back to the palace, Eleanora suggested that they

walk along the docks while she tried to unravel and understand the seers' prediction. She enjoyed watching the activity and colour of the docks. The hulls of most of the merchantmen were black from the coats of pitch used to seal the hull. However, the upper portions of the fore and aft castles were painted in geometric patterns with bright colors. Most of the ships also flew trading house flags at the mast head. One ship flew a blue house flag with three white crescents arranged diagonally. The fore and aft castles were painted with red, white and black. Another ship had a yellow house flag with a red diamond in the centre; the fore and aft castles being painted red, yellow and blue.

Eleanora turned to Sergeant Giffard saying, "Giffard, do you think that what the seer said about, look for black and gold over green, white and orange could be a ship?"

Looking at the ships tied up at the docks, Sergeant Giffard responded, "Yes, Eleanora, I would say that it's a distinct possibility. The black and gold would be the house flag. The green, white and orange would be the fore and aft castles of the ship."

Grabbing Sergeant Giffard by the arm and picking up the pace, Eleanor exclaimed. "We must hurry! I have to find Jimmy right now!"

About three quarters of an hour later they found Jimmy in a small market square four blocks up from the docks. While examining Jimmy's wares, Eleanora carried on a conversation in low voices.

"I have an assignment for you, Jimmy." Eleanora said, "I want you to start watching the docks. Use as many people as you need to. What you are to look for is any ship flying a house flag of black and gold, with the fore and aft castles painted in green, white and orange."

"My Lady, what should I do when I see such a ship?"

Eleanora replied, "I want you to take note of everyone who boards or departs the ship. Find out who they are, where they go and who they see. You will then report this to me."

Eleanora then pointed to a tray of small pastries. Jimmy started to wrap two as he said, "I'll get on it right away, My Lady."

"Good, Eleanora said," As she dug into her purse and withdrew a silver royal, handing it to Jimmy, "now do you require additional funds for this?"

Jimmy, handing the pastries to Eleanora said, "I have enough for now, My Lady. If I require more, I'll come to the palace for it."

Taking the pastries, Eleanora said in a normal voice. "Thank you for the pastries, sir. I'm sure that we will enjoy them." She and Sergeant Giffard then turned and walked away.

CHAPTER 23

The winter solstice arrived and everyone celebrated the midwinter feast. Eleanora enjoyed celebrating with Prince Hugh and his family. She found great pleasure in the gift giving, and playing with the children. She now dreamed of having her own children, hopefully she would have them with Ambrose. She loved and missed him terribly. She didn't know what she would do if they couldn't marry. She didn't even want to think of an alternative.

When all her duties, responsibilities, desires and longings threatened to overwhelm her, Eleanora would seek solitude atop one of the towers overlooking the city of Dunboro and the harbor. Despite the cold winds and occasional snow, she found herself spending more time alone on the towers.

Through the winter season, Eleanora kept busy with her training, and with her intelligence network. By now it had become obvious that the shadowy figure known only as Hammer would not revive his spy network in Dunboro. Having no other options, Eleanora instructed Jimmy to focus most of his efforts on the docks, and around the White Dove brothel. Now she could only wait for something to happen.

Spring arrived. There were still cold nights, but not many near freezing. Leaves were starting to show on the trees and shrubs, and blossoms began to sprout on a few hardy plants. Everyone looked forward to getting out and participating in outdoor activities. Eleanora however, had a foreboding that trouble would soon arrive.

With warmer weather and the seasonal change in the winds, shipping started to pick up. With the arrival of more ships at Dunboro. With the increase in shipping there came an increase in reports of sightings of biremes, triremes and cogs of the Jute Empire offshore from the ships captains. The reports went through the office of the harbour master, to the palace. The news of the sightings of Jute ships off the coast soon came to the attention of Prince Hugh. He needed the services of Mistress Caitlin.

Around the basin stood Mistress Caitlin, Duke Bran, Prince Hugh, Knight Marshal Simon and Lady Eleanora. With everyone ready Mistress Caitlin let two drops of a liquid fall from a vial into the water in the basin. Replacing the vial in a pocket in a fold in her robe, Mistress Caitlin started to incant a spell. First the level of light in the room dimmed. Then a shimmering started on the surface of the water in the basin. Then a glow started within the water to coalesce into an image of everyone in the room standing around the basin holding hands as seen from above. As Mistress Caitlin continued to incant the point of view of the image started to rise up through the roof, until it was on the outside looking down at the roof of the tower. The point of view continued to rise until the whole palace was in view, then the whole city of Dunboro. The view point of the image stopped rising and started to move west, first over land, then out over the sea. As it moved it picked up speed.

Mistress Caitlin continued to incant and the view shifted forward in the direction of travel. Mistress Caitlin continued to move the view west, then north, and then south. Many ships were seen, some were legitimate merchantmen. The rest were Jute biremes, triremes and cogs, many more than would be needed for a scouting mission, and all packed with soldiers. Mistress Caitlin ended the spell, the light returning to the room.

Looking at Mistress Caitlin, Prince Hugh said, "Thank you, Mistress Caitlin, your seeing has been very revealing."

With a nod, Mistress Caitlin replied, "Thank you, Your Highness."

Now addressing everyone in the room, Prince Hugh said, "Gentlemen and ladies it appears that the Jutes are preparing to move a large force south. I will now take comments on this development."

Duke Bran was the first to speak. "Your Highness, it could be that they plan to conduct raids along our coast." Perhaps we should send out an alert, and call up the levies to help defend our coastal communities."

Knight Marshal Simon spoke next, "Your Highness, I agree with Duke Bran. I can put the legion on a war footing. That way I can have it ready to move with just a few hours' notice."

Eleanora had been listening to the exchange, and had questions. After looking and getting a faint nod of support from Mistress Caitlin, Eleanora said, "Your Highness, is this the usual manner that the Jute take when they come to raid?"

Prince Hugh now looking at Eleanora said, "Yes, Lady Eleanora, this is usually the way that they operate, although there seems to be more of them this year. Perhaps they plan more than a single raid at a time." "Or more than just a raid, Your Highness." Eleanora said.

"So, Lady Eleanora," Prince Hugh responded, "you think that the probability of invasion by sea may exist?"

Nodding, Eleanora said. "Yes, Your Highness, I feel that we foiled an invasion attempt last year when we stopped their assassin. Their plans came to naught last year, but I doubt that they would give up after just one try."

Knight Marshal Simon now spoke, "Your Highness, although an invasion by sea is unlikely, due to the massive seaborne logistics involved, it must be considered a possibility."

Prince Hugh then looked at Duke Bran saying, "What say you, Bran?" Looking at Prince Hugh, Duke Bran said, "Your Highness, as much as I doubt a seaborne invasion, we would be remiss in not being prepared for one."

Prince Hugh stood in thought for a couple of minutes, as everyone waited in silence for his decision. Finally, Prince Hugh looked at Knight Marshal Simon saying, "Simon, if there is any equipment maintenance

that needs doing take care of it now. I want the legion on full alert, and ready to march on twelve hours' notice."

With a nod, Knight Marshal Simon replied, "It will be done, Your Highness. I shall give you a daily report on the readiness of the legion." Having given Knight Marshal Simon his orders, Prince Hugh now turned to Duke Bran saying, "Bran, we need to call up the levies from all the shires. Send word to Attleton, Sallasburg, Haffendel and Kientor to muster their levies. Also call up our levies for Dunboro."

Duke Bran responded, "Yes, Your Highness, I'll see to it right away. How about Stone Bridge, do you also want them to call up their levies?"

Shaking his head, Prince Hugh said, "No, not now, Bran. If we need them there will be time to call them up."

Eleanora now said, "Your Highness, my barony has a levy of forty mounted men. They would normally marshal at Sallasburg. I would like for them to marshal here at Dunboro."

"Do you intend to command them yourself, Lady Eleanora?" Prince Hugh inquired with an inquisitive look.

Eleanora responded, "Your Highness, is there any reason why I shouldn't command my own men?"

Everyone present looked on as Prince Hugh answered, "Well, Lady Eleanora, ladies normally delegate command to a knight or other noble. However, if you want to command your men yourself, then that's your right." Prince Hugh then spoke to Duke Bran, "Bran, see that Lady Eleanora's levy reports to the palace here at Dunboro."

Nodding, Duke Bran responded, "Yes, Your Highness."

Prince Hugh looking at everyone said, "Now, if there is nothing else I will adjourn this meeting." As Prince Hugh turned to go, Duke Bran and Knight Marshal Simon bowed while Eleanora and Mistress Caitlin curtsied.

Eleven days later the levy from Eleanora's barony arrived at the palace at Dunboro. The forty mounted men from Hawkers Dale were led by Sergeant Rodney. Eleanora had arranged for Sergeant Giffard to meet them and see to it that they were assigned quarters. Sergeant Giffard then had the men from Hawkers Dale assemble in the bailey.

Eleanora watched as Sergeant Giffard and Sergeant Rodney got the men in formation. For this first meeting with her command she had dressed in cobalt-blue tunic with her blazon on the left breast, black trousers and black boots. She also wore her sword and dagger. When all the men were in formation she approached.

As Eleanora came to a halt in front of him, Sergeant Giffard called out. "Troop attention!"

The troop snapped to attention. Sergeant Giffard, saluting said, "My Lady, your troop is formed."

Eleanora acknowledged Sergeant Giffard's salute saying. "Thank you, Sergeant Giffard. You may take your post."

Sergeant Giffard saluted Eleanora again, and took his place beside Sergeant Rodney to the right side of the first rank.

Eleanora took a quick survey of the men standing before her. There were some young faces, lads her age or a bit younger. There were a few who were over forty, but most were in their twenties or thirties. Most were farmers; Hawkers Dale being known for the fine wines that came from their vineyards. For a moment, Eleanora had doubts that she could lead these men, but was able to suppress the feeling. Sergeant Giffard had instructed her in advance on how to drill men. She on many occasions had observed the soldiers of the palace guard being drilled by their officers, or sergeants. Remembering what Sergeant Giffard had said about a command voice, Eleanora called out, "Parade rest!"

In unison the men assumed the position of parade rest. Eleanora followed up with the command of, "Stand at ease!" The men assumed a slightly more relaxed posture.

Eleanora now spoke in a firm-authoritative voice. "Men of Hawkers Dale, I am, Lady Eleanora a baronet of the court and your liege mistress. Now I know that ladies of the court customary turn over command responsibilities to a male member of the court. However, as your liege mistress it is my right to command, and that I shall do. Now, if any

man has an objection to being commanded by a woman I will hear it now. I do not want that to be a barrier between us."

Eleanora paused to give anyone who wanted to the opportunity to speak up. Sergeant Rodney was about to say something when, Sergeant Giffard whispered to him, "I wouldn't if I were you. Lady, Eleanora doesn't wear a sword and dagger as a fashion statement. She has killed six men with sword and dagger. One of those men was an assassin of the Brotherhood of the Black Rose. She's a terror with a sword or dagger."

With a nod, Sergeant Rodney replied, "Yes, we have heard of our ladies exploits. I just wanted to say that we are all her men. We will follow where ever she leads."

Hearing no objections, Eleanora continued. While here at Dunboro we will train to sharpen our skills in arms and tactics. But first I want to inspect every man's arms and armor, so that we can take care of any problems now. A deficiency in arms or armor makes a man a liability to his comrades. Sergeant Giffard, Sergeant Rodney prepare the men for inspection."

For the next two and a half weeks, Eleanora, with the help of Sergeant Giffard and Sergeant Rodney drilled her troop, molding it into an effective fighting force. At the same time the men grew to trust her judgment and to respect her as their commander. Eleanora also had new tabards of cobalt-blue made for her men. On the left breast they bore her blazon on a knight's shield less the coronet. With the new tabards they were a splendid sight and she was proud of them.

A message arrived from Haffendel, sent three times on three pigeons to ensure delivery. The message was immediately delivered to Prince Hugh. After reading the message, Prince Hugh called a meeting with Duke Bran and Knight Marshal Simon. Eleanora, having been in Knight Marshal Simon's office, came along for the meeting.

When everyone had arrived in Prince Hugh's library, and taken a seat, Prince Hugh held out one of the slips of thin paper that rested on the table in front of him saying, "Gentlemen, Lady Eleanora, this just came from Marquis Morgan of Haffendel. It reports of a landing in force by the Jutes between Haffendel and Kientor. The message further states that the Jutes seem to be setting up a beachhead. I believe this to mean that the invasion had begun."

Everyone nodded agreement, Prince Hugh continued. "Simon, I want your legion to leave at first light tomorrow for Haffendel. I will accompany you with the cavalry overland to Haffendel. I have sent word to the harbor master to commandeer every coastal lugger and sailing barge in the harbor. Your infantry will go by boat down the coast to meet up with you at Haffendel."

Knight Marshal Simon said, "Your Highness, I have much to do. If you have nothing more for me now, may I withdraw to attend to my duties?"

Prince Hugh nodded saying, "Yes, Simon, go along and get things started. We can talk more later on."

Knight Marshal Simon stood, bowed and departed.

Prince Hugh then turned to Duke Bran saying, "Bran, once I'm gone you will have full responsibility for everything in Dunboro. If by chance you need Juliana's council for any reason, she will be ready to assist you. I will get with you at length later before I leave."

Taking his cue, Duke Bran stood saying, "By your leave, Your Highness."

"Granted," Prince Hugh replied.

Duke Bran bowed then left.

Prince Hugh now turned to Eleanora saying, "I'm glad that you came along with Knight Marshal Simon, Lady Eleanora. It saves me some time in sending for you. The first thing I want to know is if you plan to accompany me to Haffendel, or if you plan to remain here in Dunboro for now?"

Eleanora had not yet made that decision, she asked, "Your Highness, do you want me to go with you?"

With a neutral look, so as not to influence her decision, Prince Hugh said, "Lady Eleanora, you have some role to play, as yet unknown. That is why I have given you a free hand to do whatever you think best. With me I shall have my legion, plus the garrisons and levies of both Sallasburg and Haffendel. Your troop of forty men would make little difference one way or the other. You just do what you think that you must do."

Eleanora thought about it for a couple of minutes. Her first impulse was that she should go with her prince. However, there was the question about the colours, most likely a ship that she had been looking for, but not yet found. Finally making her decision, she said, "Your Highness, I shall stay here in Dunboro for now. I can always join you later, if that is what I should do."

Prince Hugh responded, "Good, Lady Eleanora, then you stay here it Dunboro. I'm sure that you will do the right thing when the time comes.

"There is one other thing that I want to speak to you about. I have been keeping an eye on you since you took command of your levy. You have demonstrated a natural ability for leadership. However, there is a common mistake that a lot of new leaders make that you should be aware of. They try to trade on their superior's authority. Now when you give a command, do not say, the prince wants us to do this, or the duke wants us to do that. The order is coming from you, and the person that you are giving the order to must know that it comes from you. You say, I want you to do this, or I want you to do that. Your men must know that you are their commander, and that you expect them to follow your orders."

Eleanora responded, "Thank you, Your Highness, I shall remember that." Prince Hugh then said, "Good, now I have much to do. You may now withdraw, Lady Eleanora."

Without further words, Eleanora stood, curtsied, and left the room.

CHAPTER 24

Four days after Prince Hugh's departure with the legion a ship sailed into the harbor of Dunboro. After taking on a pilot, the ship proceeded to the dock. After tying up to the dock, longshoremen came on board to start offloading cargo.

A bar maid working at the Goat locker Inn noticed the ship as it docked. From the flag staff at the stern flew the flag of Quazee. The fore and aft castles were painted in a geometric pattern of green and orange separated by white. At the top of the fore mast flew the house flag, a golden-yellow wyvern on black. She knew the flag to be of a trading house in the city of Quazee.

The barmaid made an excuse to the inn keeper that she had to visit the privy. On the way to the privy she stopped at the stable to speak to the stable boy. The stable boy left the stable and made contact with a young street lass who worked as the hand off for a cut purse. A few minutes later the lass delivered the information to, Jimmy. Within thirty minutes, Jimmy had agents watching the ship, the White Dove and the sewers.

By mid-afternoon members of the crew started to depart on shore leave. As each one departed they were followed discreetly. One of the men was an older man, gaunt with grey hair and beard. He was dressed as a seaman and carried a small duffle bag. Jimmy's agents followed him to the White Dove where he was seen to enter.

Another person had also seen the ship make port. It was one of the ships whose captain would bring in correspondence, money, or other smuggled goods from the Jutes for Hammer. The meeting would take place at the White Dove brothel as usual.

One and one half hours later agents watching the sewers observed a robust woman of more than average height, with dark-brown hair and dark eyes, enter the White Dove through the trap door into the basement.

Thirty minutes later the same woman left the White Dove, retracing her route through the sewers. She now had with her a man wearing the maroon robe with buff colour cowl and sash of a priest of the order of Geraint (God of Knowledge). They were followed through the sewers to an exit five blocks over from the White Dove; then through the streets of the city to the main gate to the palace.

The agent watched the main gate to the palace until the priest exited the palace through the main gate. Going directly to the docks, he hired a swift river boat for a trip up river.

By the next morning the gaunt seaman with the grey hair and beard had not been observed leaving the White Dove brothel. Putting together the reports from his agents in the streets around the White Dove and his agents in the sewers, Jimmy realized the seaman and the priest were the same man. Jimmy headed to the palace as quickly as he could. This had to be reported to Lady Eleanora right away.

As Eleanora watched Sergeant Giffard and Sergeant Rodney drill her soldiers in the bailey, she observed Jimmy come in through the main gate.

Seeing her in the bailey, Jimmy came over to her and bowing said, "My Lady, we must talk."

Seeing by his expression and demeanor that it was serious, Eleanora said, "Come with me, Jimmy."

Eleanora led Jimmy into the palace, to a room that wasn't in use at the time. Once they were both seated in chairs, Jimmy said, "My Lady, a ship docked yesterday, the ship that we have been looking for."

"Tell me about it!" Eleanora exclaimed.

Jimmy continued, "My Lady, we have been watching everyone leaving the ship. One man with grey hair and beard, and dressed as a seaman, went to the White Dove brothal. We kept watch through the night. No one observed him leaving. Then checking reports from my crew this morning I found that a woman entered the White Dove from the sewer. Then a few minutes later left the same way, escorting a priest of Geraint. I believe that the seaman and the priest are the same man."

Eleanora interrupted saying, "Did your people follow this woman and priest?"

"Yes, My Lady," Jimmy said, "we followed them here, to the main gate of the palace. Later the priest left the palace for the docks, where he hired a swift river boat for a trip up river."

Springing to her feet, Eleanora exclaimed, "Quick, Jimmy, we haven't a moment to lose, come with me!"

Eleanora almost ran to Duke Bran's office, with Jimmy close on her heels. At the duke's office, Jimmy repeated what he had told to Eleanora, to Duke Bran. Duke Bran immediately sent for all the guards that were on duty at the main gate yesterday afternoon.

While they waited for the guards a very distraught man, the keeper of the hawks mew and the pigeon coop, entered the office. Bowing quickly to the duke he exclaimed, "Your Grace, all my pigeons are dead! I went to feed them and they were all dead!"

Duke Bran and Eleanora looked at each other. They didn't ask any questions of each other. They already knew the answers. Eleanora then got the attention of one of Duke Bran's aids and ordered him, "Go to the bailey where my soldiers are drilling and inform Sergeant Giffard and Sergeant Rodney that I need them here immediately."

Bowing the aid said, "Yes, My Lady." He then turned and rushed out of the office.

When all the guards that had been on duty at the main gate yesterday afternoon were present, Jimmy described the priest and woman that they were looking for. Right away one of the guards spoke up, addressing, Duke Bran, "Your Grace, It was Carola who walked the priest through the gate yesterday. She's the Master of Ceremony Bartholomew's maid."

With anger showing on his face, Duke Bran spoke to the corporal that had brought the guards to his office, "Corporal, you will take these men. You will find this maid, Carola, and arrest her. Take her to the cells in the lower level of the old keep, and keep her in isolation. The only ones that are to see her are the prince's interrogators, or the people in this room, no one else."

The Corporal bowed to Duke Bran saying, "Yes, Your Grace." He then turned and left, taking the other guards with him.

Within minutes, Sergeant Giffard and Sergeant Rodney arrived. Seeing them, Eleanora said, "Sergeant Giffard, Sergeant Rodney, get the men ready to move. There's a ship at the docks. Jimmy will show you the ship. I want you to take the men and impound the ship. You will also arrest everyone on board, captain, officers and crew. Bring them here to the palace and confine them in the cells in the old keep. After you seize the ship and arrest everyone, you can turn the ship over to the city watch. If Sheriff Ancel has any questions, have him contact Duke Bran's office."

Bowing, Sergeant Giffard and, Sergeant Rodney said. "Yes, My Lady."

They then turned and left to carry out their orders.

Duke Bran and Eleanora now turned back to the keeper of the hawks mew and the pigeon coop. Duke Bran said, "Now, just what did you find at the pigeon coop?"

"Well, your Grace," The bird keeper said, "I went up to feed the birds. The hawks in the mew were just fine, but all the pigeons were dead. I don't yet know how it was done, but I suspect that they were poisoned."

Eleanora now spoke, "Your Grace, it appears that someone doesn't want us to be able to communicate by messenger pigeon. Something is happening and I don't know what it is. But one thing I do know, we don't have the luxury of time. I believe that Prince Hugh should know of this as soon as possible. We need to send fast riders south to Salasbury with messages to be sent by pigeon to Haffendel."

Nodding, Duke Bran said, "I agree, Lady Eleanora. I will compose the messages then send them by riders to Sallasburg. Let's say four riders, each with a remount so that they can make better time."

Eleanora nodded agreement.

Eleanora arrived at the cell block in the lower level of the old keep. The jailer and a squad of palace guards were there to meet her. Eleanora asked the jailer, "Where is she?"

The jailer pointed to a cell door saying, "She's in there, My Lady." Eleanora responded, "Open the door."

The jailer nodded, taking a ring of keys from his belt. Inserting the key into the lock, he turned it and swung the door open wide. The woman had been sitting in the dark cell and stood as the door opened, blinking at the light.

Eleanora stood at the door watching her. The woman looked to be in her late twenties, with a youthful but otherwise unremarkable face. She was robust without being overweight. Her height equal to that of an average man, with large breast and wide hips; the sort of woman that some men lust for. Eleanora could see the look of confusion and fright. Eleanora took a couple of minutes to try to gain some insight into this woman's character; and how best to quickly break her down.

A soldier stepped into the cell and placed a torch in a sconce, on the wall next to the door. In the light, Eleanora could see that the woman was manacled to the wall. There was enough chain to allow her to lay down on a pallet, or use the slop bucket, but not to reach the door. Eleanora said, "Carola, I've been looking for you for a long time. Now, I have questions, and you have the answers. Listen to me, I will not be gentle with you. I will ask a question. If you don't give me an answer, unpleasant things will happen to you."

With a look of defiance, Carola said, "What are you going to do, have the guards beat me?"

With a hard look, Eleanora replied, "Try me and find out. Now first question, who is, Hammer?"

As an answer, Carola spat at Eleanora.

Wiping the spit from the sleeve of her tunic with a handkerchief, Eleanora said to the guards, "Remove her clothes, and strip her nude."

Carola recoiled in shock as four guards entered the cell and grabbed her. She struggled, fought and screamed like a banshee to no avail. When the soldiers had finished, Carola lay sobbing on the floor in a foetal position, trying to cover her nakedness.

"Get to your feet and look at me, woman!" Eleanora exclaimed in a forceful voice.

Carola continued to lay on the floor weeping.

"Get to your feet, woman!" Eleanora exclaimed again forcefully.

When Carola still didn't respond to her commands, Eleanora, indicating two soldiers, said, "You two, grab her by the wrist and get her to her feet."

The two soldiers responded, grabbing Carola by the wrist and jerking her to her feet. They continued to hold her by the wrist with her arms raised high over her head, so that she was helpless. Her face now registered shock and hatred.

Eleanora looked into Carola's face with an expression devoid of warmth or compassion saying, "Listen to me, woman! You think that you are inconvenienced now, just continue to try my patience! Now, who is, Hammer?"

Eleanora now stood too far back for Carola to spit on her. Instead, Carola just glared at Eleanora and uttered, "Bitch!"

Looking at Carola with absolute seriousness, Eleanora said, "Woman, I will ask you the question once more! If you do not answer me, I will have the guards throw you into the cell with the men! I'm sure that they would love to act out their cardinal fantasies on your body, all nineteen of them!"

"You wouldn't dare!" Carola blurted out with a startled look on her face.

"Now, woman," Eleanora said with deliberate firmness in her voice, "who is, Hammer?"

Eleanora waited for close to a minute for an answer, but one was not forthcoming. Finally she said, "Guards, throw her in with the men!"

Carola shrieked in dread, "No! No, you can't!"

Without words the guards grabbed her by the upper arms. The jailer took the key to unlock her fetter. Eleanora replied, "Yes I can do this, and I'm going to!"

"No!" Carola sobbed as the guards started to drag her struggling from the cell.

The jailer started to unlock the door to the men's cell. Carola tried to dig in her heals, but it was a futile effort. Screaming, she cried out, "No, please don't do it! No! No!"

The jailer threw the cell door open. Carola could see the men in the cell leering at her. She pleaded, "Please don't put me in there! Please, no!"

They had her at the door. Eleanora could see the look of stark horror on her face. Carola grabbed the door frame with a death grip and screeched, "No, please don't!"

The guards started to pry her fingers from the door frame. She was near hysterical. As they were about to shove her through the door, she cried out, "Bartholomew!"

Eleanora signalled a halt. She thought for a moment then said with firmness, "Are you saying that the Master of Ceremonies Bartholomew is, Hammer?"

Carola seemed to visibily wilt. Eleanora now knew that she had broken Carola's spirit. Carola nodded saying, "Yes, Master of Ceremonies Bartholomew is, Hammer."

"The priest that you brought through the gate yesterday." Eleanora said, "Who was he?"

Still looking at the leering faces of the male prisoners in the cell, Carola answered, "He was no priest. He was, Emperor Eimion's sorcerer."

By now everyone present was amazed at hearing of a traitor in the court. Eleanora asked another question of Carola, "Who is Lord North?"

Carola answered, "Lord North is Emperor Eimion"

Eleanora now had what she needed. She said to the jailer, "You can put her back in her cell, and let her have her clothes back. I'm sure that the prince's inquisitors will want to see her later."

The jailer bowed saying, "Yes, My Lady."

She then turned to the soldiers. Indicating two of them she said, "You two men, go to the main and postern gates. Tell the guards there that under no circumstance is Master of Ceremonies Bartholomew to leave the palace."

The two guards saluted saying, "Yes, My Lady." They then left to carry out their orders.

Eleanora then indicated two other guards saying, "You two men, come with me." She then left the cell block, with the two guards close behind.

After a few enquiries, Eleanora found Master of Ceremonies Bartholomew in the great hall, where he had just finished instructing some of his pages. Eleanora approached him with her two guards behind her. When she came to about five paces from Bartholomew she halted. After regarding him for a moment she said, "Master of Ceremonies Bartholomew, or should I call you by your other title of traitor."

Bartholomew's hand went for the hilt of his sword, but before he could draw it, Eleanora already had hers out, she said to him, "Carola has already told us everything. I am placing you under arrest for treason."

Bartholomew said in defiance, "You haven't the authority to arrest me." Eleanora responded, "I do have the authority and you have a choice. Submit and come with us, or draw your sword and I kill you."

Bartholomew seemed to weigh his options, then his hand dropped from his sword hilt to his side. As much as he would like to fight it out rather than surrender, he knew that he had to. If he drew his sword against Lady Eleanora he would be lucky to draw a last breath before he was dead. Eleanora said to her guards, "Disarm him, bind him and take him to the cells in the lower level of the old keep. Tell the jailer to keep him in isolation."

Moving forward the guards replied. "Yes, My Lady."

Duke Bran, Princess Juliana, Mistress Caitlin and Eleanora stood around the basin. Mistress Caitlin let two drops of liquid fall into the basin. After putting the vial back in a pocket in a fold in her robe, she started to incant the spell. The light in the room dimmed and the water in the basin started to glow from within. As, Mistress Caitlin continued to incant an image begin to appear. The point of view of the image rose until it was above the roof of the tower. The point of view continued to rise until the palace and a good part of the city of Dunboro was in view.

The view started to move north, up the Aber River. The image picked up speed, covering most of the distance to Stone Bridge in a few minutes. Mistress Caitlin incanted and the image slowed so that they could see what moved on the river. A few miles north of Stone Bridge, just below the first rapids they spotted a swift river boat tied up to the bank of the river. A few miles further on a man dressed as a priest of Geraint was seen moving north toward the fortress of Questers Pass.

Eleanora said, "Mistress Caitlin, keep following the river north." Mistress Caitlin continued to incant. The image began to move faster again. The image continued on past the fortress of Questers Pass. Then through the pass to a plain north of the pass. That was where they saw the tents, thousands of tents on the plain. Around the tents were more men than they could count. There were also many wagon parks.

The image faded and the light came back to the room. Duke Bran said, "An army marshals on the plain north of the pass. They plan an invasion."

Eleanora said, "Your Grace, Prince Hugh is in the wrong place. We need to send more riders with an updated message."

"I agree, Lady Eleanora," Duke Bran responded, "I'll send more riders right away."

Eleanora, after seeing the army gathered on the plain to be thrown against the kingdom knew what she must do. Looking at Duke Bran, she said, "Your Grace, I must go to the fortress at Questers Pass. I will take my men and Sergeant Rodney. I also want Sergeant Giffard and one hundred men from the palace guards."

Duke Bran, aware of the document that Eleanora carried would give her the soldiers. However, he wasn't so sure that she should go. "Lady Eleanora," Duke Bran said, "I will send reinforcements to Questers Pass, but do you have to go? I can send a knight or two with the reinforcements."

Eleanora regarded Duke Bran with a resolute look saying, "Your Grace, I cannot explain it, but I know that my destiny awaits me at Questers Pass. Whatever that destiny is, I cannot avoid it. Can you have the men in the bailey ready to ride in four hours?"

"Yes, Lady Eleanora," Duke Bran said, "they will be ready."

"Thank you, Your Grace," Eleanora said, "and I don't want baggage wagons, they are too slow. Have what we need loaded on pack mules. Also, when I get to Stone Bridge I will have Earl Gerard send word to Attleton and Duman Ford of the invasion, and to send soldiers to Stone Bridge."

"That's good, Lady Eleanora," Duke Bran said nodding, "they can wait there and join with Prince Hugh when he arrives there. You can also ask Earl Gerard to send us some of his pigeons, so that we can send him a message when Prince Hugh arrives here in Dunboro.

"I'll go now and arrange for the soldiers that will accompany you." Without waiting for the usual formalities, Duke Bran turned and left the room.

When Duke Bran had left, Mistress Caitlin turned to Eleanora saying, "I heard of your unorthodox interrogation of the prisoner, Carola."

Looking at Mistress Caitlin, Eleanora said, "Mistress Caitlin, Carola is a prideful and arrogant woman with an inflated ego. She imagined herself as better than those around her. She was ready to endure torture and pain. When it became too much for her to withstand she was prepared to lie. I had no time to let her play out her drama as a martyr. I had to get the upper hand quickly. By striping her naked I took away her dignity and made her feel completely helpless and vulnerable. I then exercised complete dominance over her. Finally I debased and humiliated her, even taking away her control of her own body. I crushed her spirit and bent her to my will."

Princess Juliana had been listening to Eleanora's account of her handling of the traitor, Carola. She now asked, "Lady Eleanora, would you have really given her to the male prisoners?"

"Well, Your Highness," Eleanora, with a little smirk replied, "the ultimate fantasy for most men is to be set upon by a group of women raging with sexual passions. To be set upon by a mob of men in the throes of sexual passion is hardly a woman's fantasy. I don't know of any woman that would like to be set upon by a gang of men who would use her for their own sexual gratification. I just let her own imagination work against her."

With a chuckle, Princess Juliana said. "Well, Lady Eleanora, it seems a terrible thing to put any woman through, but it worked." turning serious, Princess Juliana continued, "I feel that you will be going in harm's way. I and my children have come to cherish and love you, and would truly miss you if something were to happen to you."

With glistening eyes, Eleanora embraced Princess Juliana and Mistress Caitlin. Then turning for the door said, "I must go now."

CHAPTER 25

By late afternoon all one-hundred forty soldiers of Eleanora's force were mounted and ready to depart. At a command the mounted soldiers, riding two abreast, passed through the postern gate. In the lead on a grey warhorse rode Eleanora in full armour with weapons and shield. Beside her rode Sergeant Giffard who carried her personal standard. Behind her rode her men from Hawkers Dale. Behind them rode the soldiers of the Dunboro palace guard, and the baggage train. The citizenry seeing a large body of mounted soldiers, led by an officer of the court, hastened to clear the way.

They were soon out of the city riding north on the road to Stone Bridge. For the first thirty miles the road paralleled the river. The road then took a more direct route to Stone Bridge. Eleanora kept the column moving through the night, maintaining an arduous pace. At midnight they stopped to let the horses rest. In less than four hours they were on the march again.

Through the rest of the night then through the day and the next night they kept moving. They stopped only to rest and feed the horses from a store of grain carried on the pack mules. The men ate in the saddle and got what rest that they could in the saddle. After almost two days on the road they arrived at the main gate of the Palace of Stone Bridge.

The guard at the gate observed the approaching company of soldiers and noticed that most of the soldiers wore the tabards of the Dunboro palace guard. They were being led by a young noble. As they drew near the guard called out, "Who approaches!"

Sergeant Giffard, who rode beside Eleanora and carried her personal standard responded, "The Lady Eleanora baronet of the court of Dunboro and company."

The guard took a closer look at whom at first he thought a knight. On the surcoat wasn't a knight's shield blazon, but a woman's lozenge with baronet coronet. The guard came to attention and saluted saying, "You may pass, My Lady."

Eleanora dismounted at the gate, handing the reins of her horse to one of her men to take to the stable. She then turned to the guard saying, "I must see Earl Gerard immediately."

The guard called the corporal of the guard, who detailed another guard to escort her to Earl Gerard. Entering Earl Gerard's study, Eleanora bowed saying, "My lord."

Earl Gerard couldn't help but to notice that Lady Eleanora was in full battle dress. He replied, "Lady Eleanora, what a surprise to see you. What brings you to Stone Bridge?"

Having decided it best that she immediately establish her authority, Eleanora withdrew the parchment from its case and handed it to Earl Gerard saying, "My Lord, if you would please read this."

Taking the document from her, Earl Gerard began to read. As he read the document his expression changed from that of a pleasant smile to a look of serious contemplation. He knew that Lady Eleanora would not have shown him this document if the circumstance were not so grave. Handing the document back to her, Earl Gerard said, "How may I be of help to you, Lady Eleanora?"

"My lord," Eleanora said, "before I make my request, let me tell you what is happening. Prince Hugh is in Haffendel to oppose a Jute landing between Haffendel and Kientor. A few days ago a ship docked at Dunboro. A sailor from this ship entered a brothel in Dunboro. He later slipped out dressed as a priest of Geraint. He was escorted through the main gate of the palace by one of the maids from the palace. He

spent little more than an hour in the palace, then went to the docks and boarded a swift river boat for a trip up river. The boat took him as far as the first rapids. From there he went by foot to Questers Pass.

"Soon after he left, all the pigeons in the palace coop died. Later, Mistress Caitlin using her seeing basin found the boat just below the first rapids. We then found him moving on foot towards Questers Pass. Mistress Caitlin continued the seeing through Questers Pass. North of the pass stands an army on the plain. We saw thousands of tents, too many men to count and several wagon parks. My lord, that army stands ready for invasion. One last thing, the false priest is Emperor Eimion's sorcerer."

By now, Earl Gerard's face was ashen. He said, "This is most disturbing, Lady Eleanora, what do you need?"

"First thing, my lord," Eleanora said, "you need to call up all your levies.

I also want you to send messages to Attleton and Duman Ford to call up their levies, and to send every man that they can to Stone Bridge. They can wait here for the arrival of Prince Hugh. Also instruct Duman Ford to inform the king of the coming invasion."

"I'll take care of that right away, Lady Eleanora." Earl Gerard said. Eleanora continued. "I also need fresh mounts for my men. I also need as many men as you can spare to be in the saddle and ready to go in four hours." Earl Gerard pondered the request for almost two minutes before he answered. "Lady Eleanora," Earl Gerard said, "I can give you seventy-five men to include one sergeant and two corporals."

"Thank you, My Lord," Eleanora said, "I have one last request. Do you have pigeons that are trained to fly back here to Stone Bridge? I need some to take with me to Questers Pass, and you need to send pigeons to Dunboro. As many as you can spare."

"I'll see to it that you have as many pigeons as you need, Lady Eleanora." Earl Gerard said.

"Thank you, My Lord." Eleanora said, "Now, if you will excuse me, I have to see to my men."

Eleanora was about to turn to leave when Earl Gerard put a restraining hand on her arm saying, "Lady Eleanora, you are exhausted. I will see that everything is taken care of, while you and your men get some rest."

Pointing to a divan next to the wall, Earl Gerard said, "Why don't you lie down and rest for a while. I will wake you."

Allowing Earl Gerard to lead her over to the divan, Eleanora said, "Thank you, My Lord. Please awaken me in two hours." She lay on the divan and closed her eyes.

Someone touched her shoulder and her eyes came open. Earl Gerard and Countess Natalia were standing beside her. Eleanora said, "I feel as if I just closed my eyes a moment ago."

"You have been sleeping for three hours." Countess Natalia said.

Sitting up, then getting to her feet, Eleanora said, "I need to see to my men. There's a lot to be done."

Putting a hand on her shoulder, Earl Gerard said, "Don't worry about a thing, Lady Eleanora. My men have already taken care of everything. Your men are ready to march. My cooks have made a fine stew, and are feeding your men now."

Before anyone could say anything else a knock came at the door. Earl Gerard called out, "Enter."

The door swung wide and a servant entered bearing a tray with a large bowl of stew and a loaf of fresh bread. The servant placed the tray on the table, bowed to Earl Gerard, then turned and left the room. Earl Gerard then directed Eleanora to sit at the table and eat. As Eleanora started on the stew, Earl Gerard poured her a glass of wine from a decanter. As Eleanora ate, Countess Natalia sat at the table to keep her company. With the first spoon full of stew, Eleanora realised how hungry she was; not having taken much time on the march up from Dunboro to eat.

When she had finished her meal, Earl Gerard and Countess Natalia went with her to the bailey.

A few minutes later, Eleanora rode out the gate of Stone Bridge at the head of her company that now numbered two-hundred fifteen men. She also had four corporals and three sergeants. A fine company of reinforcements for Baron Clerebola of Questers Pass.

With fresh mounts, and the men having been able to get some rest, Eleanora was able to set a fast pace. She planned to push on through the night, stopping only to rest the horses. She intended to be at the fortress at Questers Pass before sundown the next day. Eleanora kept the column marching through the night. Then at about three in the morning they encountered three riders headed south to Stone Bridge. Eleanora's point riders soon found out that they were soldiers from Questers Pass. They were taken to Eleanora who said, "I am, Lady Eleanora baronet of the court of Dunboro. Who among you is the senior?"

One of the men stepped forward saying. "I am, My Lady, I'm Douglas." Eleanora then asked, "What is so urgent that you must ride through the night?"

Douglas would also have liked to ask Eleanora the same question, but felt it prudent not to, he said, "My Lady, there has been treachery and foul murder at Questers Pass."

On a hunch, Eleanora asked, "Did it by chance have something to do with a priest of Geraint?"

With an expression of surprise, Douglas responded, "How did you know of that, My Lady?"

Eleanora replied, "We have been after him since he worked his mischief at Dunboro. Now you said something about murder, tell me about it."

"Well, My Lady," Douglas said, "this priest came to Questers Pass. We showed him the hospitality that we would show anyone of the clergy. This false priest was very cordial, visiting with many of the men in the fortress, giving them the blessing of Geraint. We invited him to stay for a while, but he declined, stating pressing business elsewhere.

"The next morning, Baron Clerebola was found dead in his bed, also all of his knights and all but two sergeants and one corporal. Sergeant

Eric, being on patrol in the pass and Sergeant Giles with Corporal Amos in town, procuring supplies for the fortress. There were also twenty-seven soldiers found dead."

"How did this happen, Douglas?" Eleanora asked.

Douglas said, "My Lady, this false priest managed to poison the wine cask in the officer's mess, and the ale cask in the soldiers mess. We were fortunate that the ale cask was almost empty and that we had to tap another cask, or we all may have died."

"What about your pigeons?" Eleanora asked.

"Dead also, My Lady." Douglas said, "He got to them too."

Eleanora thought for about a minute, then looked at Sergeant Giffard who gave her an encouraging smile. She then turned back to Douglas, having made up her mind saying, "Douglas, you will return with me to Questers Pass. Your two companions will continue to Stone Bridge and report to Earl Gerard on the developments at Questers Pass. I will also pin a message to Earl Gerard that I have taken command at Questers Pass. And that I intend to block the pass against the invading army until Prince Hugh arrives."

Douglas looked at Eleanora aghast and blurted out. "But, My Lady, you can't command at Questers Pass!"

Eleanora was about to reply when, Sergeant Giffard cut in saying, "Let me tell you, Douglas, that, Lady Eleanora is not high born. She holds her rank in her own right, having earned it on her own. Do not let her gender, tender years, or pretty face fool you. She is as hard as a new forged sword, and just as deadly. I know of six men that she has killed by sword or dagger. One of these men was an assassin of the Brotherhood of the Black Rose."

"No kidding," Douglas said, "the Black Rose. How did she do it?"

With a little chuckle, Sergeant Giffard said, "The assassin died screaming with a dagger buried to the hilt in his groin."

Douglas had to resist the urge to put his hand to his groin to protect his private parts, as he said. "Please forgive my outburst, My Lady. It is not my place to question your right to command."

"Thank you, Douglas," Eleanora said, "I accept your apology."

After penning a letter to Earl Gerard, Eleanora sent the other two riders on their way. She then gave the command to resume the march.

They continued on through the night and into a dawn of a new day. They kept on moving, stopping only to feed and rest the horses. They ate cold rations in the saddle when hungry. They even dozed in the saddle when fatigue overcame them. Finally in late afternoon as the sun started to drop towards the western horizon, they rode through Questers Pass Village. Thirty minutes later they approached the main gate of the fortress.

As they approached a guard from atop the gate called out, "Halt! Who goes there?"

Sergeant Giffard called a halt. Then Eleanora rode a few paces forward and responded. "I am Lady Eleanora, baronet of the court of Dunboro. I am here to take command of this garrison."

The gate swung open and Eleanora rode through the gate at the head of her company into the bailey. Looking about, Eleanora could see soldiers on guard on the walls. Other soldiers and civilians were engaged in other duties. As she dismounted she noticed a sergeant approaching. Eleanora quickly asked, Douglas, "Who is that?"

"That's Sergeant Eric, My Lady." Douglas replied.

As Sergeant Eric came up to Eleanora she said, "Good afternoon, Sergeant Eric. I am Lady Eleanora, baronet of the court of Dunboro."

Saluting, Sergeant Eric said, "Welcome to Questers Pass, My Lady." Eleanora continued, "Sergeant Eric, as that Baron Clerebola and his command staff is dead, I am taking command of Questers Pass immediately." With an astonished look, Sergeant Eric exclaimed, "But you can't, My

Lady, You're just a lass!"

Eleanora responded, "Sergeant Eric, my age or gender is of no consideration in this. I have the rank and it is my right. We will settle this now, for I am taking command."

"But, My Lady," Sergeant Eric said, still not willing to let it pass, "this is most irregular. Questers Pass is no command for a woman."

Seeing that she was getting nowhere with Sergeant Eric, Eleanora pulled the document from its case and handed it to him saying, "Read this document, Sergeant Eric."

Sergeant Eric took the document and started to read. As he read his eyes grew wider. From the time that it took, Eleanora figured that he must have read it two to three times. Finally, Sergeant Eric looked up from the document and said, "My Lady, as you act in the name of the king, I will not dispute your right to command."

Sergeant Eric handed the document back to Eleanora. Taking the document, Eleanora said, "Sergeant Eric, of you and Sergeant Giles, who is senior?"

Sergeant Eric responded, "I am, My Lady, by two years." Eleanora then called out, "Sergeant Giffard, please join us." Sergeant Giffard responded, "Yes, My Lady."

When Sergeant Giffard had joined her and Sergeant Eric, Eleanora said, "Gentlemen, we must immediately revive the command structure, Sergeant Giffard, Sergeant Eric."

They both responded in unison, "Yes, My Lady."

"Gentlemen," Eleanora said, "from this moment on you are elevated to the rank of knight. Congratulations, Sir Giffard, Sir Eric."

After a momentary shock, they each said, "Thank you, My Lady." Eleanora said, "Prince Hugh will make it formal later on. Right now we

have other things to worry about. An army marshals on the plain north of the pass, set for invasion. Our duty is to block the pass from invasion until Prince Hugh can get here with his army. Now when the time comes we will defend these walls, to the end if necessary. However, the commander who sits safe behind his defenses has already lost the battle.

"Sir Eric, I want lines of archers as far up the pass as you can get them. Engage the enemies' point elements, slow them down, and make them deploy their infantry. Kill as many as you can, but do not

become decisively engaged. As soon as they get close, fall back past the next line of archers."

"I'll see to that right away, My Lady." Sir Eric said.

Eleanora continued, "Sir Eric, you will be my second in command, and command the soldiers of Questers Pass. Promote men to replace the sergeants and corporals that were lost."

Sir Eric said, "I'll take care of that right away, My Lady."

Eleanora now spoke to, Sir Giffard, "Sir Giffard, you will command the soldiers from Dunboro and Stone Bridge. You will also act as my adviser. Our men have just completed a gruelling forced march. Get them settled in and let them have a few hours rest. Then we shall make plans."

CHAPTER 26

The sun had been up for two hours when the soldiers spotted the lone figure dressed in the robes of a priest of Geraint walking around a bend in the trail. They immediately started to tack up the horses. By the time the soldiers had the horse ready the priest had drawn near. The soldier in command of the four man detachment called out. "Hello, Master Arfon, we have been waiting for you."

Walking up to the soldiers, Master Afron said, "Am I glad to see you. I have not walked so far in years. Even my blisters have blisters."

The soldiers laughed, then their leader said, "Then don't you worry, Master Afron. We have an extra horse for you. You can let him do the rest of the walking."

Another soldier brought a horse up to Master Afron. Taking the reins, Master Afron mounted. When everyone had mounted, they set off up the trail. The detachment commander and Master Afron in the lead, with the other three men bringing up the rear.

Shortly after the noon hour, Master Afron rode up to the emperor's pavilion, in the middle of the main camp. Dismounting and handing the reins of his horse to a groom, Master Afron rushed into the pavilion. Inside he found Emperor Eimion conferring with Lord Marshal Rhodri. When he saw his sorcerer enter the pavilion, Emperor Eimion said, "Master Afron, how went your mission?"

Bowing to the Emperor, Master Afron said, "Your Majesty, the mission went just as we had planned. Prince Hugh is at Haffendel. The palace at Dunboro has no direct contact, except by riders. And last, the fortress at Questers Pass has been dealt with as planned. The way through Questers Pass is now open."

Emperor Eimion shouted with glee, "At last! At long last! Lord Marshal Rhodri, sound the horns and beat the battle drums, we march!"

After a few hours' sleep, Eleanora felt refreshed, but still sore from the forced march from Dunboro to Questers Pass. After a quick meal, Eleanora called a meeting with her officers, to include all sergeants and corporals not on urgent duties. Sir Eric and Sir Giffard had done a good job of reviving the command structure.

Eleanora had been thinking of the defense of Questers Pass. The terrain favored them. Where the Aber River exited the pass a rise in the land to the east forced the river to flow up against a near vertical cliff that formed the western edge of the pass. At this point the trail had to cross over the river on a wooden bridge. Questers Pass fortress stood on the high ground to the east, with the river bank and bridge within range of a battery of three trebuchets in the fortress bailey. There was no way that the enemy could break out of the pass onto the open plain without first taking the fortress.

Before beginning, Eleanora took a good look at these men whom she would have to depend upon and lead if she were going to hold the pass against the invaders until, Prince Hugh could get here with his army. They were all older men, most at least twice her age. They were all rugged men used to the rigours and hardships of a soldier's life. They were bold and courageous men, and would expect the same from their leader. She had to suppress any doubts that she could lead such men. She knew that as a young woman she must not show any uncertainty or weakness before these men. If she did she would certainly lose control.

Opening the meeting she asked, "Sir Eric, what has been done so far to prepare the garrison for attack?"

Sir Eric said, "My Lady, about an hour after your arrival I dispatched two groups of skirmishers. They will set up skirmish lines to engage and slow the enemy down. Falling back one behind the other, giving ground as slowly as they can."

"The bridge across the river," Eleanor asked, "what's the plan for it?"

Sir Eric responded. "My Lady, as soon as the last skirmisher is back across, we burn the bridge. I have men making it ready now to be fired."

Eleanora turned to Sir Giffard, "Sir Giffard, how is the integration of our two forces going?"

Sir Giffard answered, "It is going well, My Lady, Sir Eric will command the north and east walls. I will command the south and west walls. With the men that we brought with us from Dunboro and Stone Bridge, we will be able to keep one third of the garrison in reserve."

"That's good, Sir Giffard." Eleanora said, "Now what about the villagers, will any of them take refuge with us?"

Sir Eric answered, "My Lady, every person in the village with a wagon or cart is hauling stores for our soldiers, or stones for our war engines. The stones are being piled up in the bailey for use. As for arrows, we have so many that we have bundles stacked like shocks of grain everywhere in the fortress that we have room. When the enemy arrives some of the villagers will take refuge here in the fortress. The rest will flee south to Stone Bridge." The rest of the meeting dealt with command control and logistics.

Eleanora could see that she had good men to work with.

Corporal Lyam could now hear the sounds of approaching troops from up the trail. One look told him that he didn't have to give any commands, as his bowmen were starting to nock their arrows. An army on the move being a very noisy creature, could be heard over the noise of the river. His men were alert now, concealed amongst the rocks and brush of the pass, ready to draw bows and let arrows fly.

One hundred-fifty yards up the pass two men appeared from around a turn in the trail. They were Jute light infantry, wearing round steel helms with nose guard, leather gambeson armor and carrying a round wooden shield with iron boss in the centre. They were armed with an eight-foot long thrusting spear and short sword with twenty-six-inch blade. They advanced about twenty to twenty-five yards when three more light infantrymen came around the turn in the trail. They were the point for the enemy column.

When the point guard came to within sixty yards of their position, Corporal Lyam gave the signal and the arrows flew. The enemy point guard, to a man, fell each with at least two arrows in him. The enemy point guard had been taken completely by surprise.

About three minutes later twelve more light infantrymen came around the turn in the trail in loose formation. Seeing their point guard lying on the ground bristling with arrows, they stopped then brought up their shields, moving into a line formation. Two of the men turned and ran back up the tail.

Even at over a hundred yards the line of infantry was still within easy range of the longbows. Corporal Lyam gave the order and the whole line of archers started shooting at the line of infantry. Under the barrage of arrows the Jute infantry withdrew. There were no more fatalities, but many received wounds in arms and legs.

More than ten minutes went by before, Corporal Lyam and his men saw the enemy again. The enemy light infantry quickly formed up into a phalanx of twenty men across and six men deep. With shields locked, and the front rank sprouting with spear points, the phalanx started to move forward.

Corporal Lyam watched the phalanx move forward, withholding the fire of his archers until the phalanx had closed to sixty yards. He then gave the signal to shoot. All the bowmen shot their first arrow in volley, forty arrows striking the front ranks all at once. The initial volley took down seven men in the front rank and four from the second rank, killing three. After faltering for a moment, the phalanx continued on.

The bowmen now started to engage their targets individualy, taking careful aim. More soldiers in the phalanx started to drop, most now with fatal wounds. The phalanx manage to get as close as twenty-five yards from the archers before, Corporal Lyam gave the order to withdraw. The line of archers broke and ran. In the short time that they had been engaged, the archers of Questers Pass had killed or wounded fifty-one Jute invaders.

Corporal Lyam knew that they had been successful so far because the enemy had not been expecting them, and had not shown them respect. He also knew that the next attack would be with a large enough force to overwhelm them. The next time they would not come with just infantry. They would also have support from archers. He would hold as long as he could, breaking contact before the enemy was upon them, taking to their horses. A quarter-mile back the other group stood ready to trigger a rock slide to block the tail as soon as his group was clear.

Eleanora had been conducting an inspection of the fortress. Atop the towers that stood above the walls at regular intervals were mangonels and onagers for hurling stones at on coming attackers. Along the walls at regular intervals were ballistas that shot a large arrow that could pass right through two or three men. She also inspected the kitchen, stores and other common areas. The inspection served two purposes, to ensure that all was ready for the coming battle, and to get to know the men that she now commanded.

As busy as she kept, she could not keep from thinking of Prince Ambrose. He had become the centre of her being. She longed to feel the comfort of his arms around her again, and his warm lips pressed against hers. She had removed the ring that he had given her from her finger. She now had it suspended safely between her breasts next to her heart, by a leather thong. If she survived the coming battle, she would again wear the ring on her finger.

The sun stood low to the western horizon. Long shadows stretched forth over the land. Eleanora stood atop the wall above the main gate with, Sir Giffard discussing their plan for defense of the fortress. A shout from one of the soldiers on the wall drew their attention. "Rider approaching!"

Eleanora and Sir Giffard, along with everyone else on the wall looked to see a rider cantering down the trail towards the bridge. By the time the rider came through the main gate, Eleanora, Sir Giffard and Sir Eric were waiting for him. The soldier pulled up in front of them, dismounted, and reporting to Eleanora said, "My Lady, we have made contact with the enemy, about twenty miles up the pass. Our ambush slowed them down for over a half an hour. We then withdrew, the group behind us causing a rock slide that should slow them down for two to three hours."

Looking at Sir Giffard and Sir Eric, Eleanora said, "Well, Gentlemen, it has started. Sir Eric, we need to alert Earl Gerard of Stone Bridge to the invasion."

"I'll send the message out right away, My Lady." Sir Eric said, "I believe that two pigeons should be enough."

Turning back to the messenger, Eleanora asked, "How did the ambush go?"

Smiling the soldier replied, "It was beautiful, My Lady. Their point walked right into our ambush unawares. Before they even knew what was happening they were pin cushions. It took them a while to get organised and push us out of our position. I don't think they were expecting any resistance." Speaking to Sir Giffard and Sir Eric, Eleanora said, "What do you think,

Gentlemen, how much can we slow them down?"

Sir Eric answered, "My Lady, they were about twenty miles up the pass from here. Now they will make changes in the lead elements of their force, more archers and engineers. They will now take less time to overcome our ambushes. However, they will still move slower, not knowing where they will encounter the next ambush. They will need the engineers to clear the rock slides. If we are lucky it will take the enemy two days to get here. If we are really lucky, two and a half days."

Eleanora now turned back to the soldier saying, "Thank you for the report. Now go to the kitchen for something to eat, then refresh yourself before returning back to your unit."

Saluting, the soldier said, "Thank you, My Lady." He then led his horse away toward the kitchen.

Eleanora watched him go for a moment, then turned back to Sir Giffard and, Sir Eric saying, "Well, Gentlemn, there's no doubt now that we are being invaded. It's time to get everyone who will be staying with us into the fortress. We can continue to bring stone into the fortress until just before the arrival of the leading Jute elements."

"Yes, My Lady." Sir Eric and Sir Giffard replied.

Emperor Eimion paced beside the trail in a rage. So far the invasion had not been going as planned. "Damn it," he swore, "more delays!"

Lord Marshal Rhodri and Master Afron stood close by in attendance, wishing that they could be elsewhere, or invisible in some way. Especially Master Afron, who had given assurance that the invasion through Questers Pass would meet with little resistance.

With a bitter glare, Emperor Eimion pointed an accusing finger at his sorcerer, Master Afron saying, "You, Master Afron, I am very displeased with you! You assured me that you had dealt the garrison at Questers Pass a fatal blow! You said that there would be so few survivors that they could not hold the pass! That there wouldn't be enough time to ride to Stone Bridge for help! You said that the invasion would be like a walk in the park!"

Master Afron started to respond. "Your Majesty, I don't understand how they recovered so quickly."

With a wave of the hand, Emperor Eimion cut him off saying, "I gave the order for my army to move on your assurance that the pass would be open! Now that I have committed the army, I can't recall it! Either we are victorious, or I am finished as emperor! Then there will be civil war to install a new emperor! Believe me, if in the end I must fall on my sword, I will not be the only one to die!"

Emperor Eimion now addressed Lord Marshall Rhodri. "My Lord Marshal, since we made contact with the enemy one and a half days ago, we have been measuring our advance in yards, not miles! We should have been past Questers Pass fortress hours ago, on the march to Stone Bridge! We have to move faster!"

"But Your Majesty," Lord Marshal Rhodri responded, "the narrowness of the pass works against us. We are limited in how many men we can deploy at one time. And the rock slides, it takes time to clear them."

With barely controlled rage, Emperor Eimion said, "I don't care how you do it, Lord Marshal! I want to be through this pass, do you understand?"

Lord Marshal Rhodri nodded, saying, "Yes, Your Majesty, I understand." Emperor Eimion continued, "If you can't get the job done, I will get myself a new Lord Marshal! Now, both of you, get out of my sight!" Lord Marshal Rhodri and Master Afron bowed and backed away.

CHAPTER 27

Eleanora watched from the wall atop the main gate as the last horseman galloped over the bridge. Turning to Sir Eric, who stood beside her, Eleanora said, "That's the last man in the first company. I figure that the other company will cross the bridge in about two hours."

Nodding, Sir Eric said, "I concur, My Lady, we can expect to sight the enemy soon after the last man crosses the bridge. I will have fires started near each end of the bridge now. By the time that the last company crosses the bridge there will be plenty of burning brands to throw on the straw."

Looking at the bridge, Eleanora said, "Sir Eric, does it always feel like this before a battle?"

Regarding her, Sir Eric responded, "Do you mean that feeling of heighten awareness?"

Nodding, Eleanora said, "Yes, that, but there are other things. I know what must be done, I believe that I can do it. However, at times I can't help feeling doubt in my abilities. I have fought men before, and taken their lives. I know that I can face men in a fight. What frightens me is that in command I may fail the men who look to me to be their leader."

Sir Eric looked at Eleanora. In the days since she had come to take command she had seemed to be so self-assured in her ability to command. He had started to forget just how young she was. He couldn't help but to admire her for her courage. He responded, "My

Lady, I would be surprised if you didn't feel that way. We all have our doubts at times. I'm sure that you will prove to be a fine commander. We have already gained almost three days by opposing their advance through the pass. I believe that we now have a good chance to hold out until Prince Hugh can get here."

"I hope you're right, Sir Eric." Eleanora said, looking south as if she could will Prince Hugh to get there faster. She said again, "I hope you're right."

Emperor Eimion had moved up to about two hundred yards behind his forward units, in the belief that his presence would inspire his soldiers to greater feats of valour. Now at last they were a little more than a mile from the Questers Pass fortress, and breakout onto the central plain of the Vernland Kingdom. Once in control of the central plain he could turn his attention first to defeating Prince Hugh in the western kingdom. He could then turn on King Harold. With the loss of Prince Hugh's army, King Harold would be severely weakened. The victory would be his, but first he had to break out of the pass and seize the central plain before Prince Hugh, or King Harold were on the field to oppose him.

Eleanora stood on the wall atop the main gate with Sir Giffard and Sir Eric by her side. Riders were coming down the trail at a gallop. It was the last company of archers. She looked at the bridge. Fires were burning on the river banks at both end of the bridge. Solders stood ready with shovels to throw live coals and burning brands on the straw as soon as the last rider crossed the bridge.

As the last rider sped over the bridge, soldiers on the far side of the river started to shovel live coals and fire brands onto the straw around and under the bridge. When the last man was across from the other side of the bridge, other soldiers started to fire the straw on the near side of the bridge. As the fires started to burn brightly, great billows of thick-black smoke started to rise into the sky. Just then, Eleanora and the others noticed the lead element of the enemy army come into view.

Seeing a column of smoke rise into the sky from down the pass. Emperor Eimion exclaimed, "They're burning the bridge! Quick, order our forward units ahead at a run! We must save as much as we can!"

Master Arfon now saw an opportunity to save the bridge and regain favor with Emperor Eimion. Taking an amulet from a pouch at his hip, he said, "Your Majesty, I can do something about it."

Moving into a clear space beside the trail, Master Arfon started to walk slowly in a circle as he waved the amulet over his head and incanted a spell. The sky darkened, storm clouds formed over the pass at an unnaturally swift speed until they were almost black. With peals of lightning and thunder the rains started to fall, quickly increasing to a deluge.

For several minutes, Master Arfon continued to incant as the rain beat down relentlessly on everybody and everything. Master Afron finally ended the spell. The rain stopped and the clouds started to clear. Turning to Emperor Eimion, Master Arfon said, "Your Majesty, the fire is out."

Eleanora watched the bridge catch fire and start to burn. The rain started just as the bridge had become fully involved. Under the unrelenting downpour of rain the flames were beaten down and the fires finally extinguished. Everyone and everything had been drenched.

As the rain let up and the sky cleared, Eleanora had a good look at the bridge. The railings had been mostly consumed by the fire. There were some holes in the bridge decking where the fire had started to burn through, but the bridge still stood.

Eleanora turned to Sir Eric who stood close at hand saying, "Sir Eric, the bridge still stands. Is there anything that we can do to keep the enemy from using it? Can we further damage it with the trebuchets?"

"Yes we can, My Lady," Sir Eric said, "but at that range we can't throw a large enough stone to damage the structure of the bridge. We can however throw stones large enough to further damage the bridge decking, and keep the enemy from repairing the bridge."

"What if they make repairs at night when we can't see them?" Eleanora asked.

"My Lady," Sir Eric responded, "they can't make repairs to the bridge without making noise. We have the range on the bridge. All we have to do is throw a barrage of stones to drive them off. Their infantry will be able to use it, but not their cavalry, wagons, or other heavy equipment. I shall give the order to have the battery of trebuchets fire a few volleys at the bridge."

A few minutes later the trebuchets commenced to hurl their deadly missiles. After four volleys the bridge decking, already weakened by the fire, had so many holes smashed in it that even the infantry would have trouble finding their way across under the cover of darkness.

By now the advance companies of the enemy column were approaching the bridge. They were light infantry. It would be dark in three hours. Eleanora knew that the enemy would have to stage a force on the same side of the river as the fortress before they could attack. They would need not just infantry, but also archers. They would not bother with siege engines. They would have to be set up on the far side of the river. Their range would also be diminished due to the fact that they would be shooting up hill. Siege towers also would not work. They would be attacking uphill against a fortress with thirty foot walls, surrounded by a dry moat. Emperor Eimion couldn't afford a long siege. He would try to overwhelm them with numbers.

Eleanora turned to Sir Giffard and Sir Eric who stood by her atop the wall saying, "Well, Gentlemen, there's not much daylight left. As soon as it's dark, Emperor Eimion will be pushing his soldiers over the river as soon as he can. I know that he will make the most use of the bridge as he can. I know that it would be difficult to get a large enough force, using just the damaged bridge, to mount a successful assault on us here in this fortress. It seems to me that, Emperor Eimion would be a fool not to have a way across the river."

"You're right, My Lady." Sir Eric said, "He would have the equipment for rope foot bridges with him. There is a place up river that's out of the range of our war engines. It's a good place to erect the rope bridges; with plenty of room to stage his troops for the assault on our north wall."

Eleanora thought for a while, looking at the bridge and the enemy force across the river, then to the north at the area that Sir Eric had mentioned. Finally she said, "Even if Emperor Eimion is able to get foot bridges across the river quickly, it will still take most of the night to get a sufficient force across the river to attack us. Let the men get as much rest as they can this evening, making sure that we have adequate security on the walls. It will probabily be the last good rest that they will get for a long time. Also have the kitchen have a good meal ready for them early. We will stand to the ramparts ready well before first light."

Sir Giffard now spoke up, "My lady, it is likely that once they have the men across to receive the lines and put up the foot bridges, Emperor Eimion will try to stage a small force to the south to attack the south wall. This will not be a serious attack, but enough of a threat to keep us from concentrating our force to repel the attack on the north wall. Once we are engaged on the north and south wall, they could even rush some men across the bridge to harass our west wall."

Considering what had been said, Eleanora asked, "Is there anything that we can do to delay them putting in those foot bridges up river?"

Sir Eric responded, "Beginning at two hours before midnight, Marta, the larger moon will rise. As you know it will be a waxing moon, but with enough light for our archers to mark their targets. Emperor Eimion will be forced to send over enough security to drive our archers back before they can finish the bridges."

"Sir Eric," Eleanora asked, "how many men would you need?"

Sir Eric responded, "I would say that thirty archers would be enough, My Lady."

With a nod, Eleanora said, "That sounds good, let's do it. Also, I want to send two dispatch riders to Stone Bridge with an updated report. I feel that it will be the last riders that we will be able to send out. Sir Eric, take care of the archers. Sir Giffard, have two riders ready at the postern gate at last light."

Sir Eric and Sir Giffard responded, "Yes, My Lady." they then left to carry out their duties.

Eleanora retired to her quarters to finish her report and to make a second copy.

When she had finished her reports, she took them to Sir Giffard to be carried by the riders. She then went to her customary place on the wall to watch the buildup of enemy forces beyond the bridge. Battle would soon be joined. As she saw it her two objectives were to defend the fortress, and to prevent the enemy from breaking out of the pass in force.

Her thoughts drifted to a subject more personal to her. She wondered what Prince Ambrose was doing now. Was he thinking of her as she thought of him? Was his love for her as strong now as it has been? Perhaps if she prevailed here at Questers Pass, she could find some way to visit him at Taverna. She would love to see Taverna someday. She didn't know what she would do if she couldn't have a future with Ambrose. As she stood thinking of Ambrose a tear started to roll down her cheek.

About one hour before moon rise, a force of thirty archers passed out through the postern gate on foot. By stealth they moved to the north of the fortress. About one quarter mile up they began to hear the faint sound of men working, over the sound of the river. The archers moved in as close as they dare and waited for the moon light to mark their targets.

A half hour later the moon rose high enough to bathe the pass in a dim light. A large workforce of men were at work anchoring the ends of two rope suspension bridges on the east bank of the river. A few soldiers stood watch with their weapons at the ready.

At a prearranged signal the bowmen let their arrows fly. Twelve enemy soldiers fell sprouting arrow shafts. Pandemonium erupted in the enemy camp, with men screaming and shouting, with everyone still on their feet and uninjured scrambling for their weapons and shields. Four more volleys of arrows were fired in quick succession, killing or wounding a few more of the enemy.

By now the enemy soldiers had become organised and formed a shield wall. Realizing that their volleys would have little more effect; a withdraw back to the fortress was ordered.

No lights shown near the bridge and very little sound could be detected, but Eleanora knew as well as everyone else that the enemy had to be using the bridge to move soldiers across the river. She had ordered the trebuchets to bombard the bridge at irregular intervals.

Once the bowmen sent out to harass the enemy that were putting up the foot bridges had safely returned to the fortress, Eleanora left Sir Eric in command and retired to her quarters.

CHAPTER 28

Eleanora stood atop the wall in full armour and arms, her knights shield on her left arm. All around the wall her soldiers stood at the ready. Archers stood ready in the towers around the wall to shoot arrows through the archer's loops to sweep attackers from the walls. Other archers were on the walls to engage the advancing enemy formations. Atop the towers mangonels and onagers would fling stones at the advancing enemy formations, as ballistas would fire large arrows that could pass through two to three men. The trebuchets in the bailey were ready to unleash their deadly barrage.

In the predawn light objects began to appear out of the darkness. When the rising sun provided sufficient luminosity for the opposing forces to see each other, horns blew and drums sounded. With battle cries and the beating of shields the enemy started to surge forward, the enemy's main effort being against the north wall. A smaller force coming against the south wall would keep those defenders occupied so that they couldn't reinforce the north wall.

The mongonels and onagers atop the towers let loose with their barrage of stones. Men fell dead or wounded, opening up gaps in the enemy formation. Next to fire were the ballistas, flinging their deadly missiles and more of the enemy died. Next the archers on the wall started to shoot from between the merlons. Finally as the attacking force started to reach the base of the fortress wall; archers in the towers started to shoot through archers loops to sweep enemy soldiers from the wall.

Following ranks of enemy soldiers rushed forward carrying scaling ladders that were quickly thrown up against the wall. Enemy soldiers started to climb the ladders. Many fell from the ladders, victims of the arrows being shot from the archer's loops in the towers.

The dead and wounded were not all on one side. Many of the defenders were struck by arrows while trying to engage the enemy soldiers at the base of the wall. The defenders took long polls with a forked end, and engaging the top rung of the ladder, pushed it away from the wall. The ladder tipped over and fell to the ground, each with several enemy soldiers on them. Some of the enemy soldiers managed to reach the top of the ladder and start to push through a crenel; only to meet the point of a spear, or the cutting edge of a sword. The defenders were hard pressed to keep the attackers off the wall, then the momentum of the attack faltered and the enemy broke and ran for the safety of their own line.

After the action, reports started to come in to Eleanora. Casualties were light, three dead and fourteen wounded. Nine will only need their wounds dressed. They would then be able to return to duty. The others would need some time for recovery.

The enemy on the other hand suffered well over two hundred, perhaps as many as three hundred men killed or wounded. It would take time to bring more men over the rope suspension bridges before they could make another assault. They had tried to run more men across the damaged bridge during the assault, but two volleys from the battery of trebuchets stopped them. They wouldn't be able to reinforce their force facing the southern wall until after sundown.

The second attack came three hours later the enemy force attacking the southern wall, having not been able to replace their earlier losses, were even less effective than the first attack. The enemy force attacking the northern wall, having been reinforced to make them an even larger force, got no further than they had that morning.

The enemy staged a third attack late in the afternoon as the sun was starting to set. The enemy could only attack the northern wall. Their

force facing the southern wall being so degraded as to be ineffective. On the north wall the enemy did manage to get a few men atop the wall, only to have them quickly cut down. As the light started to fade the enemy force withdrew and set up camp for the night.

Emperor Eimion was in a rage, everyone being afraid to come near him, unless summoned. Right now the focus of his rage was on Lord Marshal Rhodri and Master Arfon. Emperor Eimion yelled at them, "Four days! Four long Days! Since we made contact four days ago we have advanced twenty miles, only twenty miles!"

Looking at Lord Marshal Rhodri, Emperor Eimion continued, "My Lord Marshal, we should be well beyond Stone Bridge by now; yet I find myself still looking at that accursed fortress on the other side of the river! Now why is that?"

"Your Majesty," Lord Marshal Rhodri said, "the fortress was much better prepared than expected."

Turning to face his sorcerer, Emperor Eimion said, "And why is that, Master Arfon? You gave me assurances that the fortress would be in chaos from the death of their command structure, and a good many of their soldiers! Instead what I saw was an organized defense that started twenty miles up the pass! Why is that?"

With a hangdog look, Master Arfon said, "Your Majesty, I have searched the wall with my far sight. I met the commander and his staff when I was in the fortress, they are nowhere to be seen. A young nobleman, a baron or baronet by his blazon, is now in command. Some of the soldiers wore his tabard, other soldiers wore the tabards of Stone Bridge and Dunboro. I would say that they have a new commander and reinforcements. They are even stronger now than they were before."

Emperor Eimion had to pause to ponder the ramifications of what he had been told. If they had reacted so quickly to send a new commander and reinforcements, then what about, Prince Hugh. Is he already on the way? If so, then how close is he? Turning back to Lord Marshal Rhodri, Emperor Eimion said, "My Lord Marshal, we must take that fortress quickly. I want every man that you can get across the river tonight to throw against the walls at first light in the morning. Also, since we can't work on repairing the bridge deck without being bombarded, have our engineers build replacement decking in sections that can be laid over the old decking when it comes time to cross."

Bowing, Lord Marshal Rhodri said, "Permission to withdraw, Your Majesty."

With a nod Emperor Eimion said. "Granted."

Emperor Eimion then turned back to Master Arfon saying, "Master Arfon, when we make our attack in the morning I want you to use your distant eye to let me watch the battle. Now you may withdraw."

With relief, Master Arfon bowed and backed away.

At first light the next morning the horns sounded, the drums beat and the enemy soldiers surged forward shouting their battle cries and beating their shields. First the mangonels and onagers volleyed. Then the ballistas hurled their missiles of death. The enemy line continued to surge forward, to be engaged by the bowmen on the walls. Finally, they reached the base of the walls. They continued to fall dead or wounded at the base of the walls or on the scaling ladders. Defenders also fell to the arrows of the enemy archers.

From atop the west wall over the main gate, Eleanora kept watch on the battle. The south wall was holding well. The north wall was being hard pressed. From time to time an enemy soldier would reach the top of the wall, only to be cut down by a defender. Then an enemy soldier gained the top of the wall to immediately be joined by a second. Before they could be engaged a third, then a fourth and fifth enemy soldier appeared on the wall.

Realizing that if nothing was done right now the north wall, then the fortress could be lost, Eleanora acted. Moving quickly along the wall to the west end of the north wall, Eleanora grabbed every third man by the shoulder saying, "Follow me!"

Just as she reached the fighting on the north wall a defender in front of her took a blow from an enemy ax on his shield, knocking him to the floor. Just as the enemy soldier drew back his ax for the

killing blow, Eleanora stepped over the fallen man, driving the point of her sword deep into the ax man's body just below his armpit. The ax clattered to the floor, followed by the body of the ax man. Eleanora then deflected a sword blow with her shield, running her sword through her opponent's neck.

By now part of the reserve had mounted the wall and had started to push the enemy back from the east end. Slowly they started to push the enemy back to the centre of the wall. Eleanora kept in the front fighting the enemy and coming to the aid of any of her soldiers that seemed to be in trouble. Finally the last enemy soldier died on the wall. The defenders were back in control again.

With the loss of their foothold on the wall, the momentum of the assault broke. All along the walls enemy soldiers turned and fled back to the safety of their camp. A cheer went up from the defenders.

Eleanora went back to her command position over the main gate on the west wall. Villagers working for the welfare of the soldiers brought buckets of water to the soldiers. Eleanora took a cup of water offered to her by one of the village women, then washed the blood off her hands, arms and face with water from another bucket.

By then, Sir Giffard had joined her. "You took a great risk, My Lady." He said.

Eleanora started to answer him when someone on the wall called out, "Hail, Eleanora!"

Other soldiers joined in calling, "Hail, Eleanora!"

Then the whole garrison was calling out, "Hail, Eleanora! Hail, Eleanora! Hail, Eleanora!"

Turning to Sir Giffard, Eleanora asked, "Sir Giffard, what does this mean?"

With a big grin, Sir Giffard answered, "My Lady, they salute you. When you were needed, you were in the fore fighting with them; willing to take the same risk with them. You have won their respect, trust and loyalty. They are now truly your men to command."

Eleanora looked about at all the men looking at her. She then said, "Let's just hope, Sir Giffard, that I can keep as many alive as possible, while keeping, Emperor Eimion trapped here in the pass until Prince Hugh arrives."

As the attack had started, Emperor Eimion and Master Arfon stood on the far bank of the river within sight of the fortress. Master Arfon had the butt of his staff on the ground. Atop the staff was affixed a loop of thin silver wire about the size of a round shield. As, Master Arfon started to incant a spell an image started to form within the loop. The image was a magnified portion of the fortress wall. With subtle movements of the loop, Master Arfon brought the image of Eleanora into view, standing between two merlons in full armour, helm and shield. "Your Majesty," Master Arfon said, "this is the young nobleman. As you can see he is young, still with a clean-unlined face."

As the battle started to develop and their soldiers started to gain a foothold on the north wall, Emperor Eimion exclaimed, "Now we have them! The fortress will soon be in our hands and we will be free of this pass to run wild!"

But his desire was not to be. Emperor Eimion watched in dismay as the young fortress commander led the counter attack to sweep the wall clear of his soldiers. He exclaimed, "That young noble fights like a demon!"

Finally, Emperor Eimion turned away in despair realizing that to take the fortress would be no easy victory.

The defenders of the fortress turned back two more assaults that day. And one more assault about two hours after midnight.

By now the men were becoming so exhausted that they didn't even leave the walls to eat or sleep. The villagers prepared the meals and delivered them to the soldiers on the walls. They also brought water to the walls for drinking and washing. The only reason a soldier had to leave the wall was to visit the latrine.

Eleanora, through the ordeal of the siege, led from the front whenever possible. When her duties did not require her presence on the

wall, Eleanora would check on the kitchen, and any other service for the support of her soldiers to make sure that everything ran smoothly. She even found time to visit the wounded and give them comfort. A few times she held the hand of a dying man in his last few minutes of life, as in their waning awareness they would take her for their mother, wife, or sweetheart. She slept only when fatigue overwhelmed her, and only for a short time.

At the constant urging of Emperor Eimion, Lord Marshal Rhodri kept throwing wave after wave of assault troops against the walls of the fortress. Many times the enemy gained the top of the wall, only to be swept off.

During an attack on the fortress on the afternoon of the seventh day of the siege, the trebuchets in the bailey fell silent. They had run out of stones to throw at the enemy.

This development had not escaped the attention of Emperor Eimion. As soon as the last rays of light faded from the pass, teams of engineers started to run out the new sections of decking and lay them over the old bridge decking. At the same time cavalry units were brought forward for the breakout.

At first light on the eighth day, Emperor Eimion with his staff and eight hundred cavalry crossed the bridge, heading south for Stone Bridge.

Eleanora stood atop the west wall of the fortress watching the enemy cavalry stream across the bridge. She watched with a heavy heart. She had failed to keep them from breaking out of the pass before Prince Hugh could get here with his army. Turning to Sir Giffard and Sir Eric, Eleanora said, "Is there anything that we can do to stop them"

Sir Eric responded, "No, My Lady. When we exhausted our supply of stones for our war engines, we lost our only means of blocking the bridge. At least we don't have to worry about attack for a while. Now that he is past us, Emperor Eimion will not throw away any more men on us. He will just continue the siege, then come back later to deal with us."

Eleanora started to pace along the wall in thought. There just had to be something more that she could do.

Eleanora's brooding was interrupted by a shout from the top of the main keep. "My lady," the soldier shouted, "I can see a cloud of dust to the south!" Eleanora rushed to the keep and charged up the stairs as fast as she could, with Sir Giffard and Sir Eric close behind her. At the top of the keep she looked out through a south facing crenel between two merlons. There was no mistaking the dust cloud to the south. It had to be an army in the field.

"Here!" Eleanora exclaimed, "Prince Hugh is here!"

Sir Eric and Sir Giffard also took a look to assure themselves.

Stepping back, Eleanora said, "Sir Giffard, Sir Eric, I want the horses and men made ready. I plan to sally forth at the right time to block Emperor Eimion's escape, and to keep his infantry from crossing the bridge."

"Yes, My Lady," Sir Eric and Sir Giffard said in unison. They then turned and left to carry out their duties.

Eleanora took another look at the dust cloud, then went to her quarters. There she took the time to clean herself up a little and to put on a fresh surcoat.

By the time she emerged from her quarters it was being reported that the lookouts atop the keep could see Prince Hugh's cavalry coming up the road from Stone Bridge. In the bailey, Eleanora found over four hundred soldiers with their mounts. Sir Giffard had had her horse tacked up for her.

The soldiers on the main gate towers were now reporting enemy cavalry headed back to the pass. Eleanora ordered everyone to mount.

Emperor Eimion's elation at breaking out of the pass proved to be short lived. His advanced companies had gotten little more than five miles past the village of Questers Pass when they spotted a large force of mounted soldiers moving north, up the road from Stone Bridge. This was an unwelcome development. It soon became all too apparent that they were hopelessly outnumbered. The invasion had failed. With

bitterness in his heart, Emperor Eimion gave the order to withdraw back across the bridge.

It took a few minutes to get the order out, and even more time to get all the companies turned around. By then the force coming up from the south had closed the distance, and were beginning to spread out into battle formation. The banners of Prince Hugh's legion, Dunboro, Stone Bridge, Attleton and Duman Ford could be seen.

Approaching the bridge, Emperor Eimion found a line of about three-hundred archers, with spears set in the ground in front of them at an angle to discourage a cavalry charge. One end of the line anchored on the river before the bridge. At the other end of the line stood over four-hundred mounted soldiers arraigned for the charge.

Emperor Eimion's advance companies halted, unsure of what to do. To charge the line of archers and mounted soldiers would be madness. Emperor Eimion however had to do something to force a path open to the bridge, and to the safety of the pass. Without delay he ordered his lead companies to charge the enemy line to force a way open to the bridge.

Eleanora seeing the enemy companies charge the line of archers; led her mounted soldiers in an attack on the enemy flank.

The attacking enemy companies first ran into a storm of arrows. Their horses then balked and shied away from the line of spears set in front of the archers. Finally the full force of Eleanora's charge smashed into their flank. There followed a brief, but vicious melee. Eleanora found herself in the middle of the fighting with, Sir Giffard fighting hard to cover her back. The enemy faltered, then broke and ran for the safety of Emperor Eimion's lines.

Emperor Eimion seeing his last desperate gamble to win through to safety a failure, and looking at the force coming up on his rear he knew that all was lost. Just as Emperor Eimion was beginning to face the utmost humiliation of defeat, Master Arfon chose that time to speak, "Your Majesty, we must do something or all is lost!"

In a blind rage, Emperor Eimion drew his sword and shouting, "All is already lost!" swung his sword and struck Master Arfons head from his body. The head flew through the air to bounce along the ground, while the body toppled from the saddle to fall to the ground.

Dismounting from his horse, Emperor Eimion cleaned the blade of his sword on the robe of the dead sorcerer, then sheathed it. Looking at the dead body of the sorcerer he said, "You failed me, Master Arfon when it counted the most! You failed me!"

Lord Marshal Rhodri dismounted and stood watching, Emperor Eimion saying nothing.

By now they faced an overwhelming enemy force on three sides, with the river on the forth.

Without looking up, Emperor Eimion said, "Lost, everything is lost. I have nothing now, nothing."

Emperor Eimion could no longer think of his own survival; that had already been determined. Every man's hand would now be against him. He doubted if he would even survive the trip back north through that accursed pass. His body would most likely be left there for his bones to bleach in the sun. He must think of his family and his twelve year old son. As long as he lived his son would be seen by some as the heir to the throne. To keep his family safe there was but one thing that he could do. He had to have the courage to do it.

Emperor Eimion unbuckled his belt, letting his sword and dagger fall to the ground. He then removed his helm, surcoat, chain mail and gambeson armor. Dropping to his knees, he drew his dagger from its sheath. It was a long dagger with an eighteen inch blade. Placing the point of the blade to his chest he fell forward, driving the blade through his heart. His body fell to the ground, gave a couple of spasmodic jerks, then lay still.

After a minute of reflection, Lord Marshal Rhodri turned to his aids saying, "Spread the word that the Emperor is dead. Also have all the men dismount and throw down their arms and shields." What didn't need saying was that they were surrendering.

Seeing the soldiers of Emperor Eimion dismount, casting down their arms and shields, the soldiers of the kingdom knew that it was over.

Knowing that Emperor Eimion would be surrendering, Prince Hugh sent for Lady Eleanora to join him. He wanted her to be at his side to accept the surrender of Emperor Eimion.

Finally one man, unarmed except for a broad sword that he carried sheathed, left the enemy lines on foot escorted by four unarmed men.

Prince Hugh and Eleanora removed their helms, handing their helms and shields to aids. They kept their weapons with them. They then rode out to accept the surrender, accompanied by six mounted soldiers.

As Prince Hugh and Eleanora approached, Lord Marshal Rhodri was shocked to see Eleanora with her long auburn hair cascading down over her shoulders and back. This noble dressed as a man was a woman. Then he recalled the oracle's prediction. The youth whose gender could not be determined. This had to be the youth.

When they were close to Lord Marshal Rhodri, Prince Hugh and Eleanora halted, but did not dismount. Bowing to Prince Hugh, Lord Marsha Rhodri said, "Your Highness I am, Lord Marshal Rhodri."

Acknowledging Lord Marshal Rhodri with a nod, Prince Hugh said, "Lord Marshal Rhodri, I am, Prince Hugh." Indicating, Eleanora with a wave of the hand he continued, "This is, Lady Eleanora baronet of the court of Dunboro and present commander of the fortress of Questers Pass. Now, Lord Marshal, where is your emperor?"

With a bowed head, Lord Marshal Rhodri said, "Your Highness, Emperor Eimion is dead by his own hand. I am now in command. To fight now would only bring death with no chance of gain. I wish to surrender my command. However, I must first ask your terms."

Having already decided on the terms, Prince Hugh said, "Lord Marshal Rhodri, my terms are this: your common soldiers will be allowed to cross the bridge and return to their homes, but without weapons, armour or horses. As for you and your officers, you will be held for ransom."

Knowing that the terms were as generous as he would get, Lord Marshal Rhodri started to present Emperor Eimion's sword to Prince Hugh.

Shaking his head, Prince Hugh said, "Lord Marshal Rhodri, the victory is not mine, but, Lady Eleanora's. You will surrender, Emperor Eimion's sword to her."

Swallowing his pride at having to surrender to a woman, Lord Marshal Rhodri held the sword of Emperor Eimion up to Eleanora saying, "My Lady, with this the sword of our late leader, Emperor Eimion I surrender my men into your care."

Eleanora accepted the sword and the surrender was complete. Eleanora looked at the sword of Emperor Eimion. It was a beautiful weapon, with scabbard and hilt inlaid with gold, silver and precious stones. Eleanora held the sword high over her head. The kingdom soldiers seeing the sword being held high let out with a resounding cheer.

Prince Hugh gave instructions to Lord Marshal Rhodri for the disposition of his officers and men. Eleanora was given leave to take her men back to the fortress for a well-deserved rest.

CHAPTER 29

The next evening, Eleanora had dinner with Prince Hugh and a few of his officers in his command pavilion. The meal started out with light conversation. Then, Prince Hugh said, "Lady Eleanora, do you know that I almost had a rebellion on my hands when I named the new commander for Questers Pass."

With a chuckle, Eleanora responded. "Yes, Your Highness, I heard of that."

"Well," Prince Hugh said, "the whole garrison, almost to a man, said that they already had a commander and didn't want anyone else. You wouldn't by chance want to keep command of Questers Pass?"

Eleanora answered, "Your Highness, in the few days that I commanded Questers Pass I became very close to the men. I shall always have a special place in my heart for them, but I must decline."

With a grin, Prince Hugh said, "I wasn't really serious on that offer anyway, Lady Eleanora. I knew that you wouldn't want to stay." Looking thoughtfully at, Eleanora, Prince Hugh continued, "Then, Lady Eleanora, what do you want? You certainly earned the right to ask."

Eleanora put down her eating utensils, taking the time to order her thoughts, then spoke, "Your Highness, when I took command of Questers Pass, I elevated Sergeant Giffard and Sergeant Eric to knight. I would like for you to confirm this."

With a nod, Prince Hugh said, "Done, I shall swear them to fealty and give them their silver spurs."

Eleanora continued, "I also made other promotions and there are many men that I want to be recognized for exceptional valour."

Prince Hugh said, "Done, just give me the particulars." He paused for a moment then continued, "Lady Eleanora, so far you have told me what you want for others. Now what do you want for yourself?"

Eleanora took a minute before answering, "Your Highness, I already have more than I ever expected to have in this lifetime. There is nothing more that I need or desire. I wish only to continue to serve you and the king."

The other men at the dining table looked at Eleanora in awe. She had earned the right to claim a substantial reward, but had asked nothing for herself. Her selfless devotion to the royal family astounded them all.

Prince Hugh regarded her for a few seconds, then said, "The person that has done more to earn a reward, but ask nothing for herself," with a smile he continued, "I have spoken with Juliana and I am aware of what you desire the most."

With downcast eyes, Eleanora responded, "Yes, Your Highness, there is something that I desire more than anything else. If you could give it to me, I would not hesitate to ask."

There was silence at the table as everyone else wondered what Prince Hugh and Lady Eleanora had been talking about.

The trip back to Dunboro was made at a more leisurely pace. At every village and hamlet on the way the people turned out to cheer Eleanora as the heroin of Questers Pass. Upon reaching Dunboro, Eleanora rode at the head of the column next to Prince Hugh. It seemed that the whole city had turned out to cheer their return.

At the palace all the court had turned out to welcome them back. As soon as Eleanora dismounted everyone crowded around to welcome her home. It was a relief when she was finally able to retire to her apartment.

Eleanora quickly changed into a robe. She then called the maids to prepare a bath for her. Once bathed and attired in a casual gown she could relax in familiar surroundings. When Princess Juliana's children

came to welcome their Aunt Eleanora home, she knew that she was really home.

With the failure of the invasion at Questers Pass, the force of raiders between Haffendel and Kientor were withdrawn. With the death of Emperor Eimion the Jute Empire had already started to fracture into separate factions, each with its own leader with ambitions to be the next emperor. There would be civil war to determine who would next sit on the emperor's throne.

Prince Hugh now took the time to deal with the traitors, Baronet Bartholomew and the maid, Carola. At the hands of the inquisitors, Baronet Bartholomew confessed his treason. His reason for this treason being the promise of an earldom under the rule of the Jutes.

As for the maid, Carola, Baronet Bartholomew had promised her a position in his court as a dame when he became an earl. She felt it her due to be a person of esteem with others waiting on her. To try to gain leniency from Prince Hugh, she gave up the name of Halfrida the madam of the White Dove brothel as one of the conspirators. Even with the death of the cobbler, Chester, they still had certain ships that traded often with Dunboro that brought messages from the Jutes. These ships were known by Baronet Bartholomew and Carola. Meetings would be held in the White Dove brothel with the help of the madam, Halfrida. Even giving up Halfrida didn't save, Carola.

What they got was a swift trial. After being found guilty they were sentenced to death by hanging. When they went to the gallows, Bartholomew and Halfrida were stoic, having accepted their fate. Carola wept hysterically pleading for her life. The crowd cheered when the trap was sprung and they dropped to their death. Their heads were then cut off and mounted on pikes outside the main gate of the palace as a warning to all that would contemplate treason.

Three weeks after the summer solstice festival, Eleanora with Brenda, accompanying Prince Hugh, Princess Juliana and their family left for the king's court at Vanaden on the Lake. Prince Hugh had an escort of fifty mounted soldiers from the palace guard led by Sir Walter and

Sir Hal. Prince Hugh had also provided Eleanora with a twenty man honour guard, five men each from Dunboro, Stone Bridge, Hawkers Dale and Questers Pass. They were all men that she had commanded at Questers Pass. Sir Giffard commanded her honour guard.

They travelled the same route as Eleanora had travelled the last time she had visited Vanaden on the Lake. By now, Eleanora had become accustomed to all the adoration expressed by the citizens in the towns, villages and hamlets that they passed through. By now everyone in the kingdom had heard of her exploits at Questers Pass.

On arrival at the king's palace at Vanaden on the Lake, Eleanora was treated as if she were visiting royalty. The apartment given for her use was larger and more lavish than anything she had ever had. The armoires in her apartment were filled with the most exquisite gowns. There were also maids to look after her every need. In answer to her inquiry, Eleanora was told that all the gowns and other items of a personal nature were now hers.

The next morning, Eleanora awoke early and had breakfast in her apartment. Just as she had finished her breakfast, one of the queen's ladies in waiting entered her apartment followed by several maids. Curtsying the woman said. "My Lady, I am Lady Ernestine. I have been sent to help you to get ready for court."

Eleanora could see that one of the maids carried a gown made of a lustrous lavender silk brocade. The gown had a fitted bodice with full skirt and long-full sleeves. The bodice from the collar to a little below the waist and the cuffs of the sleeves were embroidered using gold and silver thread with seed pearls and small amethyst gem stones. It was the most gorgeous gown that she had ever seen.

The maids went to work, first they made Eleanora's hair up into an elaborate coiffure. Next they did her makeup. When the hair and makeup had been done, the maids helped her into the gown and matching slippers.

Lady Ernestine now produced a jewel case made of a rich reddish-brown hardwood. The case had delicate carvings of birds and flowers, inlaid with mother of pearl. She then said, "My Lady, I have been instructed to tell you that this is a gift to you from the queen, and that you are to wear them at court today."

When Lady Ernestine opened the jewel case the sight took Eleanora's breath away. The jewel case contained a diamond tiara, diamond necklace and diamond earrings. Looking at the contents of the jewel case, Eleanora said, "This is too much, I can't possibility take this."

Looking at Eleanora, Lady Ernestine said, "My Lady, you are an inspiration to all women. You are a woman who has managed to live in a man's world as an equal. You have earned everything that you can get."

With a smile, Eleanora said, "Well, Lady Ernestine, if you put it that way, I'll keep it."

Once Eleanora had the jewels on it was time for court. From one of the armoires Eleanora took the sword of Emperor Eimion.

Seeing the sword, Lady Ernestine asked, "My Lady, is that the sword of Emperor Eimion?"

Nodding, Eleanora replied, "Yes, this was the sword of Emperor Eimion."

A little hesitantly, Lady Ernestine asked, "My Lady, may I touch it?" Holding the sword out, Eleanora said, "Of course, Lady Ernestine, you may hold it."

Lady Ernestine took the sword, then said, "It's so heavy, My Lady. How do you fight with such a sword?"

Eleanora responded, "I don't use a sword like that, Lady Ernestine. I have my own sword."

Reaching in the armoire, Eleanora withdrew her own sword. Handing it to Lady Ernestine, and taking back Emperor Eimion's sword, Eleanora said. "This is my sword."

Lady Ernestine hefted the sword, then said, "It is lighter, My Lady. They say that you have never lost a sword duel with a man. How many have you killed with this sword?"

"I don't know, Lady Ernestine," Eleanora said, "Many, I've lost count." With a look of veneration, Lady Ernestine returned the sword to Eleanora. Eleanora returned her sword to the armoire. Then tucking Emperor

Eimion's sword under one arm, and lifting the front of her skirt with her free hand, she said, "Come, Lady Ernestine, it's time for court."

The nobility of the king's court had heard that Lady Eleanora had returned and would be at court. Having heard that the king planned something special for her, everyone had found a reason to be there to witness it. As Eleanora entered the grand hall people moved aside so that she could advance to the front of the crowd.

King Harold, Queen Serafina and other members of the royal family in residence entered the grand hall. Everyone in the grand hall bowed or curtsied as the king and queen took their seats on their thrones.

The Master of Ceremonies then started to call people having business with the king. After a few petitioners had been heard, the master of ceremonies called out, "Lady Eleanora, Baronet of the court of Dunboro and recent commander of the fortress of Questers Pass, come before your king!"

Eleanora advanced to the foot of the dais and curtsied to King Harold saying, "Your Majesty." Then holding out the sword with both hands, she continued, "Your Majesty, I present to you the sword of Emperor Eimion, surrendered to me on the field at Questers Pass. Your enemies have been vanquished. The kingdom is again secure."

King Harold stood, Queen Serafina standing with him. King Harold then descended the three steps to stand before Eleanora. Taking the sword from her hands, he said," I thank Lady Eleanora for her valiant defense of the kingdom, and her part in the victory. You served not for personal recognition or gain, but for love of the kingdom and the royal family. For your selfless devotion I shall set a precedent."

Offering his arm to Eleanora, King Harold said, "Lady Eleanora will you join the Queen and I on the Dais."

Handing the sword of Emperor Eimion off to a page, King Harold then led Eleanora up the steps to stand between himself and Queen Serafina on the dais.

The master of ceremonies struck the floor three times with the butt of his staff, then exclaimed. "Gentlemen and Ladies of the court, draw near and bear witness to a proclamation under the signature and seal of Harold D'Croix the second Rex!"

A herald then stepped forward and started to read from a parchment. "As, Lady Eleanora, Baronet of the court of Dunboro, and formerly an orphan of the streets of Dunboro, has often shown her devotion and love of our family. The queen and I also have a place in our own hearts and love for, Eleanora. Since Eleanora has no family, Queen Serafina and I do hereby formally adopt Eleanora as our daughter. Her name to be written on the D'Croix family rolls as, Eleanora D'Croix, daughter of King Harold D'Croix the second and Queen Serafina D'Croix. Eleanora is now our daughter and Princess of the realm."

A loud cheer went up from the court. Eleanora just stood astonished, hardly believing what had just happened. The king and queen had just taken her by the hand. Eleanora finally said. "Your Majesty, I don't understand."

With a chuckle, King Harold replied, "It's no more addressing us as, Your Majesty. You are family now, just call us, father or mother. Now, daughter, go down and accept the adoration of your subjects. I will send for you later."

Eleanora said, "Yes, father." She then descended the steps to the floor of the great hall. It still felt as though she were in a dream. It seemed that she didn't walk across the floor, but floated. Everyone bowed or curtsied to her saying, "Your Highness." All that Eleanora could manage was a smile and nod. Then, Sir Giffard stood before her.

Sir Giffard, executing a courtly bow said, "Congratulations, Your Highness."

Smiling, Eleanora said, "Sir Giffard, all of this is so startling to me. It is comforting to have a close friend near at hand."

"Your Highness," Sir Giffard responded, "I have also risen under your star. I shall always have a special place in my heart for you, and be your friend forever."

Laying her hand on Sir Giffard's forearm, Eleanora said, "Thank you, Sir Giffard. I also will always be your friend. We shall speak more later on."

Eleanora continued to move about, accepting the congratulations of the court. Soon a page came up to her and bowed saying, "Your Highness, I am here to escort you to the king's library."

Eleanora followed the page from the grand hall to the king's library. Arriving at the library the page opened the door for her to enter, then closed the door behind her. A man stood with his back to her looking out the window. Eleanora let out a gasp in recognition, then flying into his arms exclaimed, "Ambrose!"

Gathering her in his arms in a passionate embrace, Ambrose responded, "Oh my lovely, Eleanora how have I missed you." He then kissed her on the lips ardently.

Eleanora pressed her body against his, not wanting to let go. By now tears of joy had started to trickle down her cheeks. Holding tightly to Ambrose, Eleanora said, "If this is a dream, then I don't ever want to wake up."

With a laugh, Ambrose replied, "It is no dream my darling, Eleanora. You are living it, and we shall never be apart again."

What do you mean, my love?"

Ambrose answered, "After hearing of your victory over Emperor Eimion at Questers Pass; my father has had great admiration for you. However, my father didn't know what his people would think of a woman not of noble birth, and without any family, being the crown princess of Turin. When King Harold informed my father that he intended to adopt you into the royal family, and name you a princess of the realm, my father no longer had any misgivings to our betrothal. Tomorrow at court your father will formally announce our betrothal. One week later we are to be wed in the grand hall."

Now the tears really started to flow. Ambrose pulled out a handkerchief and started to dab at the tears, so that they would not fall on and stain the gown.

Finally, Eleanora got her emotions under control and said, "Oh, Ambrose, I'm sorry that I've been such a mess. Today has been a really emotionally stressful day for me. First I am elevated to a position far above anything that I could ever have imagined. Then I find that I will have that that I most desire. That I shall be your wife."

Ambrose steered Eleanora to a sofa where they both sat together.

Eleanora then said, "My love, since our last day you have never left my mind. During the darkest days at Questers Pass, it was the thought of you that kept me going."

Having heard of the battle at Questers Pass, and of Eleanora's daring leadership, Ambrose had to ask, "During the fighting were you not afraid?"

With a nod, Eleanora replied, "Yes, but what I feared the most was to never to see you again."

With a smile, Ambrose said, "Then for the rest of our lives we shall wake-up together every morning."

Eleanora then kissed Ambrose and said, "Then you will spend the night with me?"

Ambrose embraced and kissed Eleanora, then said "Of course I will. We shall spend every night together from now on. Now we must go. Your Father and Mother are expecting us for the mid-day meal."

Eleanora would have to get accustomed to thinking of the king and queen as her father and mother.

The meal was served on the same patio as before when she had dined with the king and queen. It being a beautiful day with the sunlight sparkling off the water, Eleanora decided that she would ask Ambrose to take her sailing this afternoon.

The meal started out with casual talk. It then turned to the announcement of the betrothal and the wedding during court in the morning. They would enter the grand hall with the king and queen, taking their place on the dais. Then once the court is brought to order the betrothal and wedding will be announced. King Harold then said,

"The wedding here at Vanaden on the Lake will be mostly a family affair. About four hundred guests more or less."

"So many!" Eleanora exclaimed, "I thought that you just said that it would just be a family affair, father!"

Trying to keep a straight face and not to laugh at Eleanora's remark, King Harold said, "As you will come to know, Eleanora, the royal family is quite large. You will find that you have a multitude of uncles, aunts and cousins. There are also certain people too important to ignore."

Ambrose had to laugh at Eleanora's uneasiness about such a large crowd for what she had expected to be an intimate ceremony, then said, "Oh, Eleanora, just wait until we get home to Taverna. Then we shall have a state wedding. As I am the heir apparent, our wedding will be the social event of the year, or perhaps the decade. There will be at least five times the guests, most likely more."

Eleanora just sat looking out at the lake for several seconds. She then shrugged, saying to Ambrose, "It really doesn't matter how many people are there. With you at my side, the only one I will see is you."

Everyone laughed. Queen Serafina then reached out to take Eleanora's hand, saying, "You have the right idea Eleanora, only you and Ambrose matter. It's your day."

"Thank you, mother." Eleanora said.

"One last thing, Eleanora," Queen Serafina said, "I have had five sons, but until you came along I had no daughters. I thought that I would never have a daughter to pass my wedding gown on to. It is a most lovely gown. Since you are about the same size as I was when I wed, it will need hardly any altering."

"Thank you, Mother," Eleanora said, "I shall wear it with pride."

The next morning at court, Ambrose and Eleanora entered the grand hall with King Harold and Queen Serafina. The court fell silent, knowing that something of significance would be announced. The king and queen took their places on their thrones. Ambrose and Eleanora stood on the dais beside them. When everyone was in position, King Harold gave a nod to the Master of Ceremonies.

The Master of Ceremonies struck the floor with the butt of his staff. He then said in a loud voice, "Gentlemen and Ladies of the court, give your attention to an announcement by King Harold D'Croix the second and Queen Serafina D'Croix. They are pleased to announce the betrothal of their daughter, Princess Eleanora D'Croix to Crown Prince Ambrose Jorvene of Turin."

The grand hall erupted with enthusiastic applause from the members of the court.

When the applause finally subsided the Master of Ceremonies continued. "A family wedding will take place one week from today, here in the grand hall. The couple will then travel to Turin, where a state wedding will be held in the palace of the king in Taverna."

There followed another round of applause, almost as spirited as the first round. On cue, Ambrose and Eleanora moved down the steps of the dais to accept the congratulations of the court.

Eleanora still found it strange that everyone that she encountered, even nobles of high rank such as dukes, duchesses, Earls and countesses showed deference to her by bowing, or curtsying. She still had to fight the urge to look over her shoulder when someone addressed her as, Your Highness, to make sure that they were not speaking to someone else. It seemed to Eleanora that everyone in the court was eager to be noticed by her, and to wish her happiness.

After a few minutes a page came up to Eleanora and bowed. He then handed her a note, bowed again and withdrew.

Eleanora read the note quickly, then spoke to Ambrose, "Ambrose, we have been invited to take the mid-day meal with Hugh and Juliana in their apartments."

Ambrose responded with a nod. "Good, I'm eager to meet with Prince Hugh and Princess Juliana. You have told me so much about them."

At the noon hour a page arrived to escort Ambrose and Eleanora to the apartments of Hugh and Juliana. The weather being pleasant, a table had been set up on the veranda overlooking the lake. Eleanora received a very warm reception from Hugh and Juliana, being embraced as a sister.

During the meal the conversation focused mainly on the wedding. Finally, Juliana said, "Eleanora, when you first came to us I perceived something unique about you."

Hugh spoke up, "I can say the same thing, but the main reason that I sent Eleanora to you was what Mistress Caitlin said about our destinies being linked."

"Well, whatever," Juliana said, "it was the right thing to do. It soon became apparent to me, Eleanora, that you were destined for greatness. Now you are my sister-in-law and in one week you will be a crown princess, as I am. Then some day we will rule beside our husbands as queens of neighboring kingdoms."

All this had also been on Eleanora's mind. After a pause, Eleanora said, "Yes, it's much more than I ever dreamed of having. I wonder if the spirit of my mother is aware of all that has happened to me."

Taking Eleanora's hands into his and looking her in the eyes, Hugh said, "Perhaps for such an astounding event, Odila (goddess of the dead) will make it known to your mother's shade. Don't you think so, Ambrose?"

With a nod, Ambrose replied, "My darling, Eleanora, I believe that your mother always believed that you would succeed."

CHAPTER 30

The week passed quickly with all that had to be done to get ready for the wedding. The dress, as Queen Serafina had said, needed hardly any alternation for a perfect fit. The king and queen having known that there would be a wedding even before Eleanora's arrival in Vanaden on the Lake had requested the presence of everyone that would be invited. The kitchen had also stocked up on everything that would be needed for the wedding banquet. Thanks to the advanced planning everything would be ready on time.

Other things also had to be taken care of. Eleanora turned over the responsibility for the intelligence network in Dunboro to Brenda. Jimmy would still run the operation and report to Brenda, who in turn would report to Prince Hugh. Five days before the wedding, Eleanora had a meeting with Hugh and Juliana in their apartment. After the pleasantries, Eleanora got down to business with Hugh. "Hugh, we need to speak about Brenda."

With a nod, Hugh said, "Yes we do, Eleanora. I have decided to turn Brenda over to Juliana as a personal companion. With the success that she had with you, she should have no problems with Brenda."

With a smile, Juliana said, "At least I will be getting her already partly trained."

Eleanora just had to laugh at Juliana's remark. "I wasn't that bad, was I, Juliana?"

"Well," Juliana replied, "you were really rough around the edges when I got you, but you were a fast learner."

Turning back to Hugh, Eleanora said, "Oh, Hugh it's good that you will be giving Brenda over to Juliana. However, I would like something more. I would like for you to make her a member of the peerage. It would be an advantage in running the intelligence network. That way, Jimmy and the others wouldn't question any order from her."

Hugh took a small wooden case from atop a nearby table. Opening it he withdrew a pendant badge on an indigo-blue ribbon. In the centre of the badge was a blue lozenge with a silver unicorn in the center. He then said, "I knew that you would want this, Eleanora. I plan to elevate Brenda to the rank of dame. Father has a smaller hall that we can use. We will have everyone from Dunboro in attendance. We shall do it in the morning while father is holding court in the grand hall." Giving Eleanora a crooked smile, Hugh continued, "Now, sister, Eleanora, I'm sure that you have something more in mind. Could it possibility be a betrothal?"

With a nod, Eleanora said, "Yes, Hugh, that's it. Brenda and Sir Hal have both expressed their desire to wed."

"How old is Brenda counted as of this last summer solstice festival?" Hugh asked.

"Fifteen years, Hugh." Eleanora responded, "Sir Hal has been waiting for a good time to approach Duke Bran to ask permission to wed Brenda."

With a short laugh, Hugh responded, "Most likely trying to get up the nerve to face Bran. Don't worry about it, Eleanora, they will have my blessing. After I elevate her to dame tomorrow, I shall announce the betrothal. The wedding can take place at the next summer solstice festival. Now, dear sister, is there anything more?"

"Yes," Eleanora said, "I wish to give them title to the estate of Hawkers Dale as a wedding gift."

With a nod, Hugh said, "Then I shall have a deed drawn up for you to sign."

The next morning, Prince Hugh held court in the smaller hall used by his father for more private audiences. When the members

of the Dunboro court, along with Eleanora's honour guard and any other interested members of the court were present, Prince Hugh began. Prince Hugh sat on a throne on a dais, with Princess Juliana at his side. Sir Giffard would be acting as Master of Ceremonies. Prince Hugh nodded to Sir Giffard. Sir Giffard cleared his throat, then spoke loudly, "Lady Brenda come before your prince!"

Brenda, not knowing what was in store, approached the throne. Curtsying, Brenda said, "Your Highness."

Sir Giffard then spoke again. "Gentlemen and Ladies of the court draw near and witness." Holding up a document he continued. "To all let it be known that since her arrival at court, Lady Brenda has earned our respect, trust and affection. She has worked hard in the interest of the royal family, accomplishing every task given to her no matter how difficult. Her loyalty and devotion is above reproach. We now wish to reward her steadfast service. Let it be known that the Lady Brenda is of now elevated to the rank of Dame, with all rights and duties thereunto."

Prince Hugh now stood and stepped down from the dais to stand before Lady Brenda. Two pages came forward, each holding a small blue-satin cushion. From the first cushion, Prince Hugh took the pendant badge on the indigo-blue ribbon and tied it about Brenda's neck where it hung at her throat. He then took a pair of silver spurs from the other cushion and gave them to Brenda. Prince Hugh then called out. "Sir Hal, come forward and join us."

When Sir Hal had joined Lady Brenda, next to Prince Hugh, Prince Hugh spoke to the court. "Gentlemen and Ladies of the court. I wish to announce the betrothal of Sir Hal and Dame Brenda. The wedding will be during the coming summer solstice festival. I also hold in trust the deed to Hawkers Dale, to be given to Sir Hal and Dame Brenda on their wedding day as a gift from my sister, Princess Eleanora."

The court erupted in applause as, Sir Hal and Lady Brenda stood a bit bewildered holding hands. Prince Hugh nodded to Sir Giffard. Sir Giffard then called out. "Gentlemen and Ladies, this concludes the business of the court for today!"

Eleanora was the first to come forward to congratulate Hal and, Brenda. Hal and Brenda bowed and curtsied saying, "Your Highness."

Eleanora embraced Brenda then Hal. She then said. "I am happy for the both of you. I could not leave without doing something for you. With the estate of Hawkers Dale you shall have a comfortable life."

"Your Highness," Brenda said, "I don't know what to say. This is far more than I ever expected. I don't know how I could ever thank you for all that you have done for me." Brenda looked at Hal, then continued, "Your Highness, we would like to name our first girl child, Eleanora."

Taking Brenda's hand, Eleanora said, "That would please me very much." Looking at Hal she continued, "Sir Hal, You take very good care of Brenda and give her many children."

With a blush, Brenda said, "You can count on that, Your Highness. I shall keep Hal very busy."

Now it was Sir Hal's turn to blush.

At last the day arrived, the day that Eleanora would become one with Ambrose. Eleanora found herself in the midst of a cluster of maids. They were arranging her hair in an elaborate coiffure and doing her makeup. When at last the hair and makeup was done, they helped her into her wedding gown. Eleanora had to admit that it was the most exquisite gown that she had ever seen. The gown was of shimmering emerald-green silk. It had a fitted bodice lavishly embroidered with gold thread in an intricate floral pattern from the collar down past the hips to taper down onto the full skirt at several points around the hips both front and back.

Queen Serafina arrived as Eleanora was still getting into her gown. She had with her an ornately carved jewel box of fine hard wood. "I brought something for you, Eleanora." Queen Serafina said.

"What is that, mother?" Eleanora asked.

Queen Serafina opened the jewel box. It contained a tiara, necklace and earrings, all set with emeralds and diamonds. The sight of it took Eleanora's breath away. Finally, Eleanora said, "Oh, Mother, they are so beautiful, but you have given me so much already."

"Oh my darling, Eleanora, I finally have a daughter and I want to give you everything that I can. Besides you're the daughter of a king now, you can't have too much jewellery. What would people think if we sent you off with just the clothes on your back?"

Eleanora just had to laugh at the queen's humour. Finally she said, "In that case, Mother I'll take it."

After being adorned with the jewels, Eleanora was ready. When she left her apartment with her mother, they were escorted to the grand hall by Eleanora's honour guard. At the door to the grand hall, King Harold waited. Eleanora's honour guard took up position at the door. A knight of the king's court was there at the door to escort the queen to her place in the grand hall.

After allowing enough time for the queen to be in place, King Harold presented his arm to Eleanora. "It's time my daughter." He said.

Taking her father's arm and smiling, Eleanora said, "I'm ready," Then looking at the king she said, "And, Father, thank you for everything you have done for me."

With pride in his voice, the king said. "We are family, Daughter." Ambrose waited at the altar that had been setup for the ceremony. He

wore a scarlet dress tunic lavishly embroidered with gold thread, black trousers and black boots. On his head he wore the crown of the heir apparent of Turin. As customary the high priest of Draga (god of the heavens) officiated at all royal weddings. Eleanora had also requested a priestess of Idonea (goddess of the hearth) and a priestess of Fredegonde (goddess of fertility) to bring good fortune to the union. After a brief ceremony where vows were exchanged and a cup of wine was shared between Ambrose and Eleanora, the ceremony was concluded. The priest of Draga then stepped forward and announced. "Gentlemen and Ladies, I introduce to you, Crown Prince Ambrose Joevene and Crown Princess Eleanora Joevene of Turin." The announcement was followed by a round of applause.

There followed the wedding reception and banquet. By the time that Ambrose and Eleanora were able to get away to the privacy of their apartment the sun was starting to set in the western sky.

The next morning there were the farewells to everyone. Ambrose and Eleanora set out by barge for the port city of Natenfor, accompanied by her twenty man honour guard that would serve as her honour guard during the state wedding. By mid-day of the day after, the barge arrived at Natenfor. The river barge docked at the quay near the Red Enchantress that had been dispatched to convey, Ambrose and Eleanora to Taverna.

Ambrose and Eleanora disembarked from the river barge, thanking the barge master for the pleasant trip. As they approached the Red Enchantress they could see Captain Evan and his officers standing at attention on deck near the head of the gang plank in their best uniforms, with the crew manning the rail. Seeing this, Ambrose glanced at, Eleanora saying, "Well, my love, it appears that Captain Evan has arranged a grand reception in our honour." Then with a smile he continued, "Or perhaps this is all for you. He never went to so much trouble just for me."

Ambrose's remark drew a laugh from Eleanora. She then said, "It will be good to meet Captain Evan again."

As Ambrose and Eleanora started up the gang plank there came the shrill notes of a boatswain's pipe. All the officers and men rendered a salute. Seeing Captain Evan, Eleanora smiled. "Captain Evan," Eleanora said, "the first of my new countrymen that I behold is a familiar face. I am pleased that it is your ship that we sail on."

With a bow, Captain Evan replied, "Your Highness, my crew and I are honoured to have the famous warrior princess take passage with us. Every citizen of Turin has heard of your victory over Emperor Eimion and the Jute Empire at Questers Pass."

"Don't forget that my brother, Prince Hugh was also there with his legion and the garrisons of Dunboro, Stone Bridge, Attleton and Duman Ford." Eleanora said.

With a smile, Captain Evan responded, "Your brother may have been there at the end, but the victory was yours, Your Highness."

"Captain Evan," Prince Ambrose said, "Are we ready to get underway?" "Yes, Your Highness," Captain Evan said, "the tide will turn in about two and one half hours, then we shall get underway."

After introducing his officers to Prince Ambrose and Princess Eleanora, Captain Evan had them shown to their cabin. He then set the crew to getting the ship ready to go to sea.

Two and one half hours later, Prince Ambrose and Princess Eleanora stood on the quarterdeck with Captain Evan as the lines were cast off from the quay and the Red Enchantress towed out into mid channel where it set sail and stood out to sea. Eleanora watched the port city of Natenfor fall away astern in the fading light of late afternoon. This would be her last look of the land of her birth for a long time. A land that she had come to love and had defended. Now she would have a new home with Ambrose and a new people. She made a vow to herself to do her best to be worthy to them and make them her people.

It seemed that they were blessed with fair weather and favourable winds the passage from Natenfor to Taverna being swift and without incident. Once the crew found out that Eleanora's honour guard was made up from men that she had commanded at Questers pass, the ship's crew kept after them until the whole story of the battle was known. In the wardroom, Sir Giffard kept the ships officers entertained with tales of Eleanora's daring deeds in Dunboro. The more that they learned, the more the men of Turin came to respect and love their warrior princess.

Just after the seventh bell of the morning watch the lookout at the head of the main mast called out, "Land ho dead ahead!"

Three quarters of an hour later the land could be clearly seen from the quarter deck. By now, Ambrose and Eleanora had joined Captain Evan on the quarter deck. Turning to Prince Ambrose, Captain Evan said, "Your Highness. It's time to hoist your standard."

"Okay, Captain Evan, you may hoist my standard." Ambrose said. Within a minute the personal standard of the crown prince of Turin flew at the top of the main mast.

As the ship drew closer to land, the view of Taverna became clear. Ambrose stood on the quarter deck pointing out land marks to Eleanora. The city of Taverna lay sprawled about the harbour that was protected by a stone breakwater. On a rise behind the city rose the royal palace, a magnificent edifice the colour of old ivory with high walls, many towers and turrets and roofs of red clay tile. Many standards flew from the towers and turrets. Behind all these rose mountains green with trees.

Taking Ambrose's arm, Eleanora said, "Oh, Ambrose it's so beautiful. I know that I shall love to live here."

With a smile, Ambrose replied, "Oh, my dear, we are to be wed in Taverna, but our home will be in Lavor on the island of Pendar. As crown prince I'm the prince of Pendar."

With a shrug, Eleanora said, "It doesn't matter where I live as long as it is with you."

As they entered the harbour a pilot boat came alongside. They had priority in docking and were soon approaching the pier reserved for kingdom ships. Ambrose pointed to a party standing on the pier. "Look, Eleanora," He said, "my father and mother are here to meet the ship."

Looking at where Ambrose pointed, Eleanora could see a couple in their fifties standing a couple of paces from the rest of the assemblage. It was easy for Eleanora to tell that they were the king and queen by their dress. Eleanora studied then as the ship eased up to the pier and the lines were made fast. As soon as the gang plank was in place, Ambrose and Eleanora disembarked. King Quincy and Queen Frederica were there to greet them. Ambrose bowed while Eleanora curtsied. Queen Frederica then gave her son a hug, following by giving, Eleanora a hug saying, "Welcome to the family, Eleanora. We have heard so much about you. It's so good to meet you at last."

"I'm pleased to finally be here." Eleanora replied.

King Quincy then embraced Eleanora and welcomed her to the family. He then said, "In the letter that I received from your father when the wedding was arranged; he expressed the joy at gaining a son, but expressed that he was losing a most able field commander. If the rumours are true the gain is ours."

"It is true, father," Ambrose said, "The men in her honour guard are men that she commanded at Questers Pass. I have heard that some of them fought duels to first blood to be on her honour guard."

"If that's so," King Quincy said, "I must find time to speak with some of these men."

"If you don't mind," Eleanora said, "I will now leave the making of war to the men. All I want to make now is babies with Ambrose."

Eleanora's remark drew laughter from those within hearing. King Quincy then said, "Let us be away for the palace."

For the trip to the palace they rode in an open carriage pulled by a matched team of black horses through the city. The citizens of the city stood along the sides of the road and cheered as the carriage passed by. Eleanora was pleased that she had been accepted by Ambrose's family. She looked at the people cheering as they rode by, realizing that these were her people now. She knew that she had come home.